EARLY PRAISE FOR MAP OF MY ESCAPE

"Taut, atmospheric, and unputdownable. Reed knows how to keep you turning pages!"

CANDICE FOX, INTERNATIONAL BESTSELLING AUTHOR OF *CRIMSON LAKE*, NOW AN ABC SERIES *TROPPO*

"Bending genres of police drama and adventure thriller, *Map of My Escape* is both original and breathlessly page-turning!"

WENDY WALKER, INTERNATIONAL BESTSELLING AUTHOR OF *DON'T LOOK FOR ME*

"Atmospheric and gritty, Reed's tale of a woman on the run from her own shocking past will keep you rooting for her until the end. A dark thriller with a redemptive ending from a master of suspense."

JAMIE FREVELETTI, INTERNATIONAL BESTSELLING AUTHOR OF *BLOOD RUN*

"Cheryl Reed's *Map of My Escape* is a character-driven thriller, a poignant opposites-attract love story, and a journey of self-discovery. As secrets unfold and twists abound, Reed keeps us on a razor's edge. An absolutely gripping read!"

JOHN COPENHAVER, AWARD-WINING AUTHOR OF *THE SAVAGE KIND* AND *DODGING AND BURNING*

"*Map of My Escape* combines tragic events, engaging characters, and unique locations to give readers one hell of a ride."

ELENA TAYLOR, AUTHOR OF *ALL WE BURIED* AND THE *EDDIE SHOES MYSTERIES SERIES*

MAP OF MY ESCAPE

A NOVEL

CHERYL L. REED

MAP OF MY ESCAPE

Edited by Benjamin White

Published in North America and Europe by Running Wild Press. Visit Running Wild Press at www.runningwildpress.com, Educators, librarians, book clubs (as well as the eternally curious), go to www.runningwildpress.com.

Paperback ISBN: 978-1-960018-17-5
eBook ISBN: 978-1-960018-16-8

ALSO BY CHERYL L. REED

Fiction: *Poison Girls*

Non-fiction: *Unveiled: The Hidden Lives of Nuns*

I took out the sheaf of papers and knelt down, spread them on the floor, ran my fingers over the lime-green forests, the meandering dark blue rivers, the pointy lavender mountain ranges. I had designed a whole world ... in secret.

– Jane Hamilton, *Map of the World*

For Nick,

who is always game to read one of my stories.

RILEY

We parked in the shadows of a South Side liquor store with bars on its windows. It was a chilly autumn night, and the Mustang's heater fogged the tinted windows. I rubbed at the glass. Halloween decorations lay discarded on the lawn next to us—a blowup dragon and a zombie that someone had spent good money on were crumpled in the grass. The street was empty and dark. Several overhead lights were burnt out—or shot out—heightening the creepy feeling.

"Aren't you afraid someone's going to recognize this car and know you're a cop because the drug dealer who owned it is in prison?" Reece got all his undercover cars from Vice. The interior reeked of cigarettes and Axe deodorant.

Reece shot me one of his cockeyed looks. He didn't like it when I offered street advice. After all, I was just a civilian.

"Nah. That dude probably drives something better by now," he said.

"Nobody in this neighborhood drives a souped-up car like this unless they're a drug dealer or a cop posing as a drug dealer."

"Yeah? Well, tonight I'm a drug dealer, and you're one of my ladies." He winked. "A White woman with tats and 'tude. You're like cocaine and candy all wrapped up in one." He clicked his tongue, confident he could get a rise out of me.

I rolled my eyes. I was too tired to spar with him. Reece was the only person whose crude jokes I tolerated. He was the only man who could make me drop everything with a phone call. Surviving a massacre together has a way of tethering you.

"Who is this guy, anyway?" I asked. Reece had promised me this stakeout would be worth my while.

"You'll see."

"If I can stay awake." I looked at my watch and sighed. It was well past midnight.

"*Awww*. Are you missing your booty call with Finn?" He flashed a sinister grin. Reece disapproved of Finn, whose Boy Scout demeanor and conservative politics rubbed him the wrong way. Worse, he didn't understand my attraction to someone who espoused views so opposite my own. If I'd said it was the sex or the thrill of sneaking around with a politician, Reece would have understood. But I preferred not to lie to Reece, and the truth was much more complicated.

"This better be worth it, is all I'm saying."

"Don't you give me that attitude, girl. This right here is a gift. This fucker has the mother lode." Reece's face was animated, his eyebrows on high alert, his green eyes dancing. I called them river eyes because they reminded me of the Chicago River on a sunny day when the phosphorus was blooming.

Reece liked to play up the mystery and wouldn't say who we were meeting. He'd hinted it was a well-placed source or snitch who could talk about the fed's investigation into the Chicago police department. That was all Reece and me—or anyone in Chicago—could talk about. I thought maybe the guy knew which cops were about to be indicted and which cases were suspect. Reece was all about drama, but he rarely disappointed.

I sat quietly, watching the dark storefront. Then a line of men came out the front door, their hands empty.

"Where are these guys coming from?"

Reece shushed me.

"Where are we supposed to meet *your guy*?"

He shrugged and gave me a hangdog face.

I knew that guilty look.

"You didn't tell him we were coming, did you?"

He threw up his hands. "That's not how it works. No calls, sweets. I just show up."

A tall, barrel-chested man wearing a full-length leather coat walked out of the store. The other men had vanished. He stopped under the streetlight and lit a black and mild. Even parked a hundred feet away, I could see the chunky gold rings on his hands and the rope chain around his neck, gleaming beneath the yellow streetlight. The man looked straight at us, his eyes flickering with recognition at the car.

Most snitches were skinny and strung-out, cowards who peddled in rumors, trading information for money or favors. But this guy wore money on his fingers and looked like somebody's boss. Why would he tell Reece—or me—anything?

"Is that your guy?" We watched as he disappeared down a dark alley behind the liquor store.

"Just wait. He'll be here."

The heater fan made the only noise as we both watched the dark storefront.

I fidgeted in my seat. Something didn't feel right. No one else had come out of the liquor store. Reece's lips tightened, and I could hear him grinding his teeth. This wasn't going how he'd expected either.

A shadow flitted across the car's rear window, then Reece's door flew open. Big hands pulled him from the car. "Get out here, motherfucker. Show your face!"

It was the barrel-chested man.

Reece scrambled to his feet, pulled his gun from his shoulder holster, and thrust it in the stranger's face.

The stranger jerked his head from the muzzle, stumbled backward, and fell to the sidewalk. Reece stood over him. "Who the fuck are you?"

When the man didn't answer, Reece moved toward the car. The stranger grabbed Reece's leg and pulled him to the ground. The two wrestled. The man clamped his catcher's mitt palm onto Reece's hand—the one that held the gun—and began pushing the barrel toward Reece's head.

I reached under the driver's seat looking for Reece's spare, but came up with a handful of wadded up fast-food wrappers. I opened the glove box, frantically digging beneath old registrations. My fingers wrapped around something metallic and cold. I held it up in the light: a silver revolver.

I hated guns. Hated all the pain they'd caused in my life. I glanced at Reece, his face full of fear, and swallowed my uneasiness. I checked that the gun was loaded, turned off the safety, and got out of the car.

Reece's arm shook trying to resist, but the barrel-chested man, twice his size, pushed Reece's arm steadily closer to his temple. Reece's face clenched with panic.

"Shoot him," Reece yelled. "Shoot him!"

The stranger looked up at me, surprised that Reece was not alone. I raised the gun, my hand shaking, my forefinger quivering. I picked the stranger's body part farthest from Reece's face.

"Don't bother, bitch," the man yelled. "Bro here going to eat it."

I lined up the sights, then pulled the trigger. Thunder burst in my head. I smelled the gunpowder in the night air and looked down at the warm metal in my palm. Then, it got quiet. My ears filled with an empty, underwater sound.

FINN

I waited up for hours, sitting in the dark living room, drinking Scotch and staring out the window at every passing car. The liquor mixed with jealousy made for an acidic combination. This was supposed to be our night. But, as usual, Reece had lured her away.

We'd met earlier that evening at our favorite supper club. I arrived twenty minutes early and sat in the back, sipping my first drink of the evening, imagining what we were going to do to each other after dinner. She arrived twenty minutes late and sauntered to the table, turning heads. It was hard not to stare at Riley. Her face had an ethereal quality, her skin a ghost-orchid pale. She looked as if she'd been raised in a closet —or a coffin, as the kids at school used to tease her. They called her a vampire, which wasn't far off the mark. Her pallid appearance made her hazel eyes even more radiant and set off her spiky black hair, a style most women couldn't pull off. But Riley had the attitude to match—cockiness tempered by passion.

"I can't stay long," she'd said, sliding down in the chair

opposite me, grinning with some secret. "Reece has someone he wants me to meet."

Reece was always pulling her away with some promise of finding the Al Capone of gun runners. A better man wouldn't have tolerated the competition, but Riley insisted he was the brother she gained the day she lost Ross. They had this weird survivor bond. Sometimes Riley went to a dark place in her head. Reece helped calibrate her tortured memories.

"Who is it this time?" I couldn't hide my disappointment. There was something I was aching to tell her. I'd practiced the words, even wrote out a script. I planned to confess that our relationship wasn't an accident.

She shrugged. "Reece hinted this guy knows cops who run illegal guns."

Riley's ambition in life was to rid the city of guns, an unattainable goal in my opinion since Chicago, even on a good day, had more shootings than any city in the country.

"Let's at least get you a drink." I motioned to the waiter, hoping to entice her to stay.

She shook her head. "I can't, Finn."

"So, no dinner or *dancing*?" Dancing was our code for sex.

One corner of her mouth turned up in a teasing grin. "Maybe I can come by later? For dessert?" She took my tumbler of Scotch and slugged back the last mouthful. "I wanted to tell you in person." She leaned over and kissed me discreetly on the cheek.

"Promise me you'll come over tonight," I whispered. "I don't care what time it is."

She looked at me warily. "What's the urgency?"

"There's something I need to tell you, that I've wanted to tell you for a long time."

"Oh, you can't leave it like that, Finn. Not fair."

"Neither is leaving me alone on date night."

I would soon regret not telling her, especially when she hadn't arrived by 2 a.m. or answered my cajoling texts. Sometimes Riley went quiet for days on her special projects with Reece. But that night the radio silence between us felt different.

RILEY

Three minutes. One hundred and eighty seconds. That's all it took to shatter our lives. Terror was short, but its effects were everlasting. I've relived those three minutes over and over in my head, slowing them down to milliseconds, freezing every frame, circling each angle, ticking through a parade of what-ifs to see how I might have changed our trajectories. Reece and I thought our past tragedy made us immune to further catastrophe, as if life had granted us a pass. He equated it to lightning never striking the same place twice. I've since learned that lightning does indeed strike twice, just as tragedy can be relentless.

This time I wasn't sure we would both survive.

The man I thought I'd shot rolled off Reece and crawled to his feet. He grabbed Reece's gun, glared at me, then took off down the street, swaying and stumbling like a drunk. Reece was splayed on his back, blood oozing from his neck and shoulder. For a moment, I froze, unable to believe I had just shot my best friend.

My legs moved before my mind could catch up. When I

reached him, Reece's eyes were closed, his teeth clenched. I grabbed his cell phone and tapped 911.

"An officer has been shot," I spit out.

"What's the location?" the dispatcher asked.

I looked around frantically, but there were no street signs. Where were we? "I don't know. Somewhere in Englewood." I could barely make out the liquor store sign. "In front of Markham Liquor."

"What's your name?"

Hell, no. I tapped the red button and slid it into Reece's pocket. Then I ripped open Reece's Kevlar vest. The bullet nicked the upper corner, slowing its trajectory, but penetrated the meaty shoulder muscle. I pressed my hands against the wound. Blood seeped between my fingers. He winced. When he tried to speak, the words gurgled in his mouth, and he gasped to breathe. I propped up his head and told him to keep his mouth shut. He blinked once. I forced my voice to remain steady. One hand staunched his wound; the other grasped his fingers. He clutched my hand tightly, but as we waited, his grip slackened. His chin slumped to his chest. I thought he'd stopped breathing and I shook him. His eyes flickered with pain.

"I'm so sorry, Reece," I said, my voice cracking.

He shook his head and blinked twice—telling me not to go there.

My throat caught with emotion, I looked away. In a second-story window, a tiny red light glowed. Reece and I were in the middle of the deserted street. When shots were heard on the South Side of Chicago, people scattered from the windows to avoid stray bullets. But someone was spying on us. Squinting, I could see that the red light was a video camera.

"Who are you? What are you doing?" I yelled.

The red light didn't waver.

"This man is wounded. Help me save him!"

The camera tilted down toward me; its silver casing reflected the streetlight. I searched the nearby windows, hoping for some sign of a curious neighbor, but they remained dark. With my left hand pressing on Reece's injured shoulder, I reached across the asphalt, scooped up loose gravel with my right hand, and threw it at the window.

"Coward! You want to film a man dying?" I could feel the tightness in my throat. *Damn it!* I wasn't going to cry. I shook my fist at the window. "Come help me. You sick fucker!"

I picked up a piece of asphalt, stood up to get a better aim, and lobbed the chunk at the window. It hit the corner of the windowsill and shattered, raining down pebbles. I was about to try again when Reece began coughing.

I pulled his upper body onto my lap, keeping pressure on his shoulder. "It's okay. The ambulance will be here soon." But inside, I was yelling, *Don't you die on me. I can't live if I killed you.* He squeezed my hand, and I forced a smile. We waited, listening to the night sounds of the city—distant car alarms, a barking dog. Where the hell was that ambulance?

"Maybe I should call Finn?"

Reece's eyes opened wide as if I'd suggested something heretical. He shook his head.

"Reece, we're in trouble here. I don't know what to do." I glanced up at the red light mocking me. "And then there's that asshole."

The sirens sounded in the distance. Reece jerked his head, signaling that I should leave.

"Not yet."

His mouth tried to form words.

"I will. When it gets closer."

When the sirens were a couple of blocks away, Reece gripped my hand and whispered something I couldn't make out. I leaned my ear toward his mouth. He whispered again, a hoarse gasp. "Disappear." Then he yanked my arm, pulling my face close to his, his eyes fierce. Tears wetted his cheeks. He swallowed hard and slowly enunciated each word. "You gotta get gone . . . become invisible. They gonna come after you, sweets."

Then he let go of my hand and shut his eyes.

Was he dead? I shook him gently. He didn't respond.

I could hear the roar of the sirens a block over. I picked up Reece's spare, the one I'd fired. If I threw it in the trash, there was a chance the cops or a kid or a gang member would find it. I stuffed it in my pocket, grabbed my bag from the car, and darted down the alley.

RILEY

Light from the houses lining the alley filtered through tree branches to create ominous shadows. I tripped on a pothole and fell, my face and hands scraping against the gravel. I immediately felt the sting of cuts on my palms, and the warmth of blood on my cheek. I swiped at my face and cleaned my hands on my pants. I checked the gun in my pocket. Somehow amid the chaos, I'd remembered to slip on the safety. I needed to get rid of it, just not now.

I pulled my phone from my bag, pulled out the SIM card, and stomped on the glass. It had cost me twelve-hundred dollars, but now it was useless, nothing more than a government tracking device. I tossed both in a trashcan. The noise startled a dog from a nearby backyard. He charged, scaring the shit out of me, but a chain-link fence stopped him.

I ran, fearful of what would happen if the cops found out I was with Reece—or worse—if they suspected I had shot him. If Reece lived, he'd be fired for endangering the life of a civilian by taking me to an unauthorized stakeout, and I'd be charged with attempted murder. If he died, I would be accused of murder. Either way, the outcome would be delicious double retribution for the cops—arresting an anti-gun activist for shooting a cop infamous for publicly challenging the Chicago cop culture. For both of our sakes, I couldn't get caught.

My chest hurt from the dead sprint. My breath formed a mist in the chilly air. The alley emptied onto a brightly lit street. I stopped and turned in circles, looking for something familiar.

Two men stepped from the shadows of a porch. One man wore a hoodie that concealed his face. The other pulled down a ball cap over sunglasses.

"Where you goin' so fast, bitch?" the hooded man asked.

"Leave me alone." I swerved around them on the sidewalk.

The second man snagged my arm and grinned, revealing a silver grill on his teeth that gleamed in the streetlight. I trembled at the meanness in his face. "You got any money?" He grabbed at the bag strapped across my chest.

"The police are coming," I shouted. "They're following me." I sounded crazy.

The men laughed, but turned to look down the street. That's when I pulled Reece's gun from my pocket and pointed it at them.

"Whoa!" The man with the ball cap raised his hands in front of his face. "No need to get violent, lady." He was close enough he could have lunged for the gun.

"Your hands," I yelled at the man wearing the hoodie. "Get your hands in the air, or I will fucking shoot your dick off." I aimed the gun at his crotch and slipped off the safety.

The man lifted his palms chest high. We were standing under an unusually bright streetlight. The hooded man squinted at me.

"Damn, Mickey, she looks like she done shot someone. She got blood all over her face."

"That's right. I did. I killed someone. A cop." I waved the gun from one to the other. "You want me to kill you, too?"

They looked at each other and took off running.

I took off, too, moving toward a halo of lights in the distance. Finally, I reached a busy road and saw a bus coming. I dug in my bag for a tissue, spit on it, scrubbed at my face, and then put on sunglasses. As I got on the bus, I kept my head down to avoid the camera mounted above the driver. There were only a few riders—a couple of drunk college students and a handful of weary folks getting off work. I took a seat behind the driver's cabin, a blind spot for the camera.

I felt for the gun in my pocket, fearing it would go off again, and checked the safety. I glanced around to see if anyone was looking at me. My jeans were torn at the knees where I'd fallen. Streaks of orange-red ran down both thighs. I could smell his blood on me, on my hair, my clothes.

The raw, acrid odor reminded me of that day thirteen years ago in our high school gym, the blood seeping from the bodies on the floor. I brushed my fingers through my hair and recoiled every time I touched a coagulated strand. I wanted more than anything to wash my hair, to soap my orange-stained hands, to forget what I'd done and what it was forcing me to remember.

Once we reached downtown, I caught another bus to my apartment. At home, I stripped and stared at the reflection in the bathroom mirror. My eyes were red and veiny. There were dried blood flakes at my temples. One earlobe was caked in red. Henna-colored specks dotted the base of my neck. The lack of sleep added to my crazed, hysterical look. No wonder the two thugs bolted from me.

I stepped into the shower and watched the stream flow from clear to carmine. I had tried so hard to keep it together in front of Reece. Now, alone, his blood streaming from my body, I wept uncontrollably. His shooting—the blood, the bullet wound to his upper chest, the chaos—brought back those horrific memories of the day we first met.

THERE WAS an assembly in the gym. I was sitting somewhere in the middle of the bleachers—they were the old-fashioned, accordion kind that pull out from the wall. I was reading and re-reading index cards, trying to memorize trigonometry theorems for a test. Principal Brown was at the podium talking, but it was all background noise until a loud crack resounded through the gym. The metal doors at the front of the gym—the only way in or out—opened and slammed shut. Everyone turned to look. Even Principal Brown stopped talking mid-sentence.

Darren Wallack, a guy no one paid much attention to, was standing at the gym entrance dressed like a Ninja warrior, a gun and ammo strapped across his chest, a rifle in his hands. He looked almost comical, except it wasn't Halloween.

Nancy Greene, a whisper of a girl with thick glasses and braces, let out a high-pitched squeal. She was his first victim. Then the pandemonium struck. Everyone tried to move at once. People climbed over others, trying to get away. Some hunkered down, attempting to hide. The air smelled of desperation and fear. Everyone was screaming, panicking. The gun blasted, again and again, loud, sharp cracks, like a whip cutting the air.

I noticed a guy slide his feet in between the thin slats of the bleachers. Our eyes met. He hesitated, then offered me his hand. We climbed down the support scaffolding. A few others chose to hide beneath the bleachers, too. We spread out in clumps of two and three as if we were safer with space between us. The stranger and I crouched in the corner, peaking through the gaps of the bleachers watching as Darren fired continuously, swinging his rifle from left to right like some character he'd seen in a bad movie.

"He's going to kill us," I whispered. I couldn't breathe.

I'd never met this guy next to me, but his eyes were kind, reassuring. He was Black. At our charter school, Blacks, Asians, Mexicans, and Whites didn't mix.

"It's going to be okay." He patted my back. He seemed so calm.

Through the crack in the bleachers, we could see our classmates scrambling back and forth across the basketball court, shrieking terrified screams. Darren stalked them, firing a barrage of bullets until they slumped to the floor.

I looked away. I couldn't take it anymore.

Several rounds flew over our heads. "He's coming toward us," the guy said. "Get down."

I lay on my stomach on the cold floor, the stranger next to me, convinced we were about to die. I thought about my family, my mother and father, and my older brother, who had just started college. And for a quick moment, I mourned for them. Then I thought about my younger brother, Ross. He was out there somewhere. I tried to remember where he was sitting. When was the last time I saw him?

"What is your name?" I whispered.

"What does it matter?"

"Because I don't want my last minutes on earth to be spent with a complete stranger."

"I'm Reece," he said. "You're Riley."

"How do you know my name?"

"Everyone knows who you are." He reached over and draped his arm across my back, his upper body forming a protective shield.

Darren's boots stomped above our heads. Kids screamed,

scuttled to get away. The gunfire sounded like firecrackers. I plugged my ears with my fingers. I couldn't bear to hear it anymore. If Darren came down under the bleachers, we were dead. There was nowhere to run. It was the most horrifying fifteen minutes of my life.

Then the footsteps stopped.

We didn't know if we could come out. We heard hard footfalls, police hollering as they hunted Darren down. When the police announced it was over, we walked out from under the bleachers like horror movie zombies.

That's when we saw them.

Bodies were sprawled on the bleachers. They covered the gym floor, piled three-deep in some places. I recognized many of their faces, kids I saw in literature class or passed in the hallway. I stepped around the bodies, my sneakers sticky with blood, looking for friends, anyone I knew. Then I recognized Ross's mousey brown hair. His face looked serene as if he were taking a nap. He was wearing his new White Sox jacket with black sleeves and white on the torso. Our parents had given it to him for his birthday two weeks earlier. He only took it off to go to bed. Now the white part was ruby red. And my brother was never going to wake up.

STANDING in the shower washing off Reece's blood, it was all coming back, the horror of that day, the sadness that had stalked all of us since. Surviving that nightmare together connected Reece and me in a way neither of us could explain. He never took credit for saving me. But I knew that without him guiding me under the bleachers, I would have been killed. And now I had shot him. The irony was tragic. I felt hungover with regret.

At the same time, it was clear what I had to do.

RILEY

I hovered at his bedroom door, listening to him sleep. His lips made soft cooing sounds, hypnotic whispers that tempted me: *Stay, sleep, stay, sleep.* I wanted nothing more than to curl up beside him, snuggle against the curve in his chest, and forget what had happened to Reece.

They'd come looking for me and, eventually, end up here, in his house with his children. We'd been careful, but secrets have a way of getting out. Enough people knew. Probably more suspected. It wasn't just Reece I had to protect. I was now a danger to the two most important men in my life. If suspicious eyes fell on me, they would eventually land on Finn. It could ruin his political career, his ambitions.

I debated waking him and telling him everything. I feared he wouldn't forgive me this time. Maybe he'd think I'd taken too many risks, that it was all my fault. My hands trembled as I stood in the hall, unsure of what to do. I knew he'd try his best to convince me to stay.

He said he thought of me as a *Morpho peleides*—the Blue Morpho butterfly. Finn was like that, precise, calling things by their Latin names, able to describe people with immense accuracy. That was the lawyer in him. He said I resembled the Morpho because the butterfly had two sides, iridescent blue wings, and a camouflaged undercoat; when it flew, it looked like it was alternately appearing and disappearing. He said that's how he thought of me, this free creature that appeared and disappeared from his life.

Now I had to disappear for good.

I tiptoed to his bed and stood over him, watching as the street lights flickered through the curtains and fell in waves across his face. Normally when I saw Finn, the first few seconds were a shock. His physical features—square haircut, square jaw, meaty shoulders, uniform of dark blue blazer and red tie—elicited a momentary disconnect. Then something in my brain clicked, and I remembered that Finn was a good guy wearing a Republican man suit.

Maybe my taste in men had matured. Maybe it was Finn's sharp intellect, his black humor that had sealed my affections. Maybe it was because Finn was stable, reliable, a generous lover. If I were honest, I'd admit that Finn was forbidden fruit. For a rebel like me, that was the ultimate seduction.

I longed to give him a proper good-bye, something we could both hold onto for the weeks or months—however long we would be separated. I didn't think it would be long. Not then.

Watching him sleep, I suddenly realized how seldom we'd shared a bed. There'd been so many distractions. He had constituents, fundraisers, kid sleepovers, and talky neighbors who disapproved of the unconventional, younger woman. I had meetings, demonstrations, emergency calls in the middle of the night, and of course, my lovely cat, Norma Rae. Now I wished we'd made more time. You always think you have more time.

Strands of gold and ginger fell across his forehead. I resisted the urge to sweep my fingers through his hair. I ached to touch him, to kiss him. Instead, I laid my cat at his feet, like some consolation prize. She purred and curled herself into a black circle. I could still hear his whistling breaths as I shut his bedroom door, knowing I could not go back. I had a hundred dollars in my wallet, an atlas in my car, and in my head, I was concocting the map of my escape.

FINN

I woke to smell her perfume—rose, jasmine, and sandalwood—lingering in the air. The fragrance had been my gift to her on Christmas. The woman at the Macy's counter had thrust a sample at me as I rushed by. The scent made me abruptly stop, the aroma enticingly sweet, but musky. When the clerk pronounced the name, something Japanese, and pointed to the sapphire blue butterfly on the box, I knew it matched Riley perfectly.

I was pleased when Riley adopted the fragrance as her own. I could always tell where she'd been in my house, a spicy redolence trailing her, reminding me of us having sex. That's what I thought when I smelled her perfume—that she'd finally come over and had slipped under the sheets. But when I reached across the bed, she wasn't there.

My father always told me, if a man was truly lucky in life, he might have his heart broken by the wrong kind of woman. Riley was definitely my wrong kind of woman. Riley's liberal, anti-gun agenda didn't exactly square with the expectations of my conservative constituents.

And so, we kept our opposites-attract experiment on the down-low. At first, it seemed rather tame and innocent, two single adults having *amazing* sex. Riley wasn't the sort of woman you marry or have children with or imagine growing old beside. I had no expectation that she was anything more than a fantastic fling with an expiration date. But we'd been together nearly a year, and Riley started complaining that our sneaking around made her feel like a mistress. I had begun to wonder whether we might mean more to each other than we'd let on.

I felt a humming vibration and sat up to find Riley's cat, Norma Rae, purring at my feet.

"Where's Ri?" I whispered, hoping that Riley would fling open the bedroom door naked and jump into bed. It was just the sort of thing she would do.

I felt the bedroom floor rattle as the front door shut. I got up to look out the window as her car pulled from the curb. I watched, feeling inexplicably sad, as the night swallowed her taillights. I lay awake for hours, wondering what kind of trouble she'd gotten herself into.

RILEY

I often wondered what it would be like to disappear. As a teenager, I read books like *Famous Female Fugitives* and pored over stories in my mother's magazines about women such as Bernardine Dohrn, Sara Jane Olson, or Katherine Powers, who had committed crimes with their boyfriends and ran. They changed their names, plucked birthdates off gravestones of dead babies to obtain new Social Security cards, and created new lives. I was never curious about the men who disappeared. The FBI's Most Wanted lists were full of men who'd eluded cops for years, only later to be discovered as the quiet loner next door. The women fugitives, though sparse in number, were seldom quiet. They married, raised kids, built careers. Sara Jane even joined the PTA, acted on stage, and made speeches before her state senate. They all lived their new lives in public as if they were flaunting the authorities in plain sight.

I admired their tenacity.

There had also been times in my life when I desperately wanted to disappear, when I dreamed of slipping away from the present and starting over somewhere else under a new identity. The pull became stronger after forty-four of my classmates, including my brother, and five of our teachers were killed by a guy in combat boots re-enacting his favorite video game.

I hadn't thought about my fugitive fascination for years. Of course, now it's much harder to evade police in a digital age when a person's every movement can be tracked. But I didn't consider any of that the day I ran. Running is the natural reaction—even if you do not know where you are running to. The adrenaline and animalistic self-preservation kick in, leaving your brain a scrambled mess while your body takes over.

After I left Finn's house, I drove in a daze, focused on the yellow line that I hoped would lead to a better future. Running from the cops is challenging for a normal person. But when you're an activist and your mugshot is floating on police and FBI computers, vanishing is a lot harder. In Chicago, there are police cameras on virtually every corner and security cameras outside and inside most businesses. Red-light cameras snap pictures at major intersections. Tollway cameras capture your image without warning. And if you somehow manage to elude those, banks and credit card companies track your financial transactions. What's more, your cell phone essentially is a government tracking device. In the end, we are all electronic files, avatars moving from screen to screen, followed by one entity after another.

I had to jump off those screens. That meant no electronics of any kind—no phones, no GPS, no computers. If I wanted to escape, I had to do it old school, like the women in *Famous Female Fugitives.*

I swiped at my eyes, urging myself to focus, and gripped the wheel with both hands. I took one curvy street then another that curled past Jackson Park, where Obama's presidential library was to take shape. Half a mile later, the air reeked of corn oil and burnt batter. Eight lanes of traffic skirted fast-food joints on one side while the other boasted 24-hour payday loan stores and discount liquor shops.

Then, without warning, a single lane in the middle of the road lifted onto Chicago's elevated highway, the Skyway, the quickest route out of the city and state. For five dollars, drivers could ride high above South Chicago, and, like a bird, gaze down at the tiny houses, the coal stacked up like pyramids, and the daunting cranes lining the banks of the Calumet River.

At the crest of the bridge, I pulled into the farthest right lane, opened the passenger side window, and flung Reece's gun —wrapped inside a McDonald's bag—as hard as I could. It sailed past the bridge's steel barriers and out into the black sky where I imagined it plummeted into the frigid, swirling waters, resting on the river's sandy floor. I shut the window, pulled into the speed lane, and five minutes later, I was in Indiana.

I still had to get rid of my bloody clothes, which I'd stuffed into a garbage bag and put in my trunk, just in case the cops searched my apartment. But first, I needed to put more distance between Chicago and me.

FINN

"Dad, when did you get a cat?" Nico asked, petting Norma Rae.

I sat up, remembering the strange waking moment I'd had inhaling Riley's perfume. I checked my cell phone next to the bed. No messages.

"Dad!" Nico didn't like being ignored. He was nine, and his sister Kye was six. He'd taken to acting more mature lately, reminding me when I was his age and thinking that I had to prove how much more grown up I was than my younger sisters.

Kye came running from the hallway and lunged at Norma Rae, trying to pat the cat's head. Frightened, it leaped from Nico's arms and scurried under the bed.

"Kye, you ruined it!" Nico screamed.

Kye crawled under the bed to try to grab Norma Rae. The cat darted from the room.

"Okay, you two," I said. "Let's get some breakfast, and I'll tell you all about the cat."

Kye clunked down the stairs. Nico, his shoulders hunched, followed. His sister had again outmaneuvered him. I followed in a robe, ready to play the doting father, serving hotcakes and sausage—our usual Saturday morning fare. Kye stopped at the bottom of the stairs. Behind her, Nico remained immovable.

"What's that, Daddy?" She pointed at a squat, pink plastic box.

"It's a litter box, stupid," Nico said.

Inside the litter box was a giant bag of kitty gravel. Taped to the bag was a card. I ripped it off, feeling apprehensive. Something would have to be horribly wrong for Riley to leave her cat long enough to need that much gravel. I cut through the sealed envelope with my finger. I recognized her loopy cursive writing on thick and expensive stationary, the kind that typically carried invitations to weddings and graduations—happy life events.

I read the note, sitting there on the steps, my children hanging on me begging for breakfast. When I'd reached the end a second time, the sentences blurred on the page, but the word *gun* stood out.

I got the kids dressed and loaded them into the car, ignoring their whining. I felt terrible about giving up my weekend with them. Diana, my ex, didn't even pry for details about my "emergency." God knows, she'd had enough of her own.

As I pulled into her driveway, Diana waved from the porch of her Georgian Colonial. She could afford a bigger house than me with her law partner's salary. Besides, she'd argued, the kids lived with her most of the time, and they needed more space. In some ways, I felt she was mocking me, reminding me that my civil servant salary would never provide her the style of life to which she felt entitled.

Kye unclipped her seatbelt in the backseat, flung open the car door, and ran to her mother as if she hadn't just seen her twelve hours earlier. I felt a ping of jealousy. Moms always owned their kids' hearts. Dads were ancillary.

Nico hung back in the front seat. "Dad, are you going to be okay?" My boy was becoming a sensitive young man.

I patted his knee. "Of course, buddy. A friend needs me right now. Sorry about the weekend. We'll make up for it next time."

He shrugged. "No big deal. What happened to your friend?"

I should have anticipated Nico would have more questions. "Well, my friend saw something bad happen."

"Is it Riley?"

The kids were still trying to acclimate to my having a female friend. And so, I'd compartmentalized. Riley was the other life I lived without the kids and their mother, which sometimes made me feel like a cheating spouse.

"Yes—but it's complicated, son. Let's not worry your mom about this just yet, okay?" The last thing I needed was Diana complaining that I'd dumped the kids on her because of my girlfriend. I wasn't about to tell her—an attorney and, legally, an officer of the court—that Riley was on the lam. Still, I felt like a real shit keeping secrets with my kid. Father of The Year, I was not.

"Okay, Dad. Just between us men." Nico grinned, got out, walked toward his mother, then turned around and waved, pleased with our arrangement.

If you'd told me then that I would complicate my relationship with my children and risk my career in the pursuit of Riley, I would have said you didn't know my ambitions: I loved my children, and I was three months from a shoo-in election as vice mayor, the stepping-stone to becoming mayor of the third-largest city in the United States. But life with the wrong kind of woman has a way of changing you in ways you cannot predict.

RILEY

Radio stations didn't mention anything about a cop getting shot, but it was still early. My dashboard clock showed it was five in the morning. I just wanted to know whether Reece had survived. At six a.m., WGN news radio briefly reported that a police officer had been shot. No name, no details, and damn it—no mention of whether he was alive.

I hadn't started as anti-cop. At first, I was just an interrupter, someone who shows up after gun violence to talk the injured parties out of retaliating—to *interrupt* the violence. Since Chicago racked up 4,000 shootings a year, eventually, I had to specialize. My particular skill was getting witnesses at police shootings to recount what they had seen, to rid themselves of survivor guilt. Most witnesses were standing near the victims, often within a foot or two. They were bloody, shell-shocked, and terrified the police would come after them, too. It wasn't easy to get them to talk to me, a stranger, a White woman, given that most shootings involved people of color. Sometimes, when I had to, I told them my story or enough of it that they ignored my skin color. They said they could see the pain in my eyes and knew I understood what they were going through.

I filmed the witnesses on my cell phone—before the cops could tell them what they did or did not see. I captured the truth before it was beaten or stolen from them. People on the streets saw it as protection. If something happened—and strange things tended to happen to folks who witnessed cops shooting Black men—there was a record to prove why the cops might retaliate.

Word got out about my videos. The media routinely interviewed me. I testified in several cases that resulted in cops being indicted for attempted homicide, and once, even murder.

And then the Schneider shooting happened. Robbie Schneider was a White cop who shot a Black kid sixteen times, claiming self-defense. Witnesses told me the unarmed teenager was waving a cell phone in the air—not a gun—begging the cop not to shoot. A couple of people took grainy videos, and I posted them on social media. Millions of views and massive street protests later, the Justice Department called for an FBI investigation of all cases in the last decade when a Chicago cop had fired a gun. Reece warned me to keep a low profile until things settled. Cops get defensive and jittery when they're the subject of investigation. Reece knew what I had on my interview videos, the ones never used in court. He thought the FBI would likely subpoena them. But we both knew they weren't the only ones who wanted the films.

Strong gas station coffee kept me awake as I drove the rural highways through Indiana thinking the police would be less likely to monitor those roads. Once I hit Nashville, I preferred the interstate for its numerous gas stations. I kept the radio set on strong AM stations, hoping for updates. The autumn sun began to poke through gray November skies. Fox radio, citing unidentified sources, named Reece as the wounded officer and said his condition was critical.

I felt like someone had punched me in the chest. I pulled the car to the shoulder, bent over the steering wheel, and howled. Critical condition meant Reece was near death. Worse—it meant I'd likely killed him. If Reece died, there was no way I could go back. Maybe the general public would believe I'd shot Reece accidentally. But there was no way the Chicago police were giving me a pass.

All I could think about was what Reece said before I left him lying in the street. Those words had become my mantra. They made me move forward.

Disappear. Get gone.

I pulled into a mega truck stop that touted cheap gas and free check cashing—a kitschy aspect of rural America. When I turned sixteen and started driving, my dad insisted that I keep a blank check in my car. I always argued that checks were for old ladies at supermarkets so they could hold up the line. But I kept that check for years in a slowly yellowing envelope in my glove box, mostly as a reminder of my dad from happier days. Now I was glad I had. I rummaged around the truck stop's aisles of eclectic products until I found something that piqued my interest left over from Halloween. Then I locked myself in one of the restrooms and stared at the mirror.

Something in that reflection was about to change.

FINN

Riley's father answered the phone, groggy and confused.

"Sorry to wake you, but Riley is in trouble," I said.

"What kind of trouble?" he demanded. I could hear his wife in the background asking who was on the phone.

"I'd rather discuss this in person," I said. "I'm on my way to your house."

Mr. Keane was quiet, perhaps starting to grasp the urgency of the situation. "Okay," he said, then hung up.

I wondered what he told his wife. Maybe they thought the worst—that Riley had been shot. I hated to put them through such agony, particularly given their history. If Riley were a suspect, the police would soon be at her parents' door and eventually mine. We needed to decide what we were going to tell them.

The Keanes' house was a tall Victorian bordered by an overgrown hedgerow. A cracked sidewalk led to a porch crowded with rattan furniture and clay pots with dead plants. What I knew about Riley's family, I'd learned through news stories over the years. Her father, a former chef, had run a successful downtown restaurant until the school shooting. Then he sold the restaurant, hung up his knives, and started a non-profit called Stop Illegal Guns, or SIG, a play on words since Sig Arms is one of the biggest manufacturers of guns in the U.S. The non-profit had become a family business. Riley, her mother, and her older brother all worked at the fledgling foundation. Riley was SIG's public face.

I'd never met Riley's parents in person. I'd always assumed Riley was too embarrassed to bring home a Republican and a pro-gun politician. Then again, maybe Riley didn't see me as serious boyfriend material.

Mr. Keane met me at the door, his face creased with worry, his eyes narrowed behind his oval glasses. He didn't shake my outstretched hand when I introduced myself, but nodded and waved me inside. His wife stood in the archway between the living room and dining room; a shawl draped over her shoulders. Her hair was long and gray. She had a square face like Riley's, set off by the same hazel eyes as her daughter. I stared a little too long. It was like looking at an aged-progressed image of Riley. She fidgeted beneath my gaze, then walked across the living room and extended her hand.

"I'm Emma—Riley's mother," she said. "That's Ethan."

I clasped her hand and looked her in the eye. "It's a pity we have to meet like this. I'd hoped for a happier occasion."

"Yes, and just what *is* this occasion?" asked Ethan, a scowl on his face. He leaned against a chair. Emma perched on the coffee table.

"This morning, I received a letter from Riley," I began in my formal politician voice as if I were delivering a prepared speech. I stopped and looked at their faces. They urged me on with their eyes. I hesitated. What I would say next—her words—would change all of our lives. I pulled out her letter to read aloud, though I'd already memorized her words.

"A man attacked us," I began in the middle, leaping over the part where she said she was sorry to leave me. *"I didn't know what to do. They were wrestling over a gun. I tried to shoot the attacker, but I shot Reece instead."*

"But she *loves* Reece!" Emma shrieked.

"She was trying to protect him," I explained.

"Where'd *she* get the gun?" Ethan asked.

"She didn't say. But you must realize how bad the optics are: a White woman shooting a Black man, an anti-gun activist shooting a cop. However, you want to spin it. And if this gets out, there will be plenty of spin—"

"And what if Reece doesn't live?" Ethan interjected.

"Oh, god!" Emma said. She began pacing, clasping her hands to her face. "Poor Reece."

The news was a twofold blow. Looking at Reece's multiple photos around the room, I could see that he was as much a part of the family as Riley.

"Why were they there?" Ethan asked, seemingly more confused than concerned.

"My guess is they were meeting someone from the neighborhood, maybe even a confidential informant," I said. "Something . . . went wrong."

"I'd say something went wrong," Ethan said.

"Where's Reece?" Emma asked.

"Northwestern Hospital."

"Well, where is Riley?" Ethan asked.

How did I tell them we were about to become part of a conspiracy to save their daughter?

"She took off."

This time it was Ethan who gasped. He leaned against the wall as if he might fall, pulled off his glasses, and rubbed at his eyes. "I want to talk to her."

"I haven't been able to reach her," I said. "I'm sure she's tossed her phone."

I handed the letter to Emma. She gently held the thick stationary by the tips of her fingers, mouthing the words as she followed along. She looked up at me, her face grief-stricken.

"She knows that the police will come looking for her," I said. "If Reece lives, he can vouch for her story. If he dies, I suspect she'll be charged with his death."

"Do the cops know it was her?" Ethan asked. Color had returned to his face.

"Apparently, there was a witness," I said.

"You mean the man with the video camera?" Emma asked, waving the letter. "Riley says someone was filming from a second-story window."

I stammered for a moment. "Yes... that's the most troubling aspect. We just don't know what his intentions are."

"Well, we can assume they aren't pure," Ethan said, sharply.

"Who do you think he is?" Emma asked.

"Well, I hesitate to guess," I said. "It's possible he's just someone who films crime in his neighborhood. He was using a video camera instead of a phone. My guess is he's an older man, someone who doesn't have a fancy smartphone. Maybe he's waiting for the police Crime Stoppers to post a reward."

"He could be a reporter," Ethan said. "I've heard that the *Tribune* has an undercover unit embedded on the South Side filming gangs and shootings. They're working on some big expose about the relationship between bad cops and gangs."

He stopped for a moment to gauge my reaction, but I didn't have one.

"I understand you're a former cop," he continued. "What do you know about Reece?"

Riley had always defended Reece against the rumors that

he was on the take, that he was one of those cops who, for a price, could make evidence disappear. Internal Affairs investigated him for losing a large cache of drugs and money a few years back. Eventually, IA cleared him, but the stigma remained. I didn't know whether the rap was true. Reece had always been a lone wolf, a cop who bent the rules to get results. The way Riley described him, he was a true believer, someone who thought he could change CPD from the inside.

"Sir, we never worked together. I'm several years older. I started in patrol when he was in high school." I instantly regretted bringing up high school, hoping he wouldn't connect that to the Hyde Park High School shooting and ask if I'd been one of the cops who responded that day. "I left the force to become a lawyer," I added quickly.

"Yes, but you must have heard things," he persisted.

I swallowed hard and debated what to say. I hadn't expected the two of them to be so knowledgeable about the internal workings of CPD. But Riley's parents weren't your normal mom and pop.

"What I know," I said softly, "is that Riley wouldn't have been safe if she had stayed in the city."

Ethan sighed loudly. "So, you've come here to devise a plan, is that it?"

RILEY

I ripped open the package with its Halloween theme and unpacked the chemicals. I couldn't help but think of Ross. Halloween had always been his favorite holiday. He planned for weeks, recruiting our mother into sewing elaborate costumes. Sometimes he included me, like the year he dressed as Austin Powers, and I went as Dr. Evil. We dressed our Pekinese dog as Mini-Me.

I had long hair then, and no matter how I tried to stuff it inside Dr. Evil's bald head mask, it gave me a lumpy scalp. Ross said that if I were really serious about my costume, I would shave my head. It was a dare I couldn't refuse. My mother cried as she sheered my tresses to an inch of my scalp. After that, I decided to keep it short. The style made Ross and me look even more like twins, something people were always mistaking us for, even though he was a year younger. God, how I missed him.

Someone banged on the restroom door.

I stood back from the faucet, my hair dripping cold water on my shoulders, and tried to remember where I was.

"Hurry up in there," a gravelly voice yelled. "We got a line forming out here."

"Just a minute," I yelled back.

I stuck my head beneath the hand dryer and strained to see myself in the mirror.

My black corona of hair had turned a brassy orange. It wasn't quite the look I was going for, but there was nothing more I could do. Dying black to blonde required more chemicals than a dye kit left over from Halloween. I walked out of the bathroom, ignoring the line of women glaring at me.

I asked the cashier if I could write my check for two hundred dollars to cover the Halloween dye kit, twenty dollars' worth of gas, and still have plenty left over. She asked for my ID, then stared at my hair and back at my photo.

"This is you, huh?" she asked. I felt like a college freshman trying to pass for 21 at a bar with a borrowed driver's license.

"Yep."

She wrote my driver's license number on the check, handed me my license and the change—several twenty dollar bills. "Have a good day, Riley Rae Keane—if that really is you."

I snatched the money and license from her and turned on my heel afraid I might say something I would regret. The check would eventually clear, but not as quickly as an ATM transaction.

Robotically I filled my car with gas, staring off into the clouds, considering my options. I still wasn't sure where I was headed. I had a vague notion about going to Florida, eventually making my way to Key West, a magnet for outcasts and criminals. I decided to get off the interstate, choosing instead a sparse country highway, mindlessly driving past rolling farmland and pockets of dense woods. I felt disoriented, unhinged, much like I did after Reece's gun went off. I suppose that's why I didn't immediately see the red and blue rotating lights in my rearview mirror.

For a few seconds, I considered trying to outrun the patrol car. I wasn't sure whether my newish Volkswagen Beetle could outrun his dated Chrysler. I had no desire to re-enact a Jason Bourne police chase. There wasn't much shoulder on the two-lane road, so I pulled into a church parking lot and waited.

I heard his tires crunching on the limestone gravel and watched in my rearview mirror as a short, squat officer stepped out of the patrol car. He pulled up his brown polyester pants with a little jump and tilted his hat forward before striding aggressively toward me. I opened my window. The sun's brilliant orange and purple rays were setting over the trees. I'd been driving for fourteen hours.

"Evening, Ma'am," the officer said. The voice was high-pitched with a slight drawl.

"Hello?"

"Bet you're wondering why I pulled you over, huh?" The officer was not a *he*, but a *she*.

"Well, I wasn't speeding."

"Did you get gas a while back at the truck stop?" she asked.

"Yes?" I stared off in the distance, wondering how I'd been spotted so quickly.

The officer followed my gaze to the sky, now saturated with colors like an impressionist painting.

"Some view, huh? Guess you don't see too many of these in *Chi-CA-go*?"

My back stiffened. I told myself that she'd probably read the Chicago dealer sticker on my license plate and saw my bumper stickers: "Black Lives Matter" and "The Revolution Will Not Be Televised."

"Yeah. All those buildings. Hard to see the sun go down," I said, wishing she'd get to it.

She turned back to me and stared a little too long. Maybe it was my bad dye job. Maybe she wondered if she had enough probable cause to search my car, and if she did, whether she would find marijuana or paraphernalia, items that were both legal in Chicago, but not in rebel flag territories.

"Yeah," she said. "I'm going to need to see your driver's license and registration."

"Really?"

"You didn't pay for your gas back there. That's theft." She smirked as if she'd caught a master bank robber.

"What? Of course, I paid. I'm sure I have the receipt." I began digging in my bag, but then I remembered that I'd been so rattled by the cashier that I hadn't bothered asking for a receipt. How could I have been so stupid?

"I wrote a check," I said, sweetly, reading her name badge. "Officer Baldwin."

"*Deputy* Baldwin," she corrected. "Driver's license and registration," she repeated with annoyance. I opened my glove box and dug through the old repair tickets, fighting back a distaste rising up my throat. Only hours earlier, I'd frantically searched through Reece's glove box, hoping to find a gun. Now I wish I hadn't. I swallowed hard and handed the officer a wrinkled piece of paper that no longer looked official and my driver's license, which pictured me with black hair.

"This is you?"

I forced a laugh. "Yeah, I recently went blonde."

"Hmm. Is that what you call it?" She smacked my plastic driver's license against her wrist and backed away. "I'll just be a minute."

My eyes followed her in my rearview mirror as she sauntered back to her patrol car with Georgia license plates. Her revolving lights reminded me of the red light on the video camera that filmed Reece getting shot. If the cameraman—and I assumed it was a man—wanted notoriety, the video would have gone viral on social media and been splashed all over the news by now. More likely, the photographer wanted money. He'd have to figure out who I was and how to blackmail me—or my folks.

Deputy Baldwin seemed to be taking an inordinate amount of time. The cooling fan on her car engine kicked on and off, increasing my anxiety. I worried about what she might find in her computer. She'd see all my arrests and convictions, and maybe that would give her the probable cause she needed to search my car. And then I remembered the bag with my bloody clothes in the trunk. I'd meant to ditch them at one of the truck stops, but I'd forgotten. Stupid, stupid, stupid. I slammed my fist against the steering wheel. I had to stay focused if I was going to survive on the run.

Finally, I heard her boots kicking up gravel as she made her way back to my car. Her face was stern. She stooped to look me in the eye.

"There's a problem," she announced, her jaw firmly set.

"What?" My mind did the quick math. I could pull through the field and onto the road before Deputy Baldwin could run to her car.

"The gas station clerk says you only paid for a Halloween outfit but no gas."

"I'm certain I paid." I counted out the change the cashier gave me on my lap. There were too many Andrew Jacksons. She hadn't charged me.

"She says she can take your credit card over the phone," the deputy said, clutching my registration and driver's license. "I'll wait while you call. Here's the phone number." She handed me a slip of paper.

"I don't have a cell phone," I said weakly. "Or a credit card."

"Traveling alone hundreds of miles from home with no credit card or cell phone?" She waited for an explanation.

"I'm low tech these days." Even burner phones could be tracked by cell towers, and credit cards provided instant location information to anyone with a warrant.

Deputy Baldwin chewed on the inside of her cheek. "Uh, well, you can either give me the money or go back and pay for it yourself."

I felt dizzy with relief. I wasn't going to jail, at least not at that moment. I quickly handed her a twenty. I didn't care if she pocketed the money.

"Is that all?" I started the car's engine.

"Not exactly. Your tags are out of date." She handed me a thin yellow slip of paper with my name written in all caps. "A warning." Then she stepped back and tilted her hat down in a good-bye gesture. "Not all cops are bad, Ms. Keane."

I held my breath. So, she had read my arrest record. When she finally backed away, I closed my eyes and exhaled. The deputy's stop, no doubt, would become the first pin in a police map of my escape. She would likely recognize me from any future APB put out by the Chicago police. Her report coupled with my check would provide enough detail for a savvy detective to chart where I might be headed. At the moment, that trajectory was southeast, a straight shot to Florida.

I had to change course.

No phone meant no Google maps. I dug out an old U.S. atlas—something else my father made me keep in my car—and spread it across the car hood to plot my next move. Where could I land that I wouldn't be detected? I traced the blue highway north on the wrinkled map, through the Upper Peninsula of Michigan, the United States' northern border. My finger landed on a cluster of islands in Lake Superior. The notation on the map read "Disciple Islands National Lakeshore." I tapped the small dots with my fingernail.

My family had vacationed on Angelica Island, the only habitable island in the Disciple Chain. It was a mystical place. Deer roamed like dogs. Only one paved road wrapped around the island, fourteen miles long and three miles wide. With no bridges or causeways leading to its shores, the island's only connection to the outside world was a sluggish, seasonal ferry.

What impressed me most about the island was its history. During a drought in the late 1600s, the indigenous Ojibwe tribe sacrificed its first-born daughters to the rain god. I spent most of that vacation pretending to be an Ojibwe girl hiding from men hunting me with machetes.

I stared down at the map and felt a grin spread across my face. Hiding out in the woods of Angelica Island was such an absurd idea it just might work. Surely no one would look for me on an ice cube next to Canada.

RILEY

Mine had been the only headlights on a curvy, country lane for more than an hour. It was my fourth day on the road. Reece remained in critical condition, according to news reports. Police were calling the shooting a "robbery gone wrong." Radio reports made no mention of suspects.

By midnight, I'd made it to Grand Portage, a quaint town perched on a hillside across the bay from Angelica Island. I'd missed the last ferry, which, according to the sign posted at the dock, left the mainland at ten p.m. I stood in the empty parking lot, feeling forlorn and helpless. Tufts of snow blew across the lot and into the vacant street.

Across from the ferry landing and overlooking the bay was an elaborate Queen Anne. Her upper stained-glass windows peered down like watchful eyes. Erected in the front lawn was a bed-and-breakfast marker; I trudged up the hill and rang the doorbell.

A lamp went on in the living room. A man, his face wrinkled as a morning-after bedsheet, appeared behind the glass storm door. Metal locks creaked, and the door opened.

"Can I help you?" In his bathrobe, he looked befuddled, his thin hair sticking up on one side, a hearing aid protruding from an ear. He opened the storm door slightly. We spoke through the crack.

"Sorry I woke you," I said too loudly. "I'd like a room."

"Just for tonight?" he shouted. "You won't be staying for tomorrow's dinner?"

"Dinner?"

"Yes, we offer a big spread for Thanksgiving. We're known for our cranberry stuffing."

How had I forgotten Thanksgiving? Just the word brought back warm memories: my family spread out in the living room; a fire roaring in the fireplace; Christmas music playing on the stereo; my brother, Nelson, on the floor playing with his kids; my father generously topping off wine glasses with his special port; Mom offering another piece of pie. The seed of loneliness I'd felt in the parking lot expanded to an aching black hole in my gut.

"Our guests usually come specifically for our all-day holiday party," he continued his sales pitch. "We did have a cancellation, so I am able to offer you a room."

"Well, I was hoping to go to the island..." I stuttered. "I... just missed the ferry." I still couldn't register that I'd forgotten the holiday. How could I have overlooked that?

"Oh? Do you have family on the island?"

"No."

"Well, Miss, nothing is open on Angelica Island on Thanksgiving. It's best you stay here."

Maybe he was right.

"Our Thanksgiving dinner comes with a two-night stay," he continued.

"How much is *that*?"

"It's $250 for the two nights with Thanksgiving dinner and

cocktails," he said as if quoting from a brochure. "Are you alone?" The question sounded like criticism.

"Yes."

"It's awfully late to be out, young lady. Are you in some kind of trouble? We don't want trouble here." He started to close the storm door.

"No, it's nothing like that," I said, my voice pleading. "It's just that I don't have much money… I'm… a… graduate student. Do you think you could give me a break on the price?"

My money wouldn't last long at these prices.

The man stared down his bony nose at me. "We don't make discounts, young lady. This isn't *that* kind of place."

I pulled out what cash I had in my jean pockets. "Here's a hundred-fifty dollars. If I walk away, that empty bed will get you nothing." I figured I could sleep in the car if I had to.

The old man's lips curled as if he'd tasted something bitter. "All right, you've got a deal. But be quiet about it. I don't want the other guests finding out they are paying more."

He opened the door. The warmth embraced me. The place had all the expected accouterments—antique furniture, lace doilies, grandfather clock, old-timey wallpaper, and the remnants of a fire in the fireplace. My loneliness eased a bit. We crept up two flights, the stairs creaking all the way. The innkeeper only needed a stocking cap and a burning candle stub, and he could have passed as Ebenezer Scrooge.

When we reached the third-floor landing, he opened a heavy wooden door and led me inside a dormered room that overlooked the bay. Lights from the harbor flooded the spacious room, revealing an old-fashioned poster bed and a floor to ceiling bookcase jammed with hardcovers.

"Light is here somewhere," he said, fumbling behind the door.

"No need. It's fine." I didn't want him to see my watery eyes.

"Suit yourself. My name is Bob. Breakfast is at nine a.m. *sharp*."

He held out his palm, and I thrust several bills into it, thinking he wanted payment and not a handshake.

He looked down at the money as if it were dirty laundry and shoved it back at me. "You can pay my wife, Sofia."

As soon as he closed the door, I peeled off my clothes and slid under the cool covers. All I could think about was that when I woke, it would be my family's favorite holiday, and I would not be home. It was the one day I spent with my dad in the kitchen. We always cooked on Thanksgiving together. My father used to say in a mock, genteel accent: "What's not to love about Thanksgiving? It's a made-up holiday—no church, no guilt, no gifts, just great food, wine, and pie."

I longed to call my parents and reassure them I was okay. But how could I call anyone without tipping off the police who would eventually pull the phone records of my parents and friends in order to find me? Every electronic transaction increased the risk of getting caught. I remembered from reading *Famous Female Fugitives* that slipping up just once after leading diligent lives was what ensnared them. I vowed not to get sloppy or over-confident.

That's why, after Deputy Baldwin pulled me over, I ditched the bag of bloody clothes. Then I drove to Atlanta and withdrew all my money—about five grand—from one of my bank's branches. The withdrawal would become another pin in my police tracking map. I briefly considered going to Canada instead of Northern Michigan. But I needed a passport, and I'd let mine lapse.

As I drove out of the South, I began to question whether running was the right decision. Several times, I took an exit to turn around but instead got back on the highway. Would I ever see my family again? What were they thinking of me? I missed our loud Sunday dinners and felt tortured by guilt for putting them through so much worry. Only a few days gone, and I ached with a homesickness I hadn't felt since summer camp in junior high.

I didn't fear going to prison. Lots of activists spent time behind bars. I'd been arrested enough to get a hard look at that culture. But I didn't want Reece and Finn to suffer, too. Ever since Darren Wallack shot up our high school and our lives, the only thing Reece talked about was becoming a cop. He once told me that he fantasized about being the first responder at a school shooting and taking out the predator. I was embarrassed to admit that there was a part of me that wanted that for him too. We were all wounded in some way.

My association with Finn made him just as vulnerable. Voters don't like politicians who sleep with women with rap sheets. Recently the mayor had tapped him for the vice mayor position. He was a rising star, slated to be the next mayor. I couldn't take that away from him.

On the road, I often picked up the motel phone and dialed Finn's number—all but the last—and instantly felt closer, as if all that separated us was a single digit, the single press of a button, and not the highways and states between us. I was sure Finn despised me. If the roles were reversed, I would have wanted to be a part of *his* plan, to be trusted with *his* secrets.

The grief of leaving him tugged at me. I saw Finn's face in the strangers I met on the road: in the faces of truck drivers whose hardened stares melted when I glanced their way; in the men at gas stations who talked me up and insisted on pumping my gas; in the fathers sitting with their families who smiled at me as I ate alone at roadside cafes. Like Finn, they were kind people in places I didn't expect.

I HADN'T EXPECTED to find Finn at a Take Back the Night protest. What Republican had the guts to show up at a protest involving thousands of angry women? My friends and I were marching down Michigan Avenue wearing pink crocheted pussy caps, waving our handmade signs and stabbing our fists in the air. My group chanted, "I don't want your tiny hands anywhere near my underpants!" It didn't matter that it was thirty degrees and the sky was spitting a wintry mix of sleet and snow. We felt unstoppable.

That's when I saw him passing out campaign buttons. He looked like the all-American guy next door, wearing jeans, a Cubs jacket, and a ballcap with two kids hanging off him. We'd never met before, but he was infamous: the only Republican in the Chicago City Council. We exchanged words, mine angry, his cordial. I didn't think any more of it. He handed me his card, and I stuffed it in my pocket, expecting to find it in the wash someday.

As I stepped away from him, a half dozen men in leather jackets with double lightning bolts slipped in behind my group. They called themselves Hard Boys and showed up at all our marches, causing trouble. This time they stepped on the heels of our boots and shouted at us, threatening rape. I told the women to ignore them. There were always a few hecklers. But the taunting got worse. They called us *cunts* and maliciously detailed the violence they intended to inflict upon us.

Violence is never an appropriate response to violence. I know that. But when one of the men edged up to me, stuck out his tongue, and licked my cheek, a primal instinct took over. I swung my fist as hard as I could, hitting the center of his face. He reeled and fell to the pavement. Cops came flying out of nowhere and tackled me.

It wasn't until later in the shithole they call the Cook County Jail that I found Finn's card. I stared at the city of Chicago's seal and wondered if Mr. Republican might be able to help. I used my one phone call to ring his cell, expecting that he wouldn't pick up. But he did. And within half an hour, I was staring at him through two inches of polycarbonate and acrylic. A man never looks as good as he does through jail Plexiglas.

He picked up the phone. I picked up mine.

"Didn't know you had such a powerful right hook," he said. "A peace activist who gets violent. Now that's rich."

"The man licked me! How is that *not* assault?"

Finn sat back. "You broke his nose!"

I held up my fist. The knuckles were swollen and light blue. "It hurts like hell."

"You'll be out in a couple of hours," he promised. "You can ice them then."

"I didn't mean for you to bail me out personally. I thought you could make a few phone calls on my behalf."

"It's all over the news. Marchers filmed it on their phones." He shook his head and made a face. "It doesn't look good—you on the pavement wriggling under several officers trying to handcuff you. Female protesters closing in. Male cops pushing back the women, using their batons as barriers. The women shouting: 'Protect Women Not Rapists! It Stops with Cops!'"

"They're fierce women," I said proudly.

"I called the mayor. He told me to make this go away."

We both laughed at the irony of our situation. And that's when I felt it. The sizzle up my spine, the nervousness in my belly, the bodily excitement: sexual chemistry through bullet-proof glass. Other than my lawyer and my father, no other man had ever bailed me out of jail. I wondered what else this man with opposite passions would do for me.

FINN

It was the night before Thanksgiving. I'd worked late at the office, making phone calls in my official capacity as alderman to see how Reece was faring. He had improved, but an infection got him moved to ICU. Police still didn't have any suspects, and no one mentioned anything about a video surfacing.

I wasn't sleeping much, worried about Riley, and crazy scared about where she was and what might be happening to her. I asked a cop buddy to run Riley's plates through the license plate recognition software on street and highway cameras. He'd gotten a couple of hits. One was on the Skyway, heading to Indiana. At least she'd made it out of the state.

I curled up on the couch to watch a movie. Norma Rae snuggled in the crevice of my elbow. There was a hint of Riley's perfume on her fur, and it made me think back to the first night we'd made love.

I'd bailed Riley out of jail for punching a Neo-Nazi at an anti-violence rally, and a few days later, she called, offering to buy me a drink to thank me. I suggested a biker bar near downtown on the premise that it was convenient for both of us. In truth, I'd picked it because we were unlikely to be recognized. The place was dark with a labyrinth of rooms. Its walls were yellowed from when in-door smoking was allowed. I found Riley wiping beer off a table in one of the main halls.

"You really know how to impress a girl," she said, then winced at the notion of portraying our meeting as a date, though it had that feel about it.

I let out a nervous laugh.

"I started coming here late at night while I was in law school," I said, looking around at the mostly bearded and tattooed patrons. "It's quiet during the week, and they have strong coffee."

"How long did it take you—to get through school?"

"Five years. I worked patrol during the day and went to class at night."

"You were a *cop*?"

"South Side."

"No way CPD put someone as fresh as you down there."

"Ms. Keane, do you only see people in stereotypes?"

"Mr. O'Farrell, if I thought you were a stereotypical Republican, I wouldn't be here."

On the surface, our friendly banter was similar to that I'd had with other anti-gun lobbyists over the years. Except our conversation seemed emotionally charged.

"The federal government needs to pass stricter background checks and cooling-off periods for all states," she said. "Otherwise, gun control laws in big cities like Chicago are ineffective. No one should be able to cross the border into Indiana and buy guns as easily as they can buy cheap gas. Wouldn't you agree, Alderman Finn?"

I felt uneasy under her intense stare. All I could think about was seeing her sobbing over the body of her dead brother. How could you argue with a school shooting survivor? That was the power of her position. She didn't have to say Darren Wallack had driven across the border and bought all the guns he'd used with a fake ID. Everyone knew he had. She didn't have to mention "the massacre" because everyone knew her story. She was the most famous survivor of the deadliest school shooting in history.

Listening to her brought it all back to me, the secrets, the guilt of that day. And yet, there was a part of me that so wanted to comfort her, protect her, take away her sadness. And I know it sounds strange, but I wanted to make love to her.

"Why are you doing this?" I asked after several drinks, though the question was as much for me. I was feeling less inhibited. Tipsy or not, I knew this woman, and my growing fascination with her, was trouble.

"I told you I wanted to properly thank you for bailing me out of jail," she said, matter-of-factly.

"You did that on the phone."

She pursed her lips. "Maybe I'm just curious how the other side thinks. Reece says I'm too insulated. I surround myself with people who think like me. He says it makes me weak."

"So, you're slumming with me because Detective Taylor told you to adopt a Republican?" Even then, I was uneasy with the hold Reece had over her.

"I happen to think he's right."

"Glad I could be of use." I signaled the waiter for the bill. It was my weekend with the kids, and I didn't need a hangover when I picked them up from Diana's house the next morning.

"That's not what I meant," she said. "For so long, I've thought of Second Amenders as adult boys who play shoot-em-up in the woods. They strike me as impotent men who try to make up for their lack of sexual prowess by ejaculating a lot of ammunition."

"Wow. You really know how to make a man feel special."

She laid her hand over mine on the table. Her touch sent a jolt up my arm. She looked at me for a reaction. I didn't move.

"You make smart arguments," she continued. "I need to understand constitutional purists like you."

"And why should I help you?"

"Because this is all theoretical to you. You don't own a gun, or so you've said publicly. And because I'm betting as a former cop, you saw first-hand the horrific damage guns can do."

I pulled my hand from her. What did she know? Or was she stereotyping again? I hated it when people tried to put me in the cop box or paint me as one of those crazy gun nuts. People were much more complicated. The reasons behind their sacred beliefs were much more nuanced than the media or politicians made them out to be. When something as senseless as a school shooting happens, everyone reacts differently. Riley became an anti-gun activist. Her friend Reece became a cop. I had the opposite reaction—I wanted people to be able to defend themselves. I wanted more than criminals to have access to guns.

"Come on. Let's get out of here. I've got twelve-year Scotch back at my place," I suggested, as if either of us needed more to drink.

I had sense enough to order an Uber because I might flirt with the idea of bedding a woman ten years younger than me—didn't all stereotypical politicians do that? —but a DUI would end my career.

Riley headed upstairs and straight to my bedroom, though she'd never been to my home before. I found her lying on my bed in her bra and underwear.

"You're assuming a lot," I said, unable to hide my shock and admiration.

"Am I? It's after midnight, and you've asked me back to your house. What other reason could there be?"

I didn't argue. After a night of pretense, it felt refreshingly honest. This wasn't exactly how I'd pictured our evening ending, but I wasn't complaining.

I started to turn off the bedside lamp, but she objected.

"I want to see you, really see you," she said.

I stood at the foot of the bed and slowly unbuttoned my shirt, feeling exposed. Kneeling in front of me on the bed, she traced her fingers over my chest.

"I never dated a guy with muscles before," she said in a mock damsel-in-distress voice, then jerked my shirt off.

"Yeah? What kind of guys do you normally date?" Recently divorced, I felt like I'd been married forever. I worried I wouldn't measure up to Riley's single-woman expectations.

"Let's just say that my past two boyfriends had longer hair than me and more tattoos."

"You have more tattoos than these?" I held up her wrists. She had her brother's name tattooed on one wrist, and the date of his death on the other. She had the whitest skin I'd ever seen. Any other green-blue markings would have stood out.

She smiled, undid my belt buckle, and pushed my pants low on my hips. She moved her finger just above my pelvis, drawing a line beneath my belly button. She was good at the tease, but then she'd been flirting with me all night.

I closed my eyes, waiting for her fingers to creep lower. Instead, she kissed me on my mouth. They were hungry, sloppy kisses. I pushed her back on the bed, eager to move to the next stage. I gripped her underwear with both hands and pulled them off.

That's when I saw them, small cursive letters on her upper right thigh, just below her dark pubic hair.

"What's that?" I moved closer to make out the words.

She slammed her thighs together.

"Uh-uh. Not unless you do what it says."

"Oh, a woman who comes with instructions. I like that."

"Maybe and maybe not."

I gently pulled her thighs apart and put my face between them. I could smell her vagina, a pleasant musky odor. I wanted to eat her up. I moved closer to her thigh. The tattoo was in a small font, no bigger than type on a page. The message was simple: "*Pleasure me.*"

I looked at her. She raised an eyebrow, like a question.

MY LANDLINE PHONE RANG, startling me awake. I jerked up, trying to remember where I was. That scared Norma Rae. She scratched me hard enough to bring blood. I clutched at my forearm, the skin stinging, and answered the phone.

"Finn, how are *you*? I hope I'm not calling too late."

Rod Lowenstein, the mayor's director of communications, was a man who never called with good news. Everything about him—from his nasal voice to the way he dragged out his vowels to his forced saccharine smile—screamed fraud. Among aldermen, he was known as Dr. Doom.

"Just watching TV.

"That's *special*."

"What can I do for you?"

"Well, I'm preparing your dossier backgrounder for the mayor. Congratulations again on being considered for the vice mayor running mate—"

"Rod, the mayor made the offer. It's no longer a consideration."

"Yes, well, there's just a few more things we have to clear up first."

I'd opened up my records to this slimeball in hopes he could quickly get through the vetting process, but that only exacerbated what should have been a routine stamp of approval.

"*We* like to be thorough about these things," he continued. "*We* wouldn't want the press discovering some soiled undies during the campaign."

"Soiled undies?"

"Oh, it's just a phrase we *use.* We just want to make sure that we are aware of *all* indiscretions and prepared to address *any* situations that the media might discover."

So that was it. He was calling because he wanted me to confess to the dirt, he couldn't dig up himself.

"My ex-wife said you interviewed her," I said. "You've received our divorce settlement, so you know it was all very amicable."

"*Well,* sometimes people don't admit everything during divorce proceedings. Perhaps you left out something you didn't want your former spouse to know?"

"Like what?" He was fishing.

"Well, most divorces end because someone was *unfaithful.*"

"Diane told you there were no extramarital affairs."

"Hmmm. *Yes.* But you didn't say whether you've been seeing anyone since the divorce. Is there a Ms. or *Mr.* Special Someone in your life?"

"Oh, for fuck's sake. Rod, you know I'm not gay. The mayor has had me at his beck and call for months with the promise of joining him on the ticket. In all that time, you've been crawling up my ass, and you still haven't found anything. You keep coming back asking the same damn infuriating questions. I've opened up my office to you, supplied you with all the documents you've requested. What else can I do to end this–this –*process*?"

"Well, now that you *ask,* we'd like to take a look at your personal *email.*"

"And why is that?"

"Well, now, if you don't have anything to hide, what does it matter?"

Normally I was not a man who got worked up. But Rod had called me in a vulnerable moment. "I'll tell you why it matters. I deserve to have my own space on the planet that doesn't have your fingerprints all over it."

"Would you like me to tell the mayor you're refusing to provide access to your *email*?"

I couldn't win with this guy. He wasn't going to stop until he found something that justified his existence, making him look smart and praiseworthy to the mayor. Riley and I had been diligent about keeping our internet communication free of any endearments or specifics unrelated to our official relationship. But we had used code at times. I wouldn't put it past Rod to run my emails through an algorithm that would reveal our cipher. Besides, if he found nothing peculiar in my emails, he'd be asking for text messages next. That was more problematic. Even if I managed to erase Riley's texts, he'd next want to do a forensics inspection of my phone and my computer. It just wouldn't end.

"Rod, this is going too far," I said. "Either the mayor trusts me, or he can keep his vice mayor position. The mayor needs me and my super voter constituents more than I need him."

I hung up, stunned at my sudden temerity. The vice mayor position was all I'd thought about for the past three months. Now I was about to blow it over some overprotective fear about Riley. Something inside me was shifting, and I felt absolutely powerless to control it.

RILEY

I didn't wake until I heard the clatter of dishes and the murmuring of guests filtering up through the old floor registers. I scratched through the ice on the windows until I could see cars lining up for the ferry and instantly regretted my decision to stay at the B and B for two nights. The smell of fresh-brewed coffee pushed me forward.

I threw on my jeans, quickly cleaned myself up, and lightly stepped down the stairs listening to the din of laughter coming from the dining room. I hoped to slip in without anyone paying me much attention. But when I entered, the white-haired diners stopped talking and looked at me as if I'd stumbled into a private AA meeting.

A woman with a teased gray bouffant and crimson acrylic nails stood up and smiled. "Hi there, hon. I'm Lucille, and my husband here is Raymond." She pointed at a man with a dramatic comb-over sitting next to her. "We're glad you're joining us today." The two seemed like hosts at an evangelical church.

The room erupted into a chorus of hellos. I scanned the

tables for someone—anyone—in my age bracket. In the corner, seated amid several older men, a tawny-haired guy hovered over a newspaper while mindlessly shoving toast and scrambled eggs into his mouth. He looked like he was maybe in his late thirties, graying at the temples. I smiled feebly at him and took a seat at an empty table.

"Oh, no, dear," Lucille said, waving me over. "No one sits alone. We're all family here."

The thirty-something guy looked up from his paper and shot me a pained expression.

I pulled out a chair next to Lucille. Over my right shoulder, Sofia, the innkeeper's wife, appeared with a coffee pot and asked how I wanted my eggs. Someone passed a plate of muffins, and the inquisition began.

"So, hon, where you from?" Lucille asked.

My pulse quickened. After days of being alone, it felt weird to be the center of attention. Fugitive men could be hermits and loners without raising an eyebrow, but a lone woman was cause for suspicion. I'd learned that from *Famous Female Fugitives*.

"Scrambled," I said to Sofia, then returned my attention to Lucille. "I'm a graduate student at the University of Chicago," I said. "Thought I would take a break from school." My mind raced with the lies I could spin. The intricate account poured from my mouth. It was easy as if I had lied all my life.

"Oh," said one of the women. "My son works for the University. What department are you in?" She had a head like a turtle, narrow and convex, that jutted at a right angle from her neck. Her voice was soft, as if she were afraid to draw attention to herself. But her slanted, bulging eyes suggested she was taking it all in, cataloging everything she saw.

"Archeology." My parents lived next door to the University's most famous archeologist, a guy who showed up at formal events in khaki shorts and hiking boots.

"What's your name?" the woman continued. I shifted in my chair.

"Riley . . . my name is Riley—Kennedy." *Famous Female Fugitives* said the women often used their own first names and chose a last name close to their real ones because it was easier for them to respond, especially in times of stress.

"I'll have to ask my son if he knows you," the turtle woman said.

I smiled and turned to the plate of scrambled eggs that had arrived. I wasn't expecting the women to be so prying, but if anyone knows what's going on in a small town, it's the senior citizens.

"Where do you live in Chicago?" a beige curly-haired lady inquired.

"Kenwood," I said between bites. The neighborhood was little known to most Chicagoans, even though our former President owned a house there. That didn't dissuade the women.

"What street do you live on?" the turtle woman asked in that nosy way that only old women can get away with.

"Fifty-first and Woodlawn." It was a block from where my parents lived.

"What a small world. My son lives on Woodlawn, too!" The turtle woman's eyes suddenly were even more engorged. "He's a curator with the University's Museum of Science and Industry. Do you know him? Doctor Sam Winters?"

Kenwood was a tight-knit neighborhood. I'm sure my parents knew him. I could feel the dampness collecting at my bra line. "Sounds familiar. But my life has been nothing but bones and pottery lately."

The turtle woman's eyes narrowed. "I'll be calling my son later today. I'll tell him I met his neighbor. What did you say your address was?"

There was no escaping these women. I took a sip of coffee,

feeling all their eyes on me, patiently waiting. Finally, when I opened my mouth to offer a reply, Lucille waved her hand at the women: "Let the girl eat!"

The women let out a collective giggle. The turtle woman didn't laugh. I gave Lucille a grateful smile. She nodded her teased tower of hair. A few minutes later, I slipped outside.

Leaning against my car, I furiously puffed on a clove cigarette from an old pack I found in the glove box, remnants from a night out drinking. I decided smoking would become part of my new persona. The *Famous Female Fugitive* women all smoked. They believed nothing bonded strangers as quickly as sucking on nicotine in the cold. The nicotine from my stale cigarette was easing my stress. If I became rattled by a bunch of nosy grandmothers, how would I deal with possible employers or landlords who had legitimate reasons for asking questions?

The thirty-something guy walked out of the house, lit a cigarette, then, seeing me, headed in my direction.

"Do you mind if I join you?"

I shrugged.

We silently watched the ferryboat load with people heading out to the island. He seemed anxious as if he routinely drank too much coffee and smoked too many cigarettes. His eyes darted from the boat to me as he stroked his graying goatee.

"They can be intense," he said, breaking the silence.

"They seem nice enough," I volunteered.

"They're harmless, really. It's just you're new blood, and you're so...*young*." He flashed a toothy grin. His Harley Davidson leather jacket and cowboy boots made him seem out of place in the land of parkas and snow boots. Close up, he looked much older, waterfalls of wrinkles under his eyes, worry lines on his forehead.

"And who are you?" I asked.

"I'm local. Go every year. It's sort of the happening place around here for Thanksgiving. There will be other locals this afternoon."

"You live here year-round?"

"Name's Lars Wiman." He extended a hand with thick knuckles and square, yellow fingernails stained with grease. I felt rough calluses on his palms.

"I'm Riley...Kennedy." The name still felt awkward.

"Nice to meet you, *Ms. Kennedy.*" He said it like he didn't believe it. "From the looks of it, you got a ticket a few days ago." He pointed to the yellow warning slip I'd pushed into the crevice of the windshield. It was an old habit from Chicago—based on the belief that the police wouldn't issue you a second parking ticket. Deputy Baldwin had scrawled my name in large letters with a dark pen. RILEY KEANE could be read several feet away.

"First, they interrogate me, and now you're inspecting my car? What is this, the Sherlock Holmes Club? Will there be a murder during dinner tonight?"

He shrugged. "It's okay if you don't want to give your real name. I understand. Why would you want that geriatric crowd knowing your business?"

I bit down on my bottom lip and averted my eyes. "It's not like that," I said softly, trying another tactic.

"Oh?"

"There's an ex. I just...I don't want him to find me."

"Ah," he said, nodding. "There's always a man, isn't there?"

"Weren't you young once? Didn't you ever do anything spontaneously? Take a road trip at the last minute? I just wanted to get away for a while, you know, see another part of the world, have an adventure?"

Lars took a step back and squinted at me with one eye. "This is a unique part of the world. Not sure how much fun you'll have in the snow and wind. I'm afraid this isn't the best place for an adventure, *Ms. Kennedy*."

"I guess I'll find out."

I threw the stub of my cigarette into the snow and walked toward the house. He followed, then mounted the porch stairs in front of me and held the door open.

"Just so you know, everyone gathers downstairs around one. We all drink in front of the fire, watch the game on TV and wait for dinner, around five or so."

"How do you know so much about this place?"

He grinned awkwardly. "Sofia is my aunt."

"Are you going to tell her about me?"

"What? That you're scared of the blue hairs? We're all terrified of them."

FINN

When Diana decided to spend Thanksgiving with her parents out East, Kye and Nico seemed more disappointed than I was. Since the divorce, the kids and I had created our own traditions. On Thanksgiving, I'd pick them up at six, and we'd head to Chinatown for dim sum. Afterward, we'd traipse through the various Chinese shops and survey the strange wares of dried bones and mushrooms and weird meats—snake and eel and pig's parts. The kids would titter and point and squirm. Then we'd head to an old-time movie theater in Lincoln Park with red velvet seats and a giant curtain that opened to a black and white classic film, usually, *Citizen Kane* or *His Girl Friday* or even *Nosferatu,* which thrilled and scared the kids at the same time. Nico and Kye mostly looked forward to eating the old-fashioned candy from the theater's glass cases: Milk Duds, Jujubes, and Goobers, the last one good for a few giggles.

With the kids gone, the house empty, and Riley still missing, I was at a loss how to spend the holiday. Then Emma Keane called and invited me to dinner. Her son and his family would be there, she said. I got the sense the Keanes wanted to keep me close. They didn't seem to trust me, even though I had a lot more to lose protecting their daughter's secret than they did.

I arrived at five, as Emma had instructed. From the street, the house was lit up like a stage; the curtains pulled back to display the family aglow in warm orange lights. I briefly watched from the porch as they drank wine by a roaring fire, the dining room table set with silver cutlery, antique china, and pewter candelabras—certainly not the shabby chic décor I had expected at the home of activists. Then again, Mr. Keane had been a successful restaurateur.

I punched the doorbell with my elbow. In one hand, I carried a bouquet of sunflowers, red roses, and miniature carnations. In the other, I held a bottle of Bordeaux. Wearing a navy-blue blazer, a starched shirt, and pressed jeans, I expected to be underdressed. But when Ethan opened the door, he looked completely out of character, wearing a silly Christmas sweater—one of those battery-operated pullovers with Rudolph the Reindeer on the front, its nose a glowing red bulb.

Ethan didn't immediately invite me in. The chorus of Beethoven's "Ode to Joy" spilled through the door as he stared at me as if he'd forgotten who I was. I'd surmised by his disapproving looks and the lack of conversation that Riley's father was not a fan of mine.

"Good evening," I said and bowed.

In the harsh yellow light of the porch, the fine lines around Ethan's eyes and mouth were more pronounced, his forehead creased, and his shoulders hunched forward. He waved me inside without a word.

Pine-scented candles brightened the living room. A garland stretched across the stone fireplace. Several Christmas stockings hung on the mantel, including one with Riley's name.

"This is Finn," Ethan announced. "Riley's...*friend*."

Riley's brother, Nelson, and his wife, Bree, jumped up to introduce themselves. They couldn't have appeared more opposite: He wore a pinstriped suit—looking more Republican than me—and had the signature pale Keane skin set off by flat brown hair and nerdy square glasses. She wore a stylish pink polka dot dress that showed off her sculpted biceps. Her skin was a luminous henna, and she styled her hair in a natural Afro. Their twin daughters, Mavis and Nina, danced between our legs. Bree took the wine and flowers and disappeared. Nelson motioned toward the couches.

Riley rarely talked about her older brother. So, I was happy I'd Googled him and Bree before I'd left the house. Nelson was a criminal defense lawyer who frequently worked cases with the Innocence Project, which helped free the wrongly convicted mostly through recovered DNA evidence. He also did the legal work for SIG. Bree, also an attorney, worked for the NAACP.

"How are things on the council?" Nelson asked. "And—And the m-m-mayor? How is he —uh, uh, to work for?" I couldn't tell if Nelson was normally a stutterer or if I was making him nervous. He seemed uncomfortable sitting next to me, crossing and uncrossing his legs, rapidly blinking his eyes.

"He's a tough man to work for," I said with a note of finality. The last thing I wanted to do was discuss politics, especially since his sister's disappearance was threatening my political ambitions.

Ethan poked at the fire. I looked at my watch. Only five minutes had passed.

"Happy Thanksgiving," Emma said, appearing in the living room wearing an apron that said: *Don't Kiss the Cook.* "I'm so glad you made it." She smiled and handed me a goblet of wine. "Hope you don't mind. We opened your Bordeaux. I said it needed at least an hour to breathe, but Bree decanted it and said it was fine."

"I'm sure it is," I said, happy to have the alcohol no matter how it tasted.

Everyone appeared on edge, searching for any topic other than the obvious. Eventually, I slipped into the kitchen, where I found Emma struggling with a large pot.

I grabbed an oven mitt from the counter. "Here, let me help you."

Together we hoisted a pan from the oven. Strands of Emma's hair fell into her face and sweat beaded on her cheeks.

"You really must have a big one in there."

She wiped her face on her sleeve. "This is normally Ethan's purview. I rarely ever cook, *especially* on holidays. *He's* the chef. But he said he didn't have an appetite, and he didn't want to be in here without...well, you know. They usually cooked Thanksgiving together. It was *their thing*," she said softly.

"I didn't know Riley could cook." As far as I could tell, food was the least of her interests. She seemed to subsist on grilled cheese sandwiches and take out.

Emma looked at me for a long while. "She does that, you know, hiding qualities that she thinks are too *feminine*. She's an excellent cook. Her father taught her well. I think she sees it more as a social thing, though. Lots of wine, swarms of people in the kitchen. She rarely cooks for herself..." Emma looked embarrassed as if she'd revealed too much.

"That woman continually surprises me." I had never known Riley to throw a party.

A few minutes later, we filed around the dining room table. Bree took a seat on one side of me and Nelson on the other, an arrangement that felt planned. There was small talk about the day's events, the downtown parade they'd taken the kids to earlier, chatter about the weather, and the Bears game. No one mentioned Riley's absence. I assumed the point of inviting me to dinner was to discuss our strategy. As dinner progressed, I grew increasingly anxious.

Emma had just mentioned dessert—pecan pie—when Nelson tapped his knife against his glass, muting the clamor.

"I'd like to make a toast." He held up his goblet. "To our sister, daughter, and friend, Riley. May you be safe—wherever you are on this holiday. We love and miss you."

Emma teared up. Ethan sucked on his bottom lip. Bree lowered her gaze to her plate. This part of the dinner was unplanned, apparently. They all solemnly raised their glasses in tribute; then, the room fell silent. Ethan cleared his throat.

"Finn, has the mayor or anyone at council mentioned Reece's shooting or Riley?" He spoke in an offhand way, but it struck me as contrived. The entire night had been calculated. They'd invited me so they could quiz me on what I knew and take my temperature as to how committed I was to the effort of covering for Riley.

"Uh, no, actually not. I mentioned to him that I'd heard Riley had left town on a family emergency. He seemed thrilled she wasn't around to cause problems after a cop had been shot. But that was it." It was the plan we'd all hatched on Saturday. We hadn't gotten any further because Riley's parents were convinced, they'd hear back from their daughter by now. Six days later, I could see reality was setting in. Emma looked tired and weepy. Her husband seemed even more distracted and moody.

"Do you think he believed you?" Bree asked.

"He doesn't have any reason not to. I admit it's a bit awkward having *me* tell him, but what can we do? He knows we...*are friendly*."

I didn't know how else to characterize our relationship. In the year we'd been secreting around, Riley and I had never discussed what we meant to each other. Calling her my girlfriend felt juvenile, especially in front of her family. Celebrating the holiday with them reminded me of all the things Riley and I had missed out on.

I still didn't know what she had told her family about us. Ever since I bailed Riley out of jail, the mayor had made her my problem to monitor. He assigned us to the same anti-violence and gun legislative committees. He had no idea he'd given us official cover for being near each other. I complained to him often enough about Riley to sway any suspicions.

Even my closest friends didn't know Riley's name. I usually referred to her as my "lady friend," often with a bit of winking and elbow jabbing. It seemed old-fashioned and quaint, but somehow appropriate.

I told myself that women like Riley were skittish about commitment, and talk of exclusivity or, god forbid, marriage would only frighten her. I didn't press Riley for more because I knew someone so controversial was ill-suited for my political ambitions. I'd worked hard to get where I was, years of plotting and planning. I didn't want to jeopardize all that for a relationship that was likely to be short-lived. Besides, I'd been a complete failure as a husband and wasn't eager to repeat my shortcomings. We'd gone so long without discussing what we were that it felt forced to bring it up. Now I wish we had.

Nelson dabbed his napkin at his mouth. "Going forward, what should our plan be? I mean, eventually, her friends and board members are going to notice that she's...gone." SIG's notoriety had attracted several city dignitaries as board members.

"Emma could send her friends a note, saying Riley's grandmother was ill, and she had to go see her," Bree suggested.

"Yes, but how long can we keep that up?" Nelson asked, his

tone growing more critical. "Besides, both our grandmothers are dead."

"Bree's idea is good," I said. Though they referred to our plan with a collective "we," so far, it was only me who was acting as the official conduit to the mayor, risking my political career. "Perhaps Bree could try hacking into Riley's social media accounts and posting an update about a family emergency. The more real we can make this, the better. At some point, you may need to announce an official leave of absence on SIG's website. That should come from her parents since they are officers."

"A leave of absence?" Emma asked loudly. She'd been so quiet sitting there, circling her turkey and stuffing around her plate. "Whatever for?"

"She can't just disappear without explanation," I said. I couldn't believe they were in such denial. "She's a fixture at every police shooting, every anti-gun march. People will notice. And pretty soon at that. At some point, you'll need to offer a reason why Riley was the one chosen to visit this sick relative. You'll need a lot more details, especially if it's the police asking. And eventually, it will be the police asking—probably sooner than later. You need to decide what you are going to tell them."

"Why do you say that? Do you know something you're not telling us?" Ethan asked.

"The man behind the camera will eventually surface," I said. "And when he does, it won't be good for anyone."

RILEY

I'd changed into the only formal wear I'd packed, a long, dark blue velour dress. I was sitting near the fireplace, watching two old men play chess, when Lars appeared.

"I'm surprised to see you here," Lars said. I thought he was talking to me, but he bent down to look the old man in the face. The man was at least eighty years old, bald, and hunched over the board game. He wore hearing aids and looked up at Lars with rheumy eyes, but suddenly exhibited enormous strength, grabbing Lars's wrist in a tight grip.

"Hey, old buddy. How's my favorite secret agent doing?" the old man said.

Lars' eyes widened, and he glanced at me.

"Now, now, that's no way to be talking around a young lady." Lars nodded toward me.

The old man winked. "Have you met our newest guest, Lars? She's from Chicago. Isn't your main office out of Chicago, Lars?" The old man was practically yelling. He'd apparently forgotten to turn up his hearing aid.

"I met Ms. *Kennedy* this morning," Lars said, pronouncing

my fake name with sarcasm. The old man didn't seem to notice. Lars sat down next to me, leaned over, and whispered, "Any more old ninnies interrogate you?"

I strained a smile. I didn't trust myself to speak. My ears were throbbing with the old man's voice.

Lars slapped his hands on his thighs and sat up stiffly. "Want a smoke?"

Outside, we sat on the concrete porch steps. Lars flicked his gold lighter to my cigarette. The wind whipped the embers of our cigarette tips bright red, like sparklers.

"What do you do around here?" I tried to sound casual.

He looked down at the snow collecting at his feet and flexed his shoulders. "A little of this, a little of that. I own a motorcycle shop. It's pretty much shut down in the winter."

"Why'd that old man call you a secret agent?"

Lars laughed nervously. "He was just kidding. He's a retired judge for Grand Portage County."

"A judge?"

"This might seem like some great winter paradise to you, but it's one of the closest U.S. ports to Canada." His tone was defensive. "People come through here thinking they can run from the law and slip into Canada via the lake. Doesn't work like that. We're not some podunk backwater. There are a lot of people living here off-the-grid. It's a magnet for folks who just want to be left alone and have the means to make that happen. And over there," he said, pointing to Angelica Island, "they're all hiding from something."

"Like what?"

Lars gazed out at the harbor with his hundred-yard stare. "Before you were born, there was a thing called the Vietnam War. After that, there was the Gulf War, and then the 'conflicts' in Afghanistan and Iraq. Some of the 'Nam folks were draft dodgers. The others joined in peacetime and didn't want to fight. They escaped to Canada. When the government offered them amnesty, they moved to the island, staying as close to Canada as they could in case they needed to return—they never quite believed the U.S. government. Others were protesters, and they wanted to get away from the cops and their arrest records. Some people have lived up here for years without the government knowing they even existed. People in these parts are, by nature, distrustful of outsiders.

"It's fairly easy to live off-the-grid," he added. "The island's mostly wilderness. There's timber all around for heating. Most folks have generators, solar panels, and wind turbines. You can live fairly cheaply back in the woods on the island. It's only the shoreline property that is expensive. Islanders grow their own food, and they leave people alone. If they're not breaking the law, no one cares. But once in a while..." He wrinkled his face, "they get into trouble." Lars sat up straight and grinned self-consciously. "Well, there's my class report."

He talked like a cop, but looked like a member of the Hells Angels.

"You go over there much?"

"Often enough. You know it's not every day we get someone as pretty and smart as you around here." The charm had returned to his voice.

A white ferryboat chugged in the icy waters in the distance, making its way back to the mainland. I could barely see the island, a shimmering dark mass at the horizon behind the falling snow, and wondered what mysteries it had to offer me. If Lars had wanted to scare me, it hadn't worked. The island's appeal had only grown stronger.

"Should we go back in?" I asked. The noise from the party leaked through the sheets of plastic covering the front windows.

"You eager to return to the blue hairs and their mediocre wine, eh? I've got some top-shelf Bourbon at my place. You interested?" There was an eagerness in his voice I hadn't heard before. I glanced back at the gold lights of the Inn. Turtle lady would no doubt have called her son and be poised to pump me for more information. I turned back to Lars' expectant face. I wasn't going to feel safe until I knew who he really was.

Within walking distance, Lars lived in a cottage near the bay. His motorcycle shop was next door in a former boat warehouse. The house was homey: hardwood floors, brightly colored paintings, and oversized leather furniture.

"You live alone?" I asked, leaning over the counter that connected the living room with the kitchen. Lars poured Bourbon into two crystal tumblers.

"There was a woman for a while."

"What happened?"

"Asking questions works both ways. I'm not sure you want me to start asking questions about your former *boyfriend*."

I chewed on my lip.

"How about some music?" he asked.

One wall of Lars' living room held a library of vinyl albums. I settled on the couch and watched as he slid one album cover out of a slot and then another, looking for something particular.

"I'm impressed. Most people don't bother with vinyl anymore."

"We are of different generations. I spent most of my youth collecting these."

"Come on. You're not that much older than me? Late thirties?"

He laughed. "Tack on a few more years, honey."

"Early forties?"

"That's what dirty living does. All that smoking and hard liquor have preserved me."

We laughed easily. The Bourbon was giving me a relaxed

buzz. Lars selected an album and put it on the record player. Then, he sat next to me on the couch. Something about Lars made me nervous. He had this rough, overt maleness that made me feel self-consciously feminine. We tipped our glasses to each other and listened to the music. My body softened with the heat of the alcohol rolling down my throat. With each sip, I felt a little less homesick.

"You don't strike me as a bone digger," he said.

"I like discovering other cultures."

"Hmm. I'd like to discover your culture," he said, playfully. He rested his hand on my thigh. I scooted away from him.

"Maybe I should go." I stood up.

"My bad," he said, holding up his hands in a surrender posture. "I promise, you're safe here. I know what 'no' means."

I sat back down hesitantly.

"It's been a long time since a woman's caught my attention," he said. "I'm out of practice."

"Yeah? Well, I didn't drive eight hours from Chicago to wind up in another man's arms."

"Understood."

Lars refilled our glasses. Halfway into my second glass, I was really starting to feel the liquor. I told myself to stay sober, alert. But the alcohol was the perfect elixir to soothe my self-pity. Lars was prattling on about some musician. I listened to the song, waiting for the only part I knew, and began singing along with the chorus of "Against the Wind."

"What are you running from, *Ms. Kennedy*?" he said, picking a line from the song.

Before I could make up an answer, Lars' kitchen phone rang. He gritted his teeth and got up to answer it.

"Yeah?" he barked into the receiver, then softened his voice. "Sorry. I meant to stop by. I just got caught up with visiting folks at Sofia's. I'll come over for pie, but then I gotta get back."

He hung up the phone and gave me an unhappy look. "I'll be right back. I promise."

"Your girlfriend?"

He frowned. "I'll be back in half an hour. Relax, make yourself at home."

Before I could argue with him, he'd grabbed a coat and shut the door. I waited a few minutes then, convinced he wouldn't return immediately, began to look around to find out more about "Mr. Secret Agent." I rummaged through drawers and cabinets, but didn't find much beyond cable and water bills. The cottage was spare of any personal effects—no pictures or odd mementos. His bedroom was dark, except for a nightlight beside the bed. I lay back on the bedspread for a moment. The Bourbon made me sleepy and sad. My mind wandered to my family and what they were doing at that moment.

I must have fallen asleep. When I awoke, the room seemed darker, the house quiet. There had to be a clock somewhere. I felt along the nightstand. Nothing. Not even dust. I moved my fingers until they found a knob and pulled open a drawer. I touched something leather and heavy. I lifted the triangular object from the drawer. It was a pouch of some sort. I reached inside and wrapped my fingers around something metal. That's when I realized where I'd felt that shape before—when I'd shot Reece. I looked down at my hands, and in the dim light, recognized a Glock 22—the gun of choice for law enforcement.

RILEY

Lars' gun felt cold in my hand.

Reece's spare had also felt cold the night I'd pulled it from the glove box. It wasn't the first time I'd felt a gun or shot one. Finn had made sure of that.

"WHY IS it necessary for me to handle a gun?" I had asked Finn as he drove to the shooting range. We'd been seeing each other for a few weeks, though I was still resistant to calling our outings "dates." They seemed more like debate club competitions.

He gripped the steering wheel and stared straight ahead, stifling a self-satisfied grin for having talked me into going.

"It sounds counter-intuitive, but if you're going to castigate gun enthusiasts publicly, the first criticism you need to dispel is that you've never fired a gun. It's an easy fix...and," he cast me a sideways look, "one that might make you more empathetic to their arguments."

"I don't need to be empathetic toward people whose hobby is mowing down children—or Bambis."

Finn turned down a rural road between long green fields and patches of blue spruce—hardly the setting I expected. In my mind, a gun range was a rusted trailer with a few bottles lined up on old barrels.

I dreaded the whole ordeal—holding a gun for the first time, firing it, but most of all, hearing the loud discharge. It was the sound that was the most difficult for me. Even in movies, I stiffened when I heard gunfire—or fireworks.

"Is there something you want to talk about?" he asked. His tone had softened. "I know this is going to be hard for you, that it might bring up memories that you're not prepared to deal with, but I'm here. I wouldn't push you to do this if I didn't think you needed to confront this."

Was he referring to my lack of experience handling guns or my refusal to address the massacre? Finn and I had never explicitly talked about what had happened. We referred to it in veiled references and insinuations. He'd given me subtle invitations to open up. But I never did. I saw no point in revisiting the worst day of my life.

"I don't understand why *I* have to make an effort to understand *their culture*. I don't care about these people. Their hobby, their guns have killed innocent children—including my brother—people who did not deserve to die because someone wanted *the freedom* to get their rocks off shooting a gun."

"You have a blind spot, Riley. You can't argue with a gun enthusiast reasonably unless you can acknowledge the desire to protect yourself and your family, the freedom to hold power in your hands. Most gun lovers just want a sense of security. They want to level the playing field with all the crazies, gang bangers, and criminals. They don't want to arm mass murderers. These people are not Darren Wallack."

I wrenched my head to him. No one ever spoke his name in front of me. I could feel my face grow hot, and I feared if I said anything, I would start crying.

Finn pulled into a parking space in front of a white metal building, and we walked in looking like a couple who'd just argued, me with a sour pout on my face, and him acting felicitous, trying to get me to come out of my bad mood.

"What if someone recognizes me?" I whispered.

"What if they do? They're not going to criticize you for coming on their turf to try and understand them."

"I feel very uncomfortable, Finn."

"I asked you to give me an hour. Sixty minutes. That's all."

We started with half an hour of instruction from a stocky guy named Dick, a former cop who knew Finn. He showed me how to handle a gun, load it, and stand when I fired it. Then he handed me a Glock19.

"I've read about all the problems with Glocks and their faulty trigger mechanism," I said.

Dick didn't flinch. "That's true. The gun manufacturer has worked hard at developing a better gun. This gun here," he said, pointing to the boxy black gun in my hands, "is the latest model Glock—Glock19, Gen5. It's got a lot of nine-millimeter firepower. It will certainly stop an attacker."

"You mean it will kill them?"

Dick looked a bit sheepish. "Ma'am, a gun is a weapon. It's not a toy. It's not sports equipment. It is designed to maim and kill."

"I can't do this," I said to Finn.

"Please, Riley," he pleaded. "Only thirty minutes more. You can do this."

"He's right," Dick said. "Forty percent of all gun owners are women. They own guns for protection. Learning how to handle and fire a gun just makes sense. You never know when you might be in a situation where you need to shoot one." Dick and Finn exchanged pained looks. Apparently, this wasn't in their practiced dialogue.

It took me a while to load the gun because bullets kept popping out of the magazine and falling on the floor. I slipped on the heavy-duty orange earmuffs and stepped into my assigned lane in the shooting room. Guys next to me were firing rapidly. A lone woman was shooting at the far end. The room smelled like hot lead and burnt carbon. A haze hung in the room from all the gunpowder in the spent ammunition. The noise was jarring—like putting a leaf mower to my ear. Surprisingly, it didn't sound like Darren Wallack's guns. He'd been shooting automatic rifles. At the shooting range, everyone was firing handguns.

Dick positioned me so that my torso was slightly leaning into the gun, my elbows unlocked, my feet planted.

"Relax. You shoot better when you don't tense up," he said.

I took my position, faced the bull's eye at the end of the row, scowled at Finn over my shoulder, grinned at Dick, refocused, then pulled the trigger. I felt the force of the gun in my hands. But it was the sound of the burst that jolted me.

"Hey, that was pretty good," Finn said, giving me a playful smile. "Looks like you got within the first outer ring."

Dick was less enthusiastic. "Keep your arms relaxed. Pull the trigger slowly. Keep your eye on the bull's eye. You want to hit the center mark. Aim for the red."

I exhaled loudly, planted my feet on the gray masking tape on the floor, aligned the sight on the target, and gently pulled back the trigger.

Dick switched on the chain mechanism and pulled the target sheet to us. There was a hole in the first black ring around the red center.

"That's a good start," Dick said. "Now do it another dozen times until you can hit that red dot with no problem."

My hands were shaking, my ears throbbing. My eyes felt like they were going to burst from the surge of adrenaline. I could feel that cutthroat competitiveness coursing through my body. The gun was making me aggressive. The place smelled like a men's locker room reeking with testosterone-induced sweat. The men near me did not smile. They stared at me from the corners of their eyes, inspecting me, to see how I handled myself, to see where I'd made my mark on the bull's eye. I *wanted* to make the mark, be good at this, prove I was their equal. I could be a skilled shooter *and* an anti-gun activist.

I took my stance and fired. Again, and again, in rapid succession. In my mind, my target *was* Darren Wallack. I was going to kill that mother fucker. It felt good to fire at him, to rip through the target—decimating what I imagined was his body. I admit I was a little afraid of myself. I shot two full magazines—thirty rounds—hitting the bull's eye about half the time. The others were close enough.

"Are you sure you don't want to take the police officer's exam? With your firing ability, you'd make the cut," said Dick, his lips turned up in a smile.

I winked. "No thanks. I'm good, Dick."

I discharged my magazine, feeling the men watching me, and handed the gun to Dick.

"So, what'd you think?" Finn asked when we were finally alone in his car.

"I get why people like to shoot. But that doesn't change my mind. If anything, feeling that power in my hands, seeing its path of destruction, makes me more convinced that these killing machines should be regulated."

Finn nodded. "That's exactly what I thought you'd say. And that's the argument you should make."

I LOOKED AT LARS' gun in my hand, slipped it back into its case, and returned the pouch to the nightstand. Lars' potential ties to law enforcement had just gotten more substantial in my mind.

RILEY

Walking back to the B&B, the wind lashed at my eyes and seeped through my coat, chilling me to the bone. My mind, though, wouldn't let go of how cold and heavy Lars' gun felt in my hands and the nagging question in my head: Was he a cop?

When I arrived, everyone was seated. Lucille rushed over and led me to my assigned seat.

"Here, hon," she said, pouring me a generous glass of red wine. "This will warm you up."

I told myself it wasn't so extraordinary that Lars owned a gun. This was designated wilderness territory, after all. A lot of people owned guns. But Lars' gun wasn't a shotgun or a revolver. And, sure, lots of people owned Glocks, but the model 22 was a full-size design particularly favored among law enforcement. There was a good chance that Lars was ex-military, maybe a cop, an FBI agent, or perhaps even a lowly bounty hunter. Hadn't the old judge called him a secret *agent*?

I glanced around the room until I spotted him, laughing loudly at his table. So, he'd left me at his house to come back to the B&B? Or had he come home and found me sleeping and decided not to wake me? Either scenario gave me pause. I gulped another glass of wine. By now, my velour dress and clingy tights were making me hot and itchy. I wanted to rip off the dress, tear off my stockings, put on some jeans. I wanted out of that room, away from those people. It was the first time since I'd left home that I'd felt certain I'd made a grave error. I shouldn't have left, fled, run off, whatever they were calling it back in Chicago. Fleeing wasn't brave or courageous. I'd been so sure that there was no way I'd get justice that I hadn't even tried. Now I was stuck. I couldn't go back. With a sinking feeling, I realized—I was a *fugitive.*

I excused myself, rushed upstairs, changed out of the dress, and threw everything I had into my bags. I left a hundred and fifty dollars on the nightstand, then slunk down the back stairs and out the side door. As I was rounding the house, I saw a familiar orange glow on the front steps: Lars, dragging on a cigarette. I crouched behind the evergreen bushes and watched. Was he waiting for me? He snuffed out the butt in a flowerpot, but remained motionless, staring out at the bay. Finally, he rose to his feet and plodded back inside. The storm door slammed shut with a reverberating *thwack.*

I sprinted to my car, threw my bags into the passenger seat, and slid in. I turned the ignition over, but kept the headlights off. The ferry dock was fifty yards away. I queued up behind a line of cars; Islanders who had come to the mainland for Thanksgiving were returning home. I looked in my rear-view mirror, unable to shake the feeling that someone was watching me. After several trucks pulled in behind me, I knew there was little chance Lars could spot my car crammed in among all the vans and pickups. Still, if he really looked, he could pick out the yellow Beetle. How conspicuous could I be?

"Hurry up, hurry up!" I yelled, hitting the steering wheel. The bright red numbers of the dashboard clock burned: 8:05.

The ferry was supposed to have docked already. I scanned the lake in search of the ferry lights.

I thought about leaving Grand Portage and going somewhere else. But where was I going to go where I wouldn't run into law enforcement? Besides, if Lars were suspicious of me, he wouldn't have hit on me, or would he? I couldn't keep running every time I got spooked. In *Famous Female Fugitives*, the women often panicked, but their fears were always false alarms. Even when the police finally arrested them, the women hadn't seen it coming. If Angelica Island was everything Lars said it was, it was the perfect place to hide.

Bam, bam, bam! Someone pounded on my window. I screamed and jumped back in my seat. The figure outside jumped, too. I cracked the window. "What do you want?"

"Uh, do you know what time it is?" a squeaky voice asked. I squinted at his face and realized the stranger was just a boy—a teenager with acne track marks across his cheeks.

"A little after eight o'clock," I said, softening my tone. "The ferry should be here soon."

"Thanks," he said, but remained at my window.

"Is that it?" I was eager to close out the cold.

The boy half-shrugged. "You got a light?"

"Sorry, I don't smoke," I lied, then closed the window. He stood still, staring at the glass as if he didn't believe me. Perhaps he was trying to think of another reason to pester me, to get me to open the window, to determine if I was, indeed, the woman whom Lars had sent him to find. At least that's the way I interpreted the boy's fidgeting—not the actions of an awkward, shy teenager, but that of a hired Basset Hound.

After a few moments, the kid slunk away, headed toward the nearby cottages and the B&B. Finally, the ferry lights appeared in the near distance. In a few minutes, I would be on my way to Angelica, the final stop of my escape route. None of this would matter. At least that's what I wanted to believe.

One by one, like metallic sheep, the cars and pickups wheeled up the ramp and onto the ferry. The deckhand directed us to inch our way to the back bumper in front of us. I got out of my car and stood by the railing. Lake Superior was rough, and the wind was wickedly cold. I clenched my parka around my neck and tried in vain to light a cigarette. Even though the ferry parking lot was empty, the boat's ramp remained open. Maybe the captain was feeling generous to stragglers on a holiday.

Just when the deckhand was about to raise the ramp, a motorcycle came barreling into the parking lot and roared onto the boat. The rider parked his sleek Harley Davidson and dismounted. He had a small frame and wore a dark leather jacket, just like Lars. I waited for him to take off his helmet, but he disappeared into the stairwell to the lower level. I shuddered in the icy wind. Was Lars following me?

I gripped the steel railing, staring down at the violent, frigid waters, and entertained a morbid thought: What if the ferry sank? What if this immense, dark, deep, superior lake swallowed up the boat, unable to carry all these cars, this weight, these people? It was a fleeting, ghoulish thought, the result of Bourbon, wine, despair, and the loneliness of the day. I imagined the water swallowing the cars and trucks. People's heads bobbed in the water. I pictured myself bouncing among the waves, desperately gasping for air as the icy water filled my lungs.

The idea of drowning made my stomach quiver—that and the swaying ferry, the glasses of alcohol I'd consumed, and my inflamed nerves. I doubled over the railing and retched.

I closed my eyes to the dark eddies beneath me and wiped the spittle from my mouth. When I glanced up, the faint lights of Angelica Island greeted me. And something inside me glowed with a renewed hope that my ambitious plan of escape might become a rational reality.

When the ferry landed, we took turns steering our cars down the ramp, onto the dock— about half a city block long—then onto the island. Oddly, the motorcycle rider hadn't returned to his bike, parked in a sliver of space near the front. On my turn, I pulled off the ramp, studying the motorcycle as I drove past.

Near the dock was the Angelica Inn, a sagging old house with a rusting pink Cadillac out front. The proprietor met me at the door in a pink housecoat with white feathers holding a well-groomed Pekinese. Thrilled to have a customer, she quoted a price of sixty dollars a night. She and Baxter, she said, patting the dog's head, would fix breakfast.

As soon as I closed the door to my room, I rushed to the window to see if I could spot the Harley. But the street was empty, the village quiet. Even in the dark, the island appeared much as I remembered it as a child, like an old Western town—a cluster of buildings with third-story faux fronts overlooking the main street.

Though it was getting late, I was anxious to discover the island that would be my refuge. I padded out my door and tiptoed to the front entrance without Baxter barking. The wind tickled my ears and blew hair into my eyes. I walked at a quick clip, past the cottages lining the main street. Closed until the next summer, most shops were filled with local artifacts, needless wares, and crafts that could have come from China.

At the heart of downtown—a T-intersection of two roads—and across from the gas station that appeared to serve as the year-round deli, post office, and newsstand—stood a dark-wooden tavern. Parked out front was a Harley with a sloped leather seat and a bright orange fuel tank with wings painted on the side—the same as the bike on the ferry.

My stomach clenched with nerves. I gritted my teeth and opened the door. The tavern was a cave, dark and low-ceilinged. There were fewer than a dozen patrons inside. Several sat at a long mahogany bar served by a thin rag of a barmaid. Others were throwing darts, and the remaining few were scattered among the tall, narrow tables and low booths. There was no sight of Lars.

I fished out a five-dollar bill and laid it on the bar. "Guinness. Stout."

The barmaid wrinkled her overly plucked eyebrows, grabbed a bottle from beneath the counter, popped the top, and pounded it in front of me.

I pretended to scan the room for a friend. Two motorcycle helmets rested on a table between two women. Both in their thirties, the women wore tight T-shirts beneath jean shirts.

When they noticed me staring, I turned and slugged back my beer.

"I ain't never seen you in here before. Where you from?" asked a man at the bar.

I looked away.

"Well, you come to the right place. There ain't no better bar on the island than this one. Course, this is the only bar in the winter," he continued, his mouth opened wide, exposing the dark spaces where teeth had once been.

"Sal, leave her be," the barmaid said. "Go back to yer corner, or I'll kick yer ass out."

The old man begrudgingly slid his beer back to his corner. The barmaid wiped up the streak he left in his wake and winked.

"He don't mean nothing by it. You visiting the island for the holidays, hon?"

"Yeah. Sort of. Hoping to find some work."

"On the island?" She stretched her scrawny neck over the bar. "You know they shut down the ferry in a couple weeks? You're stuck here all winter unless the lake freezes over, and some years it don't."

I smiled. "Kind of like that."

She eyed me as if I were as crazy as toothless Sal.

"What about here? You ever need any help?"

She held out her hands. "You want to work in this dump? You make nine bucks an hour, and the tips are bad."

"Looks good to me." I swiveled around, taking a census of the place.

"Then you'd have to talk to Mr. Wiman. He owns the bar."

"Lars Wiman?"

"You know him?"

"We recently met. What's he like to work for?"

She gave me a lop-sided grin, opened a beer for herself, and took a gulp. "Not a guy you want to cross. Know what I mean?"

"Yeah, I've met a few in my life. Is that his bike out front?"

"That's Ginny's." She nodded her head toward the table with the helmets.

"So, when will Lars be here?"

"Let's see." The barmaid looked up to the ceiling. "He shows up on payday, and sometimes he'll just pop in. Your best bet is if you come in about happy hour tomorrow."

One of the motorcycle women, holding an empty pitcher, appeared next to me at the bar.

"A half pitcher, Scarla."

"Hey, Ginny, this girl's looking for work," the barmaid said. "She knows Mr. Wiman. You needing anybody at the restaurant?"

"I'm Riley." I offered my hand.

"Virginia Evans." She shook mine. "You a friend of Lars?"

"I met him at his aunt's place at Thanksgiving."

"Ah," she tilted back her head and smiled knowingly. "How were the old-timers?"

I laughed. "A bit intense."

"You alone?"

I nodded.

"I'm sure they lit into you like chum." She stood back and looked me up and down. "So, Lars suggested you apply at my place, huh?"

I shrugged. "Something like that." I lied.

"You ever waitressed before?"

"My parents used to own a restaurant. My father trained me to work the front and back of the house." That part was true. I'd spent most of my life hanging out in the kitchen. My first job was polishing silverware when I was five years old. I began waitressing as soon as I could be trusted to carry dishes.

She smiled. "Then you'll appreciate the chaos of my little place. Come by in the morning about six. We're a little short on the breakfast crew. We'll see if we can put you to work."

She grabbed her half pitcher and walked back to her table.

I felt a twinge of happiness, or maybe it was simply relief. Finally, there was something to celebrate. I'd been on the island less than an hour and already had the prospect of a job. Maybe the island was welcoming me.

Scarla tapped her bottle neck to mine. "See? Sometimes it pays to know an asshole."

FINN

I arrived late for a subcommittee meeting, nauseous with nerves, and hungover from all the red wine at the Keanes' house. That morning's *Tribune* featured an artist's sketch of "a woman of interest" in Reece's shooting. The hair was too bristly and the shape of the face too narrow, but the more I studied the picture, the more I saw Riley's likeness. Her image sent me into a tailspin of anguish and worry. Would others notice the resemblance?

The meeting had already started; the only vacant seat was next to Sean McKinney, a blubbery man with a bad case of halitosis. Sean ruled our Streets Subcommittee meetings with the same brusqueness he displayed running a chain of bowling alleys on the South Side. The committee was in the throes of a heated discussion about a new way to fix potholes.

"This system uses asphalt cement, adhesive, and recycled tire rubber, and it doesn't work so good in cold temperatures," Sean argued, wiping sweat from his forehead and flipping back the bangs that continuously fell into his face.

Across the table, Elizabeth Jenner, a councilwoman from

Lincoln Park and the heir to a candy company fortune, was arguing that the city needed a more permanent and less costly solution to repair potholes. The two had been volleying arguments for several minutes when Sean noticed me reading the *Tribune* and snatched the paper out of my hands.

"This is what you think is more interesting than asphalt, Finn?"

I sat back, annoyed with his junior high tactics. "No, Sean, your analysis is riveting."

The others laughed.

"Well, let's all see what Finn finds more interesting. Can we get this story up on the screen?" Sean called to the clerks at the back of the room. The paper's front page—including the police sketch—flashed onto the conference room's giant screen. There she was, staring back at us. My throat tightened, and my tongue felt thick.

"Maybe we should approve more reward money to find this shooter?" he said. "I mean, when was the last time we had a female cop shooter?"

"The story says she's a person of interest, not the shooter," Elizabeth retorted. "It says the police are looking for a White woman who was *seen* at the detective's shooting. That's pretty vague if you ask me."

"I have to agree," I interjected. "I think the cops need to find other ways of getting people to talk besides throwing money at them. Buying witnesses by offering rewards has backfired. Their testimonies don't hold up in court."

Sean licked his chapped lips and surveyed the faces at the table. "The cops tell me that this woman was caught on a blue-light camera waving a gun." Sean was always boasting about his contacts at CPD as if he had an inside track.

"Ooooh, well, that solves the case," Elizabeth said. "Too bad they don't have any proof because if they did, the papers wouldn't be plastering some paper doll on their front pages."

Sean took off his glasses and held up the paper to an inch of his eyes. "You know who this looks like? That anti-gun protester." He shot me a look. He knew the mayor had assigned me to monitor her.

"Psst, come on?" I challenged. "Really? Riley's on the other side of the country caring for a sick aunt."

"Yeah, Sean, that doesn't look anything like Riley Keane," Elizabeth said. "You got a crush on her?"

Sean dismissed us with a wave on his hand. "Screw you guys. There are so many holes in this story, almost as many holes as an asphalt street in Chicago. Speaking of which..."

For the moment, the link between Riley and the sketch ended, but I knew it was only a temporary reprieve. The rendering of Riley's face was posted on every news website. Someone—more convincingly than Sean—would eventually point the finger at her.

RILEY

Virginia's restaurant dominated a prime lakefront plot. The Antebellum-styled building looked like it belonged in the Deep South instead of on an island on the northern edge of the United States. The front lobby was dark. The wood-paneled formal dining room was empty. I heard voices coming from deep within the restaurant, then felt a swoosh of cold air on my legs.

A waitress, smelling of cold air and nicotine, rushed in behind me. She wasn't wearing a coat, only a polyester yellow dress uniform with short sleeves. She rubbed her hands up and down her thin arms. When I told her I was looking for Virginia, she waved for me to follow. The back of the dining room opened into an airy glass atrium flooded with the faint morning light. Islanders clustered together and talked quietly while solitary diners kept company with their coffee mugs and dated newspapers.

"You'll find her in there," the waitress said, pointing to double swinging doors.

I pushed the door marked IN and was instantly met by a

clamor of pots and raised voices. At the nucleus of the chaos was a bald, muscular man with large tattoos marking his forearms. He crouched near the stainless-steel prep tables like some modern Quasimodo, his hands clenched, his back balled up in anger.

"Shit!" the man yelled, eying a gooey mess of eggs on the floor. "That's it! That is absolutely it, Adam. Out! Get out of my fucking kitchen!" He pointed his finger in my direction.

Virginia emerged from a side office just as the lanky teenager with braces threw down his apron, whisked past me, and disappeared through the swinging door marked OUT. The angry man's gaze followed the teenager then landed on me. He looked as if he were about to dress me down for invading his kitchen when Virginia rushed over.

"Oh, thanks so much for coming in," she said, her hand gently resting on my shoulders, shielding me from the man's rage. She guided me into her tiny office. "Things are a little crazy around here this morning." She laughed nervously.

Virginia looked much different than she had the night before. Her long, black tresses were pulled into a severe ponytail. Gray hairs framed her forehead. Thin wrinkles gathered under her jade-colored eyes. Her only makeup was a smear of bright red lipstick. "I'd like to say this is rare, but Javier isn't easy to work with."

I smiled. The turmoil reminded me of my father's restaurant kitchen. Like many chefs, he was known to fly into a tirade without warning.

Virginia's restaurant, she explained, had been her big venture. She'd borrowed heavily to get it going, and during the summer, it did well. The cold months were a struggle.

"Why don't you just close down in the winter?"

"Because then I'd lose my island clientele. They patronize me year-round because I stay open in the winter. In the summer, I have four other restaurants to compete with. Those restaurants cater to tourists—rich tourists. I do, too, but my bread and butter are the Islanders. Besides, I would lose money closing in the winter months, too. I just haven't figured out if the loss is greater open or closed. So, I stay open and win the gratitude of the Islanders, but not the gratitude of my bank."

"Those soulless banks will kill us all," I said.

She grinned. "Call me Ginny. Everyone does." She handed me an apron. "I had intended to try you out as a waitress, but now it looks like I need a cook's assistant. I suppose you know how to do that, too?" She didn't wait for an answer. "Listen, there's no point in having a lengthy interview. In the kitchen, resumes don't matter. You could tell me how fabulous you are, give me a list of references who claim you work miracles, but unless I see it, unless Javier likes you, you're just wasting our time. It's all about how good you are at taking orders, working with others under pressure, and giving the customers what they want. If you don't work out, I fire you on the spot. Just like Javier did today. Well, I wouldn't be so harsh. Besides, pay in the kitchen is better. And the Island's Finnish stock is not known as generous tippers. Where are you staying?"

"The Angelica Inn. Just temporarily."

She squinted. "You turned up in the dead of winter without a place to stay or a job?"

"I didn't exactly have a plan," I said weakly. "My boyfriend broke up with me, my grades were shit, and I just started driving. My parents used to take us here as kids." After the blue-haired interrogations, I was stuck playing the addled graduate student.

"I was a lot like you at your age—impetuous," she said, looking away and smiling at some far-off memory. "Enjoy it because it doesn't last long. Pretty soon, you'll have responsibilities, and then there's no escape." Her face quickly turned sad, and I felt a pang of sorrow for this woman I just met.

I tied on the apron and started for the kitchen when she grabbed my elbow.

"There's something you should know about Javier." She looked down at her square-toed motorcycle boots. "He's on parole. That scares some people. But he's a good person. You've got to give him a chance. I felt uncomfortable around him at first, too." She forced a smile, revealing a smudge of lipstick on her front teeth. "I'm not a Good Samaritan or anything." She waved her hand at the thought. "I only hired him as a favor to a friend, but then he turned out to be one of the best damn cooks we've ever had. So, *please* try to get along with him."

"I'll keep an open mind."

Plates were lined up under the kitchen heat lamps; more were set out on the dressing table. Javier was standing over the grill. I washed my hands and moved next to him. He eyed me intensely.

"Where you from?" He stood back, looking me up and down.

"Chicago," I said, jutting out my chin. "South Side."

He grinned, then threw a kitchen towel at me. "Do what I say, and we'll get along fine. And don't go crying if I yell at you. Can't stand weepy women."

That morning, Javier and I worked side by side, with me chopping onions—carefully hiding my watery eyes—cracking eggs and sautéing mushrooms. At ten-thirty, Javier went out back to smoke a cigarette. I tagged along. There wasn't a back porch, just some cement steps. The property sloped to a field of wild prairie grasses weighted with snow. We huddled with our backs to the icy wind, inhaling our nicotine. Javier cradled a mug of black coffee.

"Where'd you learn to cook?" I asked, breaking the silence.

"The Cordon Bleu."

"OK, Mr. Hostile. I thought maybe you learned to cook before you went away."

He shot me a look.

"Ginny told me about your 'unfortunate incarceration.'"

"Yeah, well then, why do I need to tell *you* anything?"

"Because if I'm going to be your assistant, I'd like to know your approach."

"I like to get paid. That's my approach." He jutted out his chin and stared at the scrub trees.

"So, do I. That's why I want to understand you, so I don't end up like that guy this morning."

"That was some bad shit, huh?" His belly jiggled. He shook his bald head, the texture and color of a football. "Look, that guy was a fucking idiot. He dropped food. He got plates mixed up. I should have fired his ass a long time ago."

He turned and stared at my chest. Then he lifted his eyes to my face. "You do what I say, and you'll be alright, *chica*."

"Yeah? Well, you keep your fucking eyes above my chin."

He mumbled something in Spanish.

"I mean it."

"OK, *chica*." He held up a hand in surrender.

We smoked a while longer.

"I was a Latin King, okay? Went to prison a kid, came out a man. Doing my pro time and then going back to Chicago." He pronounced the city like a banger: SHE-Ka-go.

I wasn't surprised. Even though it was seven hours away, Chicago was the closest big city. Detroit was a good nine hours' drive.

"What'd you do?" I asked and then immediately regretted it.

Javier bit his lip, made a fist, and rocked side to side as if he were going to punch me.

"I raped a White girl who wouldn't shut her pie hole."

It was all bluster. Whatever Javier had done, it wasn't rape. He looked to be in his mid-thirties. If he'd recently gotten out of prison, he did hard time, and it probably involved murder, drugs, or both.

The back door flung open.

One of the kitchen grunts yelled, "Hey man, we're getting slammed in here."

Javier's eyes locked on mine. "Truce, for now." He flashed me a Latin Kings' hand sign—thumb, index finger, and pinkie extended.

I flashed back the similar hand symbol for love. "Love you, too, man."

Javier snorted a laugh and shook his head. We flicked our cigarette butts onto the gravel, where they joined a pile of other dead ends.

The rush lasted until about one o'clock, breakfast morphing into lunch. Islanders ate their lunch early, starting around eleven. I would quickly learn how much life on the island was ruled by the sun. In the winter, the town was pitch black by four o'clock—not even a porch light to break the nightfall. The darkness forced people indoors, where they passed their time drinking.

As I was sweeping up, Ginny approached me. "Nice job. Even Javier approves."

"Thanks."

"By the way, I'll need you to fill out paperwork. You know, an I-9 and all that."

"Isn't there any way to do this, so we don't involve the government? Every dime I make takes away from what I can get in loans and grants."

Javier walked in carrying a box of ham from the walk-in freezer. "You a college girl, huh? Must be really smart. Guess that's why you ended up on an island in the middle of winter."

Ginny frowned. "Sorry, kiddo. Everyone here is on the books. I run a legal shop."

She tossed a yellow waitress uniform at me. "Eventually, you'll get to wear it." Then she walked into her office and closed the door.

"Don't worry about it, *chica*," Javier said. "Just give her your real number, but mix up the last two digits. You know? So no one can say that you gave a fake number." He winked at me.

I forced a smile. He was right. No one would doubt that a flighty college girl screwed up her number. That might buy me a couple of weeks or months. Eventually, I'd have to come up with a better identification, something believable. By then, I was hoping to be back in Chicago.

Just before three p.m., the night crew began to show up. The backdoor slammed with each arrival. Javier provided whispery commentary. There was Gill, a line cook. He was a tall, droop-shouldered guy with yellow-hair and a silly grin who looked like the actor Owen Wilson. But his mannerisms reminded me of Shaggy from *Scooby-Doo* cartoons—his bangs hanging in his face, one eye timidly emerging from the tangles, as if surprised. Gill came from a long line of Lake Superior fishermen, thus the weird name.

"Bluegill is a common fish in Lake Superior," Javier said, making bug-eyes and sucking in his cheeks like a fish.

Gill's sidekick was Chayton, another line cook. He was a handsome, energetic guy with dark hair and eyes and a tattoo on his neck that looked like the eagle of the Third Reich. Chayton's family was registered at the Ojibwe reservation on the north end of the island.

"Thinks he's a tough guy. Real angry, that one," Javier said.

Then there was Kayla, a short, heroin-thin woman with

tangled pink curls and an inch of black roots. Javier claimed she'd been a stripper and a drug addict before Ginny took her in.

"I'd like to do her," Javier said, thrusting his pelvis forward. "But she won't have anything to do with anyone but them people. They're like some weird cult. I heard they're all fucking each other, even the queer one," he said, gesturing toward a stork-like guy with dyed white-blond hair, who I'd later learn was Simon. "They're all real tight. No way they going to talk to you, so just leave 'em be," he said with a mixture of awe and disgust.

Javier and I started to walk out with the day crew. Ginny stepped from her office, holding her hand over the phone, and shouted: "Riley, I'll see you at the tavern for happy hour. There's someone I want you to meet."

RILEY

A tiny bell jingled when I opened the door to the gas station that also served as a general store and deli. Shelves were stocked with first-aid kits, matches, kerosene lanterns, Swiss Army Pocket Knives, and batteries. An open refrigerator case displayed bruised apples, thin-skinned oranges, iceberg lettuce, and rubbery tomatoes. A pungent, raw odor led me to a display case featuring venison, bison, sausage, and fish. Leaning over the meat section was an old man wearing an apron splattered with blood. His yellow insect eyes peered at me through thick, thumb-smeared glasses.

"Do you sell clove cigarettes?" I asked.

"Sure do." He hoisted himself off the case and walked to the front of the store, where an old, heavy cash register took up most of the checkout counter. "But we only sell *truth* cigarettes here." He stared at me with those cockroach eyes. His massive head sat directly on his shoulders. Beneath his pockmarked nose was a bushy white mustache, the ends of which he curled in his fingers.

He saw the question on my face, and continued, "Well, see,

we tell people straight out they're going to kill you. It's not the nicotine, young lady, that causes cancer, although in due time, it will get you, too. You see, it's the rat poisoning they make it with that will shut down your organs, make them fail, one at a time. *Sixty Minutes* did a big investigation, and they uncovered the truth about what you're smoking. So, I make people aware, too."

"Fair enough. I'll take two packages of your Killer Lights. I mean Djarum." I snickered.

He shook his head. "Done my job. Told you the truth, and you ignored the warning. On this island, young lady, everyone knows your business, so you better tell the truth, or they'll make you honest." Was that a warning?

I tipped my head at him. "Riley Kennedy." The name was beginning to roll effortlessly off my tongue.

"Gabe Kowalski. If there's something special you want from the mainland, you just tell me, and I'll negotiate the price."

"What are you, the island godfather?"

His face turned serious. "Something like that."

"Well, Mr. Kowalski. How about the *Chicago Tribune*? You got that?"

He smiled, displaying teeth the color of weak tea. "Every afternoon, me lady. It comes on the ferry from Grand Portage. You see, things take a little longer out here. What do you care if the news is a few days late?"

"And today's paper?"

"Right here. I keep 'em behind the counter. That way, people don't manhandle the front page to decide whether they want to buy it. I don't like my paper palmed. I like it crisp and clean with no smudges."

"I like my paper served neat, too."

Our eyes met. Kindred souls.

"My last one." He heaved the paper onto the counter. "That's three dollars."

"Three dollars for the daily?"

"Miss Kennedy, the news in this paper won't change your life on the island, but it will entertain you, make you laugh, and allow you to impress your friends with totally useless trivia. And maybe it will make you feel better about living on an island instead of that crazy world out there. Isn't keeping your sanity worth three dollars?"

I pulled out three more singles. "Good to meet you, Mr. Kowalski. I'll be sure to ask for my paper every day."

"I'll put your name on it—the Lady from Chi-raq."

I forced a grin. I hated Chicago's war zone image, and now my shooting a cop had contributed to the stereotype. I started toward the door, then stopped abruptly.

"Wait. How'd you know I'm from Chicago?"

"You're new here, ain't ya? Came off the ferry last night? Staying with that old biddy at the Inn? Went to work for Ginny this morning?"

He was starting to creep me out. "How do you know all that?"

"New faces stand out here, Miss Kennedy. People notice. Nearly everyone on this island passes through my doors. I hear *all* the gossip. And right now, they're all talking about *you*."

"Great," I said and turned toward the door. This time he hollered after me.

"If you don't pick up the *Tribune* by four, it goes on the open market. Just so you know."

The tiny bell sang as I closed the door. At first, I felt unnerved by the island's gossip and the old man's omnipresence. Then I realized if the cops showed up looking for me, the year-rounders might not cooperate, given their general distrust of government and outsiders. They might even warn me. My challenge was to be accepted by them, to be worthy of their protection.

I trudged along Angelica's empty, snow-blown street, with my *Chicago Tribune* stowed under my arm. I was beginning to feel hopeful about my future in Angelica, with its old-fashioned storefront windows and heated payphone booth. It was like I had traveled back in time. I watched the snow lighting on my skin and stuck out my tongue like a happy, stupid kid, tasting the flakes.

That warm feeling vanished when I got back to my room at the Inn and scanned the *Tribune*'s front page:

Police Seek Woman in Connection with Cop Shooting.

Police had released a sketch of a "person of interest." The drawing showed a White woman with short black hair, high cheekbones, and a tiny nose. It could have been me, and it could have been thousands of other women. The story said police had received numerous tips about the shooting after the Fraternal Order of Police offered a reward of $10,000.

So far, I was certain the cameraman hadn't come forward because any video would have been aired on television and posted on social media. What was he waiting for?

FINN

I sat down on the couch from a long day at city hall. Only Chicago would schedule city business on Black Friday to prove how hard we work for our constituents. I slipped off my shoes and was loosening my tie when my cell phone rang. It was Ethan.

"Can you come over?"

"I just got home, Ethan. What's up?" From my home on the North Side, it was at least an hour's drive to the Keane house in Hyde Park on the South Side.

"I don't think it's a good idea to talk on the phone." His voice was sharp.

I looked down at my stocking feet and Norma Rae, who was circling my legs, wanting to be fed. All I wanted to do was take some Ibuprofen and climb into bed. I still had a raging headache.

I was really hoping to extradite myself from the Keanes' plans of covering for Riley. It's not that I didn't agonize over where she was and what had happened. God, I missed her. But I also knew she could take care of herself. Riley always had a plan. I figured when she was ready, she'd come back or contact me. Until then, it seemed futile and risky for me to get involved any more than I had.

I admit I was annoyed as hell that Riley hadn't discussed her disappearing act with me. She hadn't asked me to cover for her; she just expected it. I felt a little like her bitch. What man doesn't want to be in control? As a politician, I was used to having command of any situation. But in these circumstances, I had no power. I felt impotent. And with the mayor about to announce that I was joining his re-election ticket, I needed to stay focused on my campaign.

"Are you coming?" Ethan asked.

I sighed heavily. "I'll be there as soon as I can."

It was dark by the time I reached the Keanes' front porch. Ethan opened the door before I even knocked. He stood in the doorway shoeless, his baby-fine hair sticking up in a stiff wisp and his undone bowtie hanging lopsided around his collar.

"Thank God it's you," he said. "Come in. Emma's lying down. We've had a hell of an afternoon." He wiped his forehead with a handkerchief. The shirtsleeves of his starched white shirt were rolled up.

I propped myself on the edge of the couch. The room smelled faintly of cheap perfume. Someone else had been there.

"You want a Scotch?" he called from the dining room, ice clinking into glasses.

"Please," I hollered back, unsettled by his attentiveness.

Ethan carried two beveled glasses and handed me one. The Scotch was two inches deep. Whatever he was going to tell me, it must be especially bad. He sat down in an armchair and kicked his feet up on an ottoman. He nearly finished the glass before he looked at me with liquid eyes. He slipped the bow tie from his neck and wrapped it around his left palm, like a boxer bandaging his hand before a fight.

"We had visitors today, Finn." His voice was flat with a hint of resignation.

"The police?"

He laughed cynically. "If only. *That* would be simple." He snapped the loose end of the tie in his hands. "No. We met the cameraman."

I opened my mouth to speak, but he kept going.

"He has an accomplice, too. She's a scary sort. If it were only him, I think we could work something out. I just don't think we can negotiate with criminals. I'm not going to be continually extorted."

"Who were they?" I was surprised he was confiding in me. Where was Nelson, his lawyer son?

"He was Black. She was White. He looked like a regular guy. Medium build, maybe mid-forties, clean-cut, attractive even. She looked like a prostitute, with bleached blonde hair, black roots, skin-tight dress. He was polite. She was intimidating. They both upset Emma. I refused to give them anything. Extortionists are never satisfied with the initial price, are they? Then there's further extortion and fear and more criminal acts. It's not worth it. I wonder if I'm giving up on my daughter by refusing to deal with them." His voice wavered, and he looked away.

"Did he give you a price?"

He shook his head. "We never got there. He brought the disc of the shooting. We started watching it. Emma couldn't take it. I had to ask them to leave. He left the disc. I've watched it several times. There's something I want you to see."

I wondered what Emma had seen that made her so upset. I felt anxious about what the video might show, worried that it might ruin the image of Riley in my head. Worse, I feared that viewing the video might make me complicit in a crime. As all good lawyers know, I needed to maintain a veneer of plausible deniability. It's better not to know something than to know it and not report it. But how could I worm my way out?

"You don't need to show me," I said, standing. "It's not necessary."

"No, no. Sit down. I want you to see this." He was kneeling before the DVD player. Then, suddenly, he turned around and glared at me. "Unless you think this will ruin your political career or something."

"Well, will it?" My voice was sharper than I'd intended.

"No more than you're already on the hook for, son. But if you're that worried, I can wait until Nelson arrives." He'd never called me son before.

I shut my eyes and shook my head. "Go ahead."

"Good." He fumbled with the remote control, muttering to himself, then suddenly there was static and an image on the screen. The film was dark, but I could make out two men wrestling on the ground. There was a muffled *Pow! Pow!* One man got up holding a gun and stumbled down the street. The other, who I recognized as Reece, lay lifeless on the ground. Riley ran into the frame of the camera with a crazed look, holding a handgun. The video abruptly stopped.

I sat motionless, staring at the blank screen, trying to make sense of what had transpired.

"Did you see what I saw?" Ethan asked.

"I'm not sure," I said, finding myself more curious than anxious. "Do you mind if we watch it again?"

He nodded. "I had to watch it several times myself before it all made sense."

He pressed play again, but this time he slowed the video. I noticed Reece and the man wrestling over a gun. The stranger outweighed Reece by at least fifty pounds and was probably seven inches taller. Despite the low light, I could make out the gun positioned between the two. In the few seconds, before their bodies parted, the gun was pointing toward Reece. That's when we heard the two shots, and Reece slumped over.

"Hold it there." I rushed to the television screen to get a closer look.

Ethan smiled, pleased, and played the scene again, even slower. That's when we heard the *Pow! Pow!* But this time, the gunfire sounded different. One shot sounded closer, louder, the other more distant.

Ethan and I turned to each other. "It sounds like Riley's gun and Reece's gun *both* fired," I said.

He grinned widely and patted me on my back. "Yes! I heard it too. Is there any way to tell if Riley was the one who shot Reece?"

"CPD would have ballistics of Reece's official weapon. But I'm guessing the gun in Riley's hand was Reece's spare and most likely a ghost gun—no serial number."

"And this film doesn't show Riley firing a gun," he said.

There was movement behind us. Emma walked into the living room, tears in her eyes.

"It's very damning," she said. "To me, it looks like she shot Reece."

"Really, dear? That's what you think?" Ethan asked.

"I know it was an accident," she said. "I'm sure she was trying to get that other man off of him. But that's not what it looks like."

"What did Riley do with the gun?" Ethan asked. "We may need it to prove she didn't shoot the detective."

There it was again. *We.* Riley's father was roping me in again.

"I'm sure she got rid of it," I said. "Besides, wasn't it a through and through wound? Did the police recover the bullet?

Shells? I respectfully disagree with Emma. I don't think there's anything on this video that incriminates Riley."

"But the letter you showed us—she definitely said she shot Reece," Ethan said. "She would know if her gun went off. That's not something you forget."

"I'm sure she fired," I said. "But isn't it more likely that the gun the men were wrestling over went off and hit Reece rather than Riley's gun, fired from some distance away?"

"The cameraman claimed he had more footage," Emma said. "Do you think he left that part out?"

"No, he couldn't have recorded both the struggle for the gun and Riley outside the frame of his lens, at least not with the same video camera," I said. "Why'd he leave the disc with you?"

"Maybe so we'd change our mind or to give him a reason to come back." Ethan stood up and began to pace. "What do *we* do? He says he's going to turn this over to the police for the reward money if *we* don't pay him." Ethan looked at me wide-eyed. "Maybe you could meet with him, see what else he knows, what else he might have? You were a cop. You know how to handle these kinds of guys."

I stammered for a moment, unsure of what to say.

"I don't think that's a good idea," Emma interjected.

"Well, if it's as damning as you think, Emma," Ethan said, "I don't think we should risk it getting in the hands of the police."

As much as I wanted to believe Riley was okay, watching the video had convinced me she was in deep trouble. The Keanes were out of their league trying to negotiate with some thug who could turn around and go to the police—or continue to extort them. And yet, I needed to distance myself from this mess and stay focused on my political career. But now that I'd gained the trust of her family, how could I walk away?

Ethan ejected the disk and handed it to me.

"I hate getting you entangled in all this, son. You're not quite . . . *family,* and you shouldn't be putting yourself and *your kids* at risk for a woman who isn't your wife. I can't see Riley coming out of this unscathed." He cleared his throat, pulled a slip of paper from his pants, and handed it to me. "He did leave his number, though."

RILEY

The tavern was jammed. The entire town, it seemed, had turned out to celebrate the end of the workweek. Ginny waved me over to her table.

"I want you to meet Zi," she said, pointing to a woman who was a combination beauty queen and pro wrestler: big arms, wide neck, manly fingers, long dark hair, dusky skin, dark eyes, and boney cheeks. She looked like she could whip any guy in the bar, and they'd still want to fuck her.

"Damashkawizii Bearheart." She extended her hand. When she saw me struggling with the name, she grinned. "You can just call me Zi." Her voice was deep and rough. "Pull up a chair."

Because of the music, Ginny didn't even try to participate in our conversation. Instead she stared at the door and continually looked around as if she were looking for someone in the crowd. When she noticed our empty beer bottles, she motioned to Scarla and ordered us another round. I craved a dirty Martini with olives—my usual with Finn on Friday nights. Local craft beer, however, was a source of pride in the Upper Peninsula.

"What's your name mean?" I asked.

"'Lady of strength.'" She rolled her eyes. "My mother named me after a great aunt."

I pulled out the pack of cigarettes I'd just bought. Zi held up her lighter. State law banned smoking in bars, but no one on the island bothered to enforce it. I was coming to learn how the island had its own rules.

"Truth cigarettes," I yelled over the blare of country music.

"Ah. You've met Gabe, have ya?" Zi said, nodding.

"He's *special*."

"I'm sure he took a liking to you. Did he tell you his story?"

There was a roar at the bar. Men standing below the television wearing Red Wings jerseys celebrated a goal, high-fiving each other.

"Gabe used to teach high school literature in Milwaukee," Zi said. "Used his pension money to buy the gas station. Wife's been dead for years. Lung cancer."

"So that's where he got his hokey tobacco homily?"

"Wait till you hear his poetry," she said, raising her eyebrows. "Pretty fancy stuff for a guy with a belly full of sauerkraut and sausage."

Ginny glanced at her watch, and Zi patted her on the back.

"What's wrong with Ginny?" I screamed into Zi's ear.

"Her boyfriend is late, as usual," she yelled back.

"What's he like?"

"A dick." She grinned and grabbed my thigh. "He's not my type, if you know what I mean."

People were always mistaking me as gay. It was my short hair and fuck-all attitude. I forced a smile and removed her hand. She leaned over to reveal the curve of her breasts. "If you ever want to test the waters . . ."

"No, thanks. I like men." I wanted to get that out of the way immediately.

"I know." She winked. "I'm just fucking with you."

Finally, the music stopped, and we no longer had to shout. "Listen." She cleared her throat. "Ginny tells me you're staying with the crazy lady at the Inn."

"It's just until I can find something better."

"You could do much better. There are lots of folks who'd love to have someone like you staying in their summer house for the winter, looking after the pipes and such, making sure no critters take over their million-dollar summer homes. I run a little caretaking business—if you're interested. It's a great setup if you don't mind moving around. Sometimes these people come back on short notice, and you have to get your shit out quickly. It doesn't pay much, but you get to live in a McMansion for free."

I gave her a puzzled look. "I just met you, and now you're offering me a part-time job and a place to live?"

Zi wrinkled her forehead and squinted at me. "We're desperate for workers in the winter. There aren't enough bodies. Sometimes we advertise in the Chicago and Detroit papers, but we found that attracted the wrong kind of character. And we're kind of particular about who we want to spend the winter with. There are only three hundred people here in the frozen months. Hell, I have more friends on Facebook than that. We all look out for each other here. We have to in order to survive being cut off from the mainland. You do know what you're getting into if you stay on the island after the ferry stops, right?"

"Now, don't go scaring her off," Ginny warned, finally able to hear us since the music stopped. "We have landline phones, satellite internet, and TV. And there's a prop plane that shuttles people back and forth to the mainland."

Zi waved at her dismissively. "At fifty bucks a ride, that gets expensive. And forget about your cell phone. There's no reception on the island. That's why we still have landlines and payphones."

"But Grand Portage is only three miles across the bay," I protested.

"The short answer is that the island is so rugged and hilly with dense forest that the cell phone reception was never good, to begin with. The long answer is that island culture isn't conducive to cell phones. Too many people are afraid the government is listening." Zi made a crazy face. "There was never the demand for coverage, and so cell phone companies never put up cell towers on the island. Folks here are rugged individualists. They're here for a reason. You'll understand soon enough.

"It usually takes until late January," she added, "before the lake ice has thickened enough to support snowmobiles, then we drive trucks over it." Her eyes got wide.

"How is that possible?" I couldn't even imagine the ice thick enough to support a three-quarter of a ton truck that most Islanders drove.

"We call our path across the lake, the 'ice bridge.' We plow it like a regular road and mark the edges with discarded Christmas trees."

"And I take it, you drive across the lake all the time, right?"

"Well, sure, honey," she said, slapping me on the back. "It takes a bit of swagger to drive on the ice, but you'll get used to it. We've had a few trucks sink, but hey, that's rare."

I knew she was trying to scare me. But so far, none of what I'd heard sounded any more grueling than surviving a Chicago winter waiting on a frigid El platform or clinging to ropes as you walked in wind canyons between skyscrapers.

I leaned into Zi and whispered conspiratorially. "What do I need to know that no one's telling me?"

She eyed me suspiciously. "It's kind of like that commercial. You know the one about Vegas? What happens on the island stays on the island. When the ferry stops and the ice hasn't formed, and the wind kicks up too much for the plane, it could be weeks before you get off the island or get fresh food delivered. You eat a lot of canned tuna fish, canned cream corn —canned everything. That first winter, some people go nuts. I've seen some old-timers, even island natives, crack up. There's a lot of drinking and a lot of fucking around. Not too many married people make it through a winter without splitting up. Most people here are single or divorced."

She lowered her voice even more. "By the time that ice bridge is plowed in January or February, people go racing all wide-eyed and manic over to the mainland just to see if anyone is alive. Ginny calls it Island Syndrome. I just say that people go bat-shit crazy." She widened her eyes again. "Then there are some years when the lake doesn't freeze, and we're all stuck here until late spring and—"

Someone hollered.

"The ferry just came in," Zi explained.

A line of men, most wearing bear-like parkas and construction boots, stomped through the door. They made their way through the crowd, high-fiving the regulars. The sight of one man made me do a double-take. He was slighter than the others, wearing a black scarf and a black leather jacket with a Harley Davidson logo. I breathed in my beer and choked. Beer spewed out my nose. Zi slapped my back.

"Riley, this is my boyfriend, Lars," Ginny shouted over the clamor. "I guess you two already met."

"Hello." Lars grinned sheepishly and held out his hand. "Nice to see you again. How's everyone treating you?"

Our eyes locked. He'd lied about not having a girlfriend. He also hadn't told her he'd tried to charm me into his arms on Thanksgiving. It seemed he hadn't told her anything about me, including my made-up name, for which I was thankful. From the look on his face, he was hoping we could keep our indiscretions secret.

I smiled and squeezed his hand as hard as I could, a handshake that I imagined sealed our pact; I wouldn't tell Ginny about Lars if he wouldn't tell her about me. But that's the thing about co-conspirators—someone always rats on the other to save himself.

FINN

A Chicago police officer was stationed outside Reece's private hospital room. He'd recently been moved out of ICU, where only immediate family members were allowed to visit. I was hoping he'd healed enough to understand our predicament. If there was one person who would know what to do about the blackmailer, it was Reece. He'd gotten Riley—and, by extension, all of us—into this mess by taking her to meet with an informant in the middle of the night, and now he needed to help us get her out.

The officer jotted down my name and left me standing in the hallway as he checked whether the detective could see me. I glanced at the visitor's log on the officer's chair. Besides Reece's sister, the only person who had shown up with any regularity was a Lieutenant Williams.

"The nurse says you'll have to be brief," the officer said. "He needs to rest. But he wants to see you." He did a perfunctory pat down, then waved toward the door.

Reece's room was dark, the shades drawn. Machines clustered near his bed displayed jagged lines bouncing up and down, lights blinking. There were IVs in his arms and an oxygen tube to his nose. Reece looked jaundiced and frail. His hospital gown hung loosely from his neck, making him appear small, weak. His left shoulder was heavily bandaged. His unshaved face grimaced as a nurse pricked his skin with a needle in a search for a vein. She offered me a weak smile. After collecting several vials of blood, she quietly padded out of the room. Reece and I were alone.

I was hoping he would talk first. But when the silence dragged on, I started to introduce myself.

"I know who you are," he interrupted, "otherwise you wouldn't be here." He stared at the ceiling, not even acknowledging me with his eyes.

I waited for him to say something more. He made a gurgling sound and wiped his lips.

"She talked about you sometimes," he said finally.

"She talked about you, too. She thought—thinks—highly of you. You two seem to have a special...*friendship*."

I waited for him to argue with that assessment. But he didn't.

"I'm here because—"

"I know why you're here," he interrupted, his jowls firmly set.

"Glad we got that out of the way."

He finally looked at me, his green eyes intense.

"We've got a problem," he eked out in a low, scratchy voice.

"Just one?"

"Tell me the ones you can count. I only know what I read in the papers, and most are lies the administration spins."

"You've seen the sketch that was released, right?" I asked.

"Christ, that could have been anyone."

"What does the administration know? I see you've had a few visits from Lieutenant Williams?" The city had shelled out millions to people who said Williams and his crew had beat them into making trumped-up statements. "Are the two of you friendly?"

He grunted. "You're just like her, you know. Full of questions, nosy. How is she?"

"She says she shot you, and it was an accident. She doesn't believe CPD will believe her story."

"She's right. They won't."

"What did you tell them?" I wasn't about to mention the video or that Riley had disappeared just yet. I needed to know if I could trust him first. Riley might have thought the world of Reece, but the rumors about him always made me uneasy with their friendship. And now, with Lieutenant Williams on his visitor list, I certainly had reservations.

He gave me a look of incredulity. "Why should I tell *you* anything?"

I stood at the window. It was nearly four o'clock. The sky had already darkened. The lights of the city sparkled amid a late autumn fog.

"I'm all you got right now," I said. "I'm your conduit to her. If you trusted her, you need to trust me."

The numbers on his monitors began jumping. My presence was making his heartbeat fast and his blood pressure rise. I figured the nurse would return and kick me out.

"You're risking everything coming here, you know," he said, quietly. "They keep track of who comes and goes."

I opened my suit jacket and pulled out a notebook. "I'm here in my official capacity. I'm to report back to the mayor on whether the city should offer its own reward for information about your shooting."

He wrinkled his forehead. "You have an answer for everything, don't you? How do I know you're not working with CPD to save your ass—or hers?"

"A little paranoid, aren't you?"

"That's what happens when you get shot. There were only two people who knew we were meeting with my contact that night. Me and Riley. And I sure as hell didn't tell anyone. Even my contact didn't know we were coming. So, yeah, you could say I'm a little fucking paranoid. Maybe she told you, and you're the mole."

He was trying to put me on the defensive so I'd reveal more about myself. I'd been a cop, too. Maybe he didn't know that or remember. I unknotted my tie, unbuttoned my shirt, and held it open to reveal my bare chest. "I'm not wearing a wire."

He snorted a laugh. "Put your clothes on. If you want me to believe that you know Riley, tell me something about that girl I don't know."

"Is this a test?"

He smirked. "Maybe I'm just nosy. She was pretty damn secretive about her *dating* life."

"You've known her since high school. You spent the worst day of her life with her. I should be asking you about her." Was there something he wanted to tell me, something private that he and Riley shared? I'm not a jealous man, but their relationship never made much sense to me; his motives for helping her remained murky.

"So, you know about that, huh? Did she talk about Darren Wallack?"

"She credits you with saving her."

He smiled a self-satisfied grin. "What's she like—as a *girlfriend*?"

"Why, at this moment, do you care about *that*?"

He glared at me. "You want information from me; you need to answer my questions."

I paced the room, wondering what details would satisfy his

prurient interests. "She likes girly movies, sappy romantic flicks. She gets all weepy."

"Hmm. Never saw that side of her, although she is a real sucker for crime victims. What else? What do you two do together besides meet in dark corners?"

"Sometimes we ride our bikes to the lake and spend the entire day on the rocks, reading, splashing in the water. She has to slather on layers of sunscreen. She's very fair, but she has two freckles on her ass."

He laughed for the first time.

"It's true," I said, feeling more confident. "I wonder if her parents let her run around naked as a kid." I stopped for a minute, remembering her skin, alabaster white with a light spackling of reddish freckles. Sometimes I'd map patterns in her freckles as if I were trying to find the constellations on her skin.

"Was she any good?"

I stared at him in disbelief. Normally I would have been angry, but his brashness answered a nagging question I'd had about them. I'd never asked Riley if she and Reece had slept together; now I knew they hadn't.

Most men fantasized about fucking a woman like Riley. She was as fearless in bed as she was in person. Making love to Riley was like a wrestling match. Sometimes she was on top, and sometimes I was. Sometimes we rolled around, tearing up the bed, the sheets catching in the narrow crevices between our bodies. Afterward, we slept for hours. Sometimes she woke me in the middle of the night, kissing me softly. And we'd do it again, though less aggressively. Those were my favorite. Slow and long and drowsy enough that it felt like a dream.

Reece coughed loudly, urging me to answer.

"Her mother says she's a natural in the kitchen, but she never cooked for me. Not once," I said, ignoring his question. It felt strange talking about Riley as if she were dead, as if I were being interviewed for her obituary.

"What exactly did Riley tell you about me?" His voice was cagey as if there was something particular he was trying to ascertain. When he mentioned her name, his voice was soft and gentle. His face lit up as he listened to me rattle off more details about her. Then I realized: He was jealous of *me.* He was in love with her.

"She said if anything ever happened to her that I should seek you out. That you'd know the truth. That's why I came." I lied. I had to assure his giant ego that he was still No. 1 in Riley's book. "She took off, Reece. We haven't heard from her in a week."

Reece rubbed his chin, his eyelids fluttering with some serious thought. When he spoke, his tone changed to one edged with dread.

"CPD knows Riley was there. There's a witness. So far, he isn't cooperating. That doesn't mean he won't. They're pressuring me to admit she was there, but I'm not biting. It's my word against this punk. If they had any real evidence, they'd be issuing a warrant for her arrest." He stopped and shut his eyes, his face cringing with pain. "I'm sorry I took her, that I got her involved."

"How do *we* get her out of this?" And at that moment, I meant we. I wanted to help Riley. Seeing Reece pining for her reminded me how special she was, how lucky I'd been. Nothing like competitiveness to make a man possessive. Reece saved her thirteen years ago. This time it needed to be me.

Reece fidgeted with the tubes coming out of his arm and clicked his tongue against his teeth. "Don't you mean: How do *all of us* get out of this mess? It is a crime to harbor a fugitive, to withhold information about an ongoing investigation, to lie to the police—all things you, an alderman, have done. CPD will come after you, her family, anyone helping her directly or indirectly. They'll threaten you, pressure you. They are probably following you right now, listening to your phone calls, going through your trash, monitoring your credit cards."

"There's another problem," I said. "There is evidence. There's a witness who videotaped the shooting. Maybe it's the same witness talking to the cops. In his film, it looks like Riley didn't shoot you. It was the other guy. Who was he? What do you remember about the shooting?"

"Dude, I barely remember anything. I don't know who he was or how he knew I would be there. It seemed like an organized hit, except he didn't have a gun. The details don't matter anyway. CPD never lets the truth get in the way of an indictment. Oh, sure, they might drop the charges later, citing 'new evidence,' but the damage is done by then. You, me, Riley, her family—all our reputations will be ruined."

The room got quiet. I refused to believe the Chicago police were as corrupt as Reece depicted. That wasn't my experience on the force. I believed CPD would respond to evidence. I wasn't about to argue with Reece, who'd made a career out of publicly challenging his bosses.

"So, how do we stop this guy? He's trying to blackmail Riley's parents. So far, they have not given any money. But they want me to negotiate with him."

Reece sighed heavily. "Everyone's got a goddamn camera these days. They see videos as the South Side lottery, especially anything involving the police. Make whatever deal you can afford."

"You want me to pay off a blackmailer? How do you think this is going to look if this gets out? I have an election to think about."

"Really? Your girlfriend is in parts unknown, running from corrupt police, and you're afraid of some guy with a camera who wants a few bills? Man, does Riley know how to pick 'em. Listen, *asshole,* if this guy hands over the video to CPD, to the media—to whoever—we're fucking screwed. Your political career is over. Immediately." Reece started choking. One of his machines beeped, further agitating him. He motioned for me to come closer.

"And if CPD finds out I was secretly working with the feds —Riley and I will both turn up dead."

RILEY

After the night at the bar, I spent much of the next day popping aspirin and downing ginger ale. Javier took no pity, barking commands, and banging pots and pans. The only break I got was when some men showed up at the backdoor, and Javier disappeared without explanation. Later, I saw him counting a wad of cash. I didn't ask what he was doing. I had my own theories.

By the time Zi walked in the back door at the end of my shift, I was exhausted and longed for my sagging bed at the Inn. Zi looked energetic, her big eyes alert.

"You ready to do some real estate shopping, darling?" she asked. I'd forgotten she was taking me on a tour of her care-taking properties.

When we stepped outside, the freezing air stung my cheeks, but the sunlight reflecting off the snow perked me up. Zi marched ahead in the parking lot.

"We'll take my truck," she yelled, pointing to a red four-wheel drive with oversized tires.

The cab was waist-high. I hoisted myself into the front seat using the arm of the door.

"Jesus, Zi, you think this thing is far enough off the ground?"

"When you get stuck in the snow with that little toy car of yours, you'll be calling me."

"How do you know what I drive?"

She pointed to my bright yellow Beetle in the parking lot. "Ain't that your city car with Illinois tags?"

I cringed. It was so obvious. The car was my biggest weakness.

"Yeah, it's not great with the snow. Any chance I could use a four-wheel-drive someone has stored in their garage?

She chewed on her bottom lip and nodded. "Maybe."

I strapped on my seat belt. Zi watched. "Don't trust me, do you?"

"It's the law, Zi."

"There are a lot of laws I choose not to follow."

"Yeah, I can see why you'd be suspicious of seat belt regulations."

"Ha. Ha. Not too many people around here follow government rules about *anything*."

"What about the owners of all the million-dollar houses you manage? Do those *millionaires* mistrust the government?"

She threw me a sideways look. "They don't *live* here. They come for about six weeks in the summer and some maybe on Thanksgiving or Christmas. We don't pay them much attention, aside from assessing them high taxes and taking their money." She turned up the radio, set on a country music station, and sang along to a song called "Big Ass Girls" as the truck bounced over frozen ruts of mud. I stared out the window at the majestic firs bent with heavy snow and ice.

"You don't like Lars too much, huh?" I asked.

She gave me a sour look. "You noticed?"

"Is it because he has a penis or because he's Ginny's boyfriend?"

She shook her head. "Neither. I just don't like the fucking government."

"I thought Lars owned the bar and a motorcycle shop."

"Hoo, haw. Lars is a bounty hunter—a freelance pig!"

"What?" I jerked my head toward her, pretending shock.

"He pretty much leaves his policing to the mainland, or the year-rounders would run him off the island. He mostly tracks fugitives crossing over to Canada. He has to get 'em before they enter international waters. It's illegal in Canada for a U.S. citizen to apprehend someone, same as kidnapping. They don't care for our methods of nabbing fugitives. Lars has his unorthodox ways, for sure. Hangs with a wild crowd. What's your worry?" She slapped her hand on my thigh. "You running from the *law*?" She howled a laugh.

"He just gives me the creeps, that's all."

She nodded, and I could feel her studying me out of the corner of her eye.

That afternoon, Zi took me into half a dozen homes and showed me how to check for freezing pipes, make sure the toilets had running water, and tell if the furnaces were working. Besides taking care of the cottage I'd live in, I was expected to check several other vacant homes on the island routinely.

"Don't go in after dark. You never know if you're alone," she said.

"What's that supposed to mean?"

"It means . . . there've been a few *incidents*."

"Like what?"

She nodded her head a moment, choosing her words carefully. "Sometimes—and this is rare—we've had squatters. They know the house isn't occupied, and it's heated. They figure, why not? They usually don't do any damage, but it's scary as hell to come across them. For you and them. And you never know if they're armed."

"But it gets dark at four o'clock here."

"So, go before then."

Zi pulled onto a side road that cut through dense woods. "I want to show you where I grew up."

As she drove, she recounted the island's history. As far back as the 1600s, she said, Angelica had been a major outpost for French fur traders. Then Catholic missionaries arrived to Christianize the "savages." Schools were built, and nuns taught the Ojibwe children English and religion. During the 1800s, the U.S. government split the tribe: Those who believed in the White man's God were moved off the island and settled near Grand Portage, while traditional tribe members who worshiped the Ojibwe god, Gitche Manitou, were confined to the island's reservation on the far north side. Some who stayed, like Zi's ancestors, worshiped both gods. Zi's mother, a devout Catholic, also practiced tribal rituals to ward off evil.

Eventually, the forest opened to a cluster of buildings, including a community center, a café, and a boarded-up store.

"This is the center of the reservation," she said. The place looked like a ghost town from a movie set. We stopped for a moment to look at the battered buildings, then Zi pulled onto a narrow, sandy road that meandered through tall birch trees. In the far distance, I could see the bright blue waters through the branches. As the road narrowed and the forest became denser, Zi flicked on her lights and slowly steered between giant potholes.

"Where are we?"

"Nequainie, land of spirits. This is the oldest forest on the island. Our ancestors are buried here. A few elders live out here. Their houses are hidden in the deepest part. They make sure no one desecrates the graves. During the Vietnam War, draft dodgers came here and asked for sanctuary. The government sent in the National Guard to comb the forest. They didn't find anyone." She looked at me with wide eyes. "*Dun, dun, dun, dun . . .*" Then she grabbed my leg. I jumped, my head hitting the window.

"Oh my god, Zi. You fucking scared me. I never know when you're serious."

"I am serious," she protested in a lighter tone. "There are tunnels in here. That's where the draft dodgers hid when the government came. Some say they date to colonial times when the French and the Americans fought our tribe."

"What did the government do?"

"About the 'Nam draft dodgers? Well, the feds threatened to bulldoze the forest unless the peaceniks came out. Islanders made such a fuss that the governor pulled back the Guard. Bet you won't read about that in the history books. Since then, the tribal police pretty much stick to the main reservation and leave us alone."

Zi turned onto another dirt road that led through speckled birch trees and pulled up to a series of depressed-looking cottages.

"This is home," she said. "All these houses belong to my relatives. As a kid, I dreamed about leaving the island, but now look at me. I'm a lifer."

"Why's that?"

"You'll see. You'll see."

Zi drove more back roads, telling me stories about the island and its quirky people. Finally, she stopped at a driveway with a chain across its entrance.

"This is the house I was telling you about."

I stared out the window at the giant gingerbread mansion in the distance overlooking the lake.

"It's a great job," she said. "You get to live like a millionaire while checking toilets."

She climbed out of the truck. I followed. Inside, the house was decorated tastefully with seashell knickknacks and paintings of ships in violent storms that took up entire walls. The back half of the house was floor to ceiling windows offering expansive views of the lake, framed by peeling birch trees. I stared at the lake in awe.

"I never tire of that view," she whispered.

Zi took out a bundle of sage from her pocket and lit it with her cigarette lighter. "The last person I had staying in here had an energy I didn't like."

I followed her smoky trail from room to room.

Zi held her flashlight under her chin as if she were leading a seance. "I need to warn you," she said in an ominous voice. "The island does funny things to people, Riley. People change here."

"I'm not falling for your scare tactics this time, Zi."

She pulled down the flashlight and spoke in her normal voice. "I'm just saying that the island has a way of breaking down barriers. People come here thinking they know who they are, but they leave as someone else. Sometimes it's healthy, and other times it shatters folks with fragile psyches. You want to find out what you're made of, who you really are? Spend a winter on Angelica."

FINN

He didn't sound surprised when I called, his voice calm, friendly. He also didn't sound like a street thug, more like a businessman proposing a deal. He agreed to meet me at a downtown bar called Magnolia's. It was one of those mammoth places with multiple levels, all glass and glitter, where the drinks start at fifteen dollars. People went there to see and be seen.

The bar was my suggestion. The owner was ex-Secret Service and crazy about security. He'd needed a special parking ordinance to open up the club. I'd backed his request and lobbied enough of my colleagues into passing the ordinance. Now, he agreed to return the favor, the grease of Chicago politics.

It was a risky move: a politician meeting with a blackmailer. But what choice did I have? I had to make sure the cops didn't get that video. If Riley became a suspect, they'd comb through her life, and eventually, they'd find me. If that happened, I could kiss my political career goodbye.

The cameraman showed up at the club ten minutes after I

did. He wasn't hard to spot since he was the only Black man in the bar, but he wasn't the extortionist from the 'hood I expected. Vaguely athletic-looking, he dressed like an urban hipster—black jeans and a distressed blue jean shirt unbuttoned enough to reveal a dangling gold chain. His hair was styled short with curls as Black models wear. His face sported a two-day stubble. He looked more like an actor than a hustler.

I stood up from the table. He walked over and held out his hand. "Call me Mr. Mailer."

An extortionist with a sense of humor.

"Yes, Mr. Mailer, I'm familiar with your work," I said, playing along. On the phone, I'd told him nothing about me other than I was a "family friend" who wished to discuss his "film project."

He took the stool across from me and leaned back, making no effort to speak.

"Well?" I said.

"You called the meeting. It's your agenda."

"I have to say, you don't really look like what I was expecting."

"Oh? What were you expecting? A guy with cigarettes rolled up in his t-shirt, sagging pants, and unlaced Timberlands?"

I smiled.

"I'll have to work on my ghetto attire."

"Don't make this a racist thing. I mean, who the hell films a shooting in Englewood in the middle of the night? And from the description, your associate is a real panty twister." I was getting worked up. I needed to calm down, be in control.

He suppressed a grin, pleased that he'd already riled me. "I'm glad you're interested in my film. Do you want to be a sole supporter, or are Mr. and Mrs. Keane contributing as well?"

"We need more information," I said, coolly, mad at myself for reacting.

The waitress arrived and laid cocktail napkins in front of us. "What can I get you, fellows?"

"Whiskey," I said.

"Glass of Bordeaux, 2014, if you have it."

Once the waitress left, I leaned across the table and whispered: "What is it that you want, exactly? There's nothing on that film that is incriminating."

"At best, she is a witness," he said. "At worst, she's the shooter. Regardless, it shows she's involved." He seemed arrogant as if he knew some key fact I didn't.

"The only thing that film shows is Detective Taylor wrestling with a man over his police-issued weapon, which is the gun that likely shot him."

The waitress returned with our drinks. I handed her cash with a hefty tip. "Some privacy?" I said and winked.

"Sure," she said, stuffing the fifty into her apron pocket and disappearing.

Mr. Mailer held up his glass of wine. "Thanks for the petrol, man."

"Who are you, and why were you there? How much money do you want? What are you going to do if you don't get it?" I was growing irritated.

"Did Mr. Keane say I asked for money?"

"I hear your accomplice did."

"And she's not here today for a good reason. How much is the film worth to you? It may not be a smoking gun, but it's pretty damn close. The cops aren't going to believe that a woman waving a gun that she doesn't have a license to carry is an innocent victim. The city is taking shootings very seriously these days, especially *Whites* shooting *Blacks*. Haven't you heard? Black lives matter. It would be better for your friend if that film didn't exist."

"What if I paid double the reward money? Twenty thousand dollars? That's fair. If you turn the film over to the police, the FOP may not give you the full reward, and it usually takes years and a lot of haggling."

"I was expecting an offer with a lot more zeros."

I hiccupped a laugh. "We're not rich, *Mr. Mailer*. Riley's parents run a fledgling nonprofit. I work for the city. I can give you twenty thousand now. And we can be done with this." I pulled out a large envelope. I'd taken the money out of my retirement fund, not telling Riley's parents.

He thought a minute, swirling the wine in his glass, looking around as if the sleek and glittery décor suddenly interested him. Video monitors displayed music videos. People were dancing in a distant room under yellow and blue flickering lights.

"Okay. Twenty it is."

"I'll need the original film."

He pulled a tiny video cassette from inside his jacket pocket and slid it across the table.

"That's the original," he said.

I wasn't convinced. What choice did I have? I pushed the envelope across the table.

"This better be the only copy," I said, holding up the cassette.

"Or what?" He was cocky and smug as if he held all the power.

"If you double-cross me, I'll take my video of *you* to the police."

"Of me?" He laughed.

I leaned over the table. "Your face is on these cameras." I pointed to the ceiling. The owner had promised to give me the video from his surveillance cameras. "If I want to turn you into the Chicago police, I can do just that. I hardly think the police or a judge are going to side with a blackmailer."

He stared up at the ceiling and winced. His friendly expression vanished, and he shrugged. "Doesn't matter anyway. The cops already know about me."

"Why, because you're an undercover cop? That's it, isn't it? You're working for them."

"Chicago cops typically don't beat up their own," he said, pointing to a jagged cut mark above his eye.

"You could have gotten that anywhere."

"Ever hear of a Lieutenant Williams? He's pretty famous for his methods. Crude, but effective . . . on most people."

I took a long drink. There was his name again, Lieutenant Williams. How was he involved? Something was off-kilter, something I hadn't noticed before.

"Don't look so glum, *Finn.* Oh, you thought I didn't know your name? It was pretty damn easy. Riley's Facebook account was a piece of cake to crack. Once in, I had her whole life laid out there: Her loving parents, her bestie, and you—always in the background, of course. Either you were her bodyguard or some fucking stalker. And then I saw your picture in the paper. Seems you have *ambitions.*" He said it as if it were a dirty word. You might suggest that Riley choose a more complicated password. One-one-one-one-one-one-one-one isn't very clever."

I cringed. Jesus. Now we were all in danger.

"It's an interesting number, isn't it, Finn? One-one-one-one-one-one-one-one." He sounded as if he were about to get philosophical. "It suggests it's all about her, that she's self-centered. And that's it, isn't it? I bet you're angry that she left you to clean up her mess, again, and she's not even officially in a relationship with you. I mean, her Facebook status says: 'it's complicated.' But you're the man who appears in the most pictures—in the background—so I assume there's a little ass slapping going on, eh?"

My face must have belied my shock. I opened my mouth to protest.

"Don't bother. I'm not interested in anything you have to say unless you're going to tell me where she is."

"I honestly don't..."

"Oh, I believe you don't know. But you will, won't you? You're the one she's most likely to reach out to, right? And when she does, you're going to tell me where she is."

I snorted. "You're out of your fucking mind. I gave you what you wanted, what you asked for." I sounded whiney.

He was laughing hard now, slumped over the table, holding his stomach.

"I'm so glad this is entertaining you."

"For the record, Finn, I never asked you for money. But now that I have it, it's kind of nice. Lets me know you got skin in the game." He patted the envelope and stuck it inside his jacket. "If you don't tell me when you hear from her—and I'll know—the police will be the least of your worries."

That's when he reached in his jacket pocket and retrieved pictures he fanned out on the table. They were of the kids—Kye and Nico—playing in Diana's front yard.

"What the hell? Don't you fucking go near my family." I reached over the table and grabbed his neck with both my hands, choking him. He stuck his elbows in my face and pushed me off. I fell back in my chair. He was strong for such a slim build. I could still take him.

He rubbed at his neck, then faced me with a triumphant look in his eyes.

"You'll report to me regularly. You'll tell me what the Keanes tell you, whether she's contacted them or you. The future of your family depends on me finding Riley. Got it?"

"But why? What's in it for you? Why do you need to find her?" He clearly wasn't motivated by money, but what was driving him?

"I'd like to help you out here, Finn. I would. Trust me; once you get home and mull over the situation, it's going to be clear what you need to do to protect your family. You're a smart man in a bad situation. I know you'll do the right thing."

I was sweating profusely, my mind racing. "I could report your extortion to the police," I threatened in desperation. "Blackmailing a public official is a felony."

"And then they'll arrest you for withholding evidence and helping a fugitive." He was enjoying the leverage he had over me. "No one will fault you for protecting your kids, even if it means cooperating with a punk like me. Go home, hug Nico and Kye, and think about how you're going to help me find Riley."

RILEY

It was early December. In just a few weeks, the ferry would cease its crossings for the winter. Zi said it usually stopped just after Christmas, but not always. After that, we would all be stuck on the island until an ice road formed. While everyone else at the restaurant dreaded the ferry stopping, I looked forward to the isolation. I thought I would be safer cocooned on the island all winter.

Alone at night at the cottage was the scariest time. I'd stand on the back porch in that dreamy twilight, listening for the slightest sounds, a twig snapping, a bird's startled caw, imaging cops in night goggles swarming my place. Each night I'd listen as Lake Superior gently licked at the rocky shore, as if in slow motion. Snow began to fall, dusting the pine needle carpet, forming a sound barrier around the house. Under the pines' drooping arms, the air was still. Then the lake stopped moving entirely.

One night I woke to what sounded like gunfire and rushed outside. The air was cold and prickly, stinging my face. Moonlight spread a blue sheen across the lake's undisturbed snow.

Another series of explosions erupted beneath me, and I realized: the lake was freezing, an eerie crackle and boom that sounded like muffled firecrackers or, as I liked to imagine, an angry whale moaning beneath the ice.

At the restaurant, Ginny seemed pleased to have found someone capable of withstanding Javier's mercurial moods. Since that first day, she hadn't brought up government paperwork again. And I didn't mention it. Any detective worth his badge would be monitoring my Social Security number to figure out my location. I needed to borrow a real Social Security number that wouldn't draw attention. The fact I hadn't withdrawn any more money or used my credit cards might indicate I'd found another source of money—or that I was dead.

Each day after work, I stopped by the gas station to pick up supplies. I gave Mr. Kowalski a list of things I needed, including a hair dying kit. He was able to secure everything on my list. After bleaching my hair again—twice—the color no longer looked clownish orange, but light blonde. I'd even started wearing makeup, one shade darker than my skin. I was still white, but not zombie pale. I stared in the mirror, hardly believing the results: a blonde woman with fair skin to match. It looked completely natural. My hair had grown two inches in a matter of weeks. I was wearing it as a short bob and intended to let it keep growing. I looked at my Illinois driver's license that I kept hidden in my wallet. The woman who stared back—jet black, spiky hair, ghost-white skin—was gone. No one would mistake me for her now.

FINN

It wasn't my night to take the kids, but Diana had a late-night meeting. I'd agreed to pick them up after my talk with Mr. Mailer. I was so agitated by his threats that when I pulled into Diana's driveway, I couldn't remember how I'd gotten there. Outside her front door, I could hear the television, Kye's giggling, and Nico's squeaky titter. I swallowed hard and knocked.

Diana opened the door and squinted at me in the glare of the porch light. Kye hollered: "Daddy, Daddy!" Even Nico ran to the door, his little-man face beaming. How could I risk their lives for Riley, the wrong kind of woman who would likely never be mine?

"My God, you look terrible. Is everything okay?" Diana asked as she ushered me inside.

My clothes were soaked, my glasses fogged. Water dripped from my hair. I must have walked in the rain after I left the bar. I remembered passing the club owner on the way out, feeling his eyes on me, and turning quickly so he couldn't see the despair in my face. I'd been turned, recruited to spy on Riley's family, my kids held hostage in the deal.

Kye wrapped her arms around my cold, wet pant legs. "Daddy, don't you have an umbrella? Do you want mine?" She pulled a pink nylon cylinder from the coat closet.

"No thanks, sweetie. Daddy's okay." I ran my hand across her mess of blonde curls.

Diana stared at me, her face stern. There was no way I could fool my ex-wife. Her concern for me was always indirect: Whatever tsunami engulfed me, the waves would eventually wash over our children.

"You don't look good, Finn. What's wrong? What happened?" The apprehension in her voice was replaced by fear.

I took off my glasses and wiped them on my shirt, trying to avoid her intense gaze.

"Are the polls not good? Did someone die? Did that activist break up with you?"

I wrenched my head toward her.

"Yeah, I know about Riley."

"How?"

"A wife knows. I've seen the way you look at her at public meetings. You used to look at me like that."

I shook my head like a dog after a bath. The water lighted on Kye's face. She held her head up toward me, giggling.

"Do it again, Daddy," she screamed and danced.

Diana waited, her arms crossed, her lips pressed into a hard, straight line.

"Just a bad day at work. The city is beyond bankrupt. We're talking drastic measures, including layoffs. You know how much that bothers me."

She stared a while longer but leaned in to give me a half-hug, avoiding my wet clothes as much as possible. "Their bags are packed," she said. "They just need to be dropped off at the Y tomorrow morning for swim lessons."

I nodded solemnly. The kids had a three-day weekend because of a late-semester teacher conference. Diana was always arranging organized activities for the kids. It was like she feared them having any free time. Diana didn't see the value in letting kids invent their own entertainment; worse, she saw unstructured afternoons as wasted time, especially when they could be learning or perfecting some skill, like swimming, playing the piano, soccer, or archery. I argued that kids needed time to dream, let their imaginations wander, doodle, and create fantastic stories, ride their bikes in the summer, and build snow forts in the winter. But Diana didn't buy my logic. It was an argument I'd long ago lost and a sore subject that I took pains to avoid rehashing.

"I'll take them on my way to work," I promised, knowing that I had no intention of either going to work the next day or parting with my children. I wanted to spend as much time with them as possible.

I couldn't depend on the promises of this mysterious man. What was to prevent him from taking my children even if I cooperated? The questions kept running through my mind: Should I tell the mayor? What would I say? Some guy has pictures of my kids and is trying to get me to tell him where my secret girlfriend is? And, oh, by the way, she's that anti-gun activist you asked me to manage? There was no good outcome. Besides, what was the blackmailer's end game?

Then there was this one incessant question that had nagged me for weeks, like a fly biting my skin: Would Riley ever return? I missed her in ways I'd never thought possible. I woke in the middle of the night, worried, longing to be with her. The weeks were turning into months. I was starting to have doubts that I would ever see her again.

RILEY

Whenever he got a stack of *Chicago Tribunes*, Mr. Kowalski reserved one for me. Some days there were no papers, then suddenly, there would be multiple days' worth. Every time he handed me the newspaper, he addressed me as "Me Lady from Chiraq." I grew fond of the moniker. It made me feel closer to home. Sometimes Mr. Kowalski and I discussed the headlines, the major news stories. Mostly I begged off, saying I had to check my houses before it got dark. But the real reason was so I could get to my car and rip through the paper for updates about Reece.

On December 9, a story on the front of the Metro section included a series of photos of a "woman of interest" connected to Reece's shooting. A blue-light camera captured the images several blocks from where Reece was shot. One was a grainy shot of me, staring up at the camera, my face washed out by the streetlight and blurred by movement. A second photo showed me waving a handgun at the two guys who had tried to rob me.

The men must have known about the camera because they had concealed their faces. I looked more closely at the better photo. My leather coat was bunched around my ears, and my eyes were half-closed. It wasn't a clear image, but my mother and friends would recognize me.

I sat in my car, my fingers numb, my breath visible, and wondered: how much longer before someone identified me as the "woman of interest"?

FINN

The next morning, I played hooky from work. I was enjoying breakfast with my kids when Rod Lowenstein called. I hadn't heard from him since I refused to turn over my emails. The mayor dismissed Lowenstein's intrusiveness as that of an overzealous loyalist. "Just try to humor him," he advised.

This time Rod's tone was different.

"Mr. O'Farrell, sorry to bother you at home—"

"Yes, I'm with my children, so we'll need to do this another time," I said, cutting him off.

"But I have some good *news*!" he squealed into the phone so loud that my kids looked up from their blueberry pancakes.

"Daddy, who is that man on the phone?" Kye asked.

"It's all right, honey. Eat your breakfast. I'll be back in a minute."

I walked into the living room, ready to give Rod an earful. Rod just kept talking, probably afraid that if he came up for air, I'd either yell at him or hang up.

"Mr. O'Farrell, several media outlets would like to do a story on you as the *presumptuous* candidate for vice mayor," he said jovially. "Of course, we're not confirming the choice until the scheduled announcement next week, but the mayor thought it would be good to get some pre-event publicity. What do you *say*?"

Now Rod was asking my permission. The mayor must have had a come-to-Jesus meeting with him.

"That will be fine," I said. "Let's confer on Monday when I'm back in the office."

"*Great*! I've sent you a prepared biography if you could just check your email. It will just take a second. I've set up a series of interviews for Monday morning."

I reluctantly pulled up his email and the attachment on my phone. It all looked routine: local boy becomes a cop, becomes defense lawyer, becomes alderman.

"My concern," Rod stammered, "is whether you have clients who are going to come after you in public or any cases that will damage the mayor's agenda in any way."

"We've gone over this, Rod. Most of my clients sued their companies based on infringement of their constitutional rights, mostly employment matters. I went against big corporations with horrendous reputations for employee safety and those who discriminated against women and minorities. I don't think voters in this city will have a problem with that."

"Hmm. And what about the cases you had as a cop?"

"I mostly arrested drug dealers and gang members. You're really concerned about that?"

"Your police career was *exemplary*. I wanted to highlight one of your *commendations* that you overlooked on your official bio."

I knew what was coming, but I asked anyway. "Which one was that?"

"The Blue Star Award is given for an act of *bravery*. You apprehended Darren Wallack in the Hyde Park High School shooting. That's a big *deal.* I'm stunned you've never mentioned this. I think that will appeal to voters."

I didn't respond.

"Why would you leave that off your bio?"

"First of all, the details of that award have never been made public. So, I'm not sure what little birdy tweeted in your ear. Yes, I apprehended a man who then killed himself in my custody. If I'd been successful at my job, he would have lived to face true justice."

"*Oh,* Mr. O'Farrell, I think you're being a bit harsh on yourself. The police department doesn't hand out the Blue Star awards without cause. You're just *modest.*"

"No!" I yelled and instantly regretted it. "I'm not modest," I said more softly. "This is my history, my biography, and I choose not to discuss it. I would appreciate it if you would refrain from ever mentioning it again."

There was a long pause. "Well, that's going to be hard to do."

"What did you do?" I walked outside onto the porch. "You fucking asshole. You call back every mother fucking reporter you talked to and tell them you got your information wrong."

"But..." his voice quaked.

"But what?"

"It didn't come from me. I read it this morning in the *Chicago Tribune.*"

I looked down at the morning paper still in its blue wrap on the porch. I dropped the phone and peeled off the plastic covering. On the front page above a large photo of me in my police dress uniform was the headline "Vice Mayor Candidate Cornered School Shooter."

I sunk to the porch, sitting in the damp, wet snow. I could hear Rod's voice through the phone: "I tried to reach you last night. The newspaper wanted to talk to you. You didn't answer your phone. Mr. O'Farrell? Are you there, sir?"

When Darren Wallack killed forty-nine people at the high school, everyone was in such grief. No one asked how such a monster had killed himself in a room alone with a single police officer. They were just glad he was caught, that he wouldn't be murdering any more children, that they could bury the horrors instead of dragging them out in endless trials and appeals, subjecting the families to the painful details again and again. It was a neat ending to a horrendous ordeal. The police chief decided that it was best not to reveal the identity of the officer who had cornered Darren. He felt that if the details got out, I would be branded righteous or evil for the rest of my career.

Now, thirteen years later, people would be asking much tougher questions. They'd want to know why Darren Wallack wasn't taken alive.

RILEY

More nervous young men showed up at the restaurant's back door. Javier spoke to them in hushed Spanish and stuck folded pieces of paper into their hands after he'd counted out wads of tens and twenties they handed him. It looked to me like Javier was selling drugs.

Many people used drugs on the island, and I wondered if that was why no one gossiped about Javier or questioned why he frequently disappeared in the middle of his shift. Zi told me that many year-rounders grew their own marijuana stash. The island was populated with hippies or the children of hippies, or wannabes who drove beaters with bumper stickers, like "VOTE FOR MARY JANE" or "YES, WE CANNABIS!" or, my favorite: "GOT POT?"

One day Javier and I were out on the stoop taking a smoke break. He sat a couple of steps below me; one hand held a cigarette while the other scratched at the snow. December in Northern Michigan is gray and cold and bleak.

Spread across the back of his neck was a tattoo of a seraphim, its wings tapering down under his chin. The edges of the angel were smooth and precise, unlike most prison tats. The angel stared out with eerie dark eyes, a single teardrop suspended beneath the angel's left eye. Its ominous gaze elicited a sense of doom.

"What are you looking at?" he growled. He turned toward me, his chest twice as wide as his waist, his neck squat and beefy, his hands big and leathery.

"Nothing," I said.

"What's up with you? Your time of the month or something?"

I shook my head. I wasn't going to let him get a rise out of me.

"Come on. You can tell me," he poked me on my side. "What's bothering you, *chica*?"

"Stop it!" I stood up.

"Whoa. The little lady gets angry."

I tossed my cigarette butt into the snow and turned toward the door. He pulled my arm hard. "I asked you a question."

"Ok. You want to know what's wrong with me? I think you're being really risky."

"Risky?"

"You know. Those folded up pieces of paper you hand out from the back door? You think no one notices what you're doing?"

He threw back his head and roared. "What you know about that? Ain't you just some dumb fucking college student who flunked out of school?"

"I never said 'flunked.'"

"You didn't have to. You just made everyone think that you were too *stupid* to know that the only reason people come to Angelica in the middle of winter is to ice fish." The word stupid shot from his mouth like spit.

"Aren't you afraid you're going to get caught and sent back to prison?"

He squinted at me. "What do you care?"

I shrugged. "Just trying to look out for you."

He shook his head. "No. That's not what this is about." He pointed his finger at me. "If I get caught, you're afraid they'll start looking at you. Ain't that the truth?"

"I don't know what you are talking about." I could feel my breath growing shallow. What did he know?

He fixed his dark eyes on mine. "Okay, *Riley Keane*. How long did you think it was going to take me to figure *you* out? You're driving a neon sign, you idiot. A yellow Beetle! Jesus! Didn't you think anyone would notice, run your fuckin' tags, figure out you ain't who you say you are?"

"Maybe Keane is my married name."

"And that's why you didn't want Ginny to have you on the books? You tell so many goddamn lies." He began pacing circles in the snow.

I hid my face in my hands. "How'd you find out?"

"It don't take a genius, *monita chiquita*, to figure out you're running from something."

The back door banged open, and there was Ginny. "What's going on? We got orders piling up."

Javier trudged inside. I followed.

For the rest of the afternoon, we worked next to each other, both of us fuming. At one point, our hands wound up on the same plate, mine holding a bun and his dispensing a burger. He let the meat fall to the plate then grabbed my wrist, forcing me to look at him.

"Meet me tonight," he whispered. "Eleven. Back harbor parking lot." Then he turned to the row of burgers spitting grease on the grill. I stared at him. He wasn't asking.

About ten-thirty, I backed my car into a space at the harbor parking lot. I considered not showing up, but given how much Javier already knew about me, I figured it was better to keep him as an ally. My hands nervously drummed the steering wheel. There was no sign of Javier or his jacked-up four-wheel drive pick-up truck. My windows soon fogged up. When I heard rapping against the glass, I jumped in my seat, then cracked open my window.

"Let me in."

I unlocked the door. Javier slid into the passenger seat. He rubbed his bare palms together and blew on them. "Damn, it's cold. Start the car. Keep the lights off."

Still raw from our earlier fight, I didn't say a word but did as he instructed. The light from a single parking lot light cast a sinister shadow across his face. We sat in silence for a few minutes.

"I had to check you out. I thought you might be undercover —some girl informant sent to set me up."

"What?

"I know you ain't no secret agent. You're legit...well, a legitimate *fuckup*. That's why you gotta get rid of this car. It tells anybody who wants to know who you really are."

He was right, of course. My car was the last vestige of my former life.

"I can't risk you getting caught," he said. "The feds be lookin' at everyone in the restaurant. It wouldn't take long before their beady eyes focused on me. I'd be the real catch. You'd just be the guppy." He smiled, his gold-capped eyetooth gleaming in the light of the dashboard.

"What am I going to drive now?"

"Don't worry, *chica*." He pinched my cheek. "I have something good for you."

"What do I owe you?"

Javier shrugged. "Nothing. I just don't want to have to train another ass in the kitchen." *Ass* was Javier's abbreviation for assistant.

"And that's all I am to you? Another *ass* in the kitchen?"

Before he could answer, a pair of lights approached. Javier told me to turn on my yellow parking lights. A Jeep pulled up on Javier's side as he rolled down his window. The men spoke in Spanish for several minutes. It was moments like these I wished I'd learned Spanish instead of French in college.

Javier turned to me: "Get your shit out. Everything."

I stared at him. My car was crammed with my things: CDs, books, notebooks, clothes.

"C'mon, now!" he yelled. He pulled out a garbage bag from his coat pocket and threw it at me. He yanked on the glove box, dumping its contents into another garbage bag. I popped the trunk, grabbed an armload of stuff, and shoved it into a bag. I was still digging in the dim light of the trunk when I heard my car start.

Javier pulled my arm from the trunk and slammed the trunk lid, then waved through the back glass at his friend in the driver's seat.

"Later, amigo," Javier yelled.

I stood in the cold, clutching an armload of odds and ends, and watched the stranger drive away in my car.

"I loved that car," I said, trying not to cry.

Javier stuffed the garbage bags into the back of the Jeep. "Here you go, *chica*." He held out a set of keys.

When I didn't take them, he dropped them into my coat pocket. Then he disappeared. I was alone, standing in the empty, frozen parking lot. I opened the door of the Jeep and slid behind the steering wheel. On the dashboard was a folded square like I'd seen Javier handing out the kitchen's back door.

I unwrapped the paper. Inside was a picture of me. I recognized the unflattering shot. It was my Illinois driver's license mug, except my hair had been digitally altered from black to blonde. The Michigan state driver's license bore the name Riley Kennedy with an Angelica Island address. Behind the license was a Social Security card with my fake name and a new number. I opened the glove box and found the title bearing my phony name and my real island address.

So, all those men who showed up at the back door were buying new identifications. Just like me, they were running from something. The stories about the island were true. It was the last refuge for draft dodgers, undocumented workers, criminals, and fugitives trying to start a new life.

I put my head against the steering wheel and sobbed. It wasn't about the loss of my car, but rather what losing it meant. I wasn't going back to Chicago any time soon.

FINN

When I arrived at my district office on Monday morning, reporters were spilling out the front door. Apparently, Lowenstein's "a few reporters" had multiplied after the *Tribune* story. They rushed toward me, some pushing microphones within inches of my face. One of the television cameras blinded me with its light.

"Is it true you were with Darren Wallack when he killed himself?" asked a pretty brunette I recognized as a reporter from the leading television station.

"Did he talk to you? Did he tell you why he killed his classmates?" someone else yelled.

I raised my hands. "I will answer your questions. But let's do it inside. Please. Take a seat, and we'll begin the press conference in a minute."

My assistants had arranged five folding chairs before a table in the main room. We'd never filled those seats for any press conference. Now, at least twenty or more reporters were elbowing each other for a good position.

I shut my office door and scrolled through my phone. He answered on the fifth ring.

"What the fuck, Rod? I got two dozen reporters in my office asking questions."

"*Well*, good morning to you, Finn." He'd never called me by my first name. It was always Mr. O'Farrell. "I tried to tell you what might happen. Perhaps next time, you won't hang up on me."

"Rod, I did not hang up on you. I was...in shock. The school shooting was a very traumatic time, and that, that story brought it all back."

"If you had told me about this tragic event during your vetting, I could have drawn up thoughtful responses. This is why we ask so many questions. It's not for prurient interest."

"Okay. I'm sorry. But reporters are here now. What should I say?"

He howled spitefully. "I can't do anything *now*. My advice? Don't embarrass the Mayor." Then he hung up.

"Shit." I had to explain the biggest secret in my life with no talking points. Riley would have known what to do. She was great in the spotlight, articulate, charming, her eyes flirting with the camera. But me? I was stiff and lawyerly. I read the notes I'd jotted down during the night when I couldn't sleep. But looking at them in the daylight, they seemed weak, and nothing those jackals outside my door would accept. They wanted real answers.

It wasn't the media or the mayor or even my constituents I was concerned about. Wherever Riley was, I knew she was tracking what was happening in Chicago. By now, she'd probably read yesterday's *Tribune* story and was furious with me for never having told her about my role in the worst day of her life. But there'd never been a good time to say, "You might not remember me, but I first saw you when you were weeping over your dead brother." It's not exactly a pickup line. She would think I'd dated her to satisfy some morbid curiosity. And it's true, in the beginning, I just wanted to see how she was doing after all these years. But now that my secret had surfaced, I feared it would ruin us.

RILEY

Pick-up trucks fanned out in front of Mr. Kowalski's deli. More were parked along the road. I'd never seen the place so jammed. I parked in front of one of the shuttered souvenir stores and walked into the deli. A crowd of mostly older men gathered below the television suspended from the ceiling. Though he had satellite service and better reception than most, Mr. Kowalski rarely turned on the TV in his shop. He said there was no money in it. He preferred folks bought day-old newspapers.

But today, the television was on, and the volume was turned up. I sidled up to a man I recognized as a regular at the restaurant.

"What's going on?" I whispered.

"It's the former cop who caught Darren Wallack, the school shooter in Chicago," he whispered back.

And that's when I heard his voice.

Finn.

"I followed the suspect into a classroom," Finn said, his voice cracking. He was sitting behind a table, his forehead beaded with sweat, his hair mussed, and his tie askew. He looked like a stockbroker who'd just lost a fortune.

"I thought he was going there to reload," he continued. "When I entered, he was sitting in the corner. He had something in his hand—"

"What was it?" asked a reporter.

"Let him speak," someone at the press conference hollered.

"Give the man space," one of the men in the deli yelled at the television. Others in the store murmured agreement.

"It was an automatic rifle, an AK-47," Finn said. He stopped and wiped his forehead with an embroidered handkerchief that he always kept in his jacket pocket. Then he cleared his throat. "He pointed it at me, told me to lower my weapon, and not to come closer."

My stomach tightened, and there was a bitter taste in my mouth. How could this be Finn? Why had he never told me?

"Why didn't you shoot him?" someone at the press conference yelled.

Loud moans came from the men in the deli, many of whom were war veterans.

"What was his demeanor?" another reporter asked.

"He...he seemed rattled, in shock. I...wanted to get him to put down the rifle. He was waving it at me." Finn shook his head and held out his hands in that dramatic way he always did when he spoke. "Then he started shooting at me. One struck me in the chest, stopped by my bulletproof vest."

"Were you injured?" a voice shouted at the press conference.

"Did he have other guns?" another reporter asked.

"He had two other guns. I couldn't see them. There were desks and computers between us," Finn said. "I was trained to keep the shooter talking. He told me to lock the door so no one could come in. That seemed to make him feel safer. He knew there were a lot of police at the school. We could hear them running in the hallway, yelling. I radioed my commander that I was alone with the suspect and told him to keep everyone away. The suspect was on one side of the room. I was on the other. I sat down inside the doorway, and we talked."

"What did he say?" a reporter asked.

Finn looked out at the reporters with wild eyes. "I'm not sure I should discuss what was said. I...I don't want to cause any more pain for the survivors and their families. I will say that his comments were not reflective of someone who had just taken the lives of forty-nine people."

The reporters shouted questions over one another.

"When did he kill himself?" a reporter yelled when the commotion died down.

"We talked for about twenty minutes. He told me many things about himself, about the grudges he had against kids at school, how he thought they'd mistreated and bullied him. He was angry and bitter. He saw no way out of his situation, no matter what I said. He was intent on killing himself and me with him."

"What did you say to him before he shot himself?"

"That's really all I can say." Finn stood up and started to leave the room.

"How did this affect you?" a reporter shouted.

Finn turned, a strange expression on his face. "It's not easy to see someone kill himself, no matter who they are. The scene in the gymnasium—the bodies..." he started to choke up, then cleared his throat. "I decided then that I would become a legislator, to change laws, to make sure that perpetrators can't have access to military-grade weapons and also to make sure they aren't the only ones armed."

Then he walked out.

I stood staring at the television as the men in the deli

conferred with each other. Some thought Finn should have shot Wallack in the arm or leg, something to distract him so that Finn could tackle him and arrest him. Other men argued that Finn followed the manual for how to deal with a distraught shooter. A couple of young men said Finn should have shot and killed the bastard when he had the chance.

"You okay, gal?" It was Mr. Kowalski.

I nodded, but I didn't trust myself to speak.

"It's a lot, isn't it? I remember that day so well. I was teaching, you know, in Milwaukee. Not so far from Chicago. My heart goes out to those families, the students, the teachers, the cops. It's why I eventually quit teaching. Kept having these nightmares that a shooter was going to come into my classroom."

I looked at him.

"I bought a gun. I took lessons. I kept it locked in my desk even though it was against school policy. I wasn't going to be one of *them*, and I wasn't going to let some video game maniac mow down my students."

He lightly touched my shoulder. "Someone you knew was killed, right? I can see it on your face. I'm sorry. It's a tragedy. One that keeps happening."

I turned away and filed out the door with the rest of the men.

Outside, the cold air stung my face. My brain was exploding with a collision of thoughts: Finn. Darren Wallack. The gun. My brother Ross. My parents. That day. The gym. The blood. Ross's jacket.

Looming the largest was Finn. He had been there.

Everything about our relationship suddenly felt like a fraud. My heart was breaking into a million pieces. Had he targeted me? Was he some sort of ghoulish fan? Or did being with me make him feel better about what had happened with

Wallack? And what did happen with Wallack? Why wouldn't Finn say what they talked about? The court cases were settled years ago. Nothing was in jeopardy. Or was there? Was this about his political ambitions? I wanted answers. I felt foolish for having trusted him, for having fallen for a politician—a Republican and Second Amender at that. He'd manipulated his way into my life and my heart.

What kind of man preys on a mass shooting survivor?

FINN

I was standing next to the mayor outside city hall. The wind laced with wet snow whipped at our faces. Not exactly the ideal weather to announce your campaign for mayor and vice mayor. It didn't matter. Dozens of reporters and cameras surrounded us. Curious pedestrians stopped to gawk. City and county workers stepped out of their cubicles and braved the cruel temperatures to witness a bit of history. The mass swelled to several hundred, spilling across the sidewalk and onto the street.

A week had passed since the press conference that I thought would end my political career. I half expected to be called down to police headquarters and re-interrogated about what had transpired in my twenty minutes alone with Wallack.

Some of the more liberal columnists and TV pundits, of course, raised questions about what happened in that room with Wallack. Some even demanded that an investigation be opened into whether Wallack's civil rights had been violated. But the police chief at the time had long since retired, and the new one said the case was closed and would remain so unless convincing new evidence surfaced that indicated some wrongdoing.

"Officer Finn O'Farrell was not only cleared of any mishandling of Darren Wallack but awarded the Blue Star for apprehending one of the city's most vicious killers in history," the current police chief said in a statement.

The chief was buttressed by public opinion polls that showed Chicagoans approved of my handling of Wallack. The majority saw me as brave and honest. According to Rod's magical analysis of the numbers, the public thought I would make a terrific vice mayor and heir to the mayor. For the past week, any public event I attended, even the mundane, generated crowds who held up handmade signs like "We love you Finn!" and "Out of peril with O'Farrell!"

You'd think most people would have forgotten Darren Wallack or the Hyde Park High School shooting by now. It happened thirteen years ago. But Chicagoans have long memories. They still celebrate the Bears' 1985 Super Bowl win, for Christ's sake, and most of those guys are in wheelchairs or dead. The Hyde Park High School slaughter still retains its odious title as the deadliest school shooting in history. It is referenced in news reports every time another shooter enters a school, which unfortunately is often.

My public accolades and the voluminous press coverage got the mayor's attention. He acted as if he'd never considered running with anyone else. But I knew his loyalty hinged on my popularity. Even Lowenstein had become downright obsequious. And so, here we were, right on schedule, announcing our platform for the February elections.

The mayor grinned at the TV lights. "This guy," he said, throwing his arm around my shoulder, "is a terrific alderman! He's a man who really stands up for us. A man who isn't afraid to be alone with a child killer. He will go to great lengths to protect Chicagoans and make sure crime victims are treated with respect and accorded the justice they deserve."

I dug my fingernails into my palms and forced a grin. I didn't feel brave cornering Darren Wallack. I hadn't been a hero. If people knew what had really happened in that room, they wouldn't be holding me up to praise. Oh, some would think that justice was served, that Wallack deserved to die. But the only person whose opinion mattered to me would no doubt be furious that I'd kept the biggest secret of my life from her.

I didn't expect her to forgive me. But like everyone else, she only knew half the story. My political success depended on me making damn sure no one ever learned the rest.

RILEY

The ferry only crossed the lake twice a day now. Each morning, the Coast Guard cleared a path amid the forming ice. The mid-December sky remained a constant gray, temperatures hovered in the twenties, and several inches of snow fell every day. It was getting harder and harder to get supplies on the island. Mr. Kowalski was lucky if he received days-old newspapers if he got them at all.

Still eager for updates about Finn and Reece, I showed up at the deli every afternoon, hoping that Mr. Kowalski had received a stack of newspapers.

"As much as I hate to lose your business," he said after three straight days of no news, "you should try the library."

The island's library was a repurposed church with white clapboard shingles and a steeple, but no bell. A sign outside stated: "Reading, like whiskey, can help you survive the winter and won't give you a hangover." I tried going in once, but stopped when I read a sign that said adults must show an official government ID to enter. Now, I had a shiny new driver's license with my fake name.

"There are a few things you should know before you go," Mr. Kowalski said, posing in what I called his professor stance. "There's only one librarian, Ms. Fuchs." He looked at me over his glasses. "It sounds like Fucks, which, as you can imagine, has all the little kids snickering behind her back. Most people just called her Ms. F., which she seems to tolerate."

As soon as I stepped inside the library, I was met by the imperious Ms. Fuchs reigning from her throne at the checkout desk. She seemed like a stereotype: in her sixties, her hair in a bun, her reading glasses on the tip of her nose.

Ms. Fuchs didn't look up from the book she was reading or even say hello. She just held out her hand for my ID. When I asked about the library's computers, she frowned.

"You've come too late, dear. You see that gaggle of middle school boys?" She pointed at a half dozen or so boys hanging over a bank of computers across the room. "They monopolize the computers every afternoon, scrolling for sports scores, sending emails to one another and laughing at Youtube videos of kids doing dangerous and insidious pranks." Ms. Fuchs rolled her eyes and let out a long sigh. "If you want to snag a terminal, I suggest you get here before school lets out at 2:05."

The next day, I ran out of the restaurant five minutes before the end of my shift at two o'clock, drove as fast as I could to the library, and secured my spot at one of the three computer terminals. I watched as the horde of pubescent boys came bounding in, laughing and roughhousing until they saw me. Their look of surprise was precious.

My joy was short-lived, though, when I learned that I couldn't access the *Tribune* because of its stringent paywall. I found other news sites that pilfered liberally from the newspaper. I also discovered a trove of information on the Chicago Police Department's website. After clicking through pages of crime data and photos of wanted criminals, I found a small item about Reece. He'd just been released from a lengthy hospital stay after contracting an infection. There was a thumbnail picture of him. He looked thinner, his green eyes held less light, but he was smiling. I bowed my head to the computer and said a little prayer of gratitude.

The boys were throwing a small football, and when I sat up, it smacked me in the ear.

"Ow!" I yelled.

Ms. Fuchs rushed over and snatched the football off the floor. "This is a library, not a gymnasium," she scolded. "You boys are *banished* from the library for one week! And if you don't know what banished means, look it up in the dictionary." She pointed to the door. The boys reluctantly gathered their bags and slunk out.

"Thank you, thank you, Ms. F.," I whispered.

"Mr. Kowalski called me," she said and winked.

So, the island godfather had called in a favor. I didn't care what he'd promised. Kicking out those delinquents meant I had hours of undisturbed time to search online every afternoon. That's how I discovered all the fanfare over Finn's campaign as vice mayor. In his interviews, he effused the right amount of regret about not arresting Darren Wallack. Every story made him out to be a heroic figure who confronted a crazy man with multiple weapons, the ideal narrative the mayor wanted to be spun. Why wasn't anyone asking the obvious questions: If Finn had been so courageous, why all the secrecy at the time and since? Why hadn't they celebrated the officer who had cornered a monster?

One part of Finn's story resonated with me. Like him, I never wanted to relive that day. Over the years, I ignored news articles and documentaries, of which there were many. I turned down multiple requests for interviews. In my anti-gun work, I referenced the shooting, but I refused to discuss it further. "I want to live in the present, not the past," was my stock answer. By then, most people knew my story, thanks to the media, which dredged up the old news clips at every anniversary and after every significant school shooting.

I wondered what I might find now in the old news stories. Were there clues about Finn I just hadn't seen?

When I told Ms. Fuchs I was searching for Chicago newspaper articles from 13 years ago, she looked at me with an eye of appreciation and delivered loads of dusty microfiche. I spent days in the library's archive room scrolling through the rolls of brown film. Chicago's newspapers had covered the shooting for weeks. There were eyewitness accounts and feature stories about Wallack and each of his victims, as well as comparisons with other mass shootings across the country. It was painful to read the stories, especially those about my brother. But I found no mention of Finn. Anywhere.

After several days of scrolling, I found a picture of Reece and me. It was on the bottom of an inside page in an opinion article marking the shooting's first anniversary. Reece's skinny arms were wrapped around me. My back was to the camera. I recognized my favorite purple paisley shirt I had worn that day. I never again wore paisley of any kind or purple in any pattern. In the dark archive room, I leaned toward the screen. The photo was grainy and dark. We were standing at the edge of the gymnasium. Other survivors were near us. Off to the right was a row of police officers in combat gear. In the middle stood a tawny-haired cop. He held his police helmet in his hands, his chin sunk to his chest. I recognized his square jaw, his steady gaze. He wasn't looking at the camera, as the others were.

He was staring at Reece and me.

FINN

I hadn't expected the police to question me first. I figured they'd approach Riley's parents. But there they were: two homicide detectives sitting in my ward office.

"When was the last time you saw Ms. Keane?" Detective Davies asked. He had a hardened, pock-marked face and never broke a smile.

I leaned back and looked out the window. Snow was coming down in large clumps, piling on the sidewalk. It was a Friday, a week before Christmas. Traffic would be hell going home. I wondered what the weather was like wherever Riley was. I imagined her in some sunny outpost, maybe Mexico or Central America, sitting on a beach, drinking a Mai Tai.

"I'm not sure," I said.

"According to jail records, you bailed her out of an arrest earlier this year," Detective O'Brien said. Her long black hair was pulled back into a severe ponytail, highlighting her worst feature—Dumbo ears. "Why would a Republican alderman bail out an anti-gun protester?"

"That's simple: the mayor asked me to."

"Have you heard from her? Has she emailed or called you?" Davies asked.

I thought carefully; if I said she'd sent me an email, then they'd want to see it. But if I said she phoned me at the ward office, that would be harder to track down.

"She called here and said she had to leave town. We both serve on several anti-crime and violence committees together. I haven't heard from her since."

"What did she say," O'Brien leaned forward, "exactly?"

"Oh, I don't remember the exact words." I shrugged. "Something about a sick aunt, and she'd be gone for a while. Oh, and she said she misplaced her cell phone. That was it."

"Do you think she could have been at the shooting with Detective Reece Taylor?" Davies asked. He slid a screengrab from the blue-light video across my desk as if I hadn't seen it in the newspapers or on television.

I pretended to study the grainy photo. "She would have been on her way to her aunt's by then. Did someone say that they thought this looked like her?" I held up the photo. "Because, in my opinion, it doesn't look like her at all."

"Do you expect she'll be contacting you again?" O'Brien asked. A few hairs had come loose from her ponytail. She wrapped them around her wide, unadorned ears.

"Doubt it."

"When did she say she would return?" Davies asked.

"She didn't." I leaned across my desk. "How is it that Riley came to your attention?"

The two detectives glanced at each other. Davies coughed. "She's a woman of interest," he said. "Now, could you tell us who her friends are?"

"Why would I know?"

"We've heard you were *close*," O'Brien said, playing with her hair again.

I guessed that they'd talked with Rod Lowenstein. "We've worked on a few committees together. The mayor asked me to keep tabs on her. He likes to pair up folks on the opposite sides of an issue. He calls it 'facilitating dialogue.'"

"And did it work?" Davies asked.

I shook my head. "My stance against gun control is public knowledge."

"Why is it you don't seem all that concerned about her?" O'Brien asked.

"Concerned? Riley has practically given me an ulcer with her arrests and altercations with cops. I have had to manage some of these situations, so they don't blow up in the media and make the city look bad. *Then* I was concerned. But traveling to visit a sick aunt? No, I can't say that I thought more than a minute about it. I'm relieved she's not in town."

"Aren't you *concerned* that she never arrived at her aunt's place?" she asked.

"This is news to me. Maybe she changed her mind. She is unpredictable."

Davies leaned forward, eyebrows puckered as if he were Columbo, the clumsy but curious detective on TV, trying to understand something. "So, you're not worried that Riley is lying in some ditch somewhere dead?"

"If she were dead, there's not much I could do for her, is there?" I felt sick with the thought. She drove like a race car driver, whipping around bends and white-knuckling it through sharp curves.

O'Brien referred to notes in her hands. "Says here you posted $2,000 to get her out of jail. Weren't you worried you'd lose that money?"

I chuckled. "The charges were dropped. They usually are in cases like that."

"Cases like what?" Davies asked.

"Where a protester has been threatened or harassed," I said.

"Don't you mean in cases that attract a lot of media attention? It's my understanding that she assaulted a man and several police officers during her arrest," he said.

I looked out my glass office at my assistants watching from their cubicles.

O'Brien followed my gaze. "Don't worry. We'll talk to them, too."

"Did you see Riley on a social basis?" Davies asked. He had a way of staring, full eyes, unblinking.

"I'm not sure where this conversation is going. But I don't like the ridiculous insinuation that Riley—a well-known peace activist—is a suspect in the shooting of a police officer and that perhaps she's engaged me in a coverup. Riley has not been popular with your police department." I stood up, indicating that they should leave. But they didn't move. "I've told you all I know. I'm afraid I won't be able to assist you any further."

"I don't think you're in a position to throw us out," Davies said. "*The mayor* has given us permission to talk to whomever we want. We're waiting for a couple of subpoenas. Then we'll bring you down to the station. Hopefully, there won't be a cluster of reporters because that wouldn't be good for the image of a city councilman, *or* a vice mayor candidate, would it?"

RILEY

I desperately wanted to talk with Reece. He would have the connections to find out what happened between Finn and Wallack and why it had been kept secret. Since Reece survived, did that mean it was safe for me to go home? The thought gave me hope, something I hadn't felt in a long while. I had lots of questions. I didn't know who filmed the shooting or what happened to that video. Maybe my parents had paid to keep the video from surfacing. Maybe Reece knew about that too.

I thought of creating an email account and sending a coded message to Reece or my parents, but if the police were monitoring online accounts, they'd surely trace my IP address to the island. Using electronic devices was the quickest way to be discovered. I could leave the island, just long enough to drive a few hours away and call the foundation's lawyer, Mr. Sanders, from a payphone. He would tell me if it was safe to come back. If I were a suspect, and my gut told me I was, the police would have tapped my parents' phones, and possibly Finn's. But I doubted the police could get court approval to tap the phones of a lawyer. That would be interfering with attorney-client privilege.

I spent a day plotting what highway to take, what city I would drive to, how long it would take to get there. I packed my car with a survival kit in case I ran off the road: water, a blanket, batteries, sandwiches. I would go after work the next day.

When I arrived at the restaurant the next morning, there was a lot of commotion in the kitchen. Javier was bringing up plywood from the cellar. Waitresses were stocking the upstairs pantry and walk-ins.

"What's happening?" I asked Beverly, an older waitress who was always dishing out advice. She didn't stop to answer. I followed her into the breakfast room. People were clustered near the doors, waiting for a table to open up. Normally, there were only a few customers that early in the morning.

"Haven't you heard, dear?" Beverly asked. "We're supposed to get a big snowstorm. It's set to hit this afternoon." She looked out the window at the large snowflakes coating the glass. "It looks like the weatherman's miscalculated again. It's already here. By this afternoon, you won't be able to see to drive home. Hope you brought a change of clothes."

I had brought a change of clothes, but not to stay at the restaurant.

"I don't understand. How did you find out?"

"Native News," she said.

I looked at her blankly.

"The reservation's radio station? Their weather reports are better than anyone else's. Although they didn't get this one exactly right either."

I followed her as she moved from table to table, collecting plates, taking orders. I was still in a bit of shock, disbelieving that something I hadn't prepared for was going to happen. Despite the weather, no one seemed in a big hurry. Folks had come into town to stock up on supplies, and many stopped by the restaurant to talk about the approaching storm and catch up before they spent the next several days shut up in their cabins. Their energy—and fear—was contagious.

"A snowstorm on the island isn't something to take lightly, dear," Beverly said. "I hope you are stocked up at your house. They've halted the ferry in Grand Portage for the season."

"But it's a week before Christmas," I protested in a childlike voice. "The ferry doesn't shut down until *after* Christmas."

She shrugged. "Sometimes. Sometimes not. Sorry, dear. That's the island for you. Usually, the electricity gets knocked out for days. Winter storms are when we get to use all our survival skills. That's what makes us hardy folks." She gave me a sympathetic smile.

Just when I was ready to leave, I was trapped. I'd spent so much time in the library's archive room researching the past that I hadn't paid attention to the present. It had been snowing for days, and I hadn't even noticed. If I'd been going to Mr. Kowalski's every afternoon, he would have prepared me.

I trudged back to the kitchen, where the crew was standing around the prep station eavesdropping on an argument between Ginny and Javier in her office. Javier wanted to close the restaurant, nail plywood over the windows, and conserve food if the storm turned out to be another Great One. A few years back, that snowstorm knocked out electricity on the island for a week, killing several residents. Ginny intended to keep the restaurant open round the clock, so people could have a warm place to congregate.

"These are my people, Javier," she said. "We need to offer the restaurant as a place of refuge."

"And what are you going to do, Ginny, when we don't have any food? Who is going to stop them from busting through the kitchen when we tell them we don't have what they want?"

He stormed out of her office, ripped off his apron, and went out the back door, slamming it behind him.

"He'll be back," Ginny said. Her hair looked uncombed, and her eyes were bloodshot. She'd likely been up all night.

We stared at her with disbelief. Javier had always been the fearless one. If he was afraid, we were in trouble.

Ginny laid out a plan: We'd work in shifts with a skeletal crew at night, turning the nighttime dining room into a makeshift shelter with cots and sleeping bags. The breakfast room, closest to the kitchen, would serve a limited menu.

Fifteen minutes later, the back door flung open. Javier stumbled in. Snow covered his hair. His eyes looked manic. "It's landed."

We ran to the back windows. White sheets of snow blew horizontally.

"This snow is different," Javier said, his cheeks red and raw. "It's like raining ice, stabbing your face." He stared at Ginny, expecting her to change her mind.

Beverly burst in from the breakfast room. "They keep coming. We don't have enough chairs."

We rushed to the In and Out doors and peered out their tiny port windows. Customers tumbled into the restaurant, their faces blistered, ice on their eyelashes, icicles dangling from their hair.

"We are staying open," Ginny announced emphatically, her hands on her hips.

Javier puffed up his cheeks. "Do what you want. I got people I gotta protect, too." He heaved a bag of rice onto his back, opened the back door, and disappeared. A few seconds later, the wind blew open the back door, piling snow in the doorway. Ginny pushed the door closed and locked it. She turned to me, and I saw the panic in her eyes.

"Get coffee and juice out to folks first," I ordered the wait staff.

I grabbed a menu and, using a charcoal pencil, began crossing off what would take too long to make or gobble up our critical supplies: no three-egg omelets or meat lovers' specials.

"We'll serve cereal, fruit cups, toast, pancakes, plain scrambled eggs, one or two at a time, a sausage patty if they insist, and one piece of bread per person. Everyone needs to conserve."

The staff looked at each other and then at Ginny, silently questioning my authority. Ginny loudly cleared her throat. "You heard the woman. Get going."

Our immediate problem was bodies. Without Javier, I'd need at least two more cooks to fill orders. As I began scrambling eggs and whipping pancake batter, I heard Ginny in her office rousting the evening staff. It was barely seven a.m. Within half an hour, though, the cool kids—that's what I called them—arrived: Gill, Chayton, Kayla, and Simon.

Though the line cooks Gill and Chayton didn't know me, neither balked at my orders. They bantered between themselves and entertained the crew with circus theatrics—tossing sharp utensils and catching them by their handles and lighting food on fire. Their tricks provided comic relief.

It was too cold and windy to go outside for a smoke. During a lull, I snuck down the basement stairs only to find the cool kids huddled between the cans of anchovies and capers. The air reeked of marijuana. Chayton tried to hide a blunt behind his back.

"What? You not even going to offer me a hit?" I asked.

He shook his head. "Uh . . . it's not like . . ."

"Save it," I said. "I couldn't even if I wanted to. Ginny'd smell it on me for sure."

I lit a clove cigarette, feeling their eyes on me as they tried to decide whether they should trust the new girl. No doubt they'd tagged me as a spy for Javier. Though I wanted to be loyal to him—he had protected me by getting me the Jeep and the new IDs—I was furious that he'd left us to fend for ourselves. Befriending this clique might be the quickest route to being accepted on the island.

Gill took the blunt from Chayton and inhaled. "That's some scene up there, huh?" he said, through the smoke. One animated eye poked through the hair hanging in his face.

"Should have been here when Ginny and Javier were going at it," I said. "Now that was a *scene*."

"Why the hell did he leave?" Chayton asked.

Up close, I could see why the young waitresses gushed over him. He had thick dark hair, mesmerizing gray eyes, and a coy, lopsided smile. His bad-boy disposition, his sullenness, his ready-to-fight posture made women swoon. Across the front of his neck was a tattoo of an eagle. The regal bird's symmetrical wings fanned out in perfectly horizontal lines. Its head was turned to the left, its only visible eye glaring at observers. I'd seen the same tattoo on other men's hands and arms on the island and wondered what it meant.

"What's he got to take care of during a fucking blizzard?" Chayton said.

"That guy's an asshole," Kayla said. Even when called out of bed, she'd taken the time to draw thick black circles around her eyes, setting off her green irises and her shock-white skin. "From what I hear, he's got himself quite the operation here." She looked at me, daring me to disagree.

They were testing my loyalties. There was a division between the morning and the night crews. Javier led the first camp, and Matthew, the dinner chef, led the second. I felt guilty for not defending Javier.

There were bumping and scraping sounds above our heads. The basement door opened.

"What the hell are you guys doing down there?" Ginny yelled. "We got a casualty."

Mr. Kowalski was splayed on a pallet in the middle of the kitchen. Lying on his belly, Mr. Kowalski wrenched his face sideways in agony. A gash on the back of his balding head was bleeding.

"Get the first aid kit," Ginny ordered.

I hustled to her office and searched under the stacks of books and kitchen supply catalogs. That's when I noticed the white box with the red cross. Near it, perched in the corner, was a double-barrel shotgun. I cracked open the loader and saw two bullets in the chambers.

When I returned to the kitchen, Ginny was kneeling over Mr. Kowalski, dabbing a wet rag at his matted hair.

"He was trying to check the levels of his gas tanks when he fell," she said.

"I didn't fall," he argued, his voice muffled by the blanket near his mouth. "Someone hit me. They wanted the gas."

"How'd you get here?" I asked.

"Walked in the snow," he said. Blood soaked his collar.

"You two," Ginny yelled at Gill and Chayton. "Go to Gabe's and lock up his store and the tanks. Here are the keys. See if anyone is hanging around."

"Hanging around? In a blizzard?" Chayton asked incredulously.

"Do it," Ginny ordered.

I dug through the medical kit and found suture tape and latex gloves. I used a pair of scissors and trimmed the hair around the four-inch gash that kept oozing blood.

I tried not to think of Reece, how I'd sopped up his blood with his shirt, how I'd covered his entry wound with my hands. I kept my face down, my eyes tearing up. I had been so close to seeing him again, getting off the island, and now I was stuck here, probably for months.

I was about to apply suture tape to Mr. Kowalski's scalp when the lights went out.

Kayla screamed.

We sat in darkness, the wind howling around the restaurant like a monster circling.

"Don't panic," Ginny said, her voice loud over the murmurs of others in the room. "The generator will switch on in a second."

A few lights flicked on.

I helped Mr. Kowalski sit up. He grabbed my hand and, with surprising force, pulled my face close to his. I stared at his narrow yellow eyes.

"It's Javier," he whispered. "He hit me. Ginny doesn't want anyone to worry."

"Are you sure?"

"He dropped this," Mr. Kowalski said, slipping a piece of paper from his pocket. It was a receipt for several packs of Red Man chewing tobacco and a carton of Marlboros, dated that morning. "It's Javier's. I remember because I thought it was strange for him to buy chewing tobacco *and* cigarettes. He demanded gas for his truck. I told him I didn't have any. He called me a 'cheap old man' and said that he knew I had a reserve tank."

I tried to hand back the receipt, but Mr. Kowalski refused to take it.

"You keep it. In case I get...you know...*loopy*."

I helped him to his feet. He leaned against me as he hobbled through the breakfast room. I scanned the faces of Islanders, wondering if one of them had clobbered Mr. Kowalski. I didn't want to believe it was Javier.

"I don't get it," I said as I helped Mr. Kowalski lay on a cot in the formal dining room. "If Islanders are used to snowstorms, then why are people freaking out and looting your gas?"

He leaned toward me and spoke in a hushed tone. "What's it like in Chicago during the first snowstorm of the season?"

I chuckled. "People go crazy, trying to stock up. They get scared remembering some snowstorm in 1978 when the electricity cut out for weeks, and people were eating expired can goods."

"That's exactly it," he said. "Except this has novice all over it. That's why I know it's Javier. No Islander would have done this."

WE WORKED STEADILY all day in the kitchen as the wind swirled outside and the snow piled under the windows.

"Where's Zi?" I asked Ginny as the light outside started to dim. It would be dark soon.

She shook her head and looked away.

"She's probably at the reservation," I said, rubbing her arm, though I knew it was just as likely Zi was trapped in a snowbank on the way to check one of her houses.

We stood at the prep counter for the dinner meal and, in factory-like motions, made sandwiches—corned beef, turkey, tuna fish—and wrapped them in wax paper. Kayla and Simon stuffed them, along with bags of chips, into wicker baskets to hand out, as if we were at a picnic. In the dining room, people sat like stones staring out the windows at the blackness. They spoke in serious voices and whispers. The place felt funereal.

Only a few lights were burning in the restaurant. The generator made a racket as it ground out energy. Everyone said we were lucky the county had finally laid natural gas lines, or things could be a lot worse. At least in town, we had gas to heat and cook with. People outside of town still relied on propane from tanks in their yards.

In a corner of the kitchen, the crew threw down sleeping bags. Gill laid his bag next to mine, and his friends settled around us. Ginny stretched out in her office and shut the door. She'd been trying to reach Lars all day, but her cell couldn't get a signal; the landline was dead. We wondered if anyone on the mainland knew of our situation.

The wind whistled in the eaves and seeped through cracks around the windows.

"What was is it like out there?" I whispered to Gill. He was lying on his side, his eyes gleaming in the dim light.

"Shit is flying around, shingles, roof parts, chairs. It's like a hurricane."

"And Mr. Kowalski's place?"

He closed his eyes. "Not good. His shelves are empty."

"Yeah, when I drove by early this morning, he'd already posted a hand-written sign out front that said NO GAS in giant letters. What about his reserve tank?"

"I don't know how much is left."

"What about getting a helicopter in, supplies from the mainland?"

He shook his head. "Winds are too fierce. There's no satellite service. A few of the guys are trying to work their CB radios. But to tell you the truth, I think most of these folks would rather freeze to death than ask the Mainlanders to rescue them."

FINN

Detectives Davies and O'Brien were again in my office, their second visit in five days. I complained to the mayor. He chided me, saying that it would look like I was hiding something if I refused to talk. Besides, he said, it was better that they interviewed me in my office rather than hauling me down to the police station. We couldn't afford any hint of scandal, given that the election was less than two months away.

"We're just making the rounds to see if you've heard anything further from Ms. Keane," O'Brien said, scooting to the edge of her chair. Earlier that week, detectives had summoned Riley's parents to police headquarters. Emma was thoroughly shaken, convinced that the police knew they were lying. Ethan kept me informed with burner phones he had passed out.

"I haven't heard from Riley, and I don't expect to," I told the detectives. "If Riley were going to contact someone, I assume it would be her family. Have you spoken with them?"

The corners of Davies's mouth turned up ever so slightly. "We have. But I'm sure you already knew that."

"Why would I know who you interview, or care, for that

matter?" I sounded defensive. I wondered why they hadn't asked about my visit to Reece in the hospital. They hadn't asked anything about him.

"Are you saying that you haven't spoken to Riley's parents?" O'Brien asked. She'd recently cut her hair short; the new do only enhanced her big ears.

"Who I have conversations with in the course of business is none of your concern."

"Well, if it's just a matter of business, then why not tell us who you've spoken to about Riley?" Davies said, moving aggressively toward me in his chair.

"Why do you keep trying to involve me?"

"We know you and Riley were seeing each other," he said, daring me to disagree. "Why didn't you tell us about that previously?"

I sat back in my chair and looked over my glasses at them. "You working for the tabloids now? It's not a crime to see someone socially. We're both single. Don't try to make this into something slimy. Because it isn't."

Davies grinned. It was the first time I'd actually seen his teeth. "I'm sure the mayor would not look kindly at his running mate dating an outspoken critic of the police department. I'm sure you wouldn't want the press to find out about that, either."

This was why they were pursuing me—I was the proxy for Riley.

O'Brien turned to Davies. "Maybe there's a way we could keep this evidence among ourselves?"

"What evidence?" I asked, leaning across my desk.

Davies handed me a large envelope. I stared at the yellowish-brown packet, then reluctantly opened it and pulled out a grainy photo that looked like it had come from a security camera. If Davies thought the image would induce fear, he was mistaken. The picture showed Riley and me kissing outside the supper club.

I studied the photo. I remembered that night. We hadn't been seeing each other long and rarely ever kissed in public. There was something about the way she looked in that moment, like she was genuinely happy. Her joy matched mine. My heart fluttered, my eyelashes felt wet. That night, when we made love, I pushed her arms over her head and, in the candlelight, read the inscription under her upper inner arm. It was my favorite of her tattoos. Inked in small print, it read: *The man who reads these words owns my heart*.

O'Brien coughed loudly, bringing my mind back to the room. I felt my throat catch, and I swallowed my emotions. I could feel them studying me.

"Go ahead and show it to the mayor," I said, standing up. I was done with them and their threats. "Give it to the press. I don't fucking care. I'm not embarrassed about my relationship with Riley."

They knew as well as I did that if they informed the mayor or outed me in public, it would force me to lawyer up, and that would end our conversations. As a former cop, I knew you did everything to keep your target talking. In my calculations, though, I hadn't considered how pressured Davies and O'Brien might be to break me or what deals they might strike with others to get what they wanted.

RILEY

I lay awake on my makeshift bed on the kitchen floor, listening to the mysterious thuds outside. It was our second night sleeping at the restaurant. The storm continued to rage. My thoughts drifted back to the photo of Reece and me in the gym after the shooting, Finn staring at us. Who was this man I'd been sleeping with for nearly a year?

I woke the next morning to the sounds of coffee pots gurgling and the rustling of nylon sleeping bags. Others were waking, too. Snow had piled high against the windows. It was like we were living in an ice cave.

We moved a little slower that day, serving significantly scaled back meals. Several people were camped in the dining room, unable to get home. Most insisted they weren't hungry, no doubt wanting to conserve dwindling resources. Javier was wrong about how Islanders would react to our decreasing food stock. Gill said that news of Mr. Kowalski's attack—and the theft of his reserve gas—was making the rounds in the restaurant, putting everyone on edge. Stealing was not part of island culture.

As night approached, Ginny turned the heat down to 55 degrees, and we bundled up in our sleeping bags. That night, our conversations turned bleaker. Kayla questioned whether we'd survive. Gill predicted that the state would send in the Air National Guard. Simon insisted there was no way the state would expend valuable resources to rescue a few hundred people on an island no one cared about until July. Chayton talked about an airplane crash in the Andes where the survivors ate the dead.

"What do you think human flesh tastes like?" Chayton asked, sitting up.

"Raw or cooked?" Gill asked. "With butter or garlic?"

"Dude, I am not eating you raw," Chayton said.

"I hear it tastes like chicken," I volunteered.

"You guys are disgusting," Kayla insisted and turned her back.

"Chay, I'd eat you *raw*," Simon said, sticking out his tongue.

"Ewe," Gill said.

"Yuck," Chayton said. "Sorry I asked."

We fell silent. I listened as the others' breathing became more shallow. I lay awake mired in a separate worry. If I died on the island, how would my parents ever know what had happened to me?

GLINTS of the sun streamed through the snow-plastered windows and awakened me the next morning. The wind had stopped. I gently shook Gill awake. We grabbed our coats, hurried to the front doors, and rushed outside. The air pricked our skin. The men had kept the entrance clear, but seven-foot-high snowdrifts surrounded the rest of the restaurant. In the distance, several shapes moved toward us in the sky. Then we heard the noise: helicopters overhead.

Gill grabbed my arms. We jumped up and down.

"We survived!" he screamed.

"Yeah! And you didn't have to carve me up for dinner!"

Even with the Grand Portage Sheriff's helicopters flying in supplies and utility workers, it took two days to restore the island's electrical lines and clear the main roads, forcing us to stay at the restaurant. It was wearing being cooped up with strangers, living on cream cheese sandwiches, bitter coffee, and snippets of sleep.

On the last day of our captivity, Zi arrived at the restaurant as if nothing had happened. She'd waited out the storm in her yurt on her family's ancestral lands. Others gathered at the restaurant too. It was like one big reunion, everyone sharing how they had endured the past five days without electricity and, for many, without gas to heat their houses. Javier also surfaced, offering no explanation or apology for having deserted us. When she saw him, Ginny closed herself in her office. Sheriff Kustwin interviewed Javier, but could find no evidence to charge him with Mr. Kowalski's assault. It didn't matter, Gill said, because on the island, Javier was deemed guilty. He warned that Islanders, who had ignored Javier's less-than-covert business, would now mete out their own justice.

FINN

On Christmas Eve, I worked in the office, trying to keep busy and not think about what I was missing with Riley. Diana had the kids, and I'd given the day off to my staff. Around six o'clock, I heard a pounding at the door. Couldn't they read the posted notice?

"We're closed," I yelled from my office. When the banging continued, I went to the door, ready to chew out some holiday revelers. But standing there were Detectives Davies and O'Brien.

"Don't you two have anything better to do?" I said stiffly. When they didn't answer, I held the door open for them. They took their usual spots in my office.

"We have a development," Davies said, stifling a grin.

"It better be fucking good for you to show up like this on Christmas Eve."

O'Brien took out a folder and slid it across my desk. Inside was a grainy photo of Riley lobbing something out the passenger side window of her car stopped on the Skyway

Bridge. I looked closer at the object and could make out the iconic arches.

"Looks like Riley's littering to me," I said and pushed the folder back to O'Brien. She was wearing lipstick and smelled nice, either on her way to a party or pulled from one.

Davies scooted to the edge of his chair. "We think it's the gun she used to shoot Detective Taylor."

I leaned back in my chair and chewed on a pen. "And if you are so confident, then why haven't you sent divers down to retrieve it?"

Davies looked at O'Brien.

"Before we call out divers," Davies said, "we wanted to give you and Riley's family a chance to tell us what you know and what you think is in that bag."

I snorted a laugh. "So, you need one of us to say there's a gun in that bag to convince your higher-ups to incur the expense of a dive team? If you're asking me, I think Riley tossed the remains of her dinner out the window. It's a McDonald's bag. I'd say you have an excellent case to charge her with littering."

"Listen," he said sternly. "We're giving you a chance to tell us what you know. The State's Attorney has given us authority to offer immunity to the first person who tells us what they know about Riley's involvement in the shooting. This is a Christmas gift. Take it."

O'Brien leaned on my desk. She wore sparkly purple earrings that took the emphasis off those large earlobes. "She's not even your girlfriend publicly. Why are you protecting her?"

They were playing a game I called: "Who will crack?" They only needed one of us to say something that could be used to extract information from the others—or used against another in an indictment. As a former cop, I was familiar with these kinds of tactics. I'd learned long ago how to keep secrets.

It would take greater detectives than Davies and O'Brien to make me crack.

"It's a religious holiday," I said, slowly articulating each word. "I'm too much of a gentleman to tell you what you can do with your gift." I expected a fight, but the detectives quickly left as if they had somewhere else they had to be.

By the time I drove home, I felt a deep sadness tinged with paranoia. Immunity would have protected me from Riley's mess bleeding over into my political career. But I couldn't do that to her. Besides, I didn't trust those cops. But I wasn't so sure about my co-conspirators. I had no idea whether Riley's family could withstand police questioning. Nelson and his wife could shield themselves because they were lawyers. Cops hate questioning lawyers. Weepy Emma was a particularly vulnerable target, and Evan was only slightly stronger but equally naive.

The house was dark and cold, the opposite of how it had been last Christmas Eve. Riley and I had only been dating a few weeks then, but were eager to celebrate our first holiday together. We sipped champagne and enjoyed caviar, duck pate, chocolate truffles, and later the touch of each other in front of the fire. The night felt magical.

Now here I was alone. Norma Rae brushed her tail against my leg and meowed loudly. I poured food into her bowl. I wasn't even hungry, just going through the motions of living. I reheated leftovers in the microwave.

I'd been standing there for some time, watching the Tupperware container turn round and round in the machine, feeling sorry for myself, wishing the kids were home when I noticed it: A hand-drawn map stuck to my refrigerator between Kye's crude drawings of Norma Rae. The map showed the upper part of Michigan and the lower part of Ontario, Canada. It looked like a child's rendering—traced and colored with bright crayons. A red dot appeared at the Michigan city of Grand Portage, and in a cloud blurb above it, someone had written: She was here.

I knew it was his work, Mr. Mailer. Who else would break into my house? I was furious. That bastard could have hurt my children.

I texted his phone: *Don't fucking come near my house again.*

He texted back immediately: *Merry Christmas to you too.*

I hesitated for a moment. It wasn't the kind of message a vice mayor should send. But then paying a blackmailer twenty grand wasn't stellar behavior either. I was in this neck deep. If Mr. Mailer decided to go public, I was finished no matter what I said to him.

I texted back: *I will kill you.*

I waited. Three dots jumped on my phone screen for an inordinately long time. Finally, his text came through: *I'll keep that in mind. Now go find her.*

I texted back: *I have a campaign to run.*

He texted: *The police will smear your name. She's your only defense. You have to find her. Follow the map.*

So, this was how our relationship was going to work? He'd provide clues, and I'd track them down? If that were the case, I'd need a lot more to go on than an artlessly drawn treasure map. Where was he getting his information? He seemed to have better sources than the cops. Why didn't he do his own dirty work?

I looked at the map again. Grand Portage, Michigan, was next to Canada. If she had gone that far, she probably was safe in Canada by now. Part of me felt relieved, happy even at what Mr. Mailer's stupid map meant: Riley was alive—and safe.

I left my dinner in the microwave and ran upstairs. I'd kept the gift Riley had given me last Christmas in my bedside table.

It was a leather-bound journal. I was hoping one day to find inspiration to fill it. Now I had.

In the book, I cataloged what I knew about Riley's whereabouts and what the police appeared to know. I sketched a timeline and pasted in news clips about Reece's shooting, the sketch, and blue-light camera screenshots the police had released. I described what Reece had told me. I detailed my meeting with Mr. Mailer and what I thought his video showed. I recounted in detail my interviews with Detectives Davies and O'Brien, adding the latest twist about the photo of Riley tossing a bag into the river.

I taped the kissing photo Davies had handed me inside the front cover and examined it more closely. Even though the image was pixelated, we looked blissful, enrapt with each other, so unaware of how our lives would change in a matter of months. That photo gave me hope, made me feel closer to her.

Inside the back cover, I taped the map Mr. Mailer had left on my refrigerator. It was the first clue to Riley's whereabouts. But what was I supposed to do, jump in my car and head to the dot on the map and start interviewing residents like some private detective? I laughed at the thought. But then, I realized that was exactly what I had to do. *I* had to be the one to find her —before the police, before Mr. Mailer, before anyone else.

It had to be me.

RILEY

I volunteered to work the evening shift on Christmas Eve. My plan after that involved a bottle of Johnny Walker Red and a lot of self-pity. I didn't want to think about the holiday or being alone or Finn and how angry I was that he'd kept secrets from me or what it meant about us and if there even was an *us* anymore. I didn't know if I could ever forgive him or if I could forget that he'd kept something so monumental from me.

When I'd first started working at Ginny's, I expected that it would conjure up all kinds of memories from my family's restaurant. But cooking breakfast with Javier hadn't felt familiar. My family's restaurant didn't serve breakfast. So, when I showed up for my first dinner service, I wasn't prepared for the deluge of memories it stirred in me.

My father was the one who taught me how to cook. Before Ross died, my parents spent most of their time at their downtown restaurant called Evan & Emma's, though most people just shortened it to E & E's. Some restaurant critics claimed no visit to Chicago was complete without a visit to E & E's.

Dad had gone through cooking school, but decided to skip

the years of indentured servitude working in other people's kitchens. Instead, he and my mother borrowed heavily and used a small inheritance she'd come into to start the restaurant, which focused on French and Italian dishes. My father was the chef, and my mother the hostess. The restaurant, which started as a tiny storefront, expanded to nearly half a block over the years.

My brothers and I grew up there, often running between tables, playing games in the kitchen, in the cellar. It was a great place to spend your childhood. Most of the line cooks were older men who we called uncles, the female pastry chefs we considered our aunts. We didn't have any relatives in Chicago, so the restaurant employees became our extended family. They taught us to appreciate good food, fresh spices, the best ingredients. They snuck treats to us and hid us when my brothers and I played hide and seek.

In high school, Nelson and I waited tables—or worked the front of the house, as they say. Ross loved the idea of working in the kitchen, the so-called back of the house, even though the closest he got to cooking was running the industrial dishwasher or schlepping errands for the line cooks.

My father thought he was training his heirs. Sometimes when things were slow, Dad would teach us how to cook his signature dishes. He said it was important that we knew how the food was prepared, that if we were going to cook or manage the restaurant someday, we'd need to know how to do everything. That was his dream. It was my dream too.

That fantasy ended the day my brother Ross was killed. Dad fell into a stupor and refused to go to the restaurant anymore. He spent most of his time holed up in Ross's room. I was dealing with my own grief and didn't even notice that my father was drinking heavily until he went away to rehab. When he came back two months later, he announced he was selling the restaurant and would start the foundation with the proceeds. By then, I was heading to college.

I first majored in business—the appropriate degree for a restaurant entrepreneur. But that first semester, I spent most of my time at anti-violence protests and decided to major in politics. When I came home on weekends and for the summers, it seemed strange not to be at the restaurant, not to be cooking, talking with the regulars. I missed that feeling of teamwork, putting it all together, the sweat, the smells, the music in the kitchen, the pranks among staffers, the taste of the food.

From the minute I walked in the backdoor at Ginny's on Christmas Eve, I knew that night was going to be different. First, there was the aroma. Matthew, the dinner chef, was making a fish stew that smelled exactly like my father's Tuscan fish soup. He was stirring the pot singing an aria from Tosca, my favorite opera. My father used to sing like that in the kitchen. The Italian sous chef loved opera, and the music played as the cooks prepared for the evening meal. I loved my father's restaurant kitchen in the late afternoon. There was always this sense that we were getting ready for a grand show.

Matthew looked up from his pot and smiled.

"Hope you're hungry. I'm making stew for our family meal," he said, referring to the staff meal before service. I'd heard Matthew's family meals were remarkable, that he used them as a chance to experiment for creating new menus.

"Try it," he said, holding out a tasting spoon.

I dropped my bag and rushed to the stove, still wearing my coat and boots. The soup tasted amazing. "You used saffron?"

"Well, of course. Only the best for my people."

I looked around the kitchen. Chayton and Gill were standing in front of their stations with starched aprons; their hands folded neatly behind them like a pair of nuns. Simon and Kayla were hovering at the prep counter. They were all studying me. I offered a self-conscious wave, worried about how we would get along, and darted to the break room to change clothes.

At the staff meal, Matthew asked me to sit next to him. He was thin and tall, his graying dark hair neatly trimmed. He wore thick, black glasses, which might have passed as retro if they'd been new. He had an erudite air about him that reminded me of my father. But his appearance—dark snake eyes, long narrow face, and short-cropped beard—conveyed a cold, calculated persona.

Matthew spent the family meal asking me questions about where I'd learned to cook. I wasn't used to someone showing such interest in my life. I told him a version of the truth: that I'd spent my summers and weekends working at a Chicago restaurant. When he asked which one, the name slipped out. I didn't expect him to know it.

"Oh, E & E's. That's an amazing place. Did you know the chef well?"

"Evan?" I squeaked out.

"Yes. I met him at a conference once. Amazing taste. Shame what happened to his family."

I looked down, afraid to even speak.

Luckily, someone questioned Matthew about the dinner menu. That sent him into expert mode. He gave a short lecture about the main courses, all fish and a vegetarian risotto, where the ingredients were sourced, and how they would be prepared. When he finished his talk, everyone rose at once as if this were their routine.

"I don't expect much out of you tonight," he said, leaning toward me as if sharing a secret. "I just like an extra hand on holidays in case we get swamped. You never know what to expect. We're either dead and bored out of our minds or slammed and running around like squirrels. Never in between. Just watch Chayton and Gill. I'm sure the menu won't compare to E & E's, but it does take some getting used to."

Dinner service turned out to be slow. While instructing me on preparing the restaurant's main dishes, Gill and Chayton gossiped about the morning crew. It was clear they didn't like Javier or trust him. But their relationship with their boss Matthew, whom they described as mercurial, wasn't so cozy either.

Matthew kept a tight protocol in the kitchen, insisted on being called "Chef," was stringent about plate presentation, and protested grimy aprons. Violators were hit with curt words that stung so hard they'd wished Matthew had slapped them instead.

Matthew had been tapped as an up-and-coming chef at a Michelin three-star restaurant in Detroit, they said. But his ego clashed with those of the owners, and they dispatched him with his knives like an also-ran on one of those chef TV shows. Even on Angelica Island, he couldn't put his imperious nature behind him.

I wanted to tell them that every chef is volatile. Even my father could fly into a tantrum on par with a toddler. That's how chefs were taught to cook and manage their kitchens. It wasn't personal. But I kept my mouth shut. I was older than Gill and the evening crew, and I didn't want to appear as a know-it-all. It was clear they resented Matthew's expertise.

When the dining room emptied at 9 p.m., Matthew told us to go home. We'd close early.

"Thank you so much for allowing me to observe your staff," I said, sticking my head into Ginny's office. Matthew was curled up with a stack of restaurant supply catalogs. He'd been absent through much of dinner service.

He stood up and stretched out his hand formally. "It was a

pleasure, Miss Kennedy. I've heard a lot of great things about you. I'm glad we finally got to meet properly."

"The stew was great. My fath-Ethan used to cook a similar stew."

He grinned widely, happy for the compliment.

The others had already left by the time I walked through the dark kitchen. I stopped for a second to breathe in its smells one more time before bracing the cold.

I was getting into my Jeep when Gill, standing with the others in the parking lot, hollered. "Riley! Why don't you come to the tavern with us? We're celebrating Chay's birthday!"

I was already imagining the fire I would build in my living room fireplace and the warmth of the Scotch coating my throat. Hanging out with a bunch of drunk twenty-somethings did not sound fun.

"Some other time," I yelled back.

Suddenly Gill appeared at my window, smiling like a little boy. "It's Christmas Eve."

"That's just it," I said sadly. "I'd rather not be reminded."

"That's where we're at, too. We focus on Chay's birthday and try to forget that it's another holiday passing and we're still...well, you know...*alone*. Come on. You don't want to drink by yourself tonight."

I laughed nervously. "How do you know I'm not going home and straight to bed?"

He narrowed his eyes. "'Cause I know."

"One drink. That's all," I said, reluctantly, already regretting my decision.

FINN

It was nearly eleven o'clock that night when I began dialing hotels in Grand Portage. I was half-drunk and not wanting to be alone. When I was in college, we used to get drunk and call girls we were afraid to approach in the daylight. We called it dialing while drunk.

There were only a handful of hotels in Grand Portage. Most of the clerks who answered the phone sounded half-asleep. I tried to sound official, as if my calling at that hour was a matter of urgency. I identified myself as a Chicago alderman and explained that I was working on behalf of Riley Keane's family, who were searching for their missing daughter. A couple searched through their computer databases, but found nothing. One woman told me that their clients were private. When I threatened to call and wake up the hotel owners, she complied. Another bust.

Then I dialed a bed and breakfast that, judging by the internet photos, looked too fancy for Riley. The woman who answered had a cheerful voice, despite the late hour. "Well, yes, there was a young woman here on Thanksgiving. Her first name was Riley. But she had a different last name. And she didn't have black hair."

"Really? I mean, that's great news. Can you tell me anything else about her," I said, trying to retain my official demeanor.

"She stayed one night, and I don't know where she went."

"Did she say anything about what her plans were?"

"I didn't spend much time talking with her. By the way, how do I know you are who you say you are?"

Most of the time, people are deferential when I represent myself in my official capacity. I directed her to my official website.

"O.K. That doesn't prove anything," she said.

"Would you like me to send you an official email with the emblem of the city of Chicago?"

"No. I guess not. I don't know much. She told our guests that her boyfriend had broken up with her." She stopped abruptly.

"What else?"

"Mr. O'Farrell, if that is your real name, maybe she doesn't want to be found."

"Madame, why are you so suspicious? We're talking about a missing woman here."

The line went silent, and I thought she'd hung up.

"Because you aren't the first person who has called asking about her."

RILEY

I expected the tavern to be empty, but it was packed—the crowd's size risked breaking fire code, if there'd been anyone on the island to enforce such a law. Gill, Kayla, and Simon scattered as soon as we walked in. Chayton and I were left standing in the press of people. I offered to buy him a beer to toast his birthday. We waved at Scarla, but she was busy flirting at the far end of the bar.

"What does your tattoo mean?" I tried not to stare at the eagle on his neck, but it was so big and ominous.

He rubbed his fingers over the tattoo as if he needed reminding. "Mark of the Native Brotherhood. They inducted me last year. We take an oath to guard the island, to preserve our Native lands."

"Sounds . . . responsible."

"It's not to be taken lightly. It's sort of like the Masons. What we do is *secret*."

"Everything on this island is one giant secret."

He eyed me suspiciously. "Not many Mainlanders come here in the middle of winter. You gonna stick around?"

"What choice do I have? They stopped the ferry."

"You could fly to the mainland and come back when it's warm and get your car," he said. "There's no shame in that. Plenty of people have done it."

"I'm looking forward to experiencing a winter on Angelica," I said.

He shook his head. "No, you're not. Why don't you tell me the real reason you're here?"

I looked at him, unsure what answer would appease him. Finally, I said: "I love to cook."

For the first time, I was telling the truth. I'd been working ten- to twelve-hour days for the past month. My hands were cut, burnt, and so chapped that they sometimes bled. But it felt good. My wounds were a badge of honor. I wished my father could have seen me. He would have been proud.

I also hadn't been yelled at or spit on while protesting at demonstrations. I hadn't gone to jail—at least not yet. I hadn't been awakened in the middle of the night to drive to a horrific scene of women screaming and men crying over bodies riddled by bullets. It was strange to live with such calm in my life.

Kayla and Gill scurried toward us, beaming. Gill carried a stack of bills. They'd probably hustled a sucker at the pool table. Who on the island hadn't heard of Gill's skill with a pool cue?

"Let's go to Gill and Chay's house? They've got a ton of beer and a hot tub," Kayla said, widening her heavily mascaraed eyes. It was the most engaged I'd seen her in days. Much of the time, she walked around with a sneer, her eyes half-closed as if she were high.

"C'mon, please," Gill begged. "You've got to see our house. I'll even cook."

I wanted to go home and fall into bed. But getting invited to someone's house was a big deal on the island. I had to keep reminding myself that the quickest way to acceptance on the island was through these four people, the cool kids.

We climbed into Chayton's truck. Kayla sat on Gill's lap in the front seat, and Simon and I shared the cramped back seat of the truck cab. Chayton punched the accelerator, skidded sideways in the snow, then fishtailed, slamming us into each other. "Fasten your seatbelts, folks," Chayton advised, paraphrasing Bette Davis in her old movie voice. "It's going to be a bumpy ride!"

We couldn't see more than fifteen feet in front of us in the island's darkness. Chayton turned down an inland gravel road. Trees laden with snow formed a tunnel around us. Finally, Chayton's headlights splashed across the front of a spooky, three-story Gothic Victorian.

"There she is," Chayton announced. We gazed up at the cross gables, arched windows, and a round stone tower. The house looked like something from the set of *The Addams Family*.

The truck rocked as Chayton, Simon, and Kayla jumped out, leaving Gill and me alone.

"What do you think?" he asked.

"It's...amazing."

"Great. Because this is the worst view." The lights from the house seeped into the truck's cab, enough to see the earnestness in his face. "Thanks for coming. It means a lot to Chay."

"I don't think he likes me very much."

"Nah, he just doesn't trust Mainlanders."

"Is that what I am?"

"I don't think any of us have figured out what you are."

I got out of the truck and maneuvered between deep drifts of snow. Music blasted from a boombox perched on a sawhorse in the entryway. Chayton was leading Kayla and Simon through a maze of newly-erected walls. Gill and I followed. Some rooms only had drywall; a few were painted. Gill and I lingered in one of the large bathrooms, outfitted floor to ceiling in marble, his and her toilets, and a shower with a rainforest spout.

"Are you rehabbing this for someone?" It seemed a monstrous house for two bachelors.

"Yeah. Me."

"You're not planning to sell it to one of those summer trust fund babies to make a lot of money?"

"Never! It's my dream house. I've been building it in my head since I was a kid."

"But it's so far out."

"Creeps you out, huh?"

"Not so much by the woods, but the *people* who live in the woods." I hummed the jingle from the *Twilight Zone.*

"No one bothers you out here," he said. "Park rangers don't even come back this far. All this used to be part of the reservation. They're so few tribal members left that they've sold off bits and pieces. And because most Islanders don't want to live this remotely, I got a great deal. Living out here, I feel like I'm one of the island's exiles."

"It seems we're all exiles from the real world."

Gill eyed me warily. "Yes, that's exactly what we are."

I followed him up a winding staircase to the third level. The house had little furniture. I hadn't even seen a single television. At the end of a long hall in the round stone tower was an entrance to the library, furnished with mostly well-palmed paperbacks. I walked around touching the books' broken spines and reading their titles, a mix of classic and modern fiction. I pulled out a paperback copy of Henry Thoreau's *Walden*, its pages dog-eared, some passages underlined. Gill watched as I flipped through the pages, pausing at certain spots.

"It's my favorite," he said, with a hint of embarrassment.

"Me too," I whispered. "As a kid, I always dreamed of living in a cabin in the woods."

"And now you are," he said.

Our eyes met.

"That's one way of looking at it," I said.

"How do *you* see it?"

Gill had never asked me about my past, but I thought he had a right to know something since I was standing in his house, palming his private things.

"Nothing on this island belongs to me. I'm just a caretaker to someone else's dreams," I said.

"That will change," Gill said defiantly and waved for me to follow him. "Eventually, you'll feel like an Islander."

We wound our way down the stairs to the kitchen where the others were raiding beer from the Sub-Zero refrigerator. Gill leaned against the dueling ovens watching as Simon and Kayla opened and closed cabinet doors and ran their fingers over the black stone counters that Chayton had recently installed.

"It's modeled after several I've seen in chef magazines," Gill explained.

"Let's try this baby out," Kayla said, flicking a burner on the Wolf range. Flames shot up, nearly scorching her eyebrows. "Shit!" she screamed and jumped back. When she burst out laughing, so did we.

"How about something to eat?" Chayton said. "I'm starving."

"Okay," Gill said, "but only if Riley helps." He shot me a conspiratorial look.

I shrugged assent.

Chayton quickly slunk off with Simon and Kayla to the backyard hot tub, where I imagined them jumping in naked.

"You can go with them," Gill said when we were alone.

"I don't mind." The truth was I didn't relish stripping in front of my colleagues.

I opened the refrigerator. "You got anything in here besides beer and cheese-whiz?" For a man with top-of-the-line appliances, he had little food to cook.

"We don't eat here much," Gill admitted. We spent so much time at the restaurant, I bet none of us felt like cooking when we got home.

"I know what we can do," he said, pushing back the hair that hung perpetually in his eyes. "Let's pretend this is like one of those reality cooking shows, and you have to make a dish out of random ingredients."

"One caveat," I added. "No one can take all of any single ingredient. Otherwise, there's not enough here for two dishes."

We sealed the deal with our pinkies then rushed to find ingredients.

Behind the twelve-packs in the refrigerator, I found a box of butter, a bag of yellow onions, half a carton of eggs, half a carton of milk, a basket of Shiitake mushrooms—which I suspected he'd pilfered from the restaurant—and a hunk of Parmesan cheese, also likely filched.

Gill presented what he'd found in the cupboards: a couple of cans of tomato sauce, a bottle of white wine, a few cans of chicken broth, a large bottle of olive oil, half a bag of baker's flour, and a bag of rice.

We stood surveying the ingredients. Damned if I was going to make pasta. So, *pedestrian.*

I stooped to the lower cabinets, pulling out pans that appeared never to have been used.

Gill measured out his ingredients.

"Pasta, eh?" I asked.

"And, you?"

"Mushroom risotto."

A look of jealousy flashed across Gill's face. He opened a drawer to a collection of knives, pulled out the largest, and began chopping the onions.

"So, how did you guys end up hanging together?" I asked.

He shrugged. "Chay, Kayla, and I went to Grand Portage high school."

"What's Kayla's story?"

"She had a rough home life. Her father left when she was a kid, and her mother was a drunk. Kayla raised herself. She's a real badass." His voice brimmed with admiration. I wondered if he harbored a crush. I saw the way men at the restaurant ogled Kayla.

"And Simon?"

"Hmm," Gill scratched his chin. "His parents are filthy rich. They have a mansion on the north end of the island. When Simon got kicked out of some Ivy League university, his parents sent him to the island to dry out. They don't accept that he's gay, and they are always trying to set him up with their rich friends' daughters. He's got issues, for sure, but he's a fun guy, and he always has the best weed."

"And Chayton?"

"What's to say? He's my best friend. He comes from a well-known Ojibwe family, and he takes all that Native American stuff pretty seriously."

"Yeah, I found that out tonight."

"His name means falcon. But you can call him Chay. He doesn't mind. Once he's your friend, it's for life. And he'd do anything for you."

"Anything, huh? Like rob a bank or hide you from the police?" I don't know why I said that. I was tired and tipsy.

"You thinking of robbing a bank? Wait! Is that why you came to the island? You robbed a bank, and now you're hiding from the cops. That's it, isn't it?"

"Got me." I threw my hands up.

"Yeah, well, Chay is the kind of friend who'd take a bullet for you."

"Let's hope it never comes to that," I said and winked. "What should I know about *you*?"

"I'm a pretty simple guy. Determined not to be like all the men in my family, who are all commercial fishermen. Gill, by the way, is short for *Bluegill*." He laughed. "My mother named all her boys after fish in Lake Superior."

"That's special."

"Yeah, especially if you're my brother Alewife."

I couldn't help but laugh. "Oh, that must have been hard growing up."

"Nah, we all just called him Al. My other brothers are Pike, Sturgeon—we call him Sturg—and Cisco."

"That's some lineup. And what did she call your sisters?"

"I only have one. She named her after a bird, Bluejay. We call her Jay."

"And no one thought that was weird?"

"Not really. I mean, on the island, there are a lot of strange Native-American names. So naming your kid after fish and a bird felt . . . normal."

"Makes sense."

"Chay and some of his Native Brotherhood guys taught me how to build stuff. Thus, the house," he extended his arms to emphasize his point. "Chay says I have romantic ideas about what it means to be a carpenter. He keeps telling me: 'This ain't going to make you Jesus.'"

"But you do kind of look like Jesus, a Norwegian Jesus."

We both laughed.

Gill offered me half of his onions. I dropped them into the skillet. The pan sizzled and smoked. I added fresh garlic. In another skillet, I melted butter and added another handful of onions. Gill stood at the stove sautéing his garlic and onions, swinging his hips, casually bumping mine, singing along to the song "Dance the Night Away," on the boombox.

For the first time in weeks, I felt happy. It was a strange feeling. Cooking with Gill reminded me of cooking with Ross, comparing ingredients, tasting each other's recipes. We were always so competitive.

I slowly added rice and stirred the buttery concoction. The smell of onions, garlic, and mushrooms permeated the room. Gill kneaded his dough and sipped wine, all the while stealing glances at me. I grabbed the wine bottle and doused my rice.

"Hey, that was mine!" he protested.

"We agreed to share all ingredients."

I began adding small cups of my mushroom stock to the rice. After the risotto had simmered a while, I dipped in a spoon and offered him a taste.

"Mmm," he moaned, his eyes closed. "That's good . . . No. That's really, really good."

Pleased, I handed him the wooden spoon, letting him stir the rice as I poured in more stock. He dug out a mound and held it to my mouth.

"That's too much, Gill. I just want a taste."

"Sure," he said, smearing the sticky glob across my mouth and chin.

"Gill, there won't be anything left if we keep playing around." Bits of warm rice stuck to my face like paper mache.

"That's okay because we'll have my amazing pasta." He wiped the risotto off my chin with his finger and stuck it in his mouth. "Mmmm. Buttery."

Then without warning, he bent down and licked the rice

and cheese smear from my face. I closed my eyes and held my breath. His lips moved slowly over my mouth, tickling the fine hairs above my lip. He pressed his body against mine, gently. His lips felt soft, velvety. We stood there, locked in an embrace, our mouths swallowing each other as if tasting a rare delicacy.

FINN

I woke with a raging hangover the next morning. It all seemed like a bad dream, the visit from Davies and O'Brien, another grainy photo of Riley, the hand-drawn map on my refrigerator, and the cagey conversation with the B & B proprietor. They left me feeling disoriented and sad. Out my bedroom window, it was snowing. Seeing all that white made me think of an old map of North America I'd bought years ago from an antique dealer.

I climbed up to the attic and opened the cedar chest, and partially unrolled the map in my hands. It reminded me of the early cartographers who drew pen and ink masterpieces that marked U.S. territories and their boundary waters. Unlike those maps, though, this one was in color. Bodies of water, like Lake Superior, were colored bright blue and forests shaded in green. Roads were drawn in black, splintering like veins across the vast territory shaded in white.

I also found the lockbox in the cedar chest where I kept my ghost gun, the one I carried as my spare when I was a cop. It didn't have a serial number and was unregistered. I didn't have a license to carry it. The day I surrendered my badge, I'd locked up the gun and didn't think anything further about it. Until now. A blackmailer had broken into my house where my children slept. Riley and her best friend were somehow involved in a clash with one of the city's worst cops. If I was going to find her, I had to be prepared to protect myself and my family.

I tacked the map to my bedroom wall. At six-feet by six-feet, it dominated one wall. I stuck a pin at Grand Portage, Michigan, on the cusp of Canada, Riley's apparent last sighting. I sat below the map, mesmerized by its chromatic display, and held the gun in my hand. My fingers caressed its cold metal, reminding myself what it felt like to hold a weapon, what it felt like to fire something so powerful. After Darren Wallack, I didn't think I'd ever want to fire a gun again. Now I needed to summon the mindset to use it.

I looked up at my map and tried to imagine where Riley might be hiding. I stared at the black spots marking towns. Was she still there, hanging out in the backwoods? She could hide for a long time before anyone took notice. A woman alone would get a second look, but she'd also get a pass.

By now, she could be anywhere, hitchhiking across Canada's great white north, an expanse of frozen land shaded in stark white. There was so much white on my map that it looked as if a giant iceberg had subsumed Canada. If Riley was there, tracking her would be like trailing a snowflake in the Arctic.

RILEY

It was after three in the morning when Chay drove us back to town. Gill sat next to me in the truck, his fingers lightly caressing mine in the dark. We'd shared a single kiss, but it made me a wreck. I wasn't prepared for what happened. I hadn't seen it coming. Had I just cheated on Finn? Were we still together, even though he didn't know where I was? Were his secrets about Darren Wallack enough to break up over? How do you break up with someone you don't see and can't talk to? I was furious with Finn, but did that mean I could never forgive him? Did I even know what really transpired in that room between him and the boy who killed my brother? No, but I knew Finn. Or did I?

The truck radio was set at a station that played old tunes. "Free Bird" streamed from the speakers. Chay hummed along quietly. Simon was passed out in the back, Kayla's head pressed against his chest. Chay gripped the wheel with both hands; his eyes fixed ahead.

I kept my eyes on the road, impressed with Chay's ability to maneuver through wet snow, especially since he was probably legally intoxicated. No one else was on the road. Occasionally, the truck's back end slid sideways. Chay punched the gas and jerked the steering wheel, dodging one snowdrift after another. The drive was disorienting, like a dream: the thick forest enveloping the truck, the shadows leaching the bright headlights. The combination of alcohol, the effervescent bubbles of the hot tub, and the long night made me loopy. I began to question what was real and what was imagined. Had Gill and I kissed, our hands fumbling, our lips slipping over each other?

Several inches of snow had fallen while we were drinking and sitting in the hot tub. Chay and Gill wore swimming trunks, but the rest of us stripped to our underwear. Simon wore pinstriped boxers. Kayla had on a pink lace thong and matching bra. I wore a sports bra and granny panties. Except for Gill—whose kiss still lingered on my lips—the experience felt like taking a childhood bath with my cousins.

I hadn't meant to kiss him, yet I had fallen so quickly into his arms; he made me forget what day it was on the calendar and took an edge off the loneliness I felt. My disloyalty to Finn seemed doubly harsh since it happened on Christmas Eve, our first holiday together.

Finn had never said he loved me, not really. Oh, there were a few times when he whispered it in bed. Somehow articulating our feelings in the harsh light of day seemed crass and bourgeois. Now I wished we'd been a bit more shameful. I wondered if I would ever see him again and when I did, would he forgive me for leaving, for clinging to someone else? I wondered if he was growing impatient. Maybe he was convinced I wasn't coming back; maybe he'd already taken refuge in another woman's arms.

When I woke, it was late Christmas morning, and guilt consumed me. I was lying in bed, longing for Finn when the bedside phone rang.

"You going to the Orphans?" His voice made me smile.

Gill and Chay had been talking up the annual "Orphans' Party" for the past week. The celebration was held at the restaurant, officially closed, and intended for Islanders who had no family and nowhere to go for the holiday. Over the years, "The Orphans," as it was called—which made it sound like some sort of charitable benefit and not a drunken fete—had expanded to include anybody who showed up with booze and food. Having survived the snowstorm, Islanders were eager to celebrate.

"Trying to wake up," I said.

"Orphans starts at noon, so put your party pants on, girlfriend."

I couldn't speak. Did he mean I was his *girlfriend*, or was that just slang? Even though there were only seven years difference between us, it felt like a chasm. I struggled to keep up with his references to popular culture, especially since I'd led him to believe we were the same age.

"Later," I said as casually as I could.

But my panic wasn't over. The Orphans was where gourmands showed off their recipes. Year-rounders planned their dishes for weeks. Of course, I hadn't prepared anything and searched through the freezer for something to make that would establish my place among the island foodies.

Wedged behind a carton of ice cream and Ziplock bags of flour and sugar, I found a vacuum-sealed salmon. I didn't remember buying the fish, so it had to belong to the house's owners. No telling how long it had been in its cryo state. While defrosting it in the microwave, I searched the cabinets for ingredients to jazz up the dead meat. I found a box of breadcrumbs, half a bag of pecans, and a jar of solidified honey. I remembered my father glazing salmon with a crunchy nut coating. Thirty minutes later, I pulled the steaming salmon from the oven. I cut a sliver. The sweetness of the butter and honey hid the freezer burn. I spritzed the filet with lemon and sprinkled it with parsley.

When I finally arrived at the restaurant, the parking lot was full. It was after one o'clock. Dining room tables were linked together to form one long buffet. The offerings were dizzying: Spanish tapas, rosemary lamb chops, crab cakes, meat pasties, lasagna, filet of beef. People lingered over the table, nibbling on this and that, commenting as they chewed. Elvis crooned Christmas tunes over the sound system. Someone had decorated the dining room with red candles and holly and placed mistletoe over entryways. A few daring folks stood in the doorways, puckering up to whomever passed.

Zi sidled up to me with energetic eyes. "So, what do you think? Great spread, huh? Here, try this." She shoved a cocktail plate in my hands loaded with mystery meat. I wouldn't taste any of it. "Or how about this." She held a giant scoop of cheddar mashed potatoes, but I shook my head.

"Which one's your dish?" I asked.

"You got it right there in your hands. Smoked venison." Her lips turned up in a wide smile. She wanted to see me eat wild game.

I handed her the plate. "No Bambie."

"It's not Bambie," she corrected. "It's Bambie's mother." Another smirk. "It's a recipe passed down from my great-great-grandmother, Mecho."

She waited, watching.

I pulled the brownish meat that looked like a pork chop to my mouth and took the tiniest nibble. A month earlier, I would have gagged.

"It tastes tangy and smoky."

She slapped me hard on my back. "You don't have to eat it if you don't want to."

Zi pointed out the various plates made by our friends or people from the restaurant. Mr. Kowalski had cooked prune perogies. Javier brought stuffed relleno chilies. Matthew made peach crepes.

"Where's Ginny's dish?" I asked.

Zi pointed at a silver tin, half of which had already been eaten.

"Chicken Kyiv," she whispered. "I'm betting she had it flown in. 'Cause you know Ginny can't cook, and that's the real deal." She winked like it was our secret.

For a while, I simply forgot it was Christmas. There weren't any gifts—the cardinal rule no one violated. The gathering was meant to be a debauchery of food and drink. Clusters of people sat in dark corners, passing joints. At one point, I went to the kitchen to get more butter from the walk-in. When I opened the freezer door, I was met by some guy's bare ass crawling over Beverly, the older waitress, who was bent over the frozen meats. They didn't even stop when I screamed. On my way back to the dining room, Lars met me at the entryway and grabbed me by the waist.

"Looks like we're caught underneath this little weed, Riley."

"Let it go, Lars." I turned my face away, but he tightened his grip on my wrist. I hadn't expected Lars to show up on the island, but the shuttle plane was making occasional flights now.

"We had a good time on Thanksgiving?" he whispered in my ear. "Do you ever think about me? Because I think about you a lot. You don't have to pretend you don't like me for Ginny's sake."

"Pretend? You think I'm pretending?"

He hadn't considered that my reaction to him had been genuine.

"Lars, I don't want to kiss you now or *ever*."

"Aw, come on. Can't you be charitable? It *is* a day of giving." He pursed his lips.

"The rule is no gifts, Lars."

"What the hell," said Zi. She pulled at Lars' arm. "Don't fucking grope the girl."

I slipped from his grip and mouthed a thank you to her.

Zi wrapped her hands around Lars' face and pulled him toward her, smothering her lips over his and holding his head while she forced her tongue into his mouth. He lurched from her and wiped his face with his sleeve. A small crowd had gathered and loudly clapped and cheered. Zi bowed. Lars stomped from the room.

Zi was determined to introduce me to as many year-rounders as possible, especially those who didn't frequent the restaurant. I waved at Gill and the others from across the room, but my insides twisted with guilt. I drank glass after glass of homemade wine and store-bought vodka. After several hours, I went out behind the restaurant and puked.

A moon the size of a saucer lit up the sky. I hadn't expected to feel so alone amongst so many people. Overwhelmed by the silence and the beauty, my knees buckled, and I fell into the snow, sobbing. I lay there for a long while, salty tears stinging my skin, my pant legs damp from the snow, thinking of all the Christmases I'd taken for granted. I felt so pathetic, miserable, and unworthy. I didn't deserve my family or my friends. Would I ever have another chance at a life with them? Was this my future? This island? These people?

I didn't hear Gill until he was next to me. He lifted me to my knees and dusted the snow from my face. We stood silently staring at the lights above us. The sky was so low to the earth that night, the stars so brilliant. I didn't have the energy to say anything, to hear anything. After a long while, he finally spoke.

"It was a kiss, Riley. You're not having my baby."

How did he know?

"You've been avoiding me all night. You look like you lost your dog. You came here to get away from someone. But now you feel like you've stepped out on him. Right?"

"Yeah," I said. "I don't even know if we're really broken up."

"And you can't call him because you don't want him to know where you are?"

"How—"

"—do I know? You're not the first heart-broken person who's ended up on the island. Come on. Let me take you home."

He pulled me to my feet and led me to his truck. I was in no condition to drive and wondered if he was. We didn't speak during the ride. When we reached my cottage, he tried to help me out.

"I'm fine." I jumped out, my ankles folding beneath me, my butt hitting the ground hard. I lay in the snow laughing and then crying.

Gill tried to lift me, but I elbowed him in the stomach.

"Go away."

"You're just going to sit out here all night in the snow?"

"Yep."

"Not if I have anything to do with it."

He hooked his hands under my arms and looped me over his shoulders. I kicked my feet a couple of times in protest, but didn't have the energy to fight him. He carried me into the house, turning on a lamp here and there until he arrived at my bedroom. He sat me down on my unmade bed, pulled off my boots and coat, and pulled the covers around my chin. I turned my face away, pouting like a child.

He leaned over and kissed my forehead. "It will get better. I promise."

FINN

It was January first. I'd had the kids since Christmas Day. We watched movies, ate junk food, went sledding, built a snowman in the front yard, stayed up late, slept in—all the things you're supposed to do on a break. In between, I snuck in phone calls to gas stations and restaurants in Grand Portage. But no one had seen Riley; I'd reached a dead-end and hoped for more clues from Mr. Mailer.

After I dropped the kids off at Diana's—she'd signed them up for a week at swim camp—the house just felt too empty. I went to work in my ward office. The election was seven weeks away. I'd been hard at it for hours when my desk telephone rang. I figured it was some cranky resident complaining his street needed plowing.

"Working late, huh?" There was no mistaking his high-pitched, nasally voice. The last thing I needed was a chat with the mayor's communications director.

"Rod, how can I help you?" The man seemed to know every phone number of mine.

"I have a media request for *you*," he said, dragging out his vowels.

"Set it up with my assistant like the others."

"Uh, well. This isn't any sort of *normal* media request, Finn. This is from *Dan Mackay* from the *Tribune*. He's an *investigative* reporter. He wants to talk to you about your stance on gun control. *And*...he wants to know if you were working with *Riley* in any official capacity."

So, this was it. Davies and O'Brien weren't just incompetent; they were lazy. I doubted divers were able to find the gun, and, without it, they didn't have enough evidence to obtain an arrest warrant for Riley. Instead, they'd leaked the information about me dating Riley to someone who would do their work for them. No matter what I said to Mackay, he'd portray my relationship with Riley as sullied. No voter would get past the headline: Republican Alderman's Girlfriend Is Woman of Interest in Cop Shooting.

If MacKay published even a hint of my association with Riley and the police suspicion of her, it would cost the mayor and me the campaign. If I could just find Riley, bring her home, we could defend her properly. And she and I could be together. One thing I was sure of, we were not going to keep our relationship hidden any longer. That is if she would have me. When—if—I finally found Riley, I was going to tell her everything.

"Are you there?" Rod asked.

"I'll handle it. Don't worry."

I considered telling the mayor about my suspicions. But he would overreact, and Rod would go nuclear. We hadn't taken our competitors seriously. They were mostly loudmouths with little or no credibility. But a scandalous tidbit could tip the scale in their favor. And when the media finished waging their smear campaign against me, the police would feast on the leftovers. Nothing like felling a politician on the eve of an election.

RILEY

At noon on New Year's Day, Islanders stacked their Christmas trees into a giant pile at the harbor. I didn't have a tree to contribute, but I showed up for the celebration. Islanders seemed to concoct festivities as an excuse to drink.

Gill, Chay, and Kayla warmed themselves over a fire pit in the harbor parking lot. Gill waved me over. Since we worked opposite shifts, I'd only seen the night crew in passing since The Orphans party.

"What do they do with all of those?" I pointed at the growing pyramid of mangled pines, some still threaded with tinsel or a stubborn ornament or two.

"It's how we mark the ice road," Chay said, handing me a beer from a cooler at his feet. Chay seemed friendlier than he had in the past. Maybe it was sharing the hot tub on Christmas Eve, or maybe Gill had told him about our kiss?

Kayla scanned the harbor parking lot, looking for Simon, who seemed to have disappeared again. He was often MIA without an explanation. I still didn't know whether Kayla approved or merely tolerated my presence. Some women preferred being the lone female in the pack.

The ice road, Chay and Gill explained, was built gradually. Each day, Andy and Ned, the island's two-man road crew, ventured farther and farther on the lake, staking the Christmas trees beside the road they'd plowed as green guideposts in the middle of an ocean of white. The ice had to be at least a foot thick to be deemed safe enough to drive over. The shallow water near the island froze first. The great plains in the middle presented the most troublesome stretch. Usually, the ice road opened in mid-January. But there were years when the ice never thickened enough to complete the road, turning Islanders into captives.

"It's a fear we all live with," Gill said, his voice anxious and jittery. "Trapped for four months on the island."

"How do you—get through it?"

Chay narrowed his eyes: "Ice fishing, cross country skiing, hunting, snowmobiling, hockey."

"Drinking," Gill added.

"Sex," Kayla added. I wondered who she was sleeping with.

A commotion near the Christmas trees caught our attention. Simon was trying to set fire to one of the discarded pines. Gill and Chay pulled the tree from the pile and stomped on the branch that caught fire.

"Sorry, folks," Gill said to the crowd of onlookers. "He's had a little too much to drink."

Chay and Gill each grabbed one of Simon's arms and dragged him from the pile of trees. Simon didn't seem intoxicated, more like stoned. He was shivering despite his heavy parka. He mumbled to himself and then jerked his head up and yelled at the crowd.

"This is all so stupid!"

Islanders glared at Chay and Gill to do something.

"This road is never going to open," Simon continued, falling against Chay, who propped him up again. "You all are wasting your time. It's just a big excuse to employ those *retards*." He wrenched his head toward Andy and Ned, whose orange parkas and hats made them stand out.

Simon wriggled free of Chay and Gill's grip. Then he slugged back a beer, crushed the can in his hand, and threw it toward the pile of trees. It fell far short. An Islander picked it up and shook his head with disgust.

"Hey, buddy, how about we go to the tavern and get warm," Chay suggested.

Simon shook his head. "I don't know why we don't talk about the real ice road. We need to give this up and join forces with the reservation."

The mention of the reservation provoked Chay. He began pushing Simon toward his truck. "I'm not asking, Simon. Get the hell in the truck. *Now*."

I'd never seen Chay so angry. Kayla followed, clutching at Simon's coat, shushing him.

Gill held up a hand to the onlookers. "Sorry, folks. We've all been there." He leaned in the driver's side window and said something to Chay, then the truck pulled out, leaving Gill and me alone.

We hadn't spoken since Christmas, and it felt awkward between us.

"What did he mean by 'the real ice road'?" I asked after a long silence.

"It's the Smugglers' Road," he said quietly. He moved closer to me so that I could hear him whispering. "It starts on the other end of the island–" he motioned with his arms– "in reservation waters and ends at Canada."

"It's not safe," he added. "Andy and Ned aren't out there testing the ice depth. The reservation charges a hefty amount for access. It's a point of contention between the Natives and the Islanders. Islanders resent the high fees, and the Ojibwe feel it's their birthright. The government keeps trying to shut it down, claiming illegals use it to cross into Canada.

"Some say the illegals come to the island before the ferry stops, then hide out in vacant homes, waiting for the big freeze. Then they walk across or steal snowmobiles."

"Is that what Zi meant when she warned me about finding squatters in the houses? I thought she was just trying to scare me," I whispered near his face. It felt like we were having an intimate conversation standing so close, speaking so quietly.

"It's real all right," he said, looking at me. He pulled back a stray hair that had fallen in my eyes. "You should make a lot of noise when you show up. Establish a regular pattern, so they know when you're coming."

"Why would I want to make it easy for a squatter to live in one of my houses?"

"You don't want to confront them." He smiled nervously and looked around to see if anyone was listening. People were staring at us because we were standing so close. They'd all be gossiping about us now.

"It's really not one of those things people talk about," he continued. "There are those who want to help the immigrants. Other people feel the Smuggler's Road attracts criminals. During Prohibition, it was one of the routes mobsters used to smuggle in liquor from Canada. Chay said his grandfather used dog sleds in the middle of the night to transport booze. A lot of men died. During Vietnam, draft dodgers used the route to escape to Canada. And now it's drugs and illegals moving from here to Canada. It's a long trek—about eleven miles. People have frozen to death. Some have fallen through holes in the ice. People get lost in the dark."

"Have you gone on it?"

He shook his head. "Too dangerous. Chay says when you get four or five miles out, you're totally disoriented. It's all white for as far you can see." He looked up at the gray-white sky. "It's not like being on the lake between here and Grand Portage. There you can see land. But between here and Canada, the shore is too far away. At night it's nothing but a thick, black sea. The wind is blowing, snow cutting at your face. My god, what a horrible way to die."

FINN

Dan Mackay, the *Tribune's* investigative reporter, showed up late one afternoon in mid-January at my ward office. I'd rescheduled our interview several times, citing city emergencies. But after two weeks of excuses, I had to meet with him. He hardly looked intimidating—baggy khakis, a wrinkled white shirt, and a day-old scruff on his chin. My staff had left for the day, so we were alone. As soon as he sat down, he slouched as if he intended to take a nap. Rod had advised me not to take the interview, but I knew that not meeting would confirm Mackay's suspicions.

"So, what can I do for you?" I said, sitting up straight and trying to sound friendly.

He took out a slender reporter's notebook and flipped through some pages. "I wanted to go over some of your candidate positions since you and the mayor do not share the same viewpoints."

"He's a firm believer in gun control, and I don't think it works. I prefer other measures."

"Yeah, let's talk about those."

"Well, I don't think you need to mess with the Constitution to limit dangerous weapons. I believe restricting ammunition is a better means. The Constitution doesn't make any mention about ammunition."

"And are these positions you've discussed with the mayor?"

"Of course. Politics work best when people try to find more common priorities rather than being polarized and focusing on the territory they disagree on."

"And is that what you did with the anti-gun activist Riley Keane?"

"Why are you bringing her up?"

"You and she were known to be...*acquainted.* I'm just wondering what middle ground you were able to reach with someone so polarized in her views."

"Riley and I don't agree on a lot of things. But the mayor encouraged me to work with her and others who felt strongly about gun control." I pushed back from my desk. This line of questioning meant one thing. Mackay knew. And now he wanted to corner me into admitting my relationship with Riley.

"You are aware she's missing now?" he asked.

"I had heard that."

"There's been some speculation that she was involved with a cop shooting several weeks ago. You know anything about that?"

My chair groaned when I shifted forward.

"Not sure where you're going with this, Mackay."

"It just seems strange, don't you think, that you and this anti-gun activist would be friends when you represent the most conservative ward—and the only Republican ward—-in the city—"

"I'm also running with a Democratic mayor. I often work with people who do not share my politics. In a city like Chicago, where a majority are Democrats, it's required if you want to get anything done. It's one of my strengths—working with people who don't think like me."

"Some of my sources say that you and Riley were seeing each other romantically and that you may know more than you're letting on about her whereabouts."

Now we'd gotten to the real reason for the interview.

"I'm a single man, and Riley is a single woman. There's no scandal here, Dan."

"So, you admit you are—or were—seeing Riley?"

"Who I see on my own time is my business. How is this relevant? Or has the *Tribune* decided that covering politicians' personal lives will get more website clicks than stories about our political agendas?"

"I think voters will think it's relevant that a candidate for vice mayor is linked to a woman who is a suspect in a cop shooting."

I choked back a laugh. "First of all, the police officer who was shot is one of Riley's oldest friends from high school. She credits him with saving her life during the Hyde Park High School shooting. I hardly think she would be wielding a gun against a dear friend. Have you spoken to Detective Taylor?"

"I've also heard they were having an affair. Perhaps it was a lover's feud?"

"Even if that absurd theory were true—which it's not—why would Riley shoot Detective Taylor in Englewood in the middle of the night?" This part was purely inventive on Davie's and O'Brien's part.

"To make it look like it was a gang shooting."

I shook my head. "Now you're wallowing in speculation and conspiracy theories. I thought you were a man of facts."

He pulled out a piece of paper from his notebook, and skimmed it. "Here are the facts, Finn. Riley was picked up on this blue-light camera two blocks from the crime scene minutes after Detective Taylor was shot. She has since disappeared. Detective Taylor denies she was at the shooting, but a witness says a woman matching Riley's description tended to Detective Taylor after he was shot. The police have found two bullets from two different guns at the scene."

"Have you considered that maybe Riley was with Detective Taylor that night for other reasons and something went down while she was with him?" I offered. "Maybe she fled for her safety. Maybe whoever shot Detective Taylor doesn't want her as a witness. Maybe she's not safe. And maybe Detective Taylor is trying to protect his good friend?"

MacKay stared at me for a minute. I let him chew on my version of events. He didn't like my explanation because that would mean that Riley was a victim and not the perpetrator, which meant that she wasn't a valid suspect, and if she wasn't a suspect, then there was no legitimate reason to bring her up in a story about my campaign. Say what you will about the daily hunt-and-peck reporters, but investigative reporters think they are above the fray. And one thing they despise is being wrong. Besides, with an election hanging in the balance, the paper's editors would be reluctant to air theories in a criminal case that weren't solid gold. And without confirmation from Reece, this one wasn't even copper.

"Any other theories you want to present?" I asked.

MacKay grinned. "My instincts tell me you're involved in Riley's vanishing act. When I find out how, I'm publishing it regardless if it's the night before the election."

RILEY

By the second week in January, the lake still hadn't frozen deep enough. Many blamed global warming. Others speculated that it was the cyclical nature of the lake. The official weather report attributed it to strong warm winds, which created currents that prevented the lake water from freezing. The constant gale force winds also grounded the air taxi, eliminating the most expensive option of escape. Instead of the temperature sinking below zero, as was normal for that time of year, it remained a "balmy" thirty degrees—perfect for snow; the island had already set a record of one hundred and eighty inches.

Trapped on seven miles of snow and ice for a month, year-rounders had become stir crazy. Two drunken men tried to ride their snowmobiles across the lake to Grand Portage. About halfway, they met a moving stream of ice—glaciers that had detached from the central ice shelf—and had to turn back. A few people managed to walk and ski across the three miles of ice, a dangerous trek. After braving the brutal winds and faulty ice, they arrived in Grand Portage too nerve-wracked to attempt a return trip. Water temperatures and currents were shifting and unpredictable. A key ice path could "rot"—as Islanders called it—in a matter of hours.

I crossed off each day on my calendar like a prisoner marking time. More than once, I wondered if my isolation and confinement was the universe's way of punishing me for shooting Reece. There were days I wondered if I might have been better off going to prison than serving time on the island.

We felt like hostages, resigned to having to wait until April for the ferry service to resume. Most of the restaurant staff congregated at the tavern on their days off. I tried to stay away, but by Sunday evening, I was craving human interaction.

"We gotta get off this fucking island," Kayla said one night. "I'm so sick of eating walleye." She ran her chipped fingernails through her pink hair. "Jesus, what I'd do for some real Pad Thai."

"I can make that for you," Gill offered.

Kayla rolled her eyes. "Not the same."

"I say we go at night, take the Smuggler's Road," Simon said. "No one will see us."

"But how are *we* going to see?" Gill asked. "It's eleven miles. It's dark as hell out there. Besides, doesn't Homeland Security patrol the Smuggler's Road?"

"If they did, then how is it so many illegals use it?" Simon asked.

"How do you know they use it?" I asked.

They turned to me, surprised I'd jumped into their debate.

"I can see them from my deck when it's a full moon," Simon said.

"Do you ever see border guards?" I asked.

Simon shook his head. "I wouldn't even see the illegals if I wasn't looking. Sometimes I hear snowmobiles."

"How would we do it?" Kayla asked.

"And why would we do it?" I asked.

Kayla glared at me. "Because we can, that's why."

"I admit I've been against it. But I'm curious to try it out," Chay said. "I haven't been on that ice road since I was a kid."

"Next full moon is Saturday night," Simon said. "We could go after we close, take our snowmobiles."

"What's the worst that can happen?" asked Gill. "We're American citizens. We're just escaping the island for a couple of nights. We can stay in Canada and hit St. Marie's restaurants the next day."

"I don't have a passport," I objected.

Simon curled his lips. "Doesn't matter. We don't have to come ashore right at the checkpoint."

"How do you know?" Chay's tone was sharp.

"You think the illegals walk up to the checkpoint? Fuck, no. Smuggler's Road goes around the checkpoints," Simon said, then turned to me. "Don't worry."

"But what if the ice isn't frozen enough?" I hated being the adult. "I've heard there's open water in parts and that the lake never fully freezes."

"Smugglers' Road weaves between the No Man's Islands where the water's shallow and freezes," Gill explained. "Boats don't even go there. It's the stretch between the islands and the mainland that is the toughest. That's where the water is deeper and less apt to freeze and where you can't see anything."

IT WAS NEARLY midnight when we met in the restaurant parking lot. The moon was as big and bright as if a child had drawn it. The others had just closed the restaurant and were hyped up on caffeine or maybe something else. Normally in bed by nine to get up for the breakfast shift, I had drunk several cups of coffee to stay awake. I rode with Gill and Chay in

Chay's truck, which pulled a trailer with two snowmobiles. Simon and Kayla followed, pulling a trailer with one machine. No one in our truck said a word as we headed to the other side of the island.

The reservation sat high on cliffs overlooking the lake. We slowed and turned onto the narrow, dirt road that meandered through birch trees before opening at the lake. A single road wound down to the water's edge, blocked by an imposing steel gate and fence. There was only one way down, and one way up, and the reservation controlled it.

Our headlights scanned the barrier. A man stepped out of a metal shack. Chay got out and stood in the headlights talking to him.

"How are you doing?" Gill whispered.

"Nervous."

He squeezed my hand. "Relax. I'll make sure you're safe."

"And who's going to make sure *you're* safe?"

"That man." We watched as Chay pulled several bills from a wallet and handed them to the stranger. "Chay's saved me more than once. He's got a sixth sense. Maybe it's all that Ojibwe stuff. But he's got an antenna for danger."

The guard opened the gate. Chay hopped back into the driver's seat and grinned menacingly at us. The road was steep. At the bottom, we parked next to the lake where Chay and Gill unloaded the snowmobiles. I stayed in the truck, the heat blasting. The temperature had dropped to two below zero, another reason I'd asked Gill to reconsider the trip. I watched as the guys tested the machines along the shoreline.

I had debated all day about whether I should go. I woke early that morning and wrote a letter to Finn letting him go. I was gentle and blamed it all on the distance and the situation. I wished him luck in his new role. I didn't say that I couldn't forgive him for not telling me what happened between him and

Darren Wallack. What was the point of heaping all that on him? It was better to end amicably. While writing the letter, I had to stop and walk away, the emotions too intense. It felt like I was saying goodbye forever.

Chay rapped his knuckles on the window, startling me. Then he opened the door laughing. "Come on, Ice Princess. Let's get going." He cut the engine and pulled me from the truck.

I trudged through the deep snow to Gill standing next to his snowmobile. The machines were loud and rackety, like a band of high-powered leaf blowers. "It's going to be okay," he said over the pop-pop-pop-pop of the engine idling. "We'll be there in an hour." I buried my face into his chest. I was tired, physically, emotionally. I'd come for one reason: to mail Finn's letter from Canada. I wanted him to think I was free.

Gill raised my face to his and kissed me. It didn't feel like a happy kiss, rather like something mournful. I could feel him trembling, and I realized, like me, he was afraid. I wanted to stay in that moment, our faces pressed together. When he pulled back, Gill held my head in his gloved hands. It was too dark to see his eyes, but I could feel their intensity. He pulled down my ski mask, handed me ski goggles and a helmet, and adjusted them snuggly against my head. Then he put on his own. We straddled the seat. I wrapped my arms around him.

"Hold on tight," he yelled.

As he pulled back on the throttle, we glided onto the lake. Chay led the way, pulling a sled with our overnight bags. Simon and Kayla formed the middle. Gill and I completed the tail of our roaring beast sailing across the ice. Aside from the arctic air that engulfed us, the night was stunningly gorgeous. The moon was perched on the horizon, the snow and ice reflecting its glare. I turned around to take in Angelica Island, a dark mass with flickering lights. I prayed I'd see her again.

The ice road was tunnel-like, with snow piled six feet high on the sides. The snowmobile bounced up and down as Gill traversed crusty waves of ice sculpted by the wind. We were either flying in the air or slamming into our seats.

We'd been riding about half an hour when we spotted one of the No Man's Islands off to the left. Chay signaled he was slowing down and turned his snowmobile, cresting the banks of the ice road. Simon and Gill followed.

Chay circled us, killed his engine, took off his helmet, and pumped his fist in the air. "Whew! What a fucking great ride!"

"We're off the island!" Kayla yelled, then tipped back a silver canister to her mouth. Simon lit a joint.

Gill unstrapped my helmet and rubbed his gloved hands over mine. We stood on the ice, my first steps wobbly, my leg muscles twitching from the machine's vibrations. The wind whipped at us, but it felt good to walk, even in the thick snow.

Gill and Chay jumped in the air and slapped their gloved hands in a high five.

"Man, it's fucking awesome!" Chay screamed.

Kayla handed me her flask. I took a swig, feeling the whiskey warm my throat. My ears were still ringing from the memory of the blaring machines. I walked in circles, staring up at the black-blue sky with a million twinkling lights.

"Isn't it beautiful," Gill said, slinging an arm around my shoulder. "God, I love it out here. I wanted you to see this, experience it, be a part of it: the sky, the moon, the ice."

Gill felt like a constellation that had pulled me into its gravity. Inside I was bursting with affection for him. At the same time, I was aching from letting Finn go. How was it possible to feel joy and sorrow at the same time? While I was prepared to say goodbye to my old life, I didn't want to let go. And though I was raw with sadness, writing Finn had opened something within me, making space for Gill. I couldn't stop hearing the song "Love the One You're With" in my head. As we held hands, cricked our necks to the sky, and breathed in the pristine air, my insides exploded with excitement and heartache.

Simon yelled and pointed to bouncing headlights moving across the ice in the distance. If they were undocumented immigrants, they wouldn't be heading toward us. That only left the Canadian border guards or U.S. Immigration. Whose country were we in?

"Shit!" Chay screamed. "How the fuck are we going to lose *them*?"

"Why do we have to run?" I asked. "Why can't we just see who they are and explain that we're out having fun?"

They all looked at me as if I were naïve.

"We can't get back on the ice road," Gill insisted.

Simon jumped on his machine. "I know a way."

Chay and Gill followed as best they could, but Simon was far ahead, hugging the shores of the islands where the snow was more crystalized and choppier. Gill hit a snowbank, and the snowmobile went airborne. We landed with a hard thud.

"Are you okay?" he screamed.

"Yeah, just go." The lights were getting closer.

"It's not worth getting killed over," Gill shouted.

He pulled back on the throttle. There was no way we could catch up to Chay and Simon. Gill cut his lights and maneuvered slowly along the banks of an island, then turned into the woods. Beneath the cover of pine trees, he cut the ignition.

"If they have infrared sights, we're dead," he whispered.

I buried my face into his back as if that would protect me. We sat still, my heart pounding in my ears. The roar of the machines was closer. Suddenly there they were, shining searchlights into the woods. Gill had pulled far enough into the trees that their beams fell just a few feet short. I held my breath. They slowly eased along the shore. We could hear them talking, but couldn't make out their words. Then the sound of their engines began to fade as they moved away from us.

Gill and I took off our helmets, goggles, and ski masks so we could breathe easier.

"That was scary," he said.

"I thought for sure they had seen us, especially with night vision goggles."

Suddenly the engines sounded louder, closer. Their lights bore down on us, their machines blocking us, in front and back.

FINN

Personally, time was moving slowly, and I hadn't heard from Mr. Mailer. Or from Riley. Professionally, time was moving quickly, and with five weeks left before the election, the mayor decided we should ramp up our campaign events. The perfect photo op, he decided, was at the unveiling of Hyde Park High School's memorial. In the thirteen years since the shooting, the school had raised millions of dollars to replace the old gymnasium and build an expansive memorial. The big reveal was set to take place on the anniversary of the shooting, January 17.

That morning was cold and blustery. A mixture of sleet and snow whipped about our faces as we sat on the stage in the middle of the outdoor memorial crowded with city dignitaries and school officials. Forty-nine large stones representing the victims fanned out around us, much like Stonehenge. Opposite the stage were colossal marble bleachers that rose several stories. Students, teachers, and parents huddled in the cold marble seats.

The sky was that opaque gray that leaves you feeling listless and despondent. It was the first time since the shooting I had returned to the high school. I felt shameful that we were using the memory of that horrendous day to boost our public persona.

A conspiracy of ravens cawed noisily from a nearby tree. I kept thinking of that day, how we'd arrived at the school, the adrenaline quivering in my veins. The halls were dark and eerily quiet. When we got closer to the gymnasium, we heard crying and moaning. But nothing prepared us for what we would find on the other side of that door. No matter how much active shooter training a cop has, nothing prepares you for the actual moment.

Someone nudged me. The principal was calling me to the podium. I took my position and delivered the speech Rod Lowenstein had written for me: how we must develop better mental health programs for students so that another student didn't surface with a cache of guns again. I didn't believe a word I was saying. If someone wants to shoot up a school or a church or even a government office, they will figure out how to do it. And no law, metal detector, psychiatrist, or rent-a-cop was going to stop them.

I looked out into the crowd. One face stood out. It was Reece's. My voice grew shaky, and I felt unsteady on my feet. I managed to get through the speech, but my hands were trembling when I sat down.

Then the principal called Reece to the stage. He walked stiffly, favoring his left side where he'd been shot. He'd regained some weight since I last saw him at the hospital. His cheeks were puffy, his hair grayer at the temples.

"That day," he said, looking out at the audience, "changed my life and the lives of those around me. I hid behind the bleachers in the gym. About a dozen of us were there, and we watched through the slats as a student killed our friends, our teachers.

"Before that day, I thought I was going to become a hip-hop

artist. I'd recorded a sample track and had my whole life mapped out in my head. But after that day, I decided to become a cop, to hunt down bad guys. Everything changed for the girl next to me. Riley Keane planned to become a chef like her father. But after the shooting, you couldn't stop her from protesting gun violence. And I see on the stage here," he looked back at me standing next to the mayor, "the former police officer who cornered the shooter. He is now a city councilman. Finn O'Farrell gave up his badge to become a legislator and write laws to protect us. The events of that day had dramatically different effects on all of us. We're still feeling them. Today is the first time I've been back at the school, and it's taking all of my strength to stand here and face you, this place, these memories."

It was an honest speech, one I wished I had delivered. After Reece, the mayor delivered closing remarks, and forty-nine doves were released. We watched them fly into the winter sky. I wanted to get to my car as fast as possible.

But students crowded around the stage wanting to know what it was like to be alone with Darren Wallack, a name we had not been allowed to mention from the stage. I never got used to these kinds of fans and their grim questions. I repeated the talking points Rod prepared. I didn't say what I really felt: Darren Wallack was an evil mistake of a human being who didn't deserve to live.

When I looked up to shake the next student's hand, I was met by Reece's stone, cold face.

"Nice speech," he said, grabbing my arm.

"I didn't write it. That's what happens when you are running for office. Someone else tells you what you feel, puts words in your mouth."

I glanced at Rod Lowenstein, who came rushing over, his schedule flapping in the wind. "We need to roll," he said.

I looked at Reece and shrugged.

"I'll give you a ride to wherever it is you need to go," Reece said. "But you and I need to talk."

I reluctantly nodded. Rod backed away.

I followed Reece to a side street behind the school where he'd parked his unmarked detective car. We rode in silence. When we reached the stone archway, I knew where he was taking me. He drove deep into the cemetery and pulled over. He then leaned into the back seat, retrieved several bouquets wrapped in cellophane, and handed me half.

We walked on the marshy grass, soaked from the recent snow, and laid the flowers at the foot of a row of gravestones.

"This entire row," he said, "is where they buried most of my friends from the football team."

I knew the story. They had tried to wrestle Darren Wallack to the ground after he started shooting.

"I should have been with them," Reece said. "Instead, I was hiding behind the bleachers. What kind of man does that? And then I find out that you had him, and you let him kill himself."

I didn't argue with him. He seemed on edge.

"I want to know," he said, facing me, "what happened between you and Wallack." I half expected him to pull out his gun and hold it on me, force me to answer him.

"You know that's classified," I said quietly.

There was rage in his eyes. "Yes, Alderman, we both share a lot of secrets, don't we? Some of them might even cost you the election if they got out."

I sighed and closed my eyes for a moment. "I was just a beat cop, Reece. Twenty-six years old. I'd only been on the force three years. Adrenaline was high. We got to the school and fanned out, looking for him. I see him go into a room. I think he's going to reload. I follow him. He starts firing at me."

"Why didn't you shoot back?"

"You're assuming I didn't."

Reece mulled over that for a minute. "My whole life as a cop, I hoped one day I could end up in a room with a shooter like Darren Wallack. I fantasize about it, you know. Just me, some asshole, and all of my revenge. I've carried that all this time. It's what's driven me. It's what made me become a cop, licensed to kill."

"Yeah?" I asked. "How do you know what you would do? How do you know what any man is going to do when he comes face to face with a child killer?"

"I know what I would do."

"Really?"

He was quiet for a moment. "I'd probably do exactly what you did."

"I thought you didn't know."

"I read the file."

"There is no file."

He grunted. "The autopsy report."

"He died from a bullet to his head," I said. "You needed a report to tell you that?"

"He died from a bullet that was unlike any others he fired that day."

RILEY

We couldn't see their faces because of the lights in our eyes. "Step away from your machine with your hands up," a voice ordered.

I looked at Gill. He nodded. We stuck our hands in the air and stepped off the snowmobile.

"We're Americans!" Gill shouted.

"We don't care what you are," the voice yelled. "Give us what you're carrying."

The two dark figures came closer, and I could see they weren't wearing any government insignia. Ski masks covered their faces. Each held a flashlight and a gun.

"Ice bandits," Gill whispered under his breath.

"What is it you're saying there, boy?" one of the men shouted.

"We don't have anything," Gill hollered. "We're just riding on the lake."

One of the men went to Gill's snowmobile, lifted the seat, and opened each compartment. The other man came closer and shined his light in my face.

"Now, who do we have here?"

I flinched and held my hands in front of my eyes.

"Leave her alone," Gill ordered.

"Yeah? And what are you going to do about it?" He stuck his gun in Gill's face.

"There ain't nothin' here," the other guy yelled from our snowmobile.

"Where's the drugs, Big Boy?" The man stuck the gun underneath Gill's chin. "We know you are making a drop tonight. Did you dump it in the woods? We'll make you get on your hands and knees until you find it. Or maybe I'll have my way with your girlfriend here while my partner takes you into the woods." He moved his flashlight beam from Gill to me.

I could feel my lips quivering. Snot was running down my nose.

"We don't have any drugs," Gill shouted. "We just went for a ride after work."

"And what kind of work does a wussy boy like you do?"

Gill didn't flinch.

"I said where do you work?" He stuck the pistol to Gill's temple.

"We work at the restaurant," I blurted.

"Ginny's?" He turned the light to my face.

I nodded.

"I suppose those two other mobiles are with ya?" He had a distinct accent, Canadian with a hint of something else mixed in. Maybe he was from Quebec. English was not his first language. If he knew Ginny, then he was local. But there was something else. Something about him that felt familiar—his posture, his mannerism, maybe even his voice.

"They took off. You scared them," Gill said.

"Yeah, right. Did you sell the drugs to them?"

"We don't have any drugs," Gill insisted. His hair hung in his eyes. I wished we'd kept our helmets on.

"Take off your coats." The man ordered.

"It's fucking two below," Gill argued.

"Do it!"

We slowly peeled off our jackets and dropped them on the ground. My teeth chattered from the biting cold. I rubbed my hands up and down my arms and stomped in my boots. But Gill stood still staring at the man rifling through our coat pockets while his partner pointed a gun at our heads. I dreaded him finding my letter to Finn, hoping he'd disregard it as uninteresting. But criminals have a way of knowing what is of value. He pulled the card from my coat, and I could see his malevolent grin in the glare of the flashlight.

"What is this? A card? The envelope is addressed to *Alderman Finn O'Farrell* in Chicago?"

I refused to look at him, to give him the satisfaction.

He put his flashlight underneath his arm and took out a knife to slice through the envelope I'd so carefully licked and sealed. Then he pulled out the ivory stationery with the dried flowers fused into its cottony edges. He folded his knife back in his pocket, took the flashlight back in his hand and let the light fall on the letter in his other hand.

"'*Dear Finn,*'" he began in a mock theatrical voice. Then he turned to Gill. "Oh, partner, did you know she had another man?"

He licked his lips and continued reading: "'*I wanted you to know that I'm okay. I miss you, and I think about you every day. It was a hard decision to leave. But given what I've seen on television, it was the right decision.*'"

He shined his flashlight in my face. "What does that mean?"

"It means I didn't like the way the politics were going in Chicago."

"Do a pat-down and make sure she's not carrying," he ordered his partner. The other man, who was still pointing a gun at us, came over and moved one hand down my back and legs.

"Turn your pant pockets inside out," the leader ordered.

Gill and I handed the man our keys and spare change. Luckily, I'd packed my purse and ID in my overnight bag that Simon was pulling on his sled.

The leader turned back to the letter. "*I don't know if it's possible for me to come back soon or even at all.*' Oh, this is a sad love story. '*Finn, I want the best for you. Know that I'm safe.*' Yes, you are, honey. Very safe." He laughed cruelly. "'*I have a job. I'm building another life, and I want you to have a life, too. Please, go on without me. I'm sorry it turned out this way. For what it's worth, I really thought we had something special.*'"

When I glanced over, Gill was biting down on his lower lip and glaring at the lead bandit.

"Aw. Isn't this sad? Romeo and Juliet can't be together because Juliet has run away."

"Give them back their coats," he said to his partner.

We quickly put them back on.

"Now, over there," the man ordered. "Go sit next to that tree."

We walked through steep snow to a large tree. I was still shivering. We sat with our backs to the tree. The second man jerked our hands to our laps and tied them with rope. Then he wrapped another rope snuggly around our chests and tied it off behind the tree.

I winced. "You're hurting me. I can't breathe."

"Sorry, *mademoiselle*," the second man said and slightly loosened the rope.

"Now, you're going to tell us where your 'friends' went." The main bandit stood above us with his gun pointed at Gill's head.

Gill shook his head. The man slammed the gun into the side of Gill's head. Gill flew back against the tree. In the glare of the flashlight, I could see blood trickling down his face.

"Stop it!" I screamed. "I'll tell you what you want, but don't kill us."

The lead bandit twisted his mouth and nodded. "I'm listening."

"We were supposed to meet in Whitefish." I'd heard the guys discussing the town earlier.

The man moved the gun to my face. "Where exactly were you meeting them?"

"At the harbor."

"Good."

"And what are their names?"

"I don't know. They don't speak English."

"Now we're getting somewhere."

"And what are they carrying?"

"Two kilos."

"Good girl." The man caressed my cheek with the barrel of the gun. "If they're there, we'll trade your lives for the drugs. Your friends can come back and rescue you. And you better hope we find them because otherwise, no one will find your bodies until spring—or what's left of them."

Then he yelled at his partner, "Get the jar."

"Shouldn't we shoot them?" the second guy said. His accent sounded foreign as well.

"Nah," the first guy said. "Bullets leave trails. I don't want to have to get rid of this gun. We'll let the wolves deal with them."

The second man pulled out a glass jar from a satchel and

handed it to the main guy. The man unscrewed the lid and took a big whiff.

"Mmmm. So fresh," he said. "You're really going to enjoy this."

He poured the liquid over our heads. It ran down our faces. I recognized the smell.

"I hear wolves can smell blood from miles away," the leader said.

I kept my head down, so the blood didn't seep into my eyes and hoped the blood was from an animal. I heard the men's boots crunch through the snow and then the sharp whining of their machines. Then they were gone.

"Why'd you tell them the others had cocaine?" Gill asked.

"We needed a distraction."

"Yeah, but now if they can't find them, they're going to come back and kill us."

"Not if we can get out of here before they come back."

My arms had long gone numb, but I thought I might be able to wedge beneath the rope around my chest.

"I have a small Pocket Knife," Gill said. "It's in my boot. If you slide down, you can maybe get it."

After a few minutes, I'd managed to painfully wiggle my chest and shoulders enough to get my breasts below the rope and free myself. The guy who tied us up must have thought the rope was only meant to keep us until he put a bullet in each of our heads. With my teeth, I yanked up Gill's pant leg, and between my mouth and fingertips, I pulled out the knife from Gill's boot. My hands were tied at the wrists, allowing my fingers to extend a blade. Then I sawed at the rope on my hands, nicking my hands and fingers several times, blood running down my palms until I freed myself. Then I untied Gill. Gill cut a piece from his shirt's tails and wrapped it around both of my wrists to stanch the bleeding.

"Do you think they're waiting for us on the lake?" I asked, using my own shirt to wipe the wolf-bait blood from my face.

"It's a risk we'll have to take." Gill turned on the snowmobile lights, then used his knife to cut wires to start the ignition. The snowmobile sputtered, then Gill gunned the engine.

"C'mon, let's get the fuck out of here," he said.

This time we slowly made our way to the other end of the island and then snaked back to the Smuggler's Ice Road. Instead of heading north to Canada to join the others, we headed to Angelica Island.

The air was cold, and my hair was frozen with the blood. Gill sped across the ice. I buried my head in his back. Warm tears ran down my cheeks cutting through the blood on my face. It felt so much like the night I'd run in the streets as the cops arrived, the smell of Reece's blood in my hair.

RILEY

Gill drove the snowmobile along Angelica's shores then turned down the main road before looping into the restaurant parking lot. His truck and my Jeep were the lone vehicles.

Gill cut the engine, but didn't move. His hands remained clutched to the controls. I took off my helmet.

"You okay?" I asked.

He took off his helmet and turned around. There was terror in his eyes. I wrapped my arms around his chest. We held each other for a long while, shivering from the cold and the fear.

Gill said we should go to his place. Chay would call there when we didn't turn up in St. Marie. I didn't argue. I didn't have keys to my car and at the moment the last thing I wanted to do was be alone. Gill kept a spare set of keys in his glove box. We didn't speak the whole drive. My ears were still ringing from the noise of the snowmobile. I stared out the truck window until we reached his house.

I showered while Gill waited by his landline phone. Like most Islanders, he didn't own a cell phone because of the island's abysmal reception. I stood under the hot water and scrubbed the blood from my head and hands, the rust-colored liquid circling the tile before emptying into the drain. When I stepped out of the shower, I heard a voice below and opened the door slightly.

"Yeah, we're fine—now. But someone knew we were coming. And they may be waiting for you when you cross."

He went silent.

"I'll tell you about it when you get here. They were definitely ice bandits, and they intended to kill us."

Another silence.

"Yeah, she's okay. They were pretty hard on her. Leave at dawn. Be careful what you tell Simon. I don't understand why they thought we were carrying drugs."

More silence.

"It's not her. I can tell you that. I'll tell you later why. It's some fucked up mess. But it sure as hell wasn't Riley."

Another silence.

"Yeah, yeah. See you soon."

I quietly shut the door and dressed in clothes Gill had loaned me. The jeans hung off my hips, and I was swimming in the sweatshirt. I tentatively made my way down the stairs in my bare feet, dreading the conversation that was coming.

Gill sat at the kitchen table staring out the window. The coffee pot was percolating.

He turned his body toward me but kept his gaze lowered. His blond hair was streaked with blood, his face speckled with the same rust-colored liquid. Black grease from the snowmobile stained his fingers.

"That was Chay," he said, nodding toward the phone. "They're at the hotel in St. Marie. They'll leave in the morning, travel in the light to avoid the bandits."

"Who do you think they are?"

He shrugged. "How would I know?"

"Their voices sounded familiar. They knew about Ginny's. Do you think they could have come from Angelica?"

He rubbed his hands across his face. "I don't know who they were, but I'm pretty sure they meant to kill us." He was still rattled.

I poured two cups of coffee and set them on the table.

"I want to tell you about the...*letter*."

"It's your business." He looked at me for the first time since I'd walked into the kitchen.

"I didn't want to involve you in my *mess*." I borrowed the word he'd used with Chay.

"You don't owe me an explanation." His jaw was firm and his lips tight with conviction.

"I thought it was better if you didn't know the specifics."

"So, you said."

I could see the hard lines of his face softening.

"I wrote the letter, Gill, because I needed to let Finn go." I laid my hand over his on the table. He didn't pull away. "I wrote the letter to say goodbye—properly."

He nodded as if he understood, but remained silent.

Finally, he cleared his throat. "There's a saying on the island: Life begins at 47/90. It's the latitude and longitude of Angelica. It means it doesn't matter what you did or who you were before you came here because it's completely irrelevant on the island.

"What you should be worried about are those thugs," he continued. "They know a helluva lot about us—where we work and your friend's name and that he's a politician. They'll use that to blackmail him, promising to lead him to you. Riley, we haven't escaped at all."

RILEY

For the past week, breakfast business had more than doubled. Customers weren't coming for the food; they wanted to get the morning report from Andy and Ned, the snowplow drivers, who dropped in for breakfast after making their ice road checks.

Each morning the year-rounders grew edgier, confronting Andy and Ned about when the ice road would be ready as if the two men were personally keeping everyone hostage on the island. Andy and Ned were both a bit socially inept. Ginny told me they were high functioning autistic.

On Monday morning, Andy and Ned arrived an hour later than usual. A small crowd collected around their table, hoping to hear when the ice road would open, and they could escape the island. It was already January 21.

Shoveling eggs and bacon into his mouth, Andy tediously described how he and Ned had taken readings at every Christmas tree. He recounted precise measurements starting with the marker closest to the shore. Even polite year-rounders got up from their tables to listen. The only people eating were

Andy and Ned, who seemed oblivious to the growing anxiety around them.

Javier and I peered through the kitchen door windows. When Javier could no longer hear Andy's belabored report, he stormed into the dining room, pushed aside the small crowd.

"When are you going to open that goddamn road?" he screamed.

Andy pulled back his head and squinted at Javier. "Uh. It's open now."

A collective yell went up from the dining room, followed by the din of chairs scraping the floor as customers scrambled for the doors. Some forgot to pay. Others just threw cash on their tables. Javier shouted for me to cover for him in the kitchen.

The news spread quickly. Within minutes, pick-ups lined up in the harbor parking lot. I watched from the restaurant's side windows as the trucks slowly edged onto the lake's frozen surface.

As soon as my shift ended at 2 p.m., I rushed to my cottage. But when I got out of my Jeep, I saw strange footprints in the fresh snow. I followed them from the driveway to the back of the house, where they seemed to dance around, stomping down the snow, and then moved around to the other side of the house, ending at the front porch. I wasn't sure what to do. Everyone had scattered at the restaurant.

I went back to my Jeep, took out a knife Gill had put in the glove box, and went inside. I quietly stepped from room to room, turning on lights and looking through closets. I wasn't about to go into the basement. Part of me was scared; the other part of me was annoyed. I needed to get to the mainland, and I didn't need any distractions. Was it a squatter taking refuge, or had the ice bandit come back to finish me off?

I quickly stuffed a bag with clothes and pulled out my map. Then I ran to the door, slammed it shut behind me, and locked it. I sprinted to my Jeep, got in, and locked the doors. I waited to see if anyone materialized, if shadows were moving inside the house. But it was just a clear sunny day. I felt silly.

I unfolded the map and studied a route I had carefully drawn through towns in northern Wisconsin—far enough away from Angelica that the most diligent cop wouldn't trace me back to the island. For my scheme to work, I needed a working payphone. I still didn't know if any of these towns had one.

It was mid-afternoon when I slowly steered the Jeep down the boat ramp and onto the plowed snow. The "road" felt bumpy. I drove slowly, the powerful wind rocking the Jeep. Puffy purple and pink clouds hovered at the horizon.

I thought I would feel ecstatic, escaping the island. But I couldn't shake an uneasiness. I feared I wouldn't get back in time, that the island would pull back her imaginary drawbridge, and I'd be stuck on the mainland. The island had been my home for two months. I had acclimated to its slow pace, its natural beauty, its ruggedness that made us all feel connected. For the first time, I realized how much I had become an Islander.

Once on the mainland, I meandered through villages without even a single stop sign. I drove in a state of mindfulness, mesmerized by the sight of rolling snow-topped pastures and woods. I'd been driving for about two hours when I reached a town marked along my route. It was just before 5 o'clock, and the sky was darkening. I spotted a public telephone booth in front of the post office and pulled into the parking lot. The phone had a dial tone. I pulled out a jar of change, plunked three dollars in quarters into the slot, and dialed the number I knew by heart.

The phone rang three times, and a message came on the line. "Thank you for calling Sanders and Sanders law offices. In observance of the Martin Luther King holiday, the office will be closed on January 21."

"What?" I yelled at the receiver. "How can that be? Was today a federal holiday? How did I not know this?"

I put the receiver down. The coins clinked loudly as they made their way through the machine, some plunking into the return slot. I put in several dollars-worth and dialed the foundation attorney's mobile phone. It rang and rang. Finally, a small voice I recognized as Mr. Sanders' came on the line and told me how important my phone call was and urged me to leave a message. I hadn't planned for this. Previously Mr. Sanders had always answered his phone. At the sound of the beep, a robotic voice said the voicemail was full.

"God damn it." I slammed the receiver down.

I couldn't call Finn's cell phone or those of my parents or my brother. Even landlines, like the one at Finn's ward office, would have been tapped by the police. Besides, Finn wouldn't be in his office anyway. It was a fucking federal holiday.

I looked out the window at the post office. Desperate times called for desperate measures. Inside the building, the post office booths were closed, but the outer part was open. There was a vending machine that sold paper, envelopes, and stamps. Ah! At least something was going my way. I inserted quarters into the machine and retrieved my writing kit. Sending a letter was risky, but I didn't have much choice. Old school methods work best, I'd remembered from *Famous Female Fugitives*.

I didn't use any salutations—no dearest Mom or Dad. I got to the point. *I've found a place to live and a job. Please don't worry about me. I wish I could come back. But I need to know that it is safe first. I love and miss you and think about you all the time.* And then, as if an afterthought, I wrote: *I'm sorry.*

When I'd finished, I read it like a cop to see if I'd revealed anything that could be used against me. I read it like my mother, imagining how she would receive the news. I read it like my father as he parsed each word, looking for some hidden meaning. The letter was cryptic, reassuring, but vague.

I sealed the envelope, stamped it, kissed it, and dropped it into the mailbox slot in the wall. As I was leaving, I noticed the name of the town on the door and smiled, remembering why I'd chosen the village: Luck, Wisconsin.

I jumped into the Jeep and turned the key. The motor groaned and sputtered. I turned the key again and again and got the same whirring noise. I pumped the gas and turned the key again.

"Come on! Come on!" Nothing.

I put my head against the steering wheel and muttered a desperate prayer. I tried starting the Jeep several more times. Each time it failed. Now I was at risk of flooding the car. I took my foot off the gas and waited, my breath steaming up the windows. I debated whether to go back to the payphone and call a tow truck. There wasn't a gas station in town, and I hadn't seen another person since I arrived.

RILEY

I climbed out of the Jeep, opened the hood, and shined a flashlight on the engine as if I knew what I was doing. Headlights scanned the parking lot. I held up my hand in front of my face to block the light. A truck pulled next to me. A window went down.

"Car trouble?" The voice sounded croaky.

"Yeah, I left it for a minute. Now it won't start." I squinted at him, tracing the shadow of a man's face.

"Let me take a look." He swung down from the cab of his truck, a rusted Ford. Strands of brown hair poked out the sides of his orange wool cap. From neck to toes, he was covered in hunting camouflage. Even his thick rubber boots were speckled green and black. He got into the Jeep and turned the key. Nothing.

"You're not from around here," he said, more a statement than a question.

"Just passing through."

"I got some jumper cables." He went to the back of his truck. He was close to my age. He rubbed at his eyes with his palms. Tall and boney, his face seemed skeletal, menacing. In a kinder light, he might have been attractive.

I trailed him prattling on, grateful for his help. "Wanted to mail a card to my grandmother," I volunteered. "She's superstitious and plays the slots. She'd think it was funny to get a birthday card from Luck."

He grunted a laugh. "Yeah, the post mark's 'bout the only thing lucky in this town."

"You from here?"

He opened the truck hood, attached cables to his battery then stretched the cables to my Jeep. His eyes landed on me with a cold heaviness. "All my life."

I hovered several feet from him, hunching my shoulders and holding my gloved hands around my mouth.

"Why don't you go sit in my truck and warm-up," he ordered.

I climbed up the sideboard. A shotgun hung in the gun rack. In the middle of the seat was a small black handgun case. I began to smell something foul and cracked the door. The dome light kicked on and illuminated a cooler in the backseat covered with bloody prints.

The man opened the door and saw me staring at the cooler.

"Deer parts. You want to see?"

I shook my head. Deer season had passed. If he had shot a deer, he was a poacher.

He lifted the cooler lid, displaying a heart, liver, kidney. A pungent, bloody smell engulfed the small space. I turned away and put my hand to my nose.

He snickered. "The carcass is in the back. But you probably don't want to look. I hit her as she was crossing the road."

I swallowed hard and faced forward, not wanting him to see me fighting nausea.

"Your Jeep's running now. Probably a weak battery."

"Thank you." I started to get out, but he grabbed my arm. His hands were stained with blood, his fingernails caked in grease.

"I'll follow you for a while and make sure it runs okay," he said, letting go. "You don't want to get stuck out here at night."

"That's *so* not necessary." The thought of this stranger trailing me in the dark made me shiver. How did I know he'd accidentally hit the deer? His truck was so banged up I couldn't tell what dents were new. And if he wasn't hunting, then why was he wearing camouflage?

"Go on. I'll be right behind you." He stared at me, waiting, his mouth set, determined.

"I'm kind of in a hurry."

"Don't go too fast, or I'll have to tow you out of a ditch," he said humorlessly.

I turned the Jeep's heat to full-blast and drove slowly at first. After fifteen minutes, his truck lights continued to blare into my rearview mirror. I tapped my brakes to indicate that he was too close. But he kept following me. I pressed on the accelerator until the speedometer read 60 mph. His lights were still burning into my mirror. As I rounded a sharp curve, the Jeep slid across the road and into the oncoming lane, finally coming to a stop with the front end of the Jeep hanging over a deep ditch. I could feel my heart in my throat, beating like crazy. I backed up the car to the shoulder. The truck eased in behind me. I stormed back to his truck.

"I can't drive like this, your headlights in my eyes. It's not safe. Stop fucking following me."

"You got a mouth on you, girl."

"Look." I took a deep breath. "I'm grateful that you helped me back there. But you need to back off."

He looked away, as if mulling over my request, and revved

his engine. "Suit yourself." Then he pulled onto the road in the direction I was headed.

Relieved, I got back on the road. It was after nine now. Except for a few rural bars with cars parked out front, no restaurants or gas stations were open. I'd been driving for about twenty minutes when a pair of headlights appeared behind me. I slowed, hoping the car would pass. It slowed, too. Then I sped up, and it sped up, too. Was it the hunter? Was he still following me? I punched the gas and moved as fast as I could on the roads, coated with a fresh sheet of snow, hoping there wasn't black ice underneath my tires. The lights followed.

I turned into a random driveway, pulled up to the garage, cut the lights, but left the car idling, then hunched down in the seat. Maybe he'd think I was home. The truck stopped in front of the house, then finally moved on.

BY THE TIME I reached Grand Portage, it was after ten o'clock. I drove along the empty streets, then turned into the harbor. My lights flashed onto the yellow barricades stationed in front of the boat ramp. A sign said the ice road would reopen at seven in the morning.

I considered moving the traffic horses and driving onto the lake. Who would stop me? Surely the lake was still frozen. The temperature had only dropped. But what if an ice shelf had broken off? How could I see that in the dark? I thought of the Jeep sinking into the black, cold waters, covering me with its freezing liquid, snatching me to the far, deep bottom. By morning, the lake would have closed up, with my body entombed in my Jeep forever on the bottom of Lake Superior like the Edmond Fitzgerald. I shivered at the thought.

I hadn't brought enough cash to stay at a motel. I hadn't expected to have car trouble or be chased by a poacher.

I drove to a late-night bowling alley on the edge of town that I'd heard Islanders talk about. Inside, the place was decorated like a disco; a twirling crystal ball hung from the ceiling casting a prism of bright, unnatural colors on people's faces, their clothes. The music was energetic and loud. Patrons laughed and yelled at each other over the retro disco tunes and crashing bowling pins.

I felt sensory overload. It was like I'd stepped from a black and white film into a colorized version. I stood still, taking in the scene as bodies swished past me. I hadn't realized how slow and quiet island life was. Even the island tavern was dark and low-ceilinged, a place more conducive to discussing secrets than dancing. I didn't see anyone I recognized. It felt weird to be in a room full of strangers.

I went up to the counter. "Can I use your phone?" I asked a bearded, tatted guy running the shoe rental desk.

"You an Islander?" he asked.

"Does it show?" I imagined we all looked a bit out of our element in that chaotic scene.

"Just had a bunch of 'em in here today. Don't none of 'em have cell phones."

"Yeah, reception's for shit on the island."

He nodded and handed me an ugly green rotary phone. I called Zi's cottage. She didn't pick up. Then I rang Ginny.

"Hey, darling," she said.

When I explained my predicament, she suggested staying at Lar's place.

"He's on the road," she said. "Tracking some bail jumper. Won't be back for days. Key is under the flowerpot on the porch."

No lights were on when I pulled in front of Lar's house. I found the key and let myself in. The door creaked loudly. I felt like an actress in some slasher film sneaking into her attacker's home while he was in the backroom oiling his chainsaw. I turned on a few lights. The house was deserted and cold, the thermostat set at fifty degrees.

I turned up the heat and got myself a glass of water. Lars' bed was made. I opened the bedside table where I'd found the gun on Thanksgiving: empty. I slipped under the blankets with my clothes on, setting the alarm for 6 a.m.

I'd been asleep awhile when I felt something cold touch my cheek and swatted at it. But it returned, this time pressing harder. I rolled over. The object followed. I swiped at it again. It shifted. Finally, I caught it in my hand. It felt heavy and metallic. My eyes opened at the sound of clicking; I was holding the barrel of a gun.

FINN

The burner phone Ethan had given me was vibrating somewhere in my desk. I finally found it. It was Emma.

"She's alive! She's alive!" Emma shrieked. Her high-pitched voice leaked through the receiver. My assistant, hovering at my computer, glanced curiously at me. We were on deadline for a report to the finance committee.

"Your daughter, you mean?" I was careful not to use Riley's name.

"Yes." Her voice cracked with emotion.

"Emma, what exactly are you trying to tell me?"

She took a deep breath. "Riley wrote us a letter. It came in the mail today. Finn, this means she's okay."

I walked into the hallway. "A letter? Really? What exactly did she say?" Just hearing Riley's name made me ache for her anew.

"She says she found a job. She's safe."

"But, where is she?"

Emma paused, and for a moment, I thought I'd lost the

connection. "She didn't say. There's no return address. The postmark is from Luck, Wisconsin. Ever heard of it?"

I'd waited so long for some nibble of news that Riley was still alive, some detail that would tell me she was coming back, that she still thought of us. I sat down on the floor and shielded my eyes as I listened to Emma read Riley's letter over and over again.

I knew then what I would do to find her, and it wouldn't involve Mr. Mailer.

RILEY

"What the hell?" I screamed, sitting up.

The overhead light came on. "Why, looky here. It's Goldie Locks. What are you doing in my house, sleeping in my bed?" He dropped the gun to his side.

"Damn you, Lars. Do you go around pulling your gun on everyone?" I rubbed my cheek where he'd poked me. Fear had changed to anger.

He plopped down on the bed next to me and flipped over the gun; the magazine had been removed. "I was just playing with you. Lighten up." He tucked the gun into the small of his back.

"Not funny, Lars. You scared the shit out of me. Didn't Ginny call you? How'd you know I was here?"

"Well, it was real hard. Your Jeep parked out front was the first clue. But the dirty footprints in the kitchen were a dead give-away."

We both laughed.

"God, you're such a bloodhound," I said.

"So, what are you *doing* here?"

"I'm trapped. The ice road closed before I could get back. Ginny said you wouldn't mind if I slept over for a few hours.

"No problem. You can sleep in my bed anytime you like." He patted my leg through the covers.

"Still chasing fugitives, or is that a euphemism for women who won't sleep with you?"

He frowned and removed his hand.

"C'mon," he said, tapping my foot. "Get up and have a drink with me."

I looked at the clock. It was 3 a.m.

"Lars, I have to go to work in three hours. I need my sleep."

"You think you are going to be able to go back to sleep now? Come on. There's something we have to talk about."

That rousted me. I followed him into the kitchen. The overhead fluorescent lights made me queasy. He took out a bag of Caribou Coffee from his freezer and began spooning the ground beans into his coffee maker. The kitchen was small but neat, the counters clear except for a few canisters and a toaster.

"What are you doing with yourself these days?" he asked.

"What do you care?"

"I like to keep tabs on people I like," he said as he added water to the coffee pot.

"You don't need to keep tabs on me."

"What does that mean? I can't watch out for you?"

"I can take care of myself."

"Really?" He sat next to me at the kitchen table. Four place settings were arranged with blue napkins in wooden ring holders as if Lars were expecting guests. Printouts from news websites were piled on one chair.

"Is this your spy headquarters?"

"Whatever you've heard about me, it's wrong."

"Zi told me you're a bounty hunter."

He took out a new pack of Marlboro Lights, pounded it against the table, peeled off the plastic strip, pulled out a cigarette, and jabbed it into his mouth. He focused one eye on me as he cupped the flame. It was a menacing look. I tried not to react.

"Sometimes I run into suspicious people, and I inquire about them and whether they are wanted by various police departments, the federal government. It's sort of a freelance job. I'm just doing my civic duty." He winked.

"Yeah?"

"Like you, for example." He leaned back in his chair and took a long drag. He was unshaven—at least two days' worth of stubble. "I already knew you gave people a false name. You said it was because you didn't want your former boyfriend to find you, and you made up a story about being a student. That's a lie."

I swallowed hard.

"Almost everything you've said about yourself isn't true."

"What's it to you, Lars?"

He frowned. "I keep track of the liars around here."

I snatched one of his cigarettes. "If you know so much, why haven't you told anyone?"

"I'll be asking the questions here, *Ms. Keane*."

My jaw tightened.

He got up and walked to the coffee maker. He poured the coffee into two mugs then brought them to the table. He bent down close to my face. I could smell liquor on his breath and the hint of motorcycle oil on his pants.

"I liked drinking with you at Thanksgiving." His voice was soft, vulnerable. "I wanted to kiss you, then." He stared at me. Our faces were inches apart. "Hell, I imagined doing a lot more to you."

I pushed my chair back. He pulled out a chair and moved it

next to mine. He put his hand on my knee. "I liked you from the minute I saw you."

I pushed his hand away. "Do you really think I'm going to sleep with you *now*? You're my boss's boyfriend."

"You seem to like having a secret life." He gently touched my cheek where only minutes earlier he'd stuck a cold, hard gun.

"What are you proposing? That I become your lover and in return, you'll keep my identity a secret?"

He stirred his muddy coffee. "I thought you felt the same towards me."

"I don't cheat."

He looked hurt.

"We should have ended it a long time ago," he said, looking in the distance. "Ginny needed to borrow money to start the restaurant. We were great friends, but I'm not her type—if you know what I mean. I co-signed the loan and told people we were getting married. Things are a little less progressive around here. A single woman taking out a loan without a lot of collateral was, well, unusual. Then we got comfortable with our arrangement. It worked for both of us. Women don't make demands of me; Ginny gets to keep her life private. But the whole thing is taking its toll."

"So how long are Zi and Ginny going to hide their relationship?" I saw the way they looked at each other, and Ginny's panic during Zi's disappearance during the snow storm hinted at a more intense relationship.

Lars shrugged. "You'd have to ask Ginny."

"But everyone on the island knows the truth about you and Ginny and Zi, right?"

He sighed and swept his fingers through his graying hair. "Pretty much."

"Did you tell Ginny who I am?"

"That first night, I Googled your real name—the one that was on the ticket you'd stuck on your car dashboard. Found out you were an anti-gun activist in Chicago. There were a lot of stories about you testifying against bad cops. One of the articles had a picture of you. I thought you'd come here under some sort of witness protection. That's why I told Ginny we had to help you, to keep your secret. I told her not to file your Social Security numbers. I was hoping in time you'd trust me enough to tell me the truth."

"You're right . . ." I stuttered. "I did want to tell you." And for a brief second, I was ready to bare everything. I was so ready to unleash this pent-up secret, and Lars seemed like a sympathetic ear.

Lars blew out a long trail of smoke. A sly smile emerged. He was pleased with himself. "Who are you testifying against next? That's why they're hiding you out here, right?"

And just like that, I lost my nerve. Lars wouldn't understand that I'd shot a cop, even though that cop was my best friend and it was an accident. The truth was too complicated.

"Can't say," I said. "He sent word from jail that I was 'a dead bitch walking.'"

FINN

The woman behind the counter looked at the envelope, then my face, then back at the envelope, then my face. She'd been doing this back and forth for an uncomfortably long time.

"Yep," the postal clerk finally said. "It was mailed from here. But I couldn't tell you who she was. Don't remember her. Maybe she just put the envelope in the dropbox."

The clerk had a long, narrow face, green dot eyes, a slit for a mouth, and a mole at the end of her chin that I wanted to pull for some strange reason.

"Well, it had to be in the last week," I insisted, hoping the intensity of my voice would convey the severity of the situation. "Your stamp here says January 22, and now it's the thirtieth."

It was three weeks before the mayoral election. I should have been in Chicago canvassing neighborhoods, passing out flyers, shaking hands with people in diners, kissing babies—doing everything to achieve what I had dreamed of for years. It was all within my reach, and yet, I had run away. I should have made up an excuse, a family emergency, anything, that would have placated the mayor. But I couldn't. I just couldn't tell one more damn lie. It's like all the lies I'd told, this other life I lived, had built up into this giant heap, and now it was crumbling and taking me with it. I'd done this risky thing. But I didn't care. And for once in my life, I respected myself for not caring.

The mayor—or Rod—called my cell phone every hour, leaving anxious messages and threatening to take out a missing person's report. It wasn't just them. Dan Mackay, the pesky investigative reporter, called numerous times, leaving ominous messages. I knew why he was calling: He'd found something damning, and he needed me to deny it or admit to it so he could publish it. I ignored them all. For eight hours of solitary peace driving to the Upper Peninsula—through little towns and next to the Big Lake—I just let it go.

Something inside me had changed. Between the detectives badgering me and Dan Mackay insisting I was lying, a part of me—that desire to be a good cop, an honest politician rose up—and I just wanted to tell the truth about the woman I loved. I wanted to come clean about Riley and me. But first I had to find her. God, I missed her. Nothing seemed more important than tracking down this one lead, this proverbial needle in a haystack—a stamp on an envelope.

"Yes, I see the stamp," she said, looking at the envelope again.

"Ma'am, what I want to know is whether you saw the woman who mailed this letter."

"Who did you say you were?" the clerk asked.

I held up a picture of Riley. "I'm a family friend. She—the woman in the photo is missing. Her family has asked me to come here to determine if the letter they received with this envelope was real. They want to know if their daughter is alive."

The woman peered again at the envelope. "Her folks in

Chicago, eh? That's a long way away." She shook her head. "Never seen her."

I pulled back the envelope and the photo. "Would it be okay if I posted this picture on your bulletin board in case someone recognizes her?"

The woman wrinkled her eyebrows. "Don't see why not."

She handed me a blank piece of paper and some tape. "You might try up at Woody's Place. It's the bar just as you get to the end of town. He probably sees more folks than I do, especially tomorrow."

"Tomorrow?"

"Super-Bowl Sunday," she barked as if I were deaf.

"Oh, yeah." The Super Bowl was practically a religious holiday in the North Woods.

I taped Riley's picture to the white paper, then in big letters wrote, "Missing: Please call if you've seen this woman." I knew it was risky posting the notice. If Riley was living in this little town, I was outing her. But I didn't know how else to get a message to her. Her letter to her mother said she needed to know if it was safe to come home. I added my cell phone number at the bottom and tacked the notice next to the FBI's Most Wanted poster.

RILEY

The ice road opened a few minutes after seven. The sun's rays had just begun to poke above the lake. Splinters of orange shot across the frozen surface, blinding me as I inched onto the freshly plowed surface. The bordering Christmas trees were losing pine needles and cresting heavily in the direction of the wind. I sped across the lake as if the ice were cracking behind me. The brilliant morning light radiated through the windshield. I was happy to be returning to the island.

Mr. Kowalski was pumping gas into a rusted pickup as I drove by. I waved. He flashed me his palm. His bug eyes followed me, the corners of his mouth turning down in disappointment when I didn't stop. I was more than an hour late.

I pulled into the parking lot and stared into the restaurant's back windows. A handful of regulars were seated at their usual places; waitresses were pouring coffee and delivering hot plates. It was as if we were all floating in the middle of Lake Superior with no intention of ever docking.

I should have rushed inside, but instead, I sat there as the Jeep turned cold, weighing my options. I could leave the island.

The ice road was open. I could pick another spot on my map and live there until I was sure it was safe to return to Chicago. I had saved enough money that I could live frugally for months. But what would I be going back to? Finn had lied about the most critical day of my life. The Chicago police were unlikely to give up on pinning me for Reece's shooting.

I walked toward the backdoor in a stupor. I'd waited for the ice road to open for more than a month now. Why was I delaying? I should go to my cottage, pack and leave.

As the door slammed behind me, Javier glanced up from whipping eggs—my job—and gave me an annoyed look.

"Ginny wants to see you. Now," he snarled. "She's in the dining room. Maybe you gonna get a talking to." He grinned savagely.

Ginny was sitting at a back table in the formal dining room, expense reports spread out in front of her. I suspected Lars had called her, and she was about to confront me about my lies.

"Good morning, Sunshine." Her voice was overly sweet.

I smiled nervously and sat down.

"I think it's time we discussed your future here, don't you?"

Shit! I was about to be canned. My decision to leave just got easier.

"You've been here a couple of months now," she said flatly.

"Going on three," I croaked out in a whisper.

"Yes." She smiled. "You've become a valued part of our staff, Riley. I was impressed with all your work during the blizzard. We couldn't have done it without you. *I* couldn't have done it without you."

I waited for the inevitable "but" that usually followed such compliments. She bent forward and peered into my face.

"It's okay, Riley. It's all good. I called you in here to talk about a *promotion*."

"Promotion?" I said it like it was a foreign word.

"Yes. I'd like to move you to the night shift. I want to train you as a sous chef. You'll be Matthew's right hand. What do you say?"

"But why?" I still couldn't get over that she wasn't firing me.

"You've done a great job, Riley. I want you to stay with us. Besides, we're coming into our busiest season. The evening shift is by far the hairiest in the summer."

"I don't know what to say."

"Well, *yes* would be good."

"Yes. I mean, yes, of course," I muttered.

We stood, and she hugged me. "You are moving up, girlfriend."

Listening to her talk about the new position stirred my ambition that had gone dormant until I came to the island. I really wanted to be a good chef. But what I was doing, this choice I was making, wasn't logical. Every instinct told me it was time to abandon Angelica. But the stubborn and determined part of me refused to run. If I couldn't make it on this island of secrets, with this collection of people who were already helping me, where could I make it? I didn't want to start anew.

When I reached the kitchen and saw the envious look on Javier's face, I realized I was taking what was rightfully his. I knew why Ginny hadn't promoted him: She was still chafing from his disappearance during the blizzard. I brushed back the flash of doubt as I surveyed the pandemonium of the kitchen, soaking in my sudden good fortune, realizing I wanted to belong to the island, these people. I wanted a home. Still, the voice in my head was Zi's, taunting me over and over:

Be careful. The island changes you, makes you someone else.

FINN

The woman smiled a mouth of spindly teeth stained with cigarette tar and handed me a mug slopping with beer suds. I held out my iPhone, its screen frozen with a picture of Riley.

"Have you seen her?" I yelled over the bar's boisterous crowd.

She shook her head. "Sorry, hun." Seeing my disappointment, she added: "You might ask those guys over there. They're the town gossips." She pointed to a table beneath a large flat-screen television. All five men were wearing Green Bay Packers shirts.

With a minute before half time, the men jumped up, waved their arms, and shouted at the television. Green Bay's quarterback connected on a near-impossible pass to set up a first down. After the men finished their high fives, I saw my opening.

"Excuse me," I said, holding out my phone. "Have you ever seen this woman?"

The men took turns squinting at the cell phone. "Geez, she don't look familiar," said one.

"Sorry, buddy," another said. "Ask Randy over there. I

think he said he met some woman in the post office parking lot last week." He pointed to a guy with a tightly drawn face, sitting alone at the next table. He wore an orange cap and a camouflage coat.

I walked over and held out my phone. The man stared at the screen longer than anyone had. He wrenched his head toward the door, and I followed. The cold outside was sharp and piercing.

"Yer her old man?" His dark eyes studied me.

I shook my head. "Family friend. She mailed a letter from Luck. She's in danger. I need to find her."

"You a cop?"

"No. We are...friends. She was a witness to a crime. Now she's being sought by some dangerous men."

"How do I know you're not one of them?"

I sighed. Now that I'd met someone who might have seen her, he wanted to play twenty questions.

"I don't suppose there's any way I can convince you that I'm a friend and not a foe?"

He turned away to spit tobacco juice into the snow. "You look like an okay guy. *She* seemed suspicious."

"So, you saw Riley?"

"Yea, I saw a woman who kind of looks like that, except this one had blonde hair."

I smiled with pride. She was smart enough to change her appearance.

"Her car broke down in the post office parking lot," he said. "I gave her a jump. I thought I should trail her for a bit, make sure there wasn't nothing wrong with the Jeep."

"Jeep? She wasn't driving a yellow Beetle?"

He raised his eyebrows. "No, sir. Wasn't no Beetle." He blinked. "It was late at night and cold." He had a nasal voice. "You end up in a ditch, and it's miles to a house. No cell phone reception, neither. You're just as likely to freeze to..." He handed back my cell phone and stared at his rubber boots. Then he looked up at me, one eye closed. "Tried to throw me off as I followed. That made me think she had something to hide."

"Maybe she was afraid of you? She was a woman driving by herself at night." I would have been terrified if this guy had tailed me.

"Nah. She was hiding something for sure. At first, I thought she might be a carrier. You know, drugs? The way she tried to lose me and speeding on these icy roads. Yea, she was trying to shake me."

"But it didn't work, right?"

He sucked on the tobacco and lowered his eyes in embarrassment. "I don't know where she went, but after about an hour, I couldn't find her no more."

"Where was she headed?"

He threw his arm up and pointed somewhere far to the left. "The U.P."

"The U.P.?"

"You're not from around here, are you?"

"Chicago."

He bounced his head up and down. "The Upper Peninsula of Michigan." He held up his palm toward me, with his thumb jutting out. "See, this is the lower peninsula," he said, looking at his hand. Then he stacked his left hand sideways on top of the right, wiggling his left thumb on top. "And this, she be the U.P. It's all wilderness. Not a lot of towns. Thousands of acres of forest. Hardly anyone lives there. Good place to hide if you ask me. Good luck finding her."

RILEY

Each day I learned a new culinary skill from Matthew, who had created most of the restaurant's signature dishes. It was like taking a crash course at The Culinary Institute. One day he instructed me how to butcher meat, the next how to correctly scale fish, then how to quarter and truss a chicken. He taught me how to make my stock and butter sauces, my own *bouquet garni*. He believed chefs cultivated creativity by working with the ingredients on hand. He taught me how to work with fewer and lesser quality ingredients since supplies were hard to come by on Angelica. My mind was blowing up from all the food facts I was committing to memory.

The dinner shift was a much tighter operation. Matthew refused to let anyone smoke while they were on duty because he said smoking destroys taste buds. Hell, he barely let anyone leave the kitchen to use the bathroom. He frequently yelled at food runners who fell behind, at cooks who under or over-cooked food, at waitresses who talked too much to diners. I listened to the others complain while I secretly reveled in my private happiness.

Sharing a stove with Matthew reminded me of cooking with my father. My dad could be just as temperamental in the kitchen. Most chefs are. But Dad was gentle with us kids. Mom said that as soon as any of us could eat solid foods, Dad was spooning samples of soups and sauces into our mouths, instructing us on what herbs and spices we were tasting. Those informal lessons eventually became serious cooking sessions on Sunday afternoons when the restaurant was slow.

Dad would pick some technique he wanted to teach Ross and me, and he'd devote several hours to our instruction. It was the one time we had our father's undivided attention. Those Sunday afternoons at the restaurant are among my favorite memories. Nelson wasn't interested in cooking, but he always turned up with Mom to try the final product.

One Sunday, Dad decided to teach us how to cook one of the restaurant's more popular dishes, Dover sole amandine with Pommes châteaux. Ross and I were intimidated by the size of this giant flatfish and the seemingly manly duty of skinning it.

We watched as Dad dipped the sole's tail in hot water and the fish skin began to curl. Then, with one hard yank, our father skinned an entire side of the fish. You would have thought he'd produced a rabbit from his sleeve. Ross thought it was magic. Of course, when Ross and I tried, we failed miserably. After several attempts, Ross—who was only fifteen at the time—managed to replicate our father's technique. Ross was so pleased, he put the fish skin on his cooking cap and ran around the kitchen, blowing air out his mouth like a blowfish. I thought my father was going to scream, but he threw back his head and roared. Ross and I laughed so hard, we gasped to breathe, each making high-pitched sucking sounds.

Although Dad was a serious, Paris-trained chef, he thought

cooking should bring joy. That was why after Ross's death, Dad refused to cook anymore. He said there was no joy left in him.

Working the dinner shift brought joy back into my life. It was like a time warp. Each night I was stepping into a warm and fuzzy three-dimensional memory and wrapping myself in its senses and smells. I was living a "what-if" dream. What-if Ross hadn't been killed? What if we still had the restaurant? What if I had become a chef instead of a professional protester?

My magical thinking didn't just exist at the restaurant. I stopped thinking about the cops coming after me, or my guilt over shooting Reece, or how Finn had lied to me. I'd even dismissed any thoughts about the bandits who left Gill and me for dead. I'd stopped reading the newspapers. I told Mr. Kowalski that I no longer needed to know what was happening *out there*. He gave me a knowing smile but didn't persist.

Gill, Chay, Kayla, and Simon included me in their late-night ramblings. We skied in the moonlight, snowmobiled through the woods. The pristine beauty of the island was most evident at night. The sky somehow seemed closer, the expanse above our heads full of twinkling lights. The snowflakes lighted on us as if we were living inside a snow globe.

I was now living at Gill and Chay's house. After our encounter with the ice bandits, I no longer felt safe alone in my cottage. If Zi knew, she pretended not to. Kayla decided that if I was going to live at *Maison Gourmande*, as we'd started calling the house, she would live there too. Simon stayed about half the time, making excuses about having to attend to his plants at his parents' house. Chay and Gill had finished enough of the house that we each had our own bedroom. At first, there was only plywood on the floors, and only Gill's and Chay's rooms had real mattresses. Then we each picked out how we wanted to decorate our rooms, the paint colors, the floor treatment, the design of the wood furniture that Chay and Gill would build.

On our days off, we worked on the house during the day, and at night we cooked and drank. I felt ten years younger, with no responsibilities, no commitments, never looking beyond tomorrow.

I'd been living at the house for about three weeks. It was late February, a Sunday afternoon, a time of the week that had once been sacred in my life when Dad would give Ross and me cooking lessons. I heard bluesy rock music wafting up the stairwell. Gill always listened to '70s music when he was cooking. I walked downstairs to see what he was up to. By then, we'd fallen into a comfortable pattern. On Sunday nights Gill and I cooked.

He was kneading a ball of dough. A stockpot was simmering.

"So, we're making pasta?"

"Tortellini."

"You're not using the pasta machine?"

"We have all afternoon." He winked.

"Where are the others?"

"They went to the tavern to watch the Wolverines play."

"And they didn't ask me if I wanted to join them?"

He laughed at the thought. "'Fraid not."

"What's my job?"

He pointed at a plate of beef and pork steaks.

I heated a large skillet, added oil, and garlic. When it sizzled, I laid in the meat.

"Why don't we have tortellini on the menu?"

"Because it's so fucking labor-intensive, that's why."

I sampled the stockpot. "Wow. This is delicious. What do you have in here?"

"The usual," he said. We were all a bit secretive about our recipes.

I loved cooking with Gill, something I couldn't do at the

restaurant. At the house, Gill and I were elbow to elbow. It felt a lot like cooking with Ross. Like him, Gill was always coming up with wild ideas and enlisting my help.

I pulled the meat off the stove to let it drain. Gill covered his yellow ball of dough to let it rise. The kitchen smelled of garlic and olive oil, an aphrodisiac for chefs.

"A break?" He pulled out a bottle of whiskey from the cupboard and poured a modest amount into two glasses.

We sat down at the table. Ever since that first night we returned from Canada, we hadn't been alone. The house was always full of our little gang. That afternoon had the feel of a setup.

"How are you adjusting—to the house, to us?" he asked.

So that's why they'd disappeared.

"Am I about to get the boot?"

"Not at all. I wanted to make sure you're okay."

"I am."

"I thought maybe you might want to be alone, especially since you just ended it with . . . *Finn*." He said his name with palpable disgust.

"That's the past."

"Here's the thing." He leaned over to me as if he were sharing a bit of gossip. "I don't know anything about your past. And that's cool if you want to keep it that way—"

"You have a right to know. I'm living in your house now."

He sat back, and I could see that he was choosing what question to ask first.

"Why'd you sour on him?"

"I think he killed a man," I blurted. I wasn't sure what happened between Finn and Darren Wallack, but it couldn't have been good if the police had hidden it all these years, and Finn himself never told me. "I mean, I don't know for sure. But my gut tells me he had some part in his death. The shooter was not a good person. But he was still a human being. I just can't decide if I can forgive Finn for it."

"You're talking about the Hyde Park School shooting."

"How do you know about all that?"

"I did my homework on Alderman Finn O'Farrell. You know it's interesting that you never come up in any stories about him. You're not in any pictures or profiles. It's like you don't even exist in his life."

I exhaled. "That was part of the problem." I wanted a cigarette, but Gill didn't allow smoking in the house. "Finn always put his political aspirations before me."

"And you came to the island to get away from him?"

This was the opening I'd been craving. I so desperately wanted to tell him the truth. I wanted to have a relationship with someone that didn't involve a string of lies. But I kept hearing that voice in my head from the *Famous Female Fugitives*: "The ones who remained free the longest told no one the truth, not even their husbands." I couldn't tell Gill the whole truth, only a bit of it. And the rest I had to twist and turn so that it fit my story or the story Gill would understand given the facts he knew.

"I was afraid," I said. That much was true. "Finn is a very powerful man."

"So, you're hiding from him?" Gill was more direct than he had ever been with me.

"I sent the letter because I wanted him to stop looking for me."

"Do you plan to go back? Or are you just biding time here?"

"At first, yes, I wanted to return. But now I don't know." It was an honest answer.

"O.K.," he said slowly. "That's fair. But here's what we need—"

"We? You've discussed this with Chay and the others?"

"Of course. We don't have secrets amongst us or in this house."

So, the others had put him up to this little *tete-a-tete.*

"Stay here as long as you need," he said. "We want you to feel safe on the island. But if you want to be a part of us, we need to know whether you want to build a life here... with us."

"Wow. This...feels like an ultimatum," I said. "I thought we were all just having a good time."

"We are having a good time." He put his hand on mine on the table. "We just don't want to get emotionally involved with someone who's going to disappear."

FINN

It had been a week since I'd returned from Luck, where I had *not* been lucky. Riley's trail ended somewhere in Michigan's Upper Peninsula's wilderness, which I learned was a million acres of remote land. During Detroit's heyday, the U.P. had thrived as the playground of car executives and well-paid union workers, a place of summer residences. "Camps," they called them, though many were sprawling mansions, lodges with quaint Native American names. After the car industry went global, the U.P. population dwindled, leaving ghost towns in the wake of the exodus. Now Nature was reclaiming the land; trees grew through the roofs of abandoned houses; vines and scrub brush swallowed up buildings along the two-lane roads that wound through forests of giant pines.

I'd driven those roads, hundreds and hundreds of miles of patched, re-patched, and unpatched asphalt, as bumpy and pockmarked as the surface of the moon. It was a beautiful, haunting place where you could stand on pristine beaches and gaze out at a lake that looked like the ocean and not see a soul for miles. I would count the minutes, ten, sometimes twenty, and, at night, even hours, before I encountered another vehicle on the road. I felt silly for having packed my gun. I sped past inland lakes during the day, reflecting the sky in iridescent shades of green and blue; their shores crowded with sweeping pines, spaces that anywhere else would have been overrun by development.

I stopped and talked with people, lifting my iPhone to their eyes. "Have you seen this woman?" I asked over and over again. They reacted the same, glancing warily from the screen to my face, taking a step back, and shaking their heads. She could have been my wife. I could have been a religious man looking for my missing spouse. But the look I got communicated a singular judgment: I was not to be trusted. I had a funny accent, wore city clothes, and drove a fancy car. If my wife or girlfriend were missing, it's because she didn't want to be found. At least, that was how I interpreted their reactions.

After several days I returned to Chicago, demoralized, worn out, and defeated. I called the mayor to apologize, saying only that I'd had a family emergency. He was angry, fuming. If the election weren't in ten days, he said, he would have dumped me from the ticket. As it was, he and I were stuck together, our relationship seriously frayed. I tried making it up to him by spending most of the remaining time campaigning. Once we won, he wouldn't remember any of this. That's how politicians' memories work.

At my ward office, I was met by stacks of mail. I found a large envelope with no return address. Inside were several photocopied pages. One photocopy was of an envelope with my address but no return address. Another page captured the outside of a card. It had a picture of a snow-covered forest overlooking a blue lake. It was the same scene I had driven past for days. The third page was a letter. I recognized the cursive, loopy handwriting. But I was not prepared for what she'd written. The message was unmistakable.

It's over.

It wasn't what I wanted to read. I wanted her to write that she still thought of me and missed me and that she loved me. Was that so inconceivable? I wasn't a man given to emotion, but I felt something break within me. My eyes brimmed, and my throat thickened. The page shook in my hand.

There was another sheet of paper in the big envelope. It was a typed letter addressed to me that said that the writer knew where Riley was. If I expected him—and I assumed it was a him—to keep quiet about her and her letter, I needed to send a money order for $7,000 to a post box in St. Marie, Canada. If I didn't send it within seven days, the letter writer would send Riley's letter to the *Chicago Tribune*. For $10,000, the blackmailer would tell me where Riley was living.

I could see from the Canadian postmark; the package had been mailed fifteen days earlier. It was past his deadline. Either he was full of shit, or Dan Mackay already had copies. If he and his editors needed outside confirmation about Riley and me, this was it.

I felt disheartened. The miles and months had broken me. The parade of wary looks on strangers' faces had crushed my spirit. I stuffed the blackmailer's demands and photocopies of Riley's letter into my leather journal. It didn't matter where Riley was. She wasn't interested in me. She'd given no reason for breaking up, but I knew. It wasn't the miles that separated us or Reece's shooting or the police looking for her.

It was because I'd never told her about Darren Wallack.

RILEY

My shift at the restaurant had ended and I'd begged off from walking over to the bar for a nightcap with the others. I so rarely had the house to myself these days. I had just gotten into my Jeep when he appeared in my rearview mirror. He wore a ski mask, but I still recognized him. I shrieked, but it wasn't loud enough for anyone to hear.

"You look so much more attractive with blood in your hair," he said.

"Fuck you." I turned around to face him in the backseat. He stuck his gun in my face.

"Ah, ah, ah. I wouldn't be so unkind to the man who is holding a weapon for killing bears." His accent sounded more ominous in the dark.

"What do you want?" I started digging through my wallet. I'd been paid that day and knew I could throw a few hundred at him.

He put a gloved hand on my arm. "There'll be plenty of time for that later."

"I'm not going anywhere with you." I opened the door and jumped out.

"Get back here!"

I ran through the parking lot. A blast pierced the air. I didn't turn around. The next shot wouldn't be a warning. I dove behind Gill's truck and watched from underneath the carriage as he came closer. I took off for the next truck, my shoulders and head bent low. The next blast was so close that it left my ears ringing.

"It doesn't have to go like this," he shouted. "I just want to talk. Maybe you'd like me to have this conversation with Gill, the two of you together, like last time?"

I could hear his heavy snow boots gnawing through the snow and the nylon of his snow pants swishing as he neared. I scanned the parking lot for my next cover. There was a long open expanse before the woods. I could hide in there. If only I could make it.

The bandit was standing at the front of Simon's truck. I was at the back, curled up with my feet perched on the bumper so he couldn't see my boots under the carriage. He fired again. The truck rocked and slumped to one side. He'd blown out one of the oversized tires. I held onto the back of the truck. If my feet slipped off the icy bumper, he'd know where I was. The next shot took out another tire. His boots crunched through the packed snow as he moved toward me. I'd have to run the length of the truck without him knowing, sprint through the open expanse, then jump down into the grasses that extended to the woods.

As he approached the middle of the truck, I let one toe slip from the bumper and lightly touched the snow, then the other foot. I crept to the other side of the truck and sprinted.

"I'm not fucking around. Stop, or I will kill you!"

I pressed harder, running through the lot. And then I heard a boom. It didn't sound like the same gunfire. I stopped and turned around. In the yellow light above the back porch, I saw the silhouette of Matthew, a shotgun in his hand. Behind me, two hundred feet away, was a dark lump in the snow.

FINN

It was the Sunday before the election. I'd been out late at a campaign rally. Since Riley's letter, I couldn't shake this terrible depression. I longed for sleep even after being in bed for ten and twelve hours. It was like my body wanted to hibernate and wake up when this was all over. That morning, my cell phone began buzzing earlier than usual. I rolled over, but it kept going off.

When I finally looked, there were dozens of texts—from the mayor, from Rod, from reporters asking me for comment on a *Chicago Tribune* story. I knew what had happened even before I picked up the paper off my front steps and pulled off the blue plastic wrap. There, above the fold, in big, bold letters, was the headline I'd dreaded for so long:

Vice Mayor Candidate Linked to Woman of Interest.

Underneath was a photo of Riley and me kissing and another of her looking up with dread at the blue light camera.

The story was a compilation of everything Dan Mackay

could dig up, mostly innuendo and gossip. Of course, all of it was attributed to "police sources." O'Brien and Davies didn't have enough evidence to charge me, so they decided to discredit me. In the process of ruining me, they'd branded Riley a criminal. The story only said Reece was recovering but didn't include a comment from him. Lousy journalism. I turned off my phone and went back to bed, overcome with malaise, knowing that nothing I said could change an election in two days.

RILEY

I ran to his body. Matthew was already there, pulling off the man's ski mask. The snow around the body was turning red. His face looked familiar, but I couldn't place him.

"It's the game warden," Matthew said, looking up at me for an explanation. His eyes were dilated, his breath raspy. "His name is John Baptiste. He's been a regular customer for years. Why the hell was he shooting at you?"

"Get Gill," was all I could say. I stared at the man's face. He had a patrician nose, a hard jawline, and dark, sinister eyes that were open to the sky as if he were taking in the stars.

"What happened?" Matthew grabbed me by my shoulders and shook me.

I looked into his face but couldn't summon the strength to say anything.

Matthew ran toward the tavern and left me next to the body. It felt too familiar. Another man shot, an entry wound to his chest, blood seeping from his body. How many times was the universe going to bring me to this point? How could someone who hates guns so much be surrounded by them? And now my life had been saved by one.

I knew he was dead, but I was terrified to be alone with his corpse, afraid he might summon up the ghost to grab me. I'd read that the brain remained functioning for several minutes after death. I stared at his open eyes.

"I don't know if you can still hear me," I said. "You left us to die in the woods. We'd done nothing to you. We didn't deserve that, and I didn't deserve you shooting at me. You brought this on yourself. So, don't go fucking haunting me, *asshole*."

I heard voices behind me.

Chay reached me first. He saw the body and threw up his hands. "Mother Fucker!" he yelled at the lifeless body. He stomped his boots in the snow. "Mother Fucker!"

Gill wrapped his arms around me. "Did he hurt you?"

I buried my face into his coat. I felt nauseous and tired. So tired. If they would leave me alone, I could lay down in the snow and fall asleep.

Matthew stood in the beam of the parking lot lights, casting a shadow over us. "You guys need to start talking. We don't have much time. I've called the Sheriff."

Gill quickly recounted how the game warden and another man had chased us into the woods, how they'd tied us up, poured blood over us, and left us to die because the two men couldn't find any drugs on our snowmobile.

"That won't do," Matthew said, shaking his head. "I know it's probably the truth—or a version of it." He looked each of us in the eyes. "But that will just make him question whether you *are* drug dealers. Riley, just say you don't know who he is. You work in the kitchen, so that's believable. Don't mention Gill or the Smuggler's Road or any of that."

When Grand Portage Sheriff Kustwin arrived, he interviewed me in the dining room while one of his deputies interviewed Matthew in the breakfast room. Kustwin asked the same question over and over. "Why was this man chasing you with a gun?"

I told him the game warden must have confused me with someone else, but it was clear the Sheriff didn't believe me.

I knew what Matthew was saying in the next room: he was doing inventory when he heard a gunshot. He thought it was someone shooting at a wolf. After the second shot, he grabbed the shotgun Ginny kept in her office and opened the back door in time to see the game warden aiming at me.

IT WAS NEARLY 6 A.M., and the sun was shining when the Sheriff said we were done. Customers had already gathered in the parking lot, no doubt hoping for tidbits about the shooting. News travels fast on the island, even without cell phones and internet service.

In my room at Gill's house, I lay on the bed in my clothes, though they were bloody and smelled of death. Gill knocked on my door and tiptoed in. Without speaking, he took off my boots, socks, and jeans. Then we climbed under the sheets, and he held me as I fell asleep.

For two days, I drifted in and out of sleep. But Gill was always there. I could feel his skin against mine. When I finally woke, I looked over at Gill, who was watching me. I vaguely remembered him applying cold compresses to my head and whispering soothing words.

"You're awake," he said, kissing my forehead.

I rubbed my head. "I have a whopping headache."

"You need water. I tried to get you to drink, but all you wanted to do was sleep."

I started to get out of bed. "I need to get to work."

Gill pulled me back. "It's 10 a.m., and even if it were later, Ginny doesn't want you and Matthew coming into the restaurant for a few days."

"What?"

"It's just a sign of respect. And to keep the fucking gawkers away."

I lay back down and stared at the ceiling, wondering what I should do now. I made mental lists of all the things I needed to pack from my cottage, what I could take, and what I should leave. I imagined saying goodbye, and that's when I got choked up.

"It's not safe here anymore, Gill," I said.

"It'll be fine. The Sheriff did what he had to do. You didn't pull the trigger. If anyone is going to be further questioned, it's Matthew."

"But the cops will go through the game warden's things. They'll find my letter to Finn." The letter connected me to a politician, and if the Sheriff connected the dots, he'd know I wasn't Riley Kennedy, the woman on my driver's license.

Gill laughed. "We have it now. While the Sheriff was questioning you, Chay and I went to Baptiste's cabin. We found your letter. There were many other letters and photos of people in compromising situations, with people who were not their partners, stuff like that. Chay is calling it the 'den of indiscretions.' I'd always heard that Baptiste bullied people into giving him bribes. It was for small stuff, not having a fishing license, shit like that. I didn't realize it was much bigger. Now the Sheriff has evidence."

"Why do you think Baptiste came back to shoot me?"

Gill shook his head. "We were loose ends, Riley. He probably would have shot me too, but Chay is like my shadow. He had better odds getting to you."

It was another opening for me to tell Gill what was really at stake. But I saw the way he looked at me, and I knew all that would change. I wanted to believe that Baptiste's death was just a speed bump in our lives.

A FEW DAYS LATER, Mr. Kowalski pulled me behind the deli counter and showed me the *Chicago Tribune's* front page. Staring back at me was an image of Finn and me kissing along with my mugshot from my last arrest.

I slumped against Mr. Kowalski. The story was dated two days before the election—nearly a week ago. Finn probably lost. And now Reece would be fired, too, if he hadn't already been let go. That one bullet I fired had killed the careers of two men.

"It's going to be okay," he said, sounding like my dad—which made me want to cry.

"By the way, your friend lost the election," Mr. Kowalski said. "I heard the results on the radio."

I tried to swallow the lump in my throat.

"No one will know," he said.

"What about people on the island?" I said, looking up at him, my voice sounding like a child's.

"Darling, most people don't read the *Chicago Tribune*. Besides, this is the only copy on the island. I burned the others."

"What about the Sheriff? I'm sure he gets the paper at the office."

"I wouldn't be so sure. Chicago isn't the center of the universe here. It's eight hours and a lifetime away. And the Sheriff, he ain't as smart as he looks. Just the same, don't go to the mainland for a while."

"But my picture is plastered on the front page. On the

internet, it will live forever. I can never hide from this." I shook the newspaper.

"Riley, you don't look anything like that photo." He grabbed a small mirror from behind the counter. "Look at yourself. You have long blonde hair. The woman in these photos has short black hair."

I stared at my reflection. My hair had grown to my shoulders. I'd kept it blonde. The woman in the mirror did not resemble the woman in the newspaper, for more reasons than what Mr. Kowalski could articulate.

"If I don't look like this photo, then how did you recognize me?"

He chuckled one of his belly-shaking laughs. "Darling, we've known who you were the moment you stepped on this island."

"What?"

"Oh sure, we didn't know your real name right away. But we knew your kind—someone who needed sheltering. In time, we filled in the details. You were driving a car registered in your real name." He narrowed his eyes, searching for a reaction. "You still don't get it, do you? The island isn't like the world out there." He pointed toward the mainland. "Haven't you learned that by now? Your secret is safe here. You are among friends."

I didn't believe in fairies and magical creatures or mystical places. Darren Wallack had killed that part of me a long time ago. The island wasn't an enchanted place; it was a twisted microcosm of the real world. Islanders had self-selected to be here. They wanted to be left alone, and, in turn, they would leave others alone. That was the island's implied contract. It's not that they were protecting my secret from the world. It's that they didn't care. If Reece had died, I think they would have thought I'd had a reason to kill him, not that I was a murderer.

Mr. Kowalski stressed that with my story and picture

floating on the web, the island was the only place I was safe. As long as I lived in the island's bubble, no one would find me; no one would know what I had done. His logic made sense, but then again, I was looking for any reason to stay, no matter how convoluted.

LOOKING BACK, that was the moment when real denial set in. I was living under a fake name with fake documents and had become involved in a homicide. Most people would have disappeared—started over elsewhere. But a constant drumbeat from Gill, Mr. Kowalski, and the others persuaded me that Baptiste's murder would blow over. The Sheriff and his deputies would go back to their world and leave us alone. And that might have happened—if I'd been the only one on the island living a double life.

FINN

After the election, I moped around the house for two days, ignoring all phone calls. Then I went back to work. I was still an alderman. I had a job to do, even if my political future looked bleak. Losing the election had defeated my American sense of invincibility, this belief that working hard for something is all that is required for success. The problem with that formula is that it doesn't take into account the actions of others. And when you are a politician, there are lots of others.

After the embarrassing defeat, I decided I was going to live how I wanted. No longer would I spend long nights at the office or take work home at night. What for? I also decided to take a more prominent role in raising my kids. I was no longer satisfied with sharing them only two weekends a month. Amazingly, Diana agreed to let the kids stay over a couple of nights a week. Although she never said, I think she pitied me after my defeat and the embarrassing coverage over Riley.

IT WAS A FRIDAY NIGHT, two weeks after the election. I came home, took off my suit, put on my pajamas and my favorite robe. I looked forward to a well-deserved night of binge-watching. I was in a good mood, the first in a long time. I made myself a peanut butter and jelly sandwich and poured a glass of milk. Norma Rae circled at my feet, whining. I poured some milk into her bowl.

When I flipped on the dining room lights, I was startled to see Mr. Mailer sitting at the dining room table and dropped my glass of milk. The glass shattered, and creamy liquid splattered across the parquet floor.

"What the hell are you doing here?" I stooped to sop up the milk with a puny napkin.

"Leave it," he said. "We got more important things to discuss."

I sat down at the table. A tumbler of Scotch was in front of him.

"You want to tell me something?" he asked. "Appears you've been racking up the miles lately. Anything to report?"

"How did you know? Forget it," I said. "I don't want to know how you know where I was or how you get in my house because this is over between us."

He laughed cynically. "It's over when I say it's over."

I shook my head. "Not this time. I'm done. You can't ruin me any more than I am."

"Yeah, man. Sorry about the election." He seemed to mean it. "Going after Snow White and you in public was really low, even for CPD. I'm shocked the paper published that bullshit so close to the election."

"I'm not going to argue with you on that one."

I reached into the oversized pocket of my robe, pulled out the leather journal that I'd kept with me for weeks, and handed him the photocopy of Riley's breakup letter. I hoped it was as clear to him that Riley had no intention of coming back.

His facial muscles drooped, and his eyebrows cinched as he read. I'm sure he'd come to the house to threaten me, to increase the scare factor. But what else can you do to a broken man?

"Good luck finding her," I said, meeting his eyes. "I'm done chasing a woman who doesn't want to be found."

RILEY

The ice road shut down in March, but there was less panic with evidence of Spring. Layer by layer, the island thawed. Crocuses and daffodils punched through crusty snow. In late April, the first ferry of the season sailed into the harbor. Angelica's little downtown rippled with energy as people reconnected and summer crews reassembled. The tavern grew more crowded as Snowbirds returned to their summer homes and to make repairs. Boards disappeared from the windows of three-season cottages; chains came down from private roads and driveways. By the end of May, all that winter dreariness seemed like a distant memory.

Four months had passed since our disastrous trek to Canada, three months since Matthew had killed the game warden, and I had been outed in Chicago as "a person of interest" in Reece's shooting. After that, I couldn't go back home, not for three years, until the statute of limitations had run out. It wasn't just to save my own ass. I'd read that Reece was still a cop. As long as the police couldn't prove I was at the shooting, they couldn't fire him for lying.

The Sheriff's investigation into the game warden's death dragged on, keeping everyone in our little band on edge, especially Gill. I knew he was waiting for me to tell him whether I would stay. After Baptiste's death, I was less fearful of being alone and began spending a few nights a week at my cottage. But we knew that Baptiste's partner was still out there, perhaps waiting to take revenge.

Ginny urged the Sheriff to close the case, arguing that it was bad for business. Actually, business had picked up since the shooting. Both Islanders and Snowbirds wanted to see where Baptiste, who had been highly unpopular, met his end. Finally, the Sheriff ruled Baptiste's death a justifiable homicide.

A few weeks later, Simon's parents' 50-foot sailboat came out of storage. The weather was still too cold for sailing, so the boat remained in the harbor. The group spent our days off bundled in coats on its deck, drinking wine pilfered from the restaurant, and smoking weed, of which Simon always seemed to have in plentiful supply. I had this strange sense that we were all waiting for something to happen.

THE FIRST SCORCHING day in June—when everyone forgets their modesty and starts stripping off clothes—I stopped by the deli. Mr. Kowalski was busy packaging a tourist's meat order while her two kids ran underfoot.

I grabbed a couple of cigarette packs, laid what I owed next to the register, and was about to leave when Mr. Kowalski yelled after me.

"Wait!" He wiped his hands on his dirty apron and ushered me outside into the blaring sun.

"You hearing anything at the restaurant?" he whispered.

"Like what?"

He shifted his weight and looked over his shoulder, though we were alone. "The Sheriff and his deputies been coming around, asking questions..."

"Yeah? It's an election year. They want to appear engaged."

"They been asking about Javier."

"And?"

"Today, they rounded up a bunch of Mexicans—illegals—in the woods."

I hadn't given a lot of credence to Mr. Kowalski's growing insinuations about Javier, chalking it up to old grievances and a bit of racism.

Mr. Kowalski wrapped his arm around my shoulder. "You be careful, girl. You hear?"

I nodded distractedly. Did he know Javier had traded my car for a Jeep and a handful of fake IDs?

DINNER SERVICE that night was slow. I busied myself stocking and taking inventory. I had just come up from cold storage when I saw Simon leaning against the prep table, lazily watching Gill blacken a walleye and Chay sear two pork chops. He yawned loudly and, with one graceful motion, dipped his hand into his pocket and retrieved a small whiskey bottle—the kind flight attendants sell—slugging back several mouthfuls.

"How about a sail tonight, guys?" Simon said, a little too loudly. "We could set off early—as soon as we dump these losers." He nodded toward the dining room where a tourist couple and their two wailing children were eating dinner. "We could sail to Thunder Bay."

By the time Matthew had finished calling in food orders, we had swept the floors, washed the dishes, put away the food, and were slumped over the prep station waiting for the family to finish their ice cream.

"You should go," I told Matthew. "Perhaps sometime this century, they'll leave."

He stared warily at the five of us. "You guys look like you're hatching a plot."

I grabbed Matthew's elbow and escorted him to the back door. Death and coverup have a way of bonding strangers; Matthew and I had become a tight-knit team.

"We'll be fine," I whispered. "You don't want them to think you don't trust me, do you?"

He hesitated. "Be careful this weekend. I have a bad feeling..." He looked back at the group. "Lots of people talking, making assumptions. There's an angry vibe on the island. Watch your back."

"Kowalski told me the Sheriff arrested some undocumented people living in the woods."

"I hear more arrests are coming. Javier may finally get his due."

I felt guilty for not defending Javier. Whatever his crimes were, he had saved me. Without him, I wouldn't have my island life. I wanted to warn him that he was in danger. But I hadn't seen him in several days and figured he had heard the same rumors and left the island.

That night as we walked to the marina, I could hear the crickets chirping in the prairie grass punctuated by whoops and hollers from Tom's Burnt Down Cafe, the remains of a bar that burned years ago. In the warm months, locals and tourists mingled in the bizarre structure that resembled a circus tent with a trailer in the middle.

Rocking back and forth in the harbor was Simon's parents' sailboat. It was white and blue with tall masts. The boat struck me as a throwback to the Kennedy era—classic and expensive.

The few times we'd slept on the boat while docked in the harbor, the guys had been kind enough to give Kayla and me the sleeping berths. Chay and Gill took the couches in the main cabin. Simon typically slept bundled up on deck.

Jacked up on strong coffee, Simon took his position at the helm, a large steering wheel. We cast off the ropes tied to the dock. Simon steered us into the dark waters of Lake Superior. Gill and Chay rushed around on deck putting up the sails. Kayla and I watched with admiration. We had no idea what they were doing or why.

I turned around to admire our island. The shadowy mass seemed no more than a clump of trees in the lake illuminated by lightning bugs. We navigated due north, cutting through rough waters, passing the uninhabited Disciple Islands, their lonely lighthouses run by computers instead of the hermit families who once tended to their lights.

Snug in our jackets, we sat on deck and sipped wine from plastic cups. Chay cranked up the music, playing old eighties tunes. Simon passed a joint. In deep water, we scanned the blackness for Isle Royal and Canada. The air smelled like rain. The moon illuminated our faces.

At that moment, it felt like a dream—as if I'd inherited someone else's life.

But that's the thing about dreams; eventually, you have to wake up.

RILEY

I felt a nudge on my shoulder and smelled the exhalation of whiskey and coffee.

"Come on, Riley," Gill coaxed. "You gotta see this. Red sky at night."

I groaned and rolled over, but he shook my shoulder again. "Come on; you'll regret it if you don't."

I flicked on the battery-powered lamp beside the bed. Gill's face was lit up with excitement, his tawny hair matted from the spray of the lake. It was the most charged I'd seen him in weeks. He grabbed my hand and pulled me toward the door. The hull was dark except for a small light at the captain's desk where Simon consulted maps and plotted our course. The high frequency radio crackled like a CB.

When I reached the deck, there above our heads were the famed Northern Lights, looping sheets of red and green auroras undulated like theater curtains. Shards of fuchsia flickered along the edges of the horizon. We gazed up at the sky, transfixed. One thrust of light after another fell toward the water.

We huddled on the deck, Gill sharing a blanket with me; Chay spooning with Kayla. It was one of the few times she allowed him to get close to her.

"This is what life is about," Gill whispered. I could feel the warmth of his breath against my cheek.

I leaned against his chest and pulled the cover to my chin. "You probably only get a handful of moments like these in a lifetime."

My mind drifted to Finn, and I wondered what he was doing. I knew he had once loved me. I had loved him too. I still loved him. But when I thought of him, which was often, it made me sad. Why had he lied? Why hadn't he trusted me with his secret?

After I'd written my letter to Finn, I thought it would free up something within me. When Finn didn't get the letter, it left me angry and nowhere to turn with these conflicted feelings. Now when I thought of Finn, I thought of Darren Wallack. I kept seeing Finn in a room with that monster. I made up conversations, things they said to each other, what they did, but no matter what the scenarios were, they always ended with a gun to Darren's head. The worst day of my life was now entangled with the man I loved.

As I lay next to Gill staring up at the light show above us, I again thought of that truism: *Love the one you're with.*

I was with Gill now. His arms wrapped around me; he smelled like baby powder and sweat. I looked over at Chay and Kayla, who were kissing. Simon clenched the steering wheel, the odd man out.

I WOKE TO A PRE-DAWN CHILL. Chay was monitoring the autopilot and radar while Simon slept below. Gill and I had fallen asleep lying on our sides, his arms wrapped around me. Now he was snoring against the back of my head. Chay and I exchanged sleepy grins. Gentle waves were lapping at the sides of the boat. Fog had wrapped its ghostly fingers around us. Visibility was maybe twenty-five feet.

Soon the sun and wind emerged, and so did the rest of the crew. Chay whipped up egg frittatas with chorizo sausage. We spent the day dashing from bow to stern, raising and lowering sails, tacking this way and that.

Gill walked me around the boat, explained the various sails, and showed me how to tie a bowline knot, the most important sailor's knot, he said. He held up the metal clips on the end of the two safety lines hanging from my life jacket and demonstrated how to properly clip them to the jackline that runs from bow to stern on both sides of the boat.

He wrapped his hands around mine and unclipped and clipped the metal clamp affixed to the nylon jackline. "Feel how it snaps to close? Wait for the snap or you may find yourself in the water," he laughed in that goofy way of his I was starting to adore.

"What's this?" I pointed to a horizontal metal arm that rested in the air, about the height of our heads. "It holds the bottom of the sail away from the mast," he explained. "And when it is loose, it can swing violently. They call it the boom, by the way, because 'boom' is the sound it makes when it hits your head. And we wouldn't want anything to hurt your pretty head." He kissed my forehead, his lips lingering. He now smelled of sweat and salt from the sea, an enticing cocktail of manliness. I felt this sudden desire spread through my body, an overwhelming urge to touch him, to feel his skin on mine, to be swept up in the moment. I still ached for Finn, but Gill was the antidote to that pain.

After my safety lesson, Gill and I lay on the upper deck, soaking in the warmth of the sun, the wind in our faces, the spray of the lake on our skin. We sipped on champagne and watched billowy clouds float lazily above us. My chest swelled with an unfamiliar happiness.

"I could live like this forever," Gill said. He enveloped my hand in his, and I could feel the callouses from the sailboat ropes and the nubby scars from kitchen knives. Neither of us moved for a long while, afraid to disturb this rare feeling of joy.

"I hope Ginny doesn't move you back to the morning shift," he said eventually.

I sat up. "Why would she?"

"You don't know?" Gill jerked up.

I shook my head. And just like that, the elation of happiness deflated. A wave of anxiousness rippled through my stomach. I tasted bile at the back of my throat. I liked working with our little crew at night. I loved that it felt like we lived and worked in a commune.

"I assume the only reason Ginny hasn't fired Javier is that she's cooperating with the Sheriff's investigation," Gill said. "The Sheriff interviewed just about everyone at the restaurant. I'm surprised he hasn't talked to you. But then again, the Sheriff doesn't trust you after what happened to Baptiste. Besides that, you're new."

"What does that mean?"

"It means you don't know island secrets. Javier has been running his little scheme for years. No one would have given him up if he hadn't beat up Gabe Kowalski during the blizzard."

"We don't know for certain he did that." I wanted to say that turning in Javier was as good as turning me in. It was another occasion when I longed to tell Gill everything. But he was finally opening up after all that had happened with Baptiste's death.

"All you need to know is that he deserted us during the storm," he said. "I heard he had some illegals stashed in a house without heat, and he had to go save them."

"You would rather he stayed at the restaurant during the storm instead of saving people's lives?"

Gill stared at something in the distance. "There's more to it than that," he said and scrambled to his feet. "Come on; we need to adjust the boom."

We sailed into Thunder Bay early the next morning. Gill, Chay, Kayla, and I went ashore to shop, leaving Simon to take care of registering the boat with the authorities. We were all charged with the promise of the evening and excitedly talked up the restaurants and bars we planned to explore.

That excitement quickly turned to fear when two hours later we walked onto the dock and saw two men in dark windbreakers stamped with Canada Border Patrol on Simon's boat. I turned around to leave, but was stopped by another border guard, who suddenly appeared behind us.

"Come with me," he said and held out his hands, corralling us toward the boat.

Simon was sitting on the deck, flanked by several Border Patrol agents. He'd hardly slept. Now he looked haggard and shifty-eyed.

"What's going on?" demanded Gill.

"You've entered the country illegally," said an officer, a red-haired woman with pasty skin. "Your friend has been denied access to Canadian ports, but he disregarded our rules and docked here anyway."

We watched as half a dozen officers who had rifled through the hull appeared on deck with black bags filled with our things. Afterward, the patrol agents told us to retrieve our IDs and come with them to the bureau downtown.

Simon was handcuffed and whisked away in a Border Patrol SUV. Officers loaded Kayla and Chay in a van. Gill and I were escorted to a black Suburban with tinted windows. I leaned over and whispered to Gill: "Do you know anything about this? What's Simon up to?"

Gill shook his head. "Don't say *anything*. Chay will call the reservation's attorney."

For the rest of the ride, he avoided my eyes and stared straight ahead.

When we arrived at a large warehouse, a guard took me to an office with a picture window that looked out at throngs of people waiting to be processed.

"Have a seat." The officer gestured to a plastic chair across from his desk. "Do you have any idea why you're here?" He peered over tiny spectacles that were too narrow for his chubby face.

"I was told we didn't register. I honestly didn't know we had to." Panic was building in my voice.

"Well, according to our records, this is your boat's third entry into this harbor this month. Does that surprise you?"

I stammered. "It's . . . not *my* boat."

"All right then. Were you on the boat on its previous trips here?"

When did Simon have time to go without us? I started counting the instances Simon mysteriously disappeared or claimed he had to meet up with his parents or friends visiting the island. Surely, he couldn't have made the trip twice without us?

"There must be some mistake. This is our first time." I didn't sound convincing.

The agent glared at me. "Young lady, we take lying very

seriously." His jowls were now resting on his chest as he studied paperwork in a folder. "What would you say if I told you we found some interesting packages on *your friend's* boat? Perhaps you'd remember something you hadn't recalled earlier?"

I swallowed hard. He was fishing for information, perhaps stalling as agents tried to intimidate the others. We all smoked marijuana, but pot was like tobacco on the island. What else was Simon into? Heroin? Cocaine? Ecstasy? Crystal Meth? I remembered him passing a brown bag once to someone at the back door. In another fragment of memory, a scruffy-looking stranger tapped Simon on the shoulder at the tavern, and, without a word, the two headed to the men's bathroom. It looked like a gay hookup. I didn't ask questions.

The agent held up my Michigan driver's license. "Where's your passport?"

I shrugged. "I don't have one. I didn't know I needed one just to go sailing."

"Doesn't anybody read in America? You've needed a passport to enter Canada since 911. This isn't even an enhanced driver's license."

There was a knock on the door, and the agent abruptly left. A few minutes later, he returned, grinning. "We're moving you to another location. We found some interesting things on your boat."

"It's not *my* boat."

"Yes, well, you can argue your case before a magistrate." The officer took me by the arm, as if I were an errant child, and escorted me to a holding cell.

"What am I being charged with?" I demanded.

"We don't have to decide that until you appear tomorrow," he taunted.

I lay on a cot in the holding cell and stared at the ceiling.

How the hell was I going to extricate myself from *this mess*? Once the Canadians learned I was on the run from Chicago police and that I'd shot a cop—how likely were they to believe I was innocent of drug trafficking?

RILEY

Several hours passed before a young female officer appeared at my cell door.

"We're releasing you," she said in her nasally Canadian accent.

I sat up on the bunk. "What?"

"Your friends can fill you in."

She led me to the lobby where Gill, Chay, and Kayla—eyeliner smeared across her cheeks—were waiting. Kayla threw her arms around me and sobbed, her tears wetting my neck. It was the most affection she'd ever shown me. Then Gill wrapped me in his arms. I started laughing so hard and then crying. I had eluded more than just the Canadian Border Patrol. Standing there in the official government lobby with its red plastic chairs, its outdated magazines, and its Canadian posters with smiling, pale faces, I could hardly contain my joy.

In the taxi van back to the harbor, Kayla filled us in while Simon sat mute next to her. Simon apparently hadn't secured the proper documents to dock, a minor infraction, she explained. But the Canadian Border patrol, which had been tracking his trips, thought it had nabbed a major drug dealer. Chay's stash of Ziploc bags containing mysterious plants he used for cooking seemed to confirm their suspicions, especially when Chay couldn't identify the herbs. They were from his mother's garden, he interjected. The Ojibwe often used herbs in their ceremonies, including some which had a hallucinatory effect. Luckily, Chay's mother was a devout Catholic who refused to grow anything illegal. Simon paid a $1,200 fine and agreed to leave immediately.

As Simon steered us out of the harbor, he still seemed sullen and moody. It was dark by then, and all we could see was a vast black sky in front of us. We were exhausted. At the wheel, Simon smoked cigarette after cigarette.

We were all sitting on the deck, scanning the water for any partially submerged debris that might strike the boat when Simon piped up.

"They were right, you know," he said, his face shrouded in the darkness. "How do you think I bankroll this lifestyle—the liquor, the expense of sailing to Canada?" His voice was teeming with contempt.

"Aren't your parents wealthy?" I asked.

"They don't give me a dime. My father says I have to *earn* my inheritance. Well, I don't need *his* money."

"But you're a waiter," Kayla said. She sounded so uncharacteristically simple.

"It's a cover, sweet cheeks," he said. "As much I like hanging out with you, serving that shit at the restaurant is the worst part of my day."

Gill flicked on the deck light. "What the fuck are you talking about?" He stooped within inches of Simon's face.

Simon brushed past Gill and began pacing the deck. I hoped the boat was on autopilot.

"You all are so fucking naïve." He was laughing, a contemptuous howl that made me shudder. "I've been transporting marijuana for years. In the summer, I use this boat, and in the winter, I snowmobile across the lake. No one has ever questioned me. Until now."

Simon's skilled navigation on the snowmobile between the No Man's Islands now made sense. It also explained why the ice bandits were waiting; they knew he was transporting drugs.

Simon's smugness, his casualness about getting us tangled up with his illicit dealings—twice—enraged me and, from the looks on their faces, the rest of the group. Growing and selling pot on the island was not risky, but transporting it across international waters and involving your friends was perilous. His illegal activities had garnered the attention of the game warden who'd nearly killed Gill and me. It had opened the island to intrusion from law enforcement. We had all been detained and threatened in Canada. And now, once the Sheriff got word of our troubles in Canada, he'd likely be all over us.

Chay and Gill lunged at Simon, wrestling him to the floor. Gill held him in a chokehold. Chay repeatedly punched him in the stomach and face. "You asshole! Who the fuck do you think you are?" Chay yelled.

Kayla jumped on Gill's back, trying to pull down his arms.

"Stop it! He didn't mean it," she screamed. "Nothing happened! C'mon, you guys. We're friends. Don't do this!"

Gill released Simon. He and Chay stood back: Simon's face was cut, his lip swollen, one eye had nearly ballooned shut. He leaned over the side of the boat and spit blood.

Simon wiped his bloody face with his shirt. Gill and Chay went below deck. I followed.

We could hear Kayla above us cooing and tending to Simon's wounds. I wondered what angered Chay more: Simon had fooled him, or Kayla had sided with Simon over him.

"We can't go to the Sheriff," I protested.

Chay looked at me as if I were stupid. "Of course, we're not going to the Sheriff. That's not how we handle things on the island. But we can't let this go. We have to tell the tribe council." His uncle served on the council along with several other relatives.

"Why do we have to do anything? Why is it our business that he's selling?" I said. "The only thing we need to be concerned about is getting off this boat as soon as possible. Guys, he's not like the only one selling weed."

Gill sighed loudly. "We smoke it; somebody's got to grow it."

"But they don't have to deliver while you're riding on their fucking boat," Chay argued.

"Or while you're riding with them on a frozen lake in the middle of the night," Gill said. He clearly blamed Simon for our encounter with the game warden, Baptiste.

"So, let's keep it between us," I said. I didn't need the Sheriff asking me more questions.

We all nodded, and I headed off to bed.

Moonlight streamed through the porthole, bathing the tiny berth with light. Disparate feelings raged inside me: joy that the Canadians had released us; anger that Simon had lied to us; worry that his disloyalty would cause suspicion to fall on all of us; sadness that the group was breaking apart. I couldn't see any of us forgiving Simon for withholding these kinds of secrets, which made me think about how the group would react to my own.

I heard a soft knock on the cabin door. Gill opened the door and wordlessly slipped under the covers. We held each other for a long while, afraid to move, unsure whether we were ready.

The moonlight through the port hole provided just enough light on our faces. His gaze held an intensity I hadn't seen since the night the game warden tied us up and left us in the woods. I wanted to take that pain away. At the same time, I longed to tell him the truth, to release this secret I'd been keeping.

Gill moved slowly, raking his fingers through my hair. He pressed his lips to mine. His mouth was on my neck and then on the curve of my breasts. I hadn't had sex for such a long time. His touch felt new as if I'd never been here before, the object of someone's lust.

He pulled off his clothes and lifted off my nightshirt. In the dim light, he tried but couldn't read the small tattoo on my side.

"What does it say?"

"Love."

"Are there others in secret places?" The tattoos on each wrist were very visible, though no one ever asked their meaning.

I rolled over and touched the base of my neck. When I had short hair, it was public.

"What does it say?" he asked.

"Survivor."

"Survive what?"

I sat up. I was done with the lies. You can't truly make love to someone while you're deceiving them. You can't fully give of yourself. I was the receiver of that lesson with Finn.

"Something happened to me a long time ago, Gill. Something that I've never gotten over. It's so attached to me; it's become part of my flesh. In a way, it's why I'm here."

He remained silent.

"I don't want to carry any more secrets. I don't want to be Simon, endangering you without your knowledge. I'm just afraid if I tell you the truth, whatever this is growing between us won't have a chance."

Gill pulled himself up straight. His eyes, black and narrow, remained on me. "I'm here, Riley. I'm listening."

"When I was seventeen, a kid from my school walked into

the gymnasium and started shooting. When he stopped, forty-nine people were dead, including my brother Ross. My best friend, Reece, survived the shooting with me. He's now a cop. In November, I shot him."

Gill's eyes widened. "Go on."

"It was an accident. A guy was wrestling for a gun in Reece's hand, and he was going to kill him. I fired, but shot Reece. Neither of us was beloved by the Chicago Police Department, and Reece, in so many words, told me to hide until everything sorted out."

"And that's why you came here?"

"Yes. I thought it would be for a few weeks, not months, and certainly not years. But a few months ago, there was a story about Finn and me. It outed me as a 'person of interest' in Reece's shooting. He's recovered, by the way. But the cops are still intent on arresting me."

"What is your plan?"

"I thought I would stay here until the statute of limitations ran out, three years. But if I stay that long I wonder what's the point of going back?"

He sucked on his bottom lip and nodded as if he were working all this out in his head.

"My driver's license is fake," I said. "I got it from Javier."

Gill moaned. "Oh, god. Don't tell me you are messed up with him?"

"He gave me the ID and the Jeep."

He didn't say anything for a while. I waited.

He pulled me close. "Can't a lawyer get you out of this?"

"It's not that easy. Shooting a cop is a felony. It's not going to go over lightly, no matter what my explanation is. Reece will most likely be fired because I shouldn't have been there with him, and the gun I used was his unregistered spare. I've already destroyed the dreams of one man—

Finn lost his election because of me. I won't destroy Reece."

He shuddered at the mention of Finn's name. "Do you still love him?"

"I don't know. I did love him. I don't think you stop loving someone suddenly. But I don't want to go back to him if that's what you're worried about."

He didn't say anything for a long time. "We'll figure this out together. OK? We'll need to come up with a backup plan in case the cops come here."

"That's my worst nightmare."

"I can't risk losing you, again."

"Again?"

"When we were in the woods tied up to that tree, I just knew that was the end. I couldn't stop thinking that the one thing I wouldn't get to do is make love to you."

He began kissing me, his lips discovering my body. I hadn't realized how much I ached to be touched, to be held, to have a man's hands on me. He pushed my arms above my head. That's when he saw the tattoo.

"What does this one say?"

"It says you own my heart."

SUN STREAMED THROUGH THE PORTHOLE, the glass creating a prism that filled the berth with a profusion of colors, mirroring my happiness. Gill lay beside me, his face pressed against my arm, his mouth agape, his blonde eyelashes fluttering with some dream. I pushed back stray hairs from his forehead and kissed his cheek.

He opened his eyes and smiled.

"I thought I was dreaming. But you are real."

"In the flesh," I said.

"I just want to stay here in bed with you all day, make love over and over."

"We'll be home soon."

We could hear Chay banging pots in the galley kitchen.

"I think he wants us to get up," I said. "What will the others think?"

"I'm not sure there's going to be 'others' after this trip." He ran his hands through his hair. "Kayla seems to be taking Simon's side. I'm pretty sure our group has shrunk to just us three, you, me, and Chay."

The three of us sat below deck most of the morning, drinking coffee, and making plans. Gill occasionally brushed his hand against my arm or leg, smiling at the secret we shared. I could see him gazing at me, swallowing me greedily with his eyes. My body shivered, remembering the pleasure of being consumed by him. I wanted to be happy, to indulge in the sweet euphoria of new love. But Simon's beating the night before felt like a hazy nightmare that left me gloomy.

The VHF radio broadcasted a warning about an approaching storm. We ascended the ladder to the deck to look at the sky. Dark clouds were bellowing on the horizon. The air was still. I could see the fear in Gill's face. Simon yelled at Chay and Gill to lower the sails.

"You're not seriously thinking about sailing through this, are you?" Chay demanded of Simon.

"We're on a sailboat. That's what you do," Simon responded.

"No, Simon, you take down the sails and motor home or to a nearby port as quickly as you can," Chay said.

Simon ignored him. He ignored all of us, even Kayla, as we pleaded with him to head back to nearby Isle Royale. He just stared straight ahead as if he couldn't hear us, as if the pounding he'd taken the night before had rendered him deaf.

The water began to get choppy. The boat rocked. The strong winds brought rain—a sideways pelting. Far off, lightning flashed. The boat began to roll with each violent wave. We donned our rain jackets and sat shivering in the cockpit, unsure of what to do. Simon ordered Chay and Gill to lower the storm sails even more, which made no sense, but Simon said we would move quicker through the squalls. Chay and Gill struggled with the sails, which were blowing like clothes on a laundry line.

"Go help them," Simon said to me, jabbing his thumb toward the mast.

I looked at him in disbelief. "Are you trying to kill us?"

"Go!" he ordered. But when Kayla started to follow, Simon pulled her back. "You, stay here."

Kayla looked at him and back at me. It seemed like a test of loyalties. Kayla pushed away his hand and grabbed hold of the back of my rain jacket. I hoisted myself on top of the boat, then attached my safety harness to the jackline. Kayla followed. The heavy rain struck us in the face, and the wind pushed us back.

Gill motioned at us.

"Too dangerous! Go back!"

A series of enormous waves struck the boat. Kayla and I hunkered down. The boat rocked to the left. Kayla's wispy body rolled over the edge, her safety strap saving her from being swept away in the water. Her legs kicked violently as she tried to work herself up from the side of the boat.

The boat rolled again. This time Kayla's body was thrown against the side of the boat. From the sound of the thud, I knew she was hurt. She'd stopped moving, hanging on the side of the boat by her safety lines.

Gill moved quickly to Kayla, stretching his safety line to its limit. Chay threw him a rope with a harness at the end. Gill clamped the harness to Kayla's life jacket. Chay pulled the rope and lifted Kayla back onto the boat. Her legs crumpled, and Gill had to hold her up as he guided her toward the safety of the cockpit. But then he stopped. His safety, tethered to the other side of the boat, had run out of line.

"Move it over here," he hollered at me over the wind and rain.

I climbed over the top of the boat, unclamped Gill's safety lines and attached them to the opposite jackline. It felt like they snapped shut in my hands. Then I gave him a thumbs-up. Another wave pounded us. This time, we were momentarily submerged. When we rolled out of the wave, Gill's safety clamps snapped off the jackline just as the boom swung wildly hitting Gill on the side of his head, throwing him overboard.

I stretched over the railing and spotted him ten feet away dangling in the water, his life jacket barely keeping him afloat. His head slumped to one side as if he were unconscious. There was blood in his hair. Another wave hit the boat. When the water retreated, Gill was gone.

RILEY

Simon radioed our coordinates to the U.S. Coast Guard. Chay was frantic, climbing up the mast to see if he could spot Gill. We circled for hours. I refused to leave the deck, my eyes continuously sweeping over the dark water, searching for Gill's body. I prayed that he was still alive. But I knew. I was responsible for another man's death—I had failed to clamp Gill's safety lines shut.

By the time the Coast Guard reached us, the storm had nearly passed. An officer came on board to take our statements. Then a larger Coast Guard boat started searching for Gill. An orange Coast Guard helicopter soon joined the search.

"It's all your fault. You killed him!" Chay screamed at Simon. "You turned the boat. You let the boom loose."

"Let's not get ahead of ourselves," the Coast Guard officer insisted. "You were in the middle of a storm. He was more likely trying to move the boat out of the squalls more quickly." He stared at us for confirmation. We returned his gaze blankly. I shook my head no. The officer wrote something in his notebook.

"I'm telling you, Simon killed Gill, and he would have killed us all if he could have gotten away with it," Chay charged.

It didn't help that Simon had a smarmy grin plastered on his face.

The officer ordered Simon to sail on to Angelica while the Coast Guard crew continued to search the waters. Chay kept threatening Simon, so the officer told Chay and me to board the Coast Guard's boat. Hours later, just as the sun was rising, a crewmember spotted Gill's life jacket floating in the water. Gill's body was not attached.

BACK ON ANGELICA, I remained ensconced in my cottage for days. Zi and Ginny brought me food and comforted me. It rained and rained. Zi said the Ojibwe believed the island was weeping over the loss of her son. Within the week, a group of Angelica fishermen recovered Gill's body. The Coast Guard closed the case, and two days later, we buried him.

They were cold, dark, damp days. The sky remained a heavy gray. The ground at the cemetery was so sodden our boots sank to our ankles in the mud. At Gill's grave, the tears that streamed down our cheeks were indistinguishable from the rain. It was as though we were still on board, our faces raw from the constant slap of water.

Gill's death changed everything on the island. Simon and Kayla both disappeared. The Grand Portage medical examiner ruled Gill's cause of death as a drowning. Chay raged that Simon had purposely sent him and Gill to lower the storm sails in order to kill them. Along with Gill's brothers and cousins, Chay made public promises of revenge and ran off to the mainland to track down Simon. Eventually, the

Sheriff agreed to investigate Gill's death. Refusing to do so would have cost him the island vote in his upcoming re-election.

After the funeral, I spent most of the time in bed. Gill's death had surfaced the other things I had lost in my life, and I was mourning them all at the same time. I'd destroyed the lives of three men. I felt like a live grenade exploding in people's lives. I refused to answer the phone at my cottage; eventually, Zi let herself in.

She coaxed me into drinking mysterious and smelly teas and lay steamy washcloths on my forehead. She waved burning incense around me and chanted strange words over me when she thought I was asleep. After a week, she convinced me to eat and shower then drove me to the restaurant. I closed my eyes and slumped against the passenger side door, hoping it would open and I would fall out.

"This is for the best. Someday you'll understand," she said as she helped me clamber down from her truck.

I walked into the kitchen alone feeling numb.

The staff abruptly stopped talking and stared at me. Matthew grinned and started clapping. Then the others joined in. They took turns hugging me and welcoming me back. Javier kissed me on the cheek and whispered: "I'm glad the Canadians didn't get you." I wondered how he knew.

Kayla never again appeared at the restaurant. Everyone assumed she had been involved in Simon's drug dealing. Chay was left emotionally crippled, only capable of expressing intermittent rage and despair. In one weekend, I'd lost four friends in one way or another.

Simon's parents put their Angelica house up for sale. The rambling mansion near the reservation had been in his mother's family for three generations. Islanders had already made up their minds. There wasn't enough room on that patch of dirt for both the dead man's family and the family of the suspected murderer, even if Gill's death turned out to be an accident.

Islanders treated me as if I were a native year-rounder. Suffering made me one of them. Strangers paid for my drinks at the tavern. People who had never spoken to me suddenly sidled up to me and whispered heartfelt empathy, as if I were Gill's widow.

I took refuge in the kitchen. It was the only place I felt at peace. I think Matthew sensed this. He often asked if I wanted to stay after work and help him create new dishes. Several times a week, we stayed for hours after the restaurant closed.

I felt safe with Matthew. We never talked much about our personal lives, and yet I felt close to him. It's hard to explain, but when someone saves your life, you share a special bond. I had that with Reece. Now I shared a similar connection with Matthew. He had killed a man to save me. And now he was rescuing me once again.

Late one night, we were finishing our creation—a salt-baked sturgeon with sautéed fennel and red pepper—when Matthew poured me a third glass of an expensive Sauvignon Blanc he'd pulled from the cellar. It was well after one in the morning.

Matthew put his feet up on a chair and swirled his wine. "So, have you decided to stay?"

"What do you mean?"

"Gill died; your little group of friends has dissolved. What's here for you?"

"Is Ginny putting you up to this?"

"It's a selfish question. I don't want you to leave."

"To be honest, I have thought about leaving. These last few weeks have been unbelievably tough."

"You've been through a string of them."

"I want to know why *you* are still here," I asked. "You're an amazing cook. You could be working in any kitchen in New York, Chicago."

He stared at the wine in his glass, considering my question. "I stay for no other reason than this place suits me. I've lived in a lot of places that didn't. Once you find your little piece of earth where you're in sync, the other stuff doesn't matter so much."

"What about love? And finding someone to spend the rest of your life with?"

"It's a good goal. But a life rich with friends is also a worthy attainment." He eyed me over his glasses. "Now it's your turn."

Since Gill's funeral, I had been weighing whether it was time to leave. Why didn't I just go home? Of course, the short answer was that the reason I fled to the island in the first place was still the reason I had to stay. That hadn't changed. But I had changed.

"I stay," I said slowly, "because of this, because of you and Ginny, and Zi. You've all helped me during my grief. I don't think until now I had the strength in me to leave. But I also stay because leaving would be running away. I've already done too much of that in my life. I stay because every day I learn something new. I stay because death is not a new pain in my life, and I know I have to keep moving forward."

That was the truth.

I held up my glass to make a toast. "To island life."

He tapped his glass to mine. "Sounds like a good theme for our next menu."

"That's a great idea," I said.

"But only if we do it together."

"Really?"

He nodded.

I took a beat and then said yes. It felt right. God, if only my dad could see me cooking and now creating dishes for a new menu.

We spent the next hour mapping out what we wanted to include. By the time I got into my Jeep, it was nearly three a.m. I was so jazzed up I couldn't sleep. The new menu was the perfect anecdote to my sadness.

I had off the next day, a Sunday, and I slept in. That afternoon sitting at my kitchen table, I mapped out more ideas for the menu. It was another cool, gray day. I stared out my kitchen window at the verdant green trees and the rain coming down and listened to the ping, ping of the water hitting the gutters. It reminded me of rainy days in Chicago, the lonely sound of water dripping onto slick sidewalks, the way cars swished through the eddies that collected at sewers.

I don't know how I remembered his home phone number. I almost always called him on his cell phone. But my fingers punched the keys on the cottage phone. I expected his line to have been disconnected. He'd long threatened to do away with his landline, like everyone else.

On the fourth ring, there was a voice, tentative and timid. "Hello?"

I recognized the uncertain masculinity, the burgeoning bass of a pre-pubescent: Nico, Finn's son. I panicked and hung up. Damn, how could I have been so stupid? Oh, God. I ran through all the possibilities: Maybe Finn wouldn't think to check his caller ID and, if he did, he'd assume it was a wrong number. Nico would tell his dad that there was no one on the line. And they'd forget all about it.

Or they wouldn't.

FINN

I'd fallen asleep on the couch, watching a Disney movie with the kids. Nico shook me awake.

"Dad, who do we know in area code 906?"

I sat up and rubbed my eyes. The light in the living room suddenly seemed overly bright.

"What?"

"It's Michigan. The northern part," he said. "I looked it up on the computer."

"I don't know, son. No one, I suppose."

"They hung up after I answered."

I got up and looked at the old caller ID attached to the phone and ran the number through Google. It belonged to a house on Angelica Island. Was it someone who had information about Riley, or could it be—and I hardly dared even to consider—*her*? I didn't want to spook whoever was on the other end of the line with a return phone call. I knew the police were still tracking my calls. Eventually, they'd discover the number, too, amid all the other numbers I'd made to the U.P. I needed to find her or whoever was protecting her before Lieutenant Williams and his men did.

It sounded crazy. Who drives eight hours to find out why someone hung up on you? But only three hundred people lived on Angelica Island year-round, according to Wikipedia. That increased the odds in my favor, especially since the island was so close to where the hunter said Riley had gone. I'd waited for this, predicted she would reveal herself in some way. It's why I hadn't stopped hoping after she'd written the letter. I knew I had to wait for Riley to find me.

I pulled out the journal that contained clues and interviews about Riley's whereabouts. I hadn't written anything in weeks. Glued to the inside of the back cover was a road map of upper Michigan and Wisconsin. I circled the city of Luck with a black pen, then I drew a line from there to Grand Portage, Michigan, where she'd stayed at the B & B. Just a puddle jump away was Angelica Island, one of the twelve Disciple Islands in Lake Superior. I pressed my pen into the small green landmass at the edge of the lake.

That's where she was.

I was sure of it.

RILEY

I was in the kitchen when Ginny caught my elbow.

"The Sheriff's on the phone. He wants to talk to you."

The nerves in my face and hands tingled. I followed her into her office and picked up the phone.

"What's up, Sheriff?" I tried to sound upbeat.

"Hi, Riley. How are you doing?"

"Ok."

"Listen, I hate to do this, but you know there's always paperwork. I need you to come to the station in Grand Portage and sign your statement about Gill's drowning."

"Well, I'm at work. We're short on staff."

"I know. I wouldn't call if it weren't important. But I need you to come now."

"To sign a form?"

"Well, there's more to it. I just need to go over a few more details before I can close the case."

"I've told you everything I know."

"Yes, but it's been my experience that witnesses remember things after a few weeks."

"OK. Can't I come tomorrow?"

"No. I need you to come this afternoon. And I need you to bring your passport. Do you want me to send an officer to pick you up?"

"No. I'm on my way."

Fuck. This was it. This was my reveal, the moment the *Famous Female Fugitives* said they all dreaded. But for them, their arrests were a relief and they felt calm in the moment. I felt panicked.

I put the receiver down and looked at Ginny.

"I'm sure it's routine," she said, rubbing my arm. But her face betrayed her. She looked worried—gray, flyaway hairs crowned her forehead. Her eyes were red and squinty. She nervously bit at her lip.

I closed my eyes and felt a cold shiver run up my neck.

"I have to go."

On the way out, I passed Matthew. "Something's come up," I said. He looked disappointed, but didn't ask any questions.

I drove straight to Chay's and Gill's house. I hadn't been there since the wake. I'd heard Chay and the others had come back empty-handed from their scorched-earth search to find Simon and were laying low.

The house looked dark when I pulled in next to Chay's truck. It was already late afternoon. I walked across the porch and was about to knock when I saw through the screen door Chay sitting at the kitchen table.

"Hey, you want some company?" I asked.

"Not really. But come on in."

I sat down opposite him and lit the candle on the table. Even in the low light, Chay looked rough. His normally short hair was long enough for a man bun. His face was sunken, his eyes hollow and dark, his mouth sagged. In front of him was a tumbler containing a spit of amber liquid.

He pulled my chair over and buried his face into my lap. I ran my hands through his hair and rubbed his back. I didn't need to ask how he was getting along.

"Chay, I'm in real trouble."

FINN

Two columns of cars squeezed onto the deck of the flat barge-like boat. Each vehicle kissed the bumper in front of it. I slithered out of my car and edged my way through the narrow spaces between cars until I reached the ferry's edge. I tried to imagine what Riley felt the first time she crossed these waters. Eight months is a long time to go without seeing your lover's face. Sometimes I had to look at a photo to remember the intensity of her green eyes.

The lake waters were a saturated sapphire, the cloudless sky cerulean blue. It was as if I were standing in a Picasso painting, his blue period. It was early morning. I'd driven all night. As I leaned over the railing, the froth wet my face. I didn't care. I was closer to finding her. I could feel it.

At the opposite end of the deck, a cluster of Sheriff deputies in dark brown pants and tan shirts stood talking. I wondered why so many were traveling to the island and silently prayed that their presence had nothing to do with Riley. The woman had a knack for attracting trouble—and the police.

I pulled out my journal. It was three-quarters full, pages

and pages of my scratchy handwriting, notes about people I'd interviewed, their physical descriptions, tics. It felt like I was a cop again, filling my little notebook with tedious facts, little monotonies that might prove valuable—or not. This time, though, the case I was covering was intensely personal.

My plan was simple. I'd go to the house, knock, and see who answered.

When we docked, the Sheriff deputies rolled off the ferry first, the lights on their patrol cars whirling as they raced through the quaint downtown. I took a different route. A mile or so out of town, I cut off the main road at the red fire marker 1255. A driveway safety chain lay on the ground. I pulled in slowly and wound through the cluster of birch and pine trees lining the drive. A black Jeep was parked in front of the house. My neck stiffened. Didn't the creepy hunter say Riley was driving a Jeep? Could she be here? After all, this time, could finding her be this easy?

I parked and slowly walked onto the porch. Beyond the house, the lake lapped at the rocky beach, and two giant egrets stalked the shore, hunting for fish.

I rang the doorbell and waited.

RILEY

Chay listened intently. When I finished, he remained quiet for a long time.

"Geez, I never would have pegged you for an anti-gun activist," he finally said.

"Really? That's your takeaway?" We both laughed. It was the release we needed at the moment.

"We'll leave on the first ferry in the morning," he said. "I'll drive you to Chicago."

"What about tonight?"

He looked at the digital clock on the stove. "Ferry shuts down early tonight for repairs."

I had forgotten entirely about "maintenance night," the first Wednesday of every month. I didn't exactly know what I'd do once we got to Chicago, but I'd figure out my next move off the island, away from the Sheriff and the immediate threat.

Chay and I had agreed to meet at my cabin early the next morning. I spent the night packing and planning. It was barely light when Chay pulled into my driveway and helped me put a couple of boxes into the back of his truck.

"I want to stop at the restaurant," I said, firmly, expecting an argument. "It's not right, me leaving without telling Ginny goodbye."

He raised his eyebrows but didn't say anything.

When we drove by the restaurant, the parking lot was full of Sheriff patrol cars.

"Oh my god," I said. It looked like Javier in the back of one of the cars.

"Get down on the floor!" Chay ordered.

He drove slowly.

"What's happening?" I asked.

"There are patrol cars everywhere. Along the road, at the deli, at the harbor. Looks like deputies are checking IDs and searching cars before letting anyone drive onto the ferry."

He pulled a blanket from behind his seat and threw it over me. "Don't say anything."

He steered the truck to the shoulder and rolled down his window.

"Hey, what's with the Sheriff cars?" Chay asked.

"The Sheriff just arrested Javier." It was Mr. Kowalski. "The Sheriff and his deputies are looking for Riley. You seen her?"

"Nah. I just got back."

"Well, if anyone knows where she is, it's most likely going to be you. They'll be coming to you next. So, you might not want to be going home so soon, if you know what I mean?"

"Thanks," Chay said. He rolled up the window and slowly drove back onto the road.

"Fuck!" I said.

"You can say that again."

"Is it safe to come out now?"

"No."

He hit the gas pedal. The truck thundered down gravel

roads. I was getting jostled on the floorboard, my head pounding the glove box.

"Now you can come out," he said.

I peeled back the cover and looked out the window. I recognized the road as the back way to the reservation. We passed a sign announcing we were entering sovereign territory.

"You'll be safe here until we can figure out our next move." I hadn't seen him so animated, so determined, since he set out to track down Simon.

We moved slowly through the trees; the forest was thick. Chay told me "they" had surveillance cameras along the route. They knew we were coming. He stretched his arm across me, opened his glove box, and pulled out a placard with a picture of an eagle that matched the one on his neck and stuck it in the middle of the dashboard.

At a clearing, a ramshackle house emerged from the shadows of the pines. A couple of German Shepherds and a Rottweiler bounded from the side of the house and clawed at the truck. I screamed and leaped toward Chay. He laughed and said the dogs were harmless. Then we heard a metal grinding noise, and the garage door opened.

Chay pulled the truck inside. The door slowly closed. We sat still in the pitch black. Finally, a light flicked on, and a withered face appeared at Chay's window.

"Hello, Brother Chayton," he said, his voice hoarse but firm. "You've come to seek refuge."

FINN

When no one answered the door, I walked around back and looked through the rear windows. There was an ugly paisley couch and masculine paintings of ships. I considered hanging around until someone came home, but I wasn't good at waiting.

If Riley lived here, someone on the tiny island likely knew her. I made my way back to town, passing a line of Sheriff patrol cars flying down the road with their lights on and sirens blaring. The whole downtown was swarming with patrol cars. I took a seat at the bar of a local tavern. It was only ten a.m., but I didn't know where else to get information. A thin woman with stringy hair served me a beer from the tap. I hadn't slept well, and the alcohol and the cool, dark room made me sleepy.

I still hadn't figured out how to bring up Riley. If I showed her photo around, people might think I was a cop, an ex-boyfriend, or a husband. Riley could have portrayed herself as a victim of domestic violence.

"What's with all the cops?"

The bartender shook her head. "We've had a lot of commotion this morning. The Sheriff arrested a cook at Ginny's restaurant."

"Lot of drama for such a little island."

"I'll say. Three weeks ago, one of the cooks at the restaurant drowned in the lake. Now the Sheriff is looking for his girlfriend."

"The police think she drowned her boyfriend?"

The bartender looked at me as if I were slow. "No. Another friend of theirs drowned Gill. The Sheriff thinks Riley is messed up with some other stuff."

"They're looking for *Riley*?"

"Yeah, you know her?"

"Not sure if it's the same one," I said.

The barmaid rubbed at her thin eyebrows. "There's only one on the island. They say she was in on it with Javier, selling fake IDs to them illegals that come to the island. It's a shame. She and Gill made a great couple."

"Couple?" I felt my throat squeezing shut.

"Yeah, they was real sweet on each other. Used to come in here all the time. Some says Gill was going to ask Riley to marry him." She bowed her head sorrowfully. "Just a sad, sad case. Now he's dead, and she's going to prison."

RILEY

Chay's plan was to hide out at the "Eagle's Nest," the Native Brotherhood's meeting house on the edge of the reservation. Then at dark we'd take a boat to the mainland. From there, he would borrow another member's truck and drive me to Chicago.

Chay spent much of the day on the landline mapping out our escape. He also fielded reports about how Sheriff deputies were conducting no-knock arrest warrants, busting through people's doors. They'd arrested several illegals. Some were well-known on the island. They cleaned houses, worked as mechanics at the garage, and one was a dishwasher at the restaurant. They were docile, polite people doing jobs nobody else wanted. Javier had supplied them with fake IDs.

Chay also learned that Sheriff deputies had searched my cottage and Chay's house. They'd gone through Zi's house and her mother's home on the reservation. That news infuriated Chay. He paced the floor, ranting about the Sheriff and Javier. It made me nervous to see him like that. He was carrying a gun, stuffed in the back of his jeans.

Members of the Native Brotherhood began to trickle into the house. They were men with tattoos of eagles on their hands, their necks, their forearms. Like Chay, they were young, angry, and armed. Many of them had helped him search for Simon and were eager for their next mission.

This kind of weaponry and high emotion made me uneasy. I smoked one after the other of the old man's hand-rolled cigarettes. I could have sworn there was more than tobacco in them, but Chay shrugged off the suggestion. "Just magic herbs," he said and winked.

The men gathered in an adjacent room. Occasionally I overheard bits and pieces of heated discussions. Someone banged on a table. Someone slammed a door. They were planning more than just our trek across the lake. Something was happening. And I didn't like the feel of it.

Eventually, a few women showed up and served us dinner of Indian fry bread and venison. I fell asleep but woke when a tribal police officer from the mainland showed up at the door.

"Have you seen her, Chay?" the officer asked. I could hear his voice in the foyer. "Sheriff deputies have a warrant for her arrest."

"The Sheriff never did a damn thing to find Gill, and now he wants my help to arrest my friend?" Chay said.

"I'm going to ask you again. Chay, do you know where Riley Kennedy is?"

There was silence.

"So, you won't mind then if I take a look around?"

That's when I heard the sound of a dozen guns moving bullets into their chambers. The Brotherhood wasn't playing around.

"Chay, I can come back with a search warrant."

"If you come back, you better have more than a piece of paper."

"I'm going. But you should know there are a lot of Sheriff's deputies out there. Turn her in before anyone gets hurt."

After the officer left, I walked into the front hallway. "I should turn myself in," I said to the men. "I don't want anyone to get shot because of me."

They laughed.

Chay threw his arm around my shoulder and walked me back to the living room. "This is all a bunch of trumped-up bullshit. I'll call our attorney."

It was well past midnight when a middle-aged man in a dark, pinstriped suit and a black ponytail arrived. Chay called him "Maajigwaneyaash," which sounded like magic-wanna-wash. I just thought of him as the Suit because no one on the island wore a suit.

The Suit said Sheriff deputies had the reservation surrounded. Javier's arrest was part of a larger investigation by the Sheriff's department and the FBI. They were focused on catching undocumented immigrants passing through Grand Portage and Angelica Island on their way to Canada.

"They hadn't been able to directly tie the immigrants' fake IDs to Javier, until yours," the Suit said. "Just dumb luck." He gave me a half-cocked smile.

The Sheriff and the FBI were willing to negotiate if I admitted I'd lied about my identity and told them what I knew about the fake identity ring. I'd have to testify against Javier.

"But I don't know anything," I protested. "Besides, how can I rat on Javier? He helped me."

"He's saying you were involved," the Suit said. "Do you have a legal title to the Jeep Javier gave you? The Sheriff found some illegal IDs, forged documents, and a gun hidden in the Jeep's wheel bed."

"What?"

"Yeah, and it's also stolen." He paused to see if the seriousness of what he was saying was sinking in.

"Don't you get it?" Chay growled. "Javier set you up. He wasn't trying to help you, Riley. He was making you his patsy."

The Suit nodded. "They've got two of Javier's right-hand guys. They'll all be looking for deals. The first one who talks will get the best offer. A number of people will go down."

His voice implied I was one of them.

FINN

Sheriff barricades blocked the road to the reservation. Lining the blockade were stone-faced deputies wearing bullet-proof vests and holding batons. A crowd had gathered on the road. Some held up hastily crafted signs:

Free Riley!

Go Home, Sheriff!

Angelica is Not a Police State!

A few banged-on drums. Dozens of curious people meandered about. I sidled up to one of the more serious protesters, a White guy with messy brown dreads.

"So, what's this all about?" I asked.

"Hey, man," he said, "the Sheriff's knocking down doors arresting people all over the island. Now he's trying to arrest this woman inside the reservation."

"What did she do?"

"*They say* she sold IDs to undocumented Mexicans," he said. "I say more power to her. The Sheriff needs to butt out of our lives." He started chanting with the others: "Hell, no, she won't go. Sheriff, get off our is-land! Hell, no, she won't go. Sheriff, get off our is-land!"

I pulled out my cell phone and scrolled to a photo of Riley. I nudged the dreadlocks guy.

"Do me a solid: Tell me if this is the woman holed up at the reservation."

The guy's eyes moved from the phone screen to me. "Yeah, that's her. But who are *you*?"

RILEY

Between sleeping, playing cards with Chay, and discussing strategy with the Suit—who'd asked me to call him Gordon—I'd lost track of the days. News of the Sheriff's standoff with the Native Brotherhood didn't take long to stir up old resentments. I watched out the living room window as the crowds grew. A shanty camp had sprung up nearby. It was like a summer festival, people milling between tents, grilling meat over wood fires—the smell of smoke constant day and night.

Chay told me that a second group of Islanders and Natives had set up camp at the edge of the reservation, near the main road. Some people were comparing it to the Standing Rock demonstration in North Dakota. Sheriff deputies and FBI agents were stationed on the reservation side, blocking protesters from entering and joining forces with the demonstrators surrounding the house. Gawkers snapped photos of the standoff.

The Islanders on the front line were likely armed, Chay warned. I knew the standoff wasn't about me. It was a showdown over who controlled the island. Tensions between the

Islanders and the Mainlanders had festered for decades. Gill's death and lack of a solid investigation by the Sheriff had only stirred up more resentment. My situation had stoked the island's anti-government fervor.

Chay's Brotherhood buddies were stationed around the house and the nearby grounds. They wore camouflage and paint on their faces to blend in with the trees and brush. I felt indebted to them; they were risking their lives for me. But Chay said this was what they needed. After returning empty-handed from their search for Simon, they'd felt incompetent. Now, he said, they felt like they mattered. They were warriors defending their island.

I wanted to go outside, if only to breathe fresh air. But Gordon worried that it might provoke the deputies and cause a dangerous confrontation. There was nothing to prevent the FBI or tribal police from coming to get me other than their fear of stirring up the protesters.

Gordon, who was full of conspiracy theories, said he feared the FBI would use any purported sighting of me as an excuse to raid the reservation.

"Really?" I said. "I accepted an illegal driver's license and apparently a stolen Jeep. It's not like we were selling cocaine, setting up terrorist cells."

Gordon shook his head. He'd just returned from yet another meeting with the task force leaders and seemed agitated.

"The feds think you and Javier were partners, that the two of you were running the enterprise together," he said. "They think Simon might have been part of your operation."

"Sure there's not a couple more unsolved murders, a missing kid they want to throw in there, too?" I should have taken it all more seriously, but the accusations were ludicrous. I wondered how much was FBI bluff and how much was Gordon mingling in his own histrionics.

"They're not going to budge until you cooperate. They ran your photo through facial recognition. And they know your real name is Riley Keane."

Chay closed his eyes and stroked the eagle tattoo on his neck, something he always did when he was nervous.

"The police in Chicago have been looking for me," I said. "They think I shot a cop. There's no arrest warrant. They are calling me a 'person of interest.'"

"Did you shoot a cop?" Gordon asked. "Never mind. I don't want to know."

"Does she look like a cop-killer to you?" Chay asked.

"She doesn't look like someone who'd be running a fake ID ring either," Gordon said. "If the police in Chicago get involved, your options for a deal with the Sheriff become much more limited."

"I'm not turning myself in," I insisted. "You need to get me a better deal, Gordon."

"And what would that look like?"

"No jail time. I will detail only what happened to me."

I knew the Sheriff had little or no evidence against me. I learned from years of getting arrested that the cops always overplayed their threats, hoping to elicit a confession. In this scenario, the cops didn't have the upper hand. A standoff at a Native American reservation wouldn't look good if it made national news, and it would look even worse if any natives or protesters were injured or killed.

Chay said he'd heard the bars, restaurants, and hotels in town were packed with local sympathizers and curiosity seekers. From Chay's accounts, the whole island seemed to be captivated by the standoff. It was the most drama they'd had in years.

"The Sheriff is going to tire of waiting for you to come out," Gordon warned. "The longer this standoff lasts, the weaker he looks." He nervously coughed. "They're bringing in an FBI negotiator. They're insisting he talk directly to you." He pulled out a bulky satellite phone from a canvas bag. "They gave this to me. He's calling tomorrow morning."

"Why would you want me to talk to the FBI?" I didn't trust Gordon's instincts.

"There really is no choice," Gordon said. "If I don't let him talk to you, they threatened to bring in troops and storm the compound. I don't think it's worth getting innocent people killed, right?" He looked me in the eye. This guy had his own agenda, and it wasn't about protecting me.

"What if the negotiator tries to trick me?"

"I'll be right here. We'll practice what you'll say, your demands."

"And what if it's a bluff to make sure I'm here. You know, proof of life, and they storm the compound?"

He shrugged. "Guess we'll find out."

FINN

For nearly a week, I'd been standing among a youngish group of protesters. They ate volumes of bean sprouts and shunned deodorant. The messy dreads guy I'd met on the first day introduced himself as Bear. When I gave him a quizzical look, he admitted, with some embarrassment, "It's short for Barron."

Bear and his friends had built a yurt and tent commune on property belonging to his parents, who lived in Green Bay and owned a chain of carpet stores. The commune was off the grid, its electricity derived from solar panels. There was a sweat lodge, Bear said, an outhouse, a meditation tent, and even outdoor showers that used rainwater. He described their rustic living with affection. They drank water from artesian springs and grew vegetables in plastic hoop houses.

"Sounds like an awesome place," I said. "Think I could get a tour sometime?"

"Sorry, man. It's sacred ground. You'd have to fast for a week to get that meat reek out of you."

Though Bear seemed to accept my story readily, others in his group gave me suspicious looks. I could tell they didn't know what to make of me in my pressed jeans and button-down shirts. But when I showed them multiple photos of Riley, pictures of us together, her smiling face, they stopped eyeing me as if I were a serial killer or, worse, an FBI agent. I told them I was a former colleague and that she'd called me just before the Sheriff tried to arrest her—which was true. I'd come because she was in trouble.

After that first day of protesting, Bear invited me to join him and his friends at Tom's Burnt Down Café, the outdoor remains of a bar that had caught fire years ago. Bear's friends discussed their protesting schemes in hushed voices, but when I picked up the tab, they invited me to join them every night.

Often it was past midnight when I'd leave the cafe and make my way to my room at the Angelica Inn, a bed and breakfast past its prime. The owner told me I was staying in the room that Riley had slept in her first night on the island. It made me feel closer to her. I was lucky to rent any space. Curiosity seekers had jammed the island. So far, the island's drama was deemed too local or unimportant to warrant national media attention, although a few journalists from towns on the mainland had arrived.

By the fifth day, I was tired and wanted to go back to Chicago. But I couldn't leave without her.

"If you hardly knew her," I asked Bear and the others one night at the bar, "then why are you protesting the Sheriff's arrest warrant?"

Bear leaned over the table in the low light and looked me in the eyes. "This ain't about your friend, dude. This is about who controls this island. We don't want the Sheriff conducting undercover investigations and swarming our homes to arrest people. That's not how we govern.

"For years, we've had an unspoken agreement with the Sheriff that unless there's a major crime—like a murder—the

Sheriff does not interfere with our self-governance. We have tribal and island councils. The investigation into Javier and your friend changed all that."

His face was yellow in the candlelight, and his eyes watery from the three whiskeys he'd downed. He lifted a flap on his cargo pants to reveal the handle of a gun.

"I thought you were peace-loving vegans?"

He threw back his head and laughed. "We all carry on the island. It's how we keep justice. If the Sheriff tries to storm the reservation to get your friend," he paused, then looked around the table at those who were quietly nodding, "he's going to be met by what we like to call the Bohemian Militia."

RILEY

The FBI negotiator didn't bring up Javier right away. At first, it was all about me, what I liked, what I didn't like. He was trying to get me to trust him, to like him, to separate himself from the local Barney Fifes. He told me his name was Thornton. It sounded made-up. Wasn't there a Dr. Seuss character named Thornton? Or was that Horton? I tried to reveal as little as possible, stonewalling his increasingly impertinent questions. What kind of movies did I like? Who was my favorite actor? What did I do in my spare time?

I was quickly tiring of the circular conversation. I gave him random answers, anything that popped in my head, especially if it was the opposite of the truth. We'd been going at it for hours.

To his credit, Gordon had predicted that the first few hours with the negotiator would be a waste of time. "The bigger the ego," he'd said, "the longer it will take him to get to the real questions. His goal is to wear you down so that you're not as sharp, so you'll lower your defenses and screw up. He's also stalling while his colleagues scour their databases. They don't want to negotiate until they know *all* your crimes."

Eventually, Thornton moved on to questions about the island. What was it like living on a remote rock in the middle of an inland ocean? What was it like to work at the restaurant? Did I like my colleagues? He inched close to Javier-related questions but never mentioned his name. I knew this game. I'd been interrogated by cops many times.

My mind began to drift. Thornton had a husky, playful tone, the kind you'd expect to hear on a late-night booty call. He was flirty and flippant, mocking the Sheriff and his deputies for not finding Simon. There was something about him that felt comfortable, familiar. He had a Midwestern accent with a slight curl at the end of his sentences that made everything he said questionable. I knew I was experiencing something like Stockholm Syndrome. I'd been trapped inside for days, and here was this person who called from out *there* and talked about everyday things, movies, and food. And for a few moments, I forgot where I was and why I was listening to this stranger's voice.

When the conversation lagged, Thornton told funny stories: How his sisters had raised him after his mother died; how they treated him like their live baby doll, keeping him in short pants well past the time he should have been wearing big boy clothes; how when he'd reached fourteen and started getting man fuzz, they'd tried to shave him and instead cut up his face, leaving a scar on his right sideburn. He was careful not to say where he grew up.

I tried to imagine what he looked like. At first, I guessed he was in his mid-forties, a TV version of an FBI guy, with square brown hair, wearing a blue blazer and a starched white shirt with a pen clipped to his pocket. Then I imagined him more as a black-ops guy with slicked black hair and metallic blue eyes, something akin to Colin Farrell. It was a silly game. But it helped pass the time. It wasn't my fault I digressed. Thornton brought up sex a lot, not directly, but in the way he inferred things. He'd whisper certain words, making them sound intimate. In that way, he reminded me of Reece and how we joked, made innuendos, flirted.

As our talk marathon dragged on, his voice became harder, edgier. "Do you think your parents miss you back in Chicago?" he asked.

It was a loaded question. It wasn't a secret that I came from Chicago, but the way Thornton said *Chicago* implied that he knew much more than he'd let on.

"How about your boyfriend? Finn? Isn't that his name?"

I didn't say anything.

"That's all right. You're probably sore that we found out who you are. It was only a matter of time. You know the Chicago Police have been looking for you for several months. Your face has been all over TV and the papers there. Let's talk about how we're going to handle this situation. Because you and I both know you've got more troubles than Javier and his little ID scam."

RILEY

Sunlight was barely skipping across the lake when Chay and I bundled up below deck in the tribal boat. Gordon sat quietly nearby, as did several of Chay's friends. The boat was fast, the lake waters choppy. By the time we reached the no-wake zone in Grand Portage, I was dry heaving in the head. I hadn't been on a boat since Gill's death.

When we docked, Gordon and the Brotherhood members got off. I waited below with Chay, listening to the radio. The sultry voice of Elvis crooned "Always on my mind."

Chay nudged me. "It's time."

We climbed to the deck then slowly made our way to the dock behind the police department. Chay and his muscle-bodied buddies fell into formation around me. Sheriff Kustwin stood at the end of the pier, his hands on his hips, his mouth stretched tight into a self-satisfied smirk. His deputies twisted my arms behind my back and handcuffed my wrists. They were about to clamp leg irons on my ankles when I heard a booming voice call out.

"Is that really necessary?"

It was the taunting, playful voice I'd listened to for hours.

The crowd parted, and a middle-aged, Black man brushed past the deputies and stood in front of me, his arms clutched against his chest, prominently displaying a snake tattoo writhing up his forearm. He had a sophisticated urban style—twisted coils that sprouted from his head, a sparse beard as if he hadn't shaved in days, and a diamond stud in one ear.

"Hello, Riley," he said. "I've been waiting to meet you for a long time."

WE SAT at a long wooden table across from the judge's podium, me in an orange jumpsuit and Gordon in his pinstriped uniform. Because the charges of conspiracy to produce false identification documents involved both federal and state laws, I was being arraigned in the Grand Portage Court before being transferred to federal court in Detroit. To my back, the gallery was sealed by two panes of bullet-proof glass. It seemed overkill for such a backwater.

There were smudge marks on the glass behind me—the perfect outline of someone's puckered lips. I craned my neck to the back of the room and saw him walking in the door—crouched as if arriving late to church.

Finn!

I could hardly breathe. After all these months, he was here. Damn it if I was going to cry. Gordon told me I was facing twenty years in prison unless I cooperated with the feds. "They throw the book at you to scare you into pleading out," he'd warned. My face felt flush in court as I listened to the long list of charges.

At the urging of the district attorney, who called me "a national security threat" and claimed I had helped manufacture over 300 false identifications and hid illegal immigrants, the judge refused bond. I glanced over my shoulder again. Finn was alone, his face chalky white. When he looked in my direction, his expression was rigid and judgmental. It was a look of utter contempt.

FINN

The Plexiglass between the court audience and where Riley sat was thick and yellowed with age. Despite the speakers piped into our side, it was hard to hear the proceedings. I hoped Riley had a good attorney. The lone man at her table looked odd. All I could see of him were his broad shoulders and a black ponytail with a bluish sheen. When they stood in court, he towered over her.

At the opposing table, two attorneys looked local, but a third had that slick, Washington D.C. bureaucratic arrogance as if he were above all these boorish people. He *had* to be from the Justice Department, probably there to make sure the locals didn't fuck anything up. Behind them sat the Sheriff, several deputies, and FBI agents. I recognized them from watching their press conference on a local newscast. They'd boasted how cooperation between local and federal authorities had broken open one of the most prolific illegal ID rings in the upper Midwest. They'd taken turns at a podium making grandiose statements while gesturing to a table in front of them spread with fake IDs and military-looking guns. The inference that

Riley had anything to do with a weapons arsenal made me furious.

In court, one of their brood looked familiar, at least from the back. He had that unique flair of Afro radiating around his head like he was a dark star. It wasn't until he turned around and our eyes met, did I realize where I'd seen him before.

He was the cameraman, Mr. Mailer.

RILEY

I lay awake all night, the light from the guard tower falling across my face. At dinner, a guard asked if I would approve a Mr. Finn O'Farrell on my visitor list for the next morning. I almost threw up. What was I going to say to him? I was sure he despised me. I'd seen it on his face in court. Why had he come? Was it curiosity or satisfaction to see me behind bars? Finn wasn't a vengeful person. He'd come looking for answers. It was the same reason I'd agreed to see him. I wanted answers, too.

At visiting hour, a guard led me to a booth. There was no one sitting on the other side.

I sat down on the metal stool and remembered the first time we'd met like this at the Cook County Jail. He'd bailed me out, saved my ass like he had so many times. I was a jumble of emotions. As much as I wanted to hate Finn for having kept his secret from me, I also understood his wanting to be close to someone who'd suffered through that unique horror show of Darren Wallack.

I stared at the empty chair on the other side of the glass.

I had only one question: Did he kill Wallack?

FINN

My legs felt limp. I couldn't focus. Everything seemed blurry. I walked into the long, narrow room and saw the number three above a cubicle window. I swallowed hard and sat down on the stool. At first, all I could see was blonde hair. For a second, I thought I had the wrong cubicle. Then I remembered how she'd looked in court: Her golden strands falling past her shoulders. I sat down and stared at her. Her head was cradled in her arm, resting on the ledge, as if she were napping.

She raised her head slowly. Her unadorned face was pale and thin. But she looked beautiful, her green eyes gleaming. She smiled, and something within me came alive; a seed of hope I'd carried suddenly cracked open.

I picked up the phone and mouthed a hoarse "hello."

"Hi," she whispered back.

"Are you okay? They treating you alright?" My voice was scratchy with nerves.

She nodded and looked down, seemingly embarrassed.

"You did good in court. I'm proud of you."

"You looked...angry."

"No! Not at you." I shook my head vigorously. How could she think that? "I was mad at how the feds had stacked the deck with all those agents sitting in court."

She peered at me with hooded eyes. "How are you?" she asked, leaning toward the window, staring at me, trying to detect changes in my face over the past eight months. "I'm sorry you lost the election. That was all my fault. That story the Sunday before the election was a real low-blow."

He shrugged. "It just wasn't my time. That's all. It's better this way. I get to spend more time with my kids, focusing on my constituents. Besides, I was getting tired of kissing the mayor's ass."

She nodded, and I could see she was trying to hold it together.

"I've missed you. A lot," I said.

Her hair cloaked her face. When she pushed back the strands, her eyes were glistening. "Why didn't you tell me?" she whispered.

My eyes locked on hers. No matter how much I practiced, I would never find the right words.

"I couldn't...I couldn't tell anyone."

"Why? You've told me lots of secrets, Finn. Why was this one so exclusive?"

"There are a lot of things I want to tell you, but not on a recorded line, okay?"

"Well, it sort of looks like this is my future," she gestured to the jail phone booth.

"You're going to be okay," I assured her. "I've called your parents. They are hiring you a good defense lawyer."

"The FBI wants me to make a deal so I can go back to Chicago and help them with their investigation of CPD."

"Riley, the cameraman?" I said. "He was in court today sitting behind the prosecution. He's FBI."

"Thornton? The Black guy?"

"Yeah, I wouldn't trust him, Riley. He tried to blackmail your parents, threatened to turn over the video of Reece's shooting to the police. I ended up giving him twenty thousand dollars. He threatened to hurt my kids if I didn't spy on your family and tell him when we heard from you. I don't know if he's cozy with the Chicago PD. But one thing I'm certain of: He's not on your side."

She wrinkled her forehead. "You gave him money?"

"We were desperate to protect you. He seemed like a real threat, went over to your parents' house with this woman—scared your mom and dad half to death. I had to stop him from badgering them. Reece told me to pay him to prevent him from going to the police."

Suddenly Riley slumped back in disbelief. "He's the FBI negotiator who convinced me to leave the reservation." Her face faltered, realizing she'd been conned. "He promised me that I wouldn't have to spend time here, that he'd make sure the Sheriff let me go."

I leaned back in my chair. "Then why, after two days, are you still sitting in jail?"

RILEY

Instead of taking me back to my cell, a guard led me to an interview room. Thornton was sitting behind a wooden table. I sat across from him. He opened a file, pulled out a statement he expected me to sign, and pushed it across the table. The document stated that I exchanged my car for a new set of IDs, that I'd come to Angelica Island because I'd witnessed a gang member shoot a Chicago cop, and I was in fear for my life. It didn't say *I'd* shot the cop. He'd left that part out, though I'd admitted to Thornton that I had shot Reece when Thornton and I were on the phone. They probably had that recorded and could pull it out any time they wanted.

"If I sign this, then what?" I hated him at that moment.

He outlined his bottom lip with a finger. "We go back to Chicago."

"And?"

He bent over the table. "*And* you're no longer in a position to negotiate, sweetheart. You should be fucking thanking me for hauling your ass out of this backwater. No telling what they'd pin on you if *they* had arrested you."

What he was saying was true, but that didn't make me trust him. I looked at the right side of his face. There was no scar. He'd made it all up to get me to turn myself in. It was all lies.

He caught me staring at his face. "If I'd told you that my parents were school teachers, and I went to an Ivy League college, would you have turned yourself in? Women always want a story, some goddamn narrative that makes them *feel* better. Think like a self-centered dickhead, and sign before everyone gets wiser."

I glared at him. I could hear Finn telling me that Thornton had been blackmailing him. "What about my friend Finn and my family? What happens to them?"

He shook his head. "Nothing is going to happen to them."

"Why did you threaten them and extort money?"

"Because I thought Reece was dying, and I didn't know where you were. And CPD was looking for you. It was better that I found you first. Now read the goddamn paper. You're getting a sweet deal here. Do you need your attorney? I can get him. But I think you know whose interest he represents."

I read over the agreement again. I was admitting to a misdemeanor—criminal possession of a forged instrument in the third degree. The catch was that in exchange, I would cooperate in two Justice Department investigations, the illegal ID ring on Angelica Island and Reece's shooting in Chicago. If I gave them my full assistance, I would receive no jail time.

Thornton grinned smugly and handed me a pen.

THAT NIGHT, a deputy rousted me from sleep. She gave me my clothes and told me to change. The next thing I knew, we were speeding through Grand Portage in a patrol car, its lights blaring. I asked where Thornton was, but the deputy ignored me. We finally stopped at an airstrip outside of town where a prop-jet brawled on the tarmac. The car door opened. Thornton pulled me out. The deputy unlocked my handcuffs. Then Thornton escorted me up the ramp. The plane's noise prevented me from asking any questions. Except for two pilots, there was no one else on the plane. Thornton directed me to a seat and handcuffed me to the armrest.

"FBI policy." He smiled maliciously, then took a seat behind me and promptly fell asleep. I stared out the window at the lights of small towns we passed over, wondering what would happen once we landed. Our generous arrangement didn't match the tenor of the man who'd arranged it.

An hour later, the plane landed at an airport in Gary, Indiana, a half-hour drive from Chicago. I was glad to be home, but terrified as to what would come next. Thornton unlocked the handcuffs, and we climbed down the stairs to a waiting black SUV. The sky was still dark. It was mid-July, and the air was humid and sticky even at that hour. There was little traffic on the road as we entered Hegewisch, the most southern Chicago neighborhood, literally a minute from the Indiana border. I expected Thornton to take me to the federal jail in downtown Chicago. Instead, the car pulled into a driveway. Thornton ordered me to get out.

He guided me toward the back door of a house that opened to an old-fashioned kitchen. The place smelled of fried rice. Bags stained brown with soy sauce lay on the counter. I hadn't eaten since lunch the previous day and felt famished. But Thornton wasn't stopping. He pulled on my arm up a set of creaky stairs.

What was this place? We walked down a hallway and up another smaller set of stairs to a low-ceilinged third floor lined with doors. Was Thornton going to keep me here, lock me away in one of these rooms until I testified?

At the end of the hallway, he lightly tapped on a door. When no one answered, he slowly turned the knob. I followed him inside. A small lamp burned on a table next to a single bed. The sheets were mangled as if someone had just gotten up. We heard the water running behind a bathroom door.

When the door opened, there was the face I had not seen since the night I fled Chicago. His hair had grayed a bit, and his shoulder slumped on one side, but his piercing green eyes were filled with the same energy they always had.

He looped an arm around my shoulder and pulled me into a bear hug. "How you doing, sweets? Heard you did some cooking up there in Siberia." He smiled that half-cocked grin. "You did good. Real good. Guess you met my cousin." He wrenched his head toward Thornton, who'd taken a chair next to the bed. "Thornton's a little rough on the edges. But he gets the job done."

"Your *cousin*? His name is really *Thornton*?"

Reece laughed. "Some things you just can't make up."

"But I don't get it," I protested. "He filmed your shooting, Reece. He blackmailed Finn, my parents."

"What did you expect me to do?" Thornton called out from his chair. "Rush down and dab at Reece's chest? I wasn't going to blow my cover to hold Reece's hand. You did that quite nicely."

"Reece," I pleaded. "He threatened my family."

"Accepting Finn's money was taking it a bit far, don't you think?" Reece said to Thornton.

"That was just so they'd be careful," Thornton said, defensively. "If they knew I was watching them, they'd be sure not to fuck up and lead the cops to *you*," he said, pointing to me. "Besides, *your boyfriend's* money is in a special government fund earning more than the current interest. He'll get it all back and then some."

"That's true, Riley. Finn will get his money back. Don't worry."

"How can you tell me not to worry? This guy—" I pointed at Thornton— "was a real gangsta terrifying my family. They didn't need that."

Reece stroked his chin. He was uneasy with the lingering tensions between Thornton and me and unsure how to settle the fireworks.

"I was in character," Thornton argued.

"What character?" I asked.

"I was working undercover," Thornton said. "We knew there was a group at CPD who were taking cuts from drugs and illegal gambling, gun-running, the whole business. They beat innocent folks into making confessions, forced others to make up stories that convicted innocent people. They even went after gang members who refused to make deals with them. Reece gave us most of our leads. He provided names and files. Some of them had first spoken to you. You filmed them."

"The night of the shooting," Reece interrupted, "I was hoping to introduce you to Thornton. I thought you might be able to help us piece together the entire picture from what we'd found and what you'd heard from the cases you were involved in. Only I never told Thornton you were coming..." He grimaced. "My bad."

"Yeah, I'll say," Thornton said, shaking his head. "I didn't know who you were when I saw you hovering over Reece's body, holding that gun. All I knew was that either you shot Reece or you were a witness. I was betting on the latter. I needed to get to you before the cops without compromising the entire investigation," Thornton explained. "Reece had already been exposed. He's a cop. He knows the risk. But you, you didn't know what you were getting into. You were out there alone, unprotected."

I walked to the window. The sky was changing from black to deep blue. It would be morning soon.

"Why didn't you ask Reece who I was?"

Thornton gargled a laugh. "You must be kidding? The guy was in intensive care with one of Lieutenant Williams' lackeys guarding the door. There was no way I was getting in. Besides, I didn't know if you were with Reece or just a Good Samaritan passing by."

"A Good Samaritan who happened to be present at a shooting in Englewood in the middle of the night?" He wasn't making sense.

This time Reece spoke up. "No matter who you were, you were a witness to the shooting. He had to find you. We knew Lieutenant Williams had his goons out looking for you. Thornton tracked down the guy who shot me."

"What? I didn't shoot you?" I felt a surge of relief.

"No sweets," Reece said, rubbing my arm. "You shot the right guy. Grazed his leg."

"All this time, I lived with this immense guilt that I nearly killed you." I hugged Reece. "But why did some stranger shoot you?"

"He was working for Williams. We now know Williams and his crew were running guns and drugs. Williams oversaw Vice. And since I used Vice cars to meet with Thornton, they were able to track my movements. Williams knew the FBI was onto him. He figured I was the leak to the feds. He sent Marquis, one of his snitches, to rough me up.

"When I finally got out of the hospital, I told Thornton about you," Reece continued. "But that was weeks after the shooting. By then, you were gone, and Thornton had already made *arrangements* with Finn."

"You mean by then he'd already extorted and threatened my family and friends?"

"Your life was at stake," Thornton argued.

"You both keep painting me like I'm some fragile girl who needs rescuing," I said. "I fucking froze my ass off on an island for eight months. I'm not *that* delicate. Don't try to smooth this out with me, either. This is all about you wrapping up loose ends, making sure your operation doesn't have *exposure,* that Langley doesn't find out you jeopardized the life of a civilian. You didn't give a shit about me, Thornton. You just wanted to make sure you got to me before the Chicago cops. This was all a game for bad boys with badges."

Reece put his hand on my arm and handed me a stack of documents. "Maybe this will make it easier for you to forgive him." It was a transcript of a grand jury testimony that Thornton had given based on evidence—photos, audio recordings, film—he'd gathered undercover. "They're picking up Lieutenant Williams and his crew right now." Reece was trying hard to get us past the awkwardness.

"Thornton has filed papers with the FBI listing you as a federal witness who was under his protection for the past eight months. He rescued you from those yahoos in Siberia. He might not look like it, but he's a superhero who has given you back your life."

FINN

I'd stayed away from the parties welcoming back Riley partly because I knew she didn't want to see me. She only wanted to hear my story. But how could I tell her? I hadn't told anyone what happened, certainly not the details that would raise questions about my moral character, my judgment. Telling her my secret was a dilemma with no good outcome. Telling her was just as likely to make her never speak to me again. So why risk it? I kept telling myself that Riley had already cost me a lot.

Walk away.

Be friendly.

Leave it.

Then Riley called me at my ward office and asked me to return Norma Rae. Riley was living at her own place again. Her parents had kept up the mortgage payments. I told her that the kids had grown very attached to the cat, and it would break their hearts to give up Norma Rae.

"Finn, she's my cat. I've missed her. I want her back."

"Maybe you could give me a little more time? Let me break it to them slowly."

"They can come here and see her any time."

She knew why I was stalling. I told the kids I had to give Norma Rae back. They cried as they hugged and petted her. Diana promised to take them to a cat shelter and pick out a kitten. She was getting to play the hero where I, once again, was the bad guy.

The next morning, I showed up at Riley's door with Norma Rae in a cat carrier. When she opened the door, she didn't even say hello but lunged for the carrier and pulled out Norma Rae. The cat meowed loudly and then purred. Riley choked back tears as she held Norma Rae to her face. Until that moment, I didn't realize how much I loved that cat. We'd shared some pretty sad days.

"Glad you two could be reunited," I said and started to leave.

"Wait! Where are you going?"

"I thought I would give you some time with Norma Rae."

"You owe me a talk. You promised."

I started to make excuses, but she shot me a look that shut me down.

I reluctantly followed her to the kitchen. It was small, but had nice morning light and looked out into a small park in the back of her building. She put on the tea kettle and fed Norma Rae. I looked around at the black and white family photos on the walls. We'd spent so little time at her place. I'd rarely ever seen it during the day.

Initially, I tried making small talk, but she cut me off.

"Look, Finn. I've waited a long time for this. Can you just get to it?"

I nodded and tried to decide which version I was going to tell. Do I tell her what I told my police commander back then? Do I tell her what I'd told Diana that night when I came home distraught? Or do I tell her what I'd told the police shrink during my mandatory visits?

"I know this is hard," she said as she reached over and touched my hand. "But I need to know. You owe me that much."

"And why do I owe you? You want me to tell you something I've never told anyone, not even my former wife."

She stared at me with dark eyes.

"Yes, Riley, this goes beyond you and me. This isn't even about you, not really."

"Why didn't you tell me you were there?"

"Because I knew you'd keep on with the questions. I know you and know how your brain works. Besides, when was the appropriate time to bring it up? When we first met? That certainly would have been creepy. Then the longer we were together, it seemed like a huge omission. To be honest, that was not the tenor of our relationship. We were about having fun. I didn't want to introduce that kind of sadness between us. When did you ever talk to me about what happened to you? Not once. Don't you think I deserved to hear that from you?"

"There are plenty of websites that tell you the whole story."

"Yes, but they wouldn't be from you. We both hid our stories from each other. You were just as guilty."

She picked up Norma Rae, circling at her feet, and stroked her while she stared out the window.

"Okay," she said. "So maybe I should have opened up more. I'll concede that. I didn't know where we were going. I felt like your fucking mistress most of the time. I expected you to break it off with me any minute, to say you had to 'dedicate yourself to your political career.'"

"Honest to god, the truth is that I was going to tell you the night you ran off with Reece. Don't you remember? I got so tired of carrying this secret. There were so many times I wanted to tell you. I worried it would destroy us. I'd worked up the courage, practiced what I would say for days. And then you arrived late at the restaurant and told me that you had some meeting you had to go to with Reece. You promised to come by that night afterward. But you never showed. Or I should say you only showed up long enough to leave Norma Rae and then you were gone."

I could see her piecing that night together. "Mostly, what I remember is firing a gun at my best friend." She sighed. "We both kept secrets. Looking back, it was apparently the basis of our relationship, although I had no idea at the time that I was keeping anything from you. But when your entire affair is a secret, there are bound to be lots of lies twisted in it."

"Yes, and that was my fault," I said. "And look what happened. I should have known keeping anything a secret as a politician is wasted effort."

"So, please, tell me what happened in that room with Darren Wallack."

I looked into her eyes. "If I tell you, we can never go back."

"Back to what? Finn, we're not together now. I tried sending you a letter from Canada, and it ended up in the hands of a bandit who later tried to kill me."

"I got the letter."

"You did?"

"Yeah, he tried to extort me too."

"Then you know. I ended us when I learned you'd kept all this from me. That destroyed us then. So, whatever you tell me is not going to affect us because there isn't an *us*."

"Then why am I doing this?"

"You deceived me for nearly a year, and now I deserve to know—"

"He needed to reload," I blurted. "That's why he went into that room. He intended to shoot at the police. I followed him.

He fired at me. I hid behind a steel desk at the front of the room. He was at the back. He told me to lock the door and to radio the other officers to stay away.

"I tried to get him to surrender. I told him we could work a deal. He wasn't having it. He was ranting. He hated all the kids in school. They'd shunned him, made fun of him. He talked about old grievances. Much of it didn't make any sense. I kept trying to maneuver to get a better shot. He sprayed several rounds at me with his automatic rifle. One of them knocked me back, lodged in my vest."

"That must have hurt."

"I momentarily lost consciousness. I came to and couldn't remember where I was. Then I heard his voice. He said that he would trade his automatic rifles for my handgun. He had an AR-15, a SIG716, and a Ruger 9mm revolver."

"I remember his guns."

"When I said I wasn't going to trade my handgun, he started firing above my head. Then suddenly, he stood up and held his arms straight out like a cross. He wanted me to kill him. I had a clear shot, but I didn't fire. He taunted me, calling me a coward.

"The police chief was on the radio telling me to take the shot, or they were coming in. I told the chief to give me more time. I was trying to negotiate with him. Then Wallack said he'd give me his rifles in exchange for one 9mm bullet. He'd run out of ammo for his revolver. He said he'd put the bullet in the chamber, spin the cylinder and see if the gun went off. 'Let's let the gun decide,' he said.

"'You mean you want to play Russian roulette with your life?' I asked him.

"'If the gun doesn't go off,' he said. 'Then I'll surrender.'"

"Tell me you didn't agree to that?" Riley said, her eyes wide with fear.

"I could hear the muffled voices of my colleagues behind the locked door. Then someone yelled: 'Finn, get out of the way, we're coming in full force.'

"I screamed back: 'Hold off, hold off.' I knew they would just execute him. I truly believed I had a chance to bring him in alive, to face justice for the people he murdered.

"I figured Wallack only had one in five chances of shooting himself—the Ruger has five chambers—and I was betting that he didn't have it in himself to pull the trigger. He slid his two rifles to the middle of the room, and I tossed him a 9mm bullet from my spare gun. He put the bullet in the chamber and gave it a spin. Then he put the gun to his head and pulled the trigger."

"Oh god."

"It didn't go off. I walked toward him, my gun pointed at his head, expecting him to let me arrest him. But he put the snout under his chin.

"'You think I'm afraid to do it, don't you?' he yelled at me.

"'I believe you,' I said. 'Now put the gun down.'

"'What if I use this bullet on you? What if I point the gun at you?' He turned the muzzle toward me. 'You'd have to shoot me. And then you'd have to live with the fact that you took away all those parents' chance for revenge. I'm not rotting my life away in prison.'

"I yelled: 'Drop the gun.' He turned the gun back on himself and pulled the trigger. Nothing. He fired again. Nothing. By this time, I was right on him. He was either going to kill himself or force me to shoot him. Then he pulled the trigger again." I looked at her. "That was the last time."

I stared out the window.

Then I felt her hand on mine. "It's not your fault, Finn," she whispered. "You were in a crazy situation with a madman."

"You don't negotiate with a serial killer. Ever. What I did was wrong and stupid in so many ways."

"He wanted to kill himself. You couldn't stop him, Finn. Most school shooters plan on killing themselves. He just ran out of the wrong bullets."

"No one asked me where he got the bullet that he used to kill himself. The bullets he used were hollow points. The one I gave him wasn't. I think the chief knew. I think that's why he decided not to reveal who the officer was in the room with Wallack. I was so young. He told me he didn't want it to ruin my career. He knew there was no way to trace that bullet to me —unless I revealed my secret. And I was too ashamed to admit my part in what happened.

"I've never told anyone this. You are the first. That's why I couldn't tell you I was at the shooting, that I was in the room with Wallack. I couldn't outright lie to you. Yes, I kept it from you, but I never lied about it."

"Why are you telling me now?"

"Because...I need you to forgive me."

RILEY

The next week I appeared before a grand jury and testified as a key witness against Marquis, the Vice snitch who'd tackled and shot Reece outside the liquor store. Faced with an attempted murder charge, Marquis testified against his handler, a Vice cop who had pressured him to take down Reece. And the dominos began to fall. More cops were arrested. Finn and Reece began working together to establish federal monitors over the Chicago Police Department.

I decided not to go back to work at the foundation. Instead, I convinced my father to rent a small storefront close to Millennial Park downtown. The place was a dump, but the whole family helped clean it up. Dad's face lit up when we went to a restaurant supply store and bought our equipment. We spent weeks cooking together in the restaurant, creating the menu. They became my new favorite memories with my father. That spark in his eyes was back, and he seemed to be wearing a permanent grin. On our opening night, I was wild with nerves. There were so many people happy to have a chance to eat my dad's cooking again.

This time, though, we decided that the restaurant would have a Northern Woods vibe. Instead of my father's favorite French and Italian dishes, we borrowed from dishes that were native to the Great Lakes. We served all kinds of fish, our version of macaroni and cheese, perogies, free-range chicken, buffalo steaks, endless dishes of vegetables. We decided to try to source all our food locally and seasonally. We called the restaurant The Woods. I decorated the place with my memories of the things that filled the cottages I had cared for: seashells, driftwood, lanterns, paintings of the lake, and the seashore. At flea markets, I bought old black and white photos of people with their families on the beach, framed them, and put them on the walls.

It was a lot of work, but I could see the joy in my father's face at the end of each long day. Our family came together at the restaurant in a joyful way. At the foundation, the work always seemed so profound, so gut-wrenching. I felt guilty for not being on the front lines of protest marches anymore. But Dad was right when he said there's a time for fighting and there's a time for baking love in a pie.

ONE DAY I received a letter from Mr. Kowalski. He'd read a review about the restaurant in the *Chicago Tribune* and promised to visit on his next trip to the city. His letter brimmed with island gossip. Javier had cut a deal with prosecutors: Seven years in exchange for particulars about his operation and those who conspired with him. Meanwhile, Chay had turned the house he inherited from Gill into a unique bed and breakfast specializing in hunting and eating wild game and lured wealthy tourists. A large portion of the proceeds went to the reservation.

Ginny and Lars split, or let the facade of a relationship slip away; I was never sure if I should have believed anything Lars said. But he was now dating Scarla, the barmaid who had always professed a particular disdain for him. Zi was now managing the restaurant. Chay received a cryptic postcard from Cyprus suggesting Simon and Kayla were sailing around the world. Sheriff Kustwin lost his re-election, primarily because Angelica residents registered in droves and voted for a last-minute candidate, a pinstriped suited attorney who called himself Magic.

Mr. Kowalski's letter brought it all back to me. I woke in the quiet of the night, my mind wandering back to my little refuge and its people. I thought of Gill and wondered what might have happened if Matthew hadn't shot the ice bandit, if the Sheriff hadn't asked about my driver's license, if Gill hadn't drowned, if I hadn't panicked and called Finn. We would have all stayed on the island in that parallel universe, floating in Lake Superior forever.

ABOUT A WEEK BEFORE THANKSGIVING, Finn showed up at the restaurant and asked to see me. He usually stopped by once a week. We were becoming friendlier, partly at the urging of Reece, who had formed a new opinion of Finn from working with him.

It was mid-afternoon. The restaurant was nearly empty. We were preparing for the dinner rush. Finn had just finished eating our newest entrée, Lake Superior Bluegill, with fingerling potatoes and a fennel salad. I called it Angelica's Dream.

"How was it?" I asked, sitting across from him and looking at his empty plate.

"Amazing. Really good. Your best yet," he said and winked.

"So, what's up?"

"I wanted you to have this." He handed me what looked like a book wrapped in red tissue paper.

"It's not my birthday."

"No, but there were a whole lot of holidays we missed when you were gone, including the one coming up."

I had noticed Thanksgiving on the calendar. I'd been back a little over four months. So much had changed in that short time, and yet, Finn and I were still orbiting around each other, doing that reticent dance of friends who wonder if they should become, once again, lovers. I hadn't yet absolved him of his role in Darren Wallack's death. Had he confessed to me before I became a fugitive, I wouldn't have forgiven him. But since I had shot a man and felt I'd contributed to the deaths of two others, I couldn't be so judgmental.

"I wanted you to have this," he said. "To mark the year and all the changes that have happened."

I started to open it, and he put his hand on mine. A shock traveled up my arm.

"Later," he said. "When you are alone. You'll want some time to read it thoroughly."

"Ok. Thank you."

I walked back to my tiny office and locked the door. I gently peeled off the crinkly paper. Inside I recognized the leather Moleskine journal I'd given him for our first Christmas. The cover was worn as if it had been held in Finn's hands many times, the oil from his fingers massaging the suede as he wrote his entries and later as he re-read them again and again. The corners of the pages were crimped, and the gold thread along their edges had frayed. I slowly turned the pages with the tip of my forefinger and a bit of thumb, delicately as if the journal were an ancient artifact.

I read through detailed accounts of the people he'd interviewed, the clues he'd collected, the threatening visits from the Chicago detectives, Thornton's menacing presence. At first, I read slowly, and then hungrily, absorbing the lines as fast as possible. In between stenography-like passages, I found pages with only a single line written in the middle. The statements—and sometimes they were questions—were written in black ink and stood out starkly on the cream-colored pages. They were brief notes he'd written as if he were conversing with me on the page, like call and response lyrics, except there was no response. Unattended, they struck me as lonely and desolate, the missives of a man in pain. *I miss you,* one page read. *Where are you?* Then, *Show me how to find you.* He'd written a list of clues, and on the next page: *Where would you go?*

The envelope from the Luck letter I'd written to my mother was neatly taped to a page and on the opposite, he'd written: *How do I get you back?* I flipped through more pages. And there it was, a photocopy of the letter I'd written to him, stolen by the game warden. On the accompanying page, he'd written only one word: *Waiting*. It pained me to read that letter again, to see his one-word response, to know how deeply I had hurt him.

Inside the back cover, he'd glued a colorful map. I peered at the notations and markings, a black line of hand-written Xs that ran north of Chicago and wound around Lake Superior's bottom. Finn had given me the vague outlines of how he'd tracked me down: Thornton's childish drawing on his refrigerator, my letter to my mother, the town of Luck, the creepy hunter, and then my hang-up phone call. It sounded so apocryphal. Now in my hands, the map struck me as prophetic, exuding a sense of urgency and secrecy, as if it were a guide to buried treasure.

At the bottom of the map, I noticed tiny letters scrawled

with the words "Map of Her Escape." That didn't sound right. The island hadn't just provided me refuge. It had given me back the life I had wanted before all the pain, before all the death. I took a pen from my desk, scratched out a word in the title, and replaced it with another.

This, I decided, was the *Map of My Return.*

ACKNOWLEDGMENTS

Map of My Escape has been a work of passion for several years. So many people have given me feedback, suggested helpful edits, and just plain encouraged me to keep going that it's hard to recall everyone who helped me. So, please forgive me if I'm remiss in mentioning someone.

My biggest supporter and the first reader of all my work is my husband, Greg Stricharchuk. A former reporter and editor with decades of experience, Greg read manuscript after manuscript for years and offered invaluable insight and suggestions as well as encouraged me not to give up. An advocate of "less is more," Greg is unmerciless in suggesting words and sentences to cut that are redundant or unnecessary. Chapters of my manuscript often came back to me with paragraphs labeled A, B, C and so on with arrows pointing to where they might fit better to improve story structure and flow. On every one of my three books, Greg and I have sparred good-naturedly with me fighting for every precious word. In the end my writing is always better with Greg's input, and for that I am grateful.

My son, Nick, also read multiple versions of the early manuscript and provided insight into the mindset of characters his age. He encouraged me, as he always does, through the grueling process of publisher rejections, insisting I would eventually find a home for *Map*.

Much appreciation goes out to Elena Hartwell, whose

editing skills were greatly needed early on. Her friendship is a bonus.

Because part of the book involved specific expertise that I do not have, I appreciated the West Point boys in Kyiv, Ukraine, who took me to a gun range and gave me a thorough lesson on shooting AK-47s and other weapons. Similarly, thanks to Michael Geissinger and Patrick Derry, experienced sailors, who spent hours teaching me proper sailing techniques and conspired with me on how best to kill someone aboard a sailboat. Any mistakes in terminology are mine.

Editor Benjamin White, a former Coast Guard lieutenant, offered expert details on rescue missions along with invaluable editing. Thanks, Ben, for making the book better.

The Chicago Writers Association honored the manuscript with its best first chapter award. Thanks for confirming that the manuscript was worthy of publishing.

Publisher Lisa Kastner and all the editors and staff at Running Wild Press, especially Evangeline Estropia, are praised for their hard work in making the book the best it could be.

Emir Orucevic from Pulp Art Studios is to be commended for designing *Map's* terrific cover.

Thanks to my friends in the thriller writing community for their support, advice and encouragement, especially Wendy Walker, Jamie Freveletti, Candice Fox, John Carpenter, and Elena Taylor.

And thank you, dear readers. Your affection for the written word and love of story keeps us writers going. Without you, we would have no audience.

Running Wild Press publishes stories that cross genres with great stories and writing. RIZE publishes great genre stories written by people of color and by authors who identify with other marginalized groups. Our team consists of:

Lisa Diane Kastner, Founder and Executive Editor
Cody Sisco, Acquisitions Editor, RIZE
Benjamin White, Acquisition Editor, Running Wild
Peter A. Wright, Acquisition Editor, Running Wild
Resa Alboher, Editor
Angela Andrews, Editor
Sandra Bush, Editor
Ashley Crantas, Editor
Rebecca Dimyan, Editor
Abigail Efird, Editor
Aimee Hardy, Editor
Henry L. Herz, Editor
Cecilia Kennedy, Editor
Barbara Lockwood, Editor
Scott Schultz, Editor

Evangeline Estropia, Product Manager
Kimberly Ligutan, Product Manager
Lara Macaione, Marketing Director
Joelle Mitchell, Licensing and Strategy Lead
Pulp Art Studios, Cover Design
Standout Books, Interior Design
Polgarus Studios, Interior Design

Learn more about us and our stories at www.runningwild-press.com.

Loved this story and want more? Follow us at www.runningwildpress.com, www.facebook.com/runningwild press, on Twitter @lisadkastner @RunWildBooks